THE CHILDREN

Edith Wharton

With an introduction by
Marilyn French

Edith Wharton

Edith Wharton was born in 1862, daughter of a distinguished and prosperous New York family. In 1885 she married a Boston socialite, Edward Robbins Wharton, and lived in Newport, Rhode Island. She became friendly with Henry James on her frequent trips to Europe. The Whartons' marriage was far from happy and she turned to writing, publishing her first novel, *The Valley of Decision*, in 1902. She was divorced in 1913 after she had moved to France permanently. By now, and for the rest of her life, she was publishing at least one book a year, her first popular success being *The House of Mirth* (1905). Her busy cosmopolitan and creative life was interrupted by energetic work during the 1914–18 war, for which she was awarded the Cross of the Legion d'Honneur and the Order of Leopold. In 1920 *The Age of Innocence* won the Pulitzer Prize; she was the first woman to receive a Doctorate of Letters from Yale University and in 1930 she became a member of the American Academy of Arts and Letters. She died in France at the age of seventy-five.

Virago

The House of Mirth
Ethan Frome
Madame de Treymes
The Reef
The Custom of the Country
The Age of Innocence
The Children
The Fruit of the Tree
Roman Fever and other stories
The Mother's Recompense
Old New York
Hudson River Bracketed
The Gods Arrive
The Glimpses of the Moon
Twilight Sleep
Ghost Stories

INTRODUCTION

EDITH Wharton declared that *The Children* was one of her favourites of her own novels, and a poignant and penetrating work it is. Yet it has remained largely unappreciated since its original publication in 1928. One reason for this is that a major theme of the work is a forbidden subject—the desire of an older man for a girl of fifteen. In addition, critics have been blindered by their perception of Wharton as not just a woman, but a lady, a *grande dame*; and they have therefore not been able to see that in this novel, the "ladylike" and mannerly, the tactful and polite is subtly but clearly found wanting, while the blunt, tactless, honest and seemingly amoral speech of a group of unrestrained children is found liberating.

The plot of *The Children* is unusual: a middle-aged man meets a group of wandering children, takes them up and tries to help them. His avuncular, benevolent feelings about the children, and his acts on their behalf, place a distance between him and the woman he has loved for many years. This plot, however, is only a skeleton, the armature upon which Wharton plays out subtle and complex conflicts.

Standing silently in the background of the book is old New York and its manners and morals. Without some comprehension of that ambience, a reader may fail to perceive the moral conflict that lies at the heart of this work. Edith Wharton was born into wealthy old New York society in 1862, and lived for the most part inside its conventions for the first forty years of her life. She therefore knew intimately the mores of this untitled aristocracy. She admired its standards of honour and probity in business affairs, but not men's exclusive control of them. She preferred its quiet rich taste to that of the *nouveau riche* class which succeeded old New York, but also found it conformist and unoriginal, even philistine. And she found the strict sexual regulation of women oppressive, killing to the spirit. But the characteristic she found most stifling and thwarting was its code of manners, which forbade discussion of any truly serious subject, especially sex and money.

Old New York society was narrow; it excluded not just the unpleasant and unmentionable, but serious discussion even of art, literature, or ideas. Readers will find vivid depictions of these attitudes in *Old New York*, a set of four short novels; in "The Touchstone", (*Madame de Treymes*); in *The Age of Innocence; The House of Mirth*; and in many other of her works. Wharton was a keen critic of the morals and the manners of the world she grew up in; but when she came to deal with the society that followed it, she tended to hold up the older ways as standards. However oppressive the old ways were, they were not vulgar, showy, pretentious, utterly irresponsible. The people who composed the *nouveau riche*—the Astors, Vanderbilts, Whitneys, and their peers—disregarded, even flouted, the old ways.

Ostentatious and showy, this society inspired Thorstein Veblen to speak of "conspicuous consumption". The men of this new aristocracy did not respect notions of honour or decency in business; nor did they, like the gentlemen of old New York, hold themselves "above" it, but pursued money avidly. Women of the new class were given as little education or occupation as those of the old; they became, however, status symbols in themselves. Decked out in the expensive gowns, jewels, the furs their husbands bought them, they were walking displays of men's wealth. In time, however, this class also altered sexual standards somewhat. Divorce became accepted, and a divorced woman was not automatically ostracised; love affairs were not utterly concealed, and flirting (after marriage) was open.

Although Wharton had suffered deeply in her life from her sexual ignorance and the fear of sex it engendered, as well as from the prohibition against divorce, she was appalled at the manners and mores of the *nouveau riche.* For her, they were not just vulgar, coarse, and tasteless, although she satirises them for these characteristics in this novel and in *The Custom of the Country*; they were, above all, irresponsible—to their society, their community, their families and spouses, and to their children. Wharton perceived the monstrousness of the code of rampant individualism, self-serving greed and aggression that was exalted by Americans of the nineteenth century. In this novel, she addresses the effects of such behaviour on the most vulnerable members of society, its children.

The novel opens on board a ship travelling from Algiers to Venice. Martin Boyne, born to genteel old New York stock, lacked money and had to take up a profession. An engineer, he has spent most of his life in a kind of exile from society, in South America, Australia, and Africa. Through many of these years, he has been in love with a married woman, Rose Sellars, who has lived in New York. On his occasional visits home, Martin has always visited Mrs Sellars, who has let him understand that she is also attracted to him, but that she intends to remain faithful to her husband. Now Rose's husband has died, and she is vacationing in Switzerland. It is to her that Martin is bound, intending to propose marriage.

But a group of children explode around him, intruding upon his meditations. They range in age from an infant to a fifteen-year-old girl who mothers them, along with a nanny, Miss Horatia Scope, Scopy, or as the children call her, Horror Scope. It takes Martin some time to make sense of the situation, but in time he discovers he has certain connections with these children. In his youth, he had been attracted to a young woman named Joyce Mervin; he flirted with her, but only so far—he had no money. She married an acquaintance of his, Cliffe Wheater. Judith, the fifteen-year-old "mother" of this group, is the daughter of the Wheaters, as are the twins Blanca and Terry, who are near eleven. Some years previously, Joyce and Cliffe divorced. Cliffe then married Zinnia Lacrosse, a film star, and they produced Zinnie, red-haired, avaricious, and lively. Joyce married the Prince Buondelmonte, who had earlier been married to a tight-rope artist who mothered two children, still very young, Beatrice and Astorre, called Beechy and Bun. The tight-rope artist died; the Prince and Joyce divorced; and somehow the children were assimilated to the Wheaters. Cliffe and Zinnia also divorced, and Cliffe remarried Joyce. He wants another son, because Terry's health is poor, and Cliffe fears he will die—he wants a male heir. Joyce obliging, produced Chipstone, the infant on Judith's arm when the novel opens.

The children have suffered through all these parental alterations—through custody battles, marital squabbles, and various arrangements for "divvying" them up. Two years before the novel opens, Judith, then thirteen, took upon herself the responsibility for caring for all the children. She is determined that they shall not be split up again; she tries to take them to places that will benefit Terry's health; and she wants to keep them as much as possible out of the grand hotels, the "Palaces" where all of them have spent their lives. She is particularly concerned about Blanca—"ever since she got engaged to the lift-boy at Biarritz". When Martin gasps that Blanca is barely eleven, Judith calmly replies, "Oh, I was engaged myself at Blanca's age—to a page at a skating rink." The difference, she says, is that her "fiancé" was sweet, whereas Blanca's wanted gifts and a real ring.

Wharton could have emphasised the poignancy of the children's situation—their vulnerability, homelessness, instability. Except for Terry, she does not. Certainly these qualities occasionally emerge, but they are not primary in her perception. She treats the children comically, even stereotypically: they are boisterous, outspoken, and without pretence; they also manifest certain characteristics of their parents as if such were carried in their genes. So Zinnie is as avaricious as her mother: nor are Blanca or even Judith free from this quality. Bun has somehow inherited his mother's gymnastic skill, and Beechy an Italian-female tendency to burst into tears at any threat to her brother. Wharton does concentrate on their lack of moral awareness: even the admirable Judith steals money from her father without compunction, and all the children except Terry betray a lack of knowledge of what is considered good and bad. This is a double-edged situation, however, for in their innocence, they blurt out truths their elders would conceal.

Martin is drawn to the children, especially to Judith, and simply slides into taking responsibility for them. This brings him into their parents' world, as he bargains with the elders for the youngsters' wellbeing. The Wheaters and their set are painted with Wharton's broadest satirical brush as they move from town to town, hotel to hotel, in search of amusement, diversion, or the "right" people. They have no sense of responsibility toward the children except a financial one; indeed they have no sense of responsibility to each other or any community.

Contrasted with the Wheaters and their set is the Princess Buondelmonte, a new wife of the Prince, an American. She is the granddaughter of a college president, with a degree in Eugenics and Infant Psychology from Lohengrin College in Texas. (Through her, Wharton satirises the eugenics movement that was gaining momentum in the United States in the early decades of the twentieth century. Although Wharton does not suggest the ominous character of that movement, which promulgated sterilization of people—mostly immigrants and blacks—who were said to constitute a threat to white American blood, the Princess does express confidence that large families will soon be prohibited by law. Wharton's naming the Princess' college *Lohengrin* suggests she may have been aware of the interest in the eugenics movement in Germany, where Hitler was soon to put it into practice. (Hitler was also a devotee of Wagner, who composed *Lohengrin*, and who was also a racist.) The Princess believes in total control over children, and justifies it by referring to the latest educational methods. She wants to take the two children of the Prince away with her and educate them in Texas. When told the children love each other and should remain together, she replies that "fondness is not everything ... it may even be a source of moral danger ... Nothing in a child's education should be left to chance. Games have to be directed even more carefully than studies." At Lohengrin, she says, "enforced obedience" has been eliminated, and adds that "when Astorre and Beatrice come to live with me the first thing I shall do is to make them both co-operate".

The Wheaters and their set and the Princess and her college constitute the two moral poles, or alternatives, for the children. Martin Boyne finds both unacceptable, and for a time, he mediates between them for the children. But Martin is torn himself, between the children and his growing attraction to Judith, and his love for Rose Sellars.

A character of great sensitivity and perceptiveness, Rose resembles a Jamesian *ficelle*, a woman who comprehends everything and demands nothing. She creates settings and waits, almost passively, for life to fill them.

> If Mrs Sellars excelled in one special art it was undoubtedly that of preparation. She led up to things—the simplest things—with the skill of a clever rider putting a horse at a five-barred gate. All her life has been a series of adaptations, arrangements, shifting of lights, lowering of veils, putting about of screens and curtains. No one could arrange a room half so well; and she had arranged herself and her life just as skilfully.

Rose's pre-eminent virtue is tact. She has the grace of the old rich at their best; she has old-rich manners and taste. Although she has been married to a mediocre man and lived without much money, she has managed to maintain an appearance of grace and leisure. She offers an unintrusive receptiveness to others; she also possesses a shuddering aversion to the crude and sensational and, with her old New York manners, avoids any reference to unpleasant or morally ambiguous subjects.

Although Rose has been for years "the one fixed pole" of Martin's life, his attitude towards her changes from the instant he meets the children. From his first acquaintance with them, he is shocked, repelled, refreshed, and enchanted by their candour, their total lack of the finish, the tact, the concern for appearance that so occupies Rose. He writes her from the ship about the children and finds her reply "jolly ... clever, understanding, humorous", but also "just a trifle mincing, self-conscious—prepared".

The contrast between Rose's manners and the childrens' could not be greater. Discovering that her twin brother must share a cabin with a middle-aged gentleman, Blanca gazes at Boyne, then turns to Terry in sympathy: "For a whole fortnight—Terry, can you *bear* it?" Their conversation touches on subjects forbidden in old New York; they are especially knowledgable about sex and the importance of money. They describe enormities in their parents' behaviour with no distress, indeed with "a detached view of human weakness".

At one point, Boyne has attempted to hire a young Oxford scholar, Gerald Ormerod, to accompany the children to Switzerland and tutor Terry. Judith doubts that this will occur, and Boyne insists the young man wants to come. The girl turns on him: "Well, then suppose it was mother who didn't want him to? ... She jolly well likes doing Venice with him." It is Martin who blushes, understanding that the child has perceived Joyce Wheater's feelings about the tutor.

Martin is anxious about bringing Rose and the children together, and considers warning his old friend, but decides that "if there were hints to be given ... there would be less risk in giving them to Judith". And the first meeting is tense. Blanca says matter-of-factly, "Oh, but when you've seen Terry you won't care for any of the rest of us." But the other children protest:

> "Yes, she will: she'll care for Beechy and me because we're Roman Princes!" Bun shouted, threatening another handspring...
>
> Zinnie pushed him aside and planted herself firmly in front of their hostess. "My mother could buy 'em all out if she wanted to, 'cos she's a movie star..."

Bun has the last word, however: "My *real* mother was a lion-tamer; but that don't matter, 'cos she's dead."

Rose finds tactful ways of silencing the smaller children, but is more threatened by Judith, who begins to speak warmly about Doll Westway, who was her best friend. Asked if she knew Doll,

Mrs Sellars says no in a tone of rejection that is "acutely familiar to Boyne". In keeping with her training, she closes the door icily on a forbidden topic—for Doll committed suicide, after having been dragged, like these children, from one grand hotel to another by her wealthy drug-addict mother. It is clear, although subtly conveyed, that Martin is well acquainted with Rose Sellars' New York manners, but that he has never seen them as anything but admirable until the children enter his life.

And it is in this area that Martin's conflict lies; moreover, it is not just a conflict between two styles, two kinds of manners—it is a moral conflict. It is vividly demonstrated in the contrast between Rose's and Judith's attitudes towards marriage. Martin proposes to Rose soon after he sees her again, and is accepted. Since he wants to go out to work again and take her with him, he wants to marry soon. Rose, however, hesitates: partly because she has spent her life being deliberate, and partly because her husband has been dead for only six months. She fears that his family would be offended at a hasty remarriage, especially an aunt who has made Rose her heir. Although Martin recognises the straitness of both their financial circumstances, he is shocked by this venality in Rose.

Judith probes to discover Martin's feelings about Rose. "If she's not as old as mother, and you've never noticed how she's dressed, you must be in love with her," she concludes. "How lovely it must be to be in love! For I suppose that's why you're marrying?" she says at a later time. "I'm sure you wouldn't marry just for position, or for money, or to regularise an old *liaison*; would you?" As so often, Martin is shocked; he emphasises the need for respect in marriage. "Oh, I can *see*. . . [that]," Judith replies. "But I can't imagine it, exactly. I should have thought wanting to give her a good hug came before anything."

Although Martin is frequently caught up short by the children's directness, he also feels liberated by it, and by them; when he goes from Rose to the children he feels he is moving from "a constrained bodily position into a natural one". He is entranced by Judith, but finds such a feeling improper and impermissible, and conceals his desire from himself. The combination of his desire and his sense of liberation gradually estranges him from Rose. In the end, unable to enter fully into the new world of the children, he is also unable to accept the old world incarnated in Rose Sellars.

The Children is, in part, about an older man's infatuation with a girl—as forbidden a subject as can be imagined. But it is also a contrast between two moral attitudes. The tragedy of Martin Boyne's life is that he cannot accept the moral world into which he was born, and which formed him; but he does not belong in the free moral world the children inhabit. It was perhaps Wharton's tragedy as well; certainly, it is a subject she returns to often in a number of variations. and this theme is characteristic of her. It places her apart from other novelists of her period who exalt the independent individual in a contest against the world or society. Some authors of Wharton's period celebrated the heroic isolated man who triumphs over or is destroyed by his circumstances; some show the forces surrounding a person to be overwhelming, and draw poignancy from the uneven contest of a person and their world. Wharton does neither. She shows the two—an individual and a world—as participating in a dynamic, shifting interaction: the world is in us as well as without; and we affect the world we live in. This insistence makes Wharton a writer for our own time. The dilemma of Martin Boyne is comprehensible and poignant in an age neither he nor his creator could forsee.

Marilyn French
New York, 1984

BOOK I

THE CHILDREN

I

AS the big liner hung over the tugs swarming about her in the bay of Algiers, Martin Boyne looked down from the promenade deck on the troop of first-class passengers struggling up the gangway, their faces all unconsciously lifted to his inspection.

"Not a soul I shall want to speak to—as usual!"

Some men's luck in travelling was inconceivable. They had only to get into a train or on board a boat to run across an old friend; or, what was more exciting, make a new one. They were always finding themselves in the same compartment, or in the same cabin, with some wandering celebrity, with the owner of a famous house, of a noted collection, or of an odd and amusing personality—the latter case being, of course, the rarest as it was the most rewarding.

There was, for instance, Martin Boyne's own Great-Uncle Edward. Uncle Edward's travel-adventures were famed in the family. At home in America, amid the solemn upholstery of his Boston house, Uncle Edward was the model of complacent dulness; yet whenever he got on board a steamer, or into a train (or a *diligence,* in his distant youth), he was singled out by fate as the hero of some delightful encounter. It would be Rachel during her ill-starred tour of the States; Ruskin on the lake of Geneva; the Dean of Canterbury as Uncle Edward, with all the appropriate emotions, was gazing on the tomb of the Black Prince; or the Duke of Devonshire of his day, as Uncle Edward put a courteous (but probably pointless) question to the housekeeper showing him over Chatsworth. And instantly he would receive a proscenium box from Rachel for her legendary first night in Boston, or be entreated by Ruskin to join him for a month in Venice; or the Dean would invite him to stay at the Deanery, the Duke at Chatsworth; and the net result of these experiences would be that Uncle Edward, if questioned, would reply with his sweet frosty smile: "Yes, Rachel had talent but no beauty"; or: "No one could be more simple and friendly than the Duke"; or: "Ruskin really had all the appearances of a gentleman." Such were the impressions produced on Uncle Edward by his unparalleled success in the great social scenes through which, for a period of over sixty years, he moved with benignant blindness.

Far different was the case of his great-nephew. No tremor of thought or emotion would, in similar situations, have escaped Martin Boyne: he would have burst all the grapes against his palate. But though he was given to travel, and though he had travelled much, and his profession as a civil engineer had taken him to interesting and out-of-the-way parts of the world, and though he was always on thc alert for agreeable encounters, it was never at such times that they came to him. He would have loved adventure, but adventure worthy of the name perpetually eluded him; and when it has eluded a man till he is over forty it is not likely to seek him out later.

"I believe it's something about the shape of my nose," he had said to himself that very morning as he shaved in his spacious cabin on the upper deck of the big Mediterranean cruising-steamer.

The nose in question was undoubtedly not adventurous in shape; it did not thrust itself far forward into other people's affairs; and the eyes above, wide apart, deep-set, and narrowed for closer observation, were of a guarded twilight gray which gave the nose no encouragement whatever.

"Nobody worth bothering about—*as usual*," he grumbled. For the day was so lovely, the harbour of Algiers so glittering with light and heat, his own mood so full of holiday enterprise—it was his first vacation after a good many months on a hard exhausting job—that he could hardly believe he really looked to the rest of the world as he had seen himself that morning: a critical cautious man of forty-six, whom nobody could possibly associate with the romantic or the unexpected.

"Usual luck; best I can hope for is to keep my cabin to myself for the rest of the cruise," he pondered philosophically, hugging himself at the prospect of another fortnight of sea-solitude before—well, before the fateful uncertainty of what awaited him just beyond the voyage. . .

"And I haven't even *seen* her for five years!" he reflected, with that feeling of hollowness about the belt which prolonged apprehension gives.

Passengers were still climbing the ship's side, and he leaned and looked again, this time with contracted eyes and a slight widening of his cautious nostrils. His attention had been drawn to a young woman—a slip of a girl, rather—with a round flushed baby on her shoulder, a baby much too heavy for her slender frame, but on whose sleepy countenance her own was bent with a gaze of solicitude which wrung a murmur of admiration from Boyne.

"Jove—if a fellow was younger!"

Men of forty-six do not gasp as frequently at the sight of a charming face as they did at twenty; but when the sight strikes them it hits harder. Boyne had not been looking for pretty faces but for interesting ones, and it rather disturbed him to be put off his quest by anything so out of his present way as excessive youth and a rather pathetic grace.

"Lord—the child's ever so much too heavy for her. Must have been married out of the nursery: damned cad, not to—"

The young face mounting toward him continued to bend over the baby, the girl's frail shoulders to droop increasingly under their burden, as the congestion ahead of her forced the young lady to maintain her slanting position halfway up the liner's flank.

A nurse in correct bonnet and veil touched her shoulder, as if offering to relieve her; but she only tightened her arm about the child. Whereupon the nurse, bending, lifted in her own arms a carrot-headed little girl of four or five in a gaudy gipsy-like frock.

"What—another? Why, it's barbarous; it ought to be against the law! The poor little thing—"

Here Boyne's attention was distracted by the passage of a deck-steward asking where he wished his chair placed. He turned to attend to this matter, and saw, on the chair next to his, a tag bearing the name: "Mrs. Cliffe Wheater."

Cliffe Wheater—Cliffe Wheater! What an absurd name . . . and somehow he remembered to have smiled over it in the same way years before. . . But, good Lord, of *course!* How long he must have lived out of the world, on his engineering jobs, first in the Argentine, then in Australia, and since the war in Egypt—how out of step he must have become with the old social dance of New York, not to situate Cliffe Wheater at once as the big red-faced Chicagoan who was at Harvard with him, and who had since become one of the showiest of New York millionaires. Cliffe Wheater, of course—the kind of fellow who was spoken of, respectfully, as having "interests" everywhere: Boyne recalled having run across Wheater "interests" even in the Argentine. But the man himself, at any rate since his marriage, was reputed to be mainly interested in Ritz Hotels and powerful motor-cars. Hadn't he a steam-yacht too? He had a wife, at any rate—it was all coming back to Boyne: he had married, it must be sixteen or seventeen years ago, that good-looking Mervin girl, of New York—Joyce Mervin—whom Boyne himself had danced and flirted with through a remote winter not long after Harvard. Joyce Mervin: she had written to him to announce her engagement, had enclosed a little snap-shot of herself with "Goodbye, Martin," scrawled across it. Had she rather fancied Boyne—Boyne wondered? He had been too poor to try to find out. . . And now he and she were going to be deck-neighbours for a fortnight on the magic seas between Algiers and Venice! He remembered the face he had contemplated that morning in his shaving-glass, and thought: "Very likely she hasn't changed a bit; smart women last so wonderfully; but she won't know *me.*" The idea was half depressing and half reassuring. After all, it would enable him to take his observations—and to have his deck-chair moved, should the result be disappointing.

The ship had shaken her insect-like flock of tugs and sailing-boats off her quivering flanks; and now the great blue level spread before her as she headed away toward the morning. Boyne got a book, pulled his hat over his nose, and stretched out in his deck-chair, awaiting Mrs. Wheater. . .

"This will do—yes, I think this will do," said a fluty immature voice, a girl's voice, at his elbow. Boyne tilted his head back, and saw, a few steps off, the slim girl who had carried the heavy baby up the gangway.

The girl paused, glanced along the line of seats in his direction, nodded to a deck-steward, and disappeared into the doorway of a "luxe" *suite* farther forward. In the moment of her pause Boyne caught a small pale face with anxiously wrinkled brows above brown eyes of tragic width, and round red lips which, at the least provocation, might bubble with healthy laughter. It did not occur to him now to ask if the face were pretty or not—there were too many things going on in it for that.

As she entered her cabin he heard her say, in her firm quick voice, to some one within: "Nanny, has Chip had his Benger? Who's got the cabin with Terry?"

"What a mother!" Boyne thought, still wondering if it were not much too soon for that maternal frown to have shadowed her young forehead.

"Beg pardon, sir—there's a new passenger booked for your cabin." The steward was passing with a couple of good-looking suit-cases and a bundle of rugs.

"Oh, damn—well, it had to happen!" Boyne, with a groan, stood up and followed the steward. "Who is it, do you know?"

"Couldn't say, sir. Wheater—Wheater's the name."

Well, at last a coincidence! Mrs. Cliffe Wheater's chair was next to his own, and his old Harvard class-mate was to share his cabin with him. Boyne, if not wholly pleased, was at least faintly excited and interested by this unexpected combination of circumstances.

He turned, and saw a little boy standing in the door of the cabin, mustering him with a dispassionate eye.

"All right—this will do," said the boy quietly. He spoke in a slightly high-pitched voice, neither querulous nor effeminate, but simply thin and a little tired, like his slender person. Boyne guessed him to be about eleven years old, and too tall and reasonable for his age—another evidence of the physical frailty betrayed by his voice. He was neatly dressed in English school-boy clothes, but he did not look English, he looked cosmopolitan: as if he had been sharpened and worn down by contact with too many different civilizations—or perhaps merely with too many different hotels.

He continued to examine Boyne, critically but amicably; then he remarked: "I'm in here, you know."

"You are? I thought it was to be your father!"

"Oh, did you? That's funny. Do you know my father?"

"I used to. In fact, I think we were at Harvard together."

Young master Wheater looked but faintly interested. "Would you mind telling me your name?" he asked, as if acquitting himself of a recognized social duty.

"My name's Boyne: Martin Boyne. But it's so long since your father and I met that he wouldn't have been likely to speak of me."

Mr. Wheater's son reflected. "Well, I shouldn't have been likely to be there if he did. We're not so awfully much with father," he added, with a seeming desire for accuracy.

A little girl of his own age and size, but whose pale

fairness had a warmer glow, had advanced a step or two into the cabin, and now slipped an arm through his.

"I've been hunting for you everywhere," she said. "Judith sent me."

"Well, here's where I am: with this gentleman."

The little girl lifted her deeply fringed lids and bent on Boyne the full gaze of two large and accomplished gray eyes. Then she pursed up her poppy-red lips and looked at her brother. "For a whole fortnight—Terry, can you *bear* it?"

The boy flushed and pulled away his arm. "Shut up, you ass!" he admonished her.

"Do let me ask Judith to tip the steward—"

He swung about on her angrily. "*Will* you shut up when I tell you to? This gentleman's a friend of father's."

"Oh—" the little girl murmured; and then added, after another fringed flash at Boyne: "He doesn't look it."

"Blanca—will you please get out of here?"

She wavered, her bright lips trembled, and she turned in confusion and ran down the deck. "She doesn't know anything—she's only my twin," said Terry Wheater apologetically.

He completed his scrutiny of the cabin, looked a little wistfully at Boyne, and then turned and sauntered away after the delinquent.

Boyne returned to the deck and his book; but though the latter interested him, it did not prevent his keeping watch, out of the tail of his eye, on the empty chair which bore Mrs. Wheater's name. His curiosity to see her had grown immensely since his encounter with her son and daughter—in the latter of whom he discovered, as the past grew clearer to him, a likeness to her mother at once close and remote. Joyce Mervin—yes, she had had those same poppy-red lips in a face of translucent pallor, and that slow skilful way of manœuvring her big eyes; but her daughter seemed made of a finer frailer stuff, as if a good deal of Mrs. Wheater's substance had been left out of her, and a drop of some rarer essence added. "Perhaps it's because the child is only half a person—there was always too much of her mother," Boyne thought, remembering Joyce Mervin as being rather aimlessly abundant. "In such cases, it's probably enough to be a twin," he decided.

But how puzzling it all was! Terry was much less like Cliffe Wheater than his twin was like their mother. There too—even more so in the boy's case—quality seemed to have replaced quantity. Boyne felt, he hardly knew why, that something obvious and almost vulgar might lurk under Blanca's fastidiousness; but her brother could never be anything but distinguished. What a pity such a charming lad should look so ill!

Suddenly, from the forward *suite,* the young lady with the baby emerged. She had her sleepy cherub by the hand and was guiding him with motherly care along the deck. She sank into the chair next to Boyne's, pulled the baby up on her knee, and signalled to a steward to draw a rug over her feet. Then she leaned back with a sigh of satisfaction.

"This is something like, eh, Chip?" she said, in her gay fluty voice.

Chip laughed a genial well-fed laugh and fingered the brim of her hat appreciatively. It was evident that the two had the very highest opinion of each other.

II

IT was none of Boyne's business to tell his new neighbour that the chair she had chosen was Mrs. Cliffe Wheater's; the less so as she might (he decided on closer inspection) turn out to be a governess or other dependent of that lady's. But no (after another look); she was too young for the part, even if she had looked or acted it—and she didn't. Her tone in addressing her invisible companions was that of command, not subservience: they were the nurses and governesses, not she. Probably she had taken Mrs. Wheater's chair because it was one of the few empty ones left, and was well aware that she might presently be asked to evacuate it. That was just what Boyne would have liked to spare her; he didn't see Joyce Wheater—the Joyce he had known—yielding her seat without a battle.

"I beg your pardon; but in case somebody should claim this chair, I might find another for you before the whole front row is taken up."

The phrase sounded long and clumsy, but it was out before he had time to polish it. He had to hear her voice again, and also to get her to turn her eyes his way. She did so now, with perfect composure. Evidently she was not surprised at his addressing her, but only at the fact he imparted.

"Isn't this my chair?" She reached for the label and examined it. "Yes; I thought it was."

"Oh, I'm sorry—"

"That's all right. They *are* filling up, aren't they?"

Her brown eyes, under deep lashes like Blanca's, rested on him in polite acknowledgment of his good will; but he was too bewildered to see anything but a starry blur.

Mrs. Cliffe Wheater, then—this child? Well, after all, why not? His Mrs. Cliffe Wheater she obviously could not be; but in these days of transient partnerships there was no reason for expecting it. The Wheaters *he* knew must have been married nearly twenty years ago; and Cliffe Wheater, in the interval, had made money enough to treat himself to half-a-dozen divorces and remarriages, with all the attendant outlay. "No more to him than doing over a new house—good deal less than running a steam-yacht," Boyne half enviously reflected.

Yes; his neighbour was obviously a later—was the latest—Mrs. Wheater; probably two or three removes from poor Joyce. Though why he should think of her as poor Joyce, when in all probability she had moved off across the matrimonial chess-board at the same rate of progression as her first husband. . . Well, at any rate, if this was a new Mrs. Cliffe Wheater, Boyne might insinuate himself into her field of vision as an old friend of her husband's; a sufficient plea, he argued, between passengers on a pleasure-cruise. Only, remembering Terry's cool reception of his father's name, he hesitated. These modern matrimonial tangles were full of peril to the absentee. . .

The question was answered by the appearance of Blanca, who came dancing toward them like a butterfly waltzing over a bed of thyme.

As she approached, the young lady at Boyne's side said severely: "Child! Why haven't you got on your coat? Go and ask Scopy for it at once. The wind is cold."

Blanca leaned against her with a caressing gesture.

"All right." But instead of moving she slanted her gaze again toward Boyne. "He says he used to know father," she imparted.

The young lady turned her head also, and Boyne felt the mysterious weight of her eyes upon his face. "How funny!" was her simple comment. It seemed to strike all the group with equal wonder that Martin Boyne should be on speaking terms with its chief. "Not smart enough, I suppose; no Bond Street suit-cases," he grumbled to himself, remembering the freight of costly pigskin which had followed his neighbour up the gangway.

The latter's attention had already turned from him. "Blanca! I tell you to go and put on your coat. And see that Terry has his. . . Don't lean on me like that, child. Can't you see that Chip's asleep?"

She spoke a little wearily, almost irritably, Boyne thought; but as she bent over the child her little profile softened, melting into something puerile and appealing. "Hush!" she signalled; and Blanca, obedient, tiptoed off.

Boyne, at this, invoking Uncle Edward, patron saint of the adventurous, risked a playful comment. "You've got them wonderfully well in hand."

She smiled. "Oh, they're very good children; all except . . . *Zinnie*—!" she screamed; and Boyne, following her horrified glance, saw a stark naked little figure with a shock of orange-coloured hair and a string of amber beads capering toward them to the wonder and delight of the double row of spectators in the deck-chairs.

In a flash the young lady was on her feet, and Boyne was pressing a soap-scented bundle to his breast. "Hold Chip!" she commanded. "Oh, that little red devil!" She sped down the deck and catching up the orange-headed child gave her a violent shaking. "*You*'ll be catching cold next, you wretch," she admonished her, as if this were the head and front of the child's offending; and having pushed the culprit into the arms of a pursuing nurse she regained her seat.

"How nicely you've held him! He's still asleep." She received back the hot baby, all relaxed and slumber-scented, and the eyes she turned on Boyne were now full of a friendly intimacy—and much younger, he thought, than Blanca's. "Did you ever mind a baby before?" she asked.

"Yes; but not such a good one—nor so heavy."

She shone with pride. "Isn't he an armful? He's nearly two pounds heavier than most children of two. When Beechy was his age she weighed only . . ."

"Beechy?" Boyne interrupted. "I thought you called her Zinnie."

"Zinnie? Oh, but she's not the same as Beechy." She laughed with something of a child's amusement at the ignorance of the grown up. "Beechy's a step—but you haven't seen the other steps," she reminded herself. "I wonder where on earth they are?"

"The steps?" he echoed, in deeper bewilderment.

"Bun and Beechy. They only half belong to us, and so does Zinnie. They're all three step-children. But we're just as devoted to them as if they were altogether ours; except when Bun is naughty. Bun is my only naughty child—oh, do hold Chip again!" she exclaimed, and once more Boyne became the repository of that heap of rosy slumber.

"There's Bun now—and I never trust him when he's by himself! I *can't*," she wailed, as a sturdy little brown boy in a scarlet jumper came crawling down the deck on all fours, emitting strange animal barks and crowings.

"He's going to do his menagerie-tricks. Oh, dear— And he can't, with the ship rolling like this. His mother was a lion-tamer. But he'll hurt himself, I know he will—oh, Scopy! Yes; do take him. . ."

A gaunt narrow-chested lady with a face hewn into lines of kindly resolution, and a faded straw hat cocked sideways on her blown gray hair, had appeared in Bun's wake and set him on his feet as firmly as the rolling deck permitted. His face, dusky with wrath, squared itself for a howl; but at that moment a very small brown girl, with immense agate-coloured eyes and a thicket of dark curls, dashed out of a state-room, and hurried to him with outstretched arms. Instantly the offender's wrath turned to weeping, and the two little creatures fell dramatically on each other's bosoms, while the governess, unmoved by this display of feeling, steered them sternly back to their quarters.

The young lady at Boyne's side leaned back with a laugh. "Isn't Scopy funny? She can't bear it when Bun falls on Beechy's neck like that. She calls it 'so foreign and unmanly.' And of course they *are* foreign . . . they're Italian . . . but I'm too thankful that Beechy has such an influence over Bun. If it weren't for her we should have our hands full with him." She hugged the sleep-drunk Chip to her bosom.

"You must have your hands rather full as it is—I mean even without Bun?" Boyne ventured, consumed by the desire to see farther into this nursery tangle, and follow its various threads back to the young creature at his side. "Travelling with them all like this—and without Wheater to help you out," he pushed on.

At this she shrugged a little. "Oh, he's not much at helping out; he loathes to travel with us," she said, slightingly yet not unkindly. Boyne was beginning to think that her detached view of human weaknesses was perhaps the most striking thing about her.

"But Terry helps—most wonderfully," she added, a smile of maternal tenderness lighting her small changeful face, in which so many things were always happening that Boyne had not yet had time to decide if it were pretty or just curiously loveable.

"My cabin-mate," Boyne smiled. "Yes; a big boy like that must be a comfort." He dared not say "a big son like that," for he could not believe that the girl at his side could be the mother of a tall lad of Terry's age. Yet she had distinctly not classed him among the "steps"! In his perplexity he ventured: "A chap of that age is always so proud of his mother."

She seemed to think that this needed consideration. "Well, I don't know that Terry's proud of Joyce, exactly —but he admires her, of course; we all do. She's so awfully handsome. I don't believe even Blanca is going to come up to her."

Joyce! Boyne caught at the familiar name as at a life-belt. Evidently his old friend Joyce Mervin was still situated somewhere within the Wheater labyrinth. But where? And who was this young thing who gave her her Christian name so easily? Everything that seemed at first to enlighten him ended only by deepening his perplexity.

"Do you know that Joyce, as you call her, used to be a great friend of mine years ago?" There could be no harm, at least, in risking that.

"Oh, was she? How jolly! She says she looked exactly like Blanca then. Did she? Of course she's a little thick now—but not nearly as much so as she imagines. She does so fret about it. It's her great unhappiness."

Boyne laughed. "You mean she hasn't any worse ones?"

"Oh, no. Not now. They've been on a new honeymoon since Chip . . . haven't they, old Chippo?"

"They. . . ?" On a new honeymoon? Since Chip? Then the sleeping cherub was not the property of the girl at his side, but of Joyce Mervin . . . Joyce Wheater . . . Joyce Somebody . . . Oh, how he longed to ask: "Joyce *who?*"

This last step forward seemed really to have landed him in the heart of the labyrinth; the difficulty now was to find his way out again.

But the young lady's confidences seemed to invite his own. Or was it just that she had the new easy way with people? Very likely. Still, an old fogey out of the wilderness might be excused for taking it as something more—a sign of sympathy, almost an invitation to meet her fresh allusions with fresh questions.

"Yes; we were friends—really great friends for a winter . . ."

("That's long, for Joyce," said his neighbour parenthetically.)

". . . such good friends that I should like to tell you my name: Martin Boyne—and to ask what your—"

"Oh—*oh! ! !*" She shrilled it out so precipitately that it cut his last word in two. At first he could not guess the cause of this new disturbance; but in a moment he discovered the young Bun walking with bare feet and a cat-like agility along the backs of the outer row of deck-chairs, while their occupants ducked out of his way and laughed their approval of his skill.

"She was also a tight-rope dancer—his mother was," the girl flung back, leaping in Bun's direction. Having caught and cuffed him, and cuffed him again in answer to his furious squeals, she dragged him away to the firm dishevelled lady who had previously dealt with him. When she returned to her seat, pale and a little breathless, she looked as if her domestic cares sometimes weighed on her too heavily. She dropped down by Boyne with a sigh. "If ever you marry," she enjoined him ("And how does she know I never have?" he wondered), "don't you have any children—that's all I say! Do you wonder mother and father don't care to travel with the lot of us?"

III

THE luncheon-signal crashed in on this interrogation, and Boyne was left alone to make what he could of it. At the first sound of the gong his neighbour was on her feet, hardly heeding his suggestion that, if she had not already chosen her seat, they might meet at a table for two in the restaurant.

"Thanks a lot; but of course I lunch with my children." And he remembered with regret that their ocean-palace had a separate dining-room for youthful passengers.

"Dash it—I should have liked a few minutes' quiet talk with her."

Instead, he drifted back to his usual place at a table of waifs and strays like himself: an earnest lady in spectacles who was "preparing" Sicily; an elderly man who announced every morning: "I always say the bacon on these big liners is better than anything I can get at home"; and a pale clergyman whose parishioners had sent him on a holiday tour, and whose only definite idea was to refuse to visit catacombs. "I do so want to lead a pagan life just for once," he confided to Boyne, with an ascetic smile which showed, between racking coughs, his worn teeth and anæmic gums.

Luncheon over, Boyne hurried back to his corner, hoping to find the seat at his side already occupied; but it was empty, and empty it remained as the long blue day curved down imperceptibly toward evening.

"Father and mother don't care to travel with the lot of us," the girl had said.

"Father and mother"? That, as far as Boyne could make out, could mean only the Cliffe Wheaters, his old original Cliffe Wheaters, in their before-the-letter state, as it were. In that case the thin eager girl at his side would be their daughter, their eldest daughter, born probably soon after a marriage which, some thirteen or fourteen years later, had produced the sturdy and abundant Chip.

"Very unmodern, all that." It gave Boyne a more encouraging view of the conjugal state than he had lately held, and made him look forward with a lighter mind to meeting the lady who awaited him in the Dolomites—the lady he had not seen for five years. It must certainly be pleasant to be the parent of a large reliable baby like Chip. . .

But no sooner did he imagine that he had solved the puzzle of the Cliffe Wheaters than the image of the enigmatic trio, Zinnie, Bun and Beechy, disarranged his neat equation. The "steps"—who on earth were the "steps," and how and where did they fit into the family group which seemed, with Judith (hadn't they called her that?) at one end, and Chip at the other, to form its own unbroken circle? Miss Wheater, he remembered, had tossed him a few details about the two brown children, Bun and Beechy. "They're foreigners. . . Italians. . ." But if so, they belonged neither to Cliffe Wheater nor to his wife; certainly not to his wife, since Judith had added, in speaking of Bun: "His mother was a lion-tamer . . ." not as if using the term metaphorically, but as stating a plain social fact.

As for Zinnie, the little red devil, she remained wholly unaccounted for, and there was nothing in her clever impudent face, with its turned-up nose and freckled skin under the shock of orange hair, to suggest any blood-relationship to the small Italians. Zinnie appeared to be sharply and completely American—as American as Beechy and Bun were Italian, and much more so than the three elder Wheaters, who were all so rubbed down by cosmopolitan contacts. The "steps," in fact, had the definiteness of what the botanists call species, whereas Judith, Blanca and Terry were like exquisite garden hybrids. The harder Boyne stared into the problem the more obscure it became.

Even the least eventful sea-voyages lend themselves to favourable propinquities, and in the course of the afternoon the gray-haired lady whom the young Wheaters addressed as "Scopy" reappeared on deck, this time alone, and seemingly in quest of a seat. Boyne instantly pointed out the one next to his, and the lady, saying with an austere smile: "I believe ours are on the other side, but I can take this while Judith's resting," settled herself at his side in an attitude of angular precision.

As she did so she gave him a look of shy benevolence, and added: "I understand from Judith that you're a friend of her people."

Boyne eagerly acquiesced, and she went on to say what a comfort it was, when they were on one of these long treks with the children, to come across anybody who was a friend of their parents, and could be appealed to in an emergency. "Not that there's any particular reason at present; but it's a good deal of a responsibility for Judith to transport the whole party from Biskra to Venice, and we're always rather troubled about Terry. Even after four months at Biskra he hasn't picked up as we'd hoped. . . Always a little temperature in the evenings. . ." She sighed, and turned away her sturdy weather-beaten face, which looked like a cliff on whose top a hermit had built a precarious refuge—her hat.

"You're anxious about Terry? He does look a little drawn." Boyne hoped that if he adopted an easy old-friend tone she might be lured on from one confidence to another.

"Anxious? I don't like the word; and Judith wouldn't admit it. But we always have our eye on him, the dear boy—and our minds." She sighed again, and he saw that she had averted her head because her eyes were filling.

"It is, as you say, a tremendous responsibility for any one as young as Miss Wheater." He hesitated, and then added: "I can very nearly guess her age, for I used to see a good deal of both her parents before they were married."

It was a consolation to his self-esteem that the lady called "Scopy" took this with less flippancy than her young charges. It seemed distinctly interesting to her, and even reassuring, that Boyne should have been a friend of the Cliffe Wheaters at any stage in their career. "I only wish you'd gone on seeing them since," she said, with another of her sighs.

"Oh, our paths have been pretty widely divided; so much so that at first I didn't know whether . . . not till I saw Chip. . ."

"Ah, poor little Chipstone: he's our hope, our consolation." She looked down, and a faint brick-red blush crossed her face like sunset on granite. "You see, Terry being so delicate—as twins often are—Mr. Wheater was always anxious for another boy."

"Well, Chip looks like a pretty solid foundation to build one's hopes on."

She smiled a little bleakly, and murmured: "He's never given us a minute's trouble."

All this was deeply interesting to her hearer, but it left the three "steps" still unaccounted for; the "steps" of whom Judith had said that they were as much beloved as if they had been "altogether ours."

"Not a minute's trouble—I wish I could say as much of the others," his neighbour went on, yielding, as he had hoped she would, to the rare chance of airing her grievances.

"The others? You mean—"

"Yes: those foreign children, with their scenes and their screams and their play-acting. I shall never get used to them—never!"

"But Zinnie: Zinnie's surely not foreign?" Boyne lured her on.

"Foreign to *our* ways, certainly; really more so than the two others, who, on the father's side. . ." She lowered her voice, and cast a prudent eye about her, before adding: "You've heard of Zinnia Lacrosse, the film star, I suppose?"

Boyne racked his mind, which was meagrely peopled with film stars, and finally thought he had. "Didn't she marry some racing man the other day—Lord Somebody?"

"I don't know what her last enormity has been. One of them was marrying Mr. Wheater—and having Zinnie. . ."

Marrying Wheater—Zinnia Lacrosse had married Cliffe Wheater? But then—but then—who on earth was Chipstone's mother? Boyne felt like crying out: "Don't pile up any more puzzles! Give me time—give me time!" but his neighbour was now so far launched in the way of avowal that she went on, hardly heeding him more than if his face had been the narrow grating through which she was pouring her woes: "It's inconceivable, but it's so. Mr. Wheater married Zinnia Lacrosse. And Zinnie is their child. The truth is, he wasn't altogether to blame; I've always stood up for Mr. Wheater. What with his feeling so low after Mrs. Wheater left him, and his wanting another boy so dreadfully . . . with all those millions to inherit. . ."

But Boyne held up a drowning hand. Mrs. Wheater had left Wheater? But when—but how—but why? He implored the merciless narrator to tell him one thing at a time—only one; all these sudden appearances of new people and new children were so perplexing to a man who'd lived for years and years in the wilderness. . .

"The wilderness? The real wilderness is the world *we* live in; packing up our tents every few weeks for another move. . . And the marriages just like tents—folded up and thrown away when you've done with them." But she saw, at least, that to gain his sympathy she must have his understanding, and after another cautious glance up and down the deck she settled down to elucidate the mystery and fill in the gaps. Of course, she began, Judith having told her that he—Mr. Boyne was the name? Thanks. Hers was Miss Scope, Horatia Scope (she knew the children called her "Horror Scope" behind her back, but she didn't mind)—well, Judith having told her that Mr. Boyne was a friend of her parents, Miss Scope had inferred that he had kept up with the successive episodes of the couple's agitated history; but now that she saw he didn't know, she would try to make it clear to him—if one could use the word in speaking of such a muddled business. It took a great deal of explaining—as he would see—but if any one could enlighten him *she* could, for she'd come to the Wheaters' as Judith's governess before Blanca and Terry were born: before the first, no, the second serious quarrel, she added, as if saying: "Before the Hittite invasion."

Quarrels, it seemed, there had been many since; she had lost count, she confessed; but the bad, the fatal, one had happened when Mrs. Wheater had met her Prince, the wicked Buondelmonte who was the father of Bun and Beechy: Beatrice and Astorre Buondelmonte, as the children were really named.

Here Boyne, submerged, had to hold up his hand again. But if Zinnie was Wheater's child, he interrupted, were Bun and Beechy Mrs. Wheater's? And whose, in the name of pity, was Chipstone? Well. . . Miss Scope said she understood his wonder, his perplexity; it did him credit, she declared, to be too high-minded to take in the whole painful truth at a glance. No; Bun and Beechy, thank heaven, were *not* Mrs. Wheater's children; they were the offspring of the unscrupulous Prince Buondelmonte and a vile woman—a circus performer, she believed —whom he had married and deserted before poor Mrs. Wheater became infatuated with him. ("Infatuated" was a horrid word, she knew; but Mrs. Wheater used it herself in speaking of that unhappy time.)

Well—Mrs. Wheater, in her madness, had insisted on leaving her husband in order to marry Prince Buondelmonte. Mr. Wheater, though she had behaved so badly, was very chivalrous about it, and "put himself in the wrong" (Boyne rejoiced at the phrase) so that his wife might divorce him; but he insisted on his right to keep Terry with him, and on an annual visit of four months from Judith and Blanca; and as there was a big fight over the alimony Mrs. Wheater had to give in about the children—and that was when Judith's heart-break began. Even as a little thing, Miss Scope explained, Judith couldn't bear it when her parents quarrelled. She had had to get used to that, alas; but what she couldn't get used to was, after the divorce and the two remarriages, being separated from Terry, and bundled up every year with Blanca, and sent from pillar to post, first to one Palace Hotel and then to another, wherever one parent or the other happened to be. . . It was that, Miss Scope thought, which had given the grown-up look to her eyes. . .

Luckily Mrs. Wheater's delusion didn't last long; the Prince hadn't let it. Before they'd been married a year he'd taken care to show her what he was. Poor Judith, who was alone with her mother during the last dreadful months, knew something of *that*. But Miss Scope realised that she mustn't digress, but just stick to the outline of her story till it became a little clearer to Mr. Boyne. . .

Well—when Mrs. Wheater's eyes were opened, and the final separation from the Prince took place, she (Mrs. Wheater) was so sorry for Beatrice and Astorre—there was really nobody kinder than Mrs. Wheater—that she kept the poor little things with her, and had gone on keeping them ever since. Their father had of course been only too thankful to have them taken off his hands—and their miserable mother too. Here Miss Scope paused for breath, and hoped that Mr. Boyne was beginning to grasp—

"Yes; beginning; but—Chipstone?" he patiently insisted.

"Oh, Chip; dear Chip's a Wheater all right! The very image of his father, don't you think? But I see that I haven't yet given you all the threads; there are so many. . . Where was I? Oh, about Mrs. Wheater's separation. You know there's no divorce in Italy, and she thought she was tied to the Prince for life. But luckily her lawyers found out that he had been legally married—in some Italian consulate at the other end of the world—to the mother of Bun and Beechy; and as the woman was still alive, the Prince's marriage with Mrs. Wheater had been bigamous, and was immediately annulled, and she became Mrs. Wheater again—"

"And then?"

"Then she was dreadfully miserable about it all, and Mr. Wheater was miserable too, because in the meanwhile he'd found out about the horror he'd married, and was already suing for a divorce. And Judith, who was thirteen by that time, and as wise and grown up as she is now, begged and entreated her father and mother to meet and talk things over, and see if they couldn't come together again, so that the children would never have to be separated, and sent backward and forward like bundles—"

"She did that? That child?"

"Judith's never been a child—there was no time. So she got Mr. and Mrs. Wheater together, and they were both sore and unhappy over their blunders, and realised what a mess they'd made—and finally they decided to try again, and they were remarried about three years ago; and then Chip was born, and of course that has made everything all right again—for the present."

"The present?" Boyne gasped; and the governess smoothed back her blown hair, and turned the worn integrity of her face on his.

"If I respect the truth, how can I say more than 'the present'? But really I put it that way only for fear . . .

for fear of the Fates overhearing me. . . Everything's going as smoothly as can be; and we should all be perfectly happy if it weren't for poor Terry, whose health never seems to be what it should. . . Mr. and Mrs. Wheater adore Chip, and are very fond of the other children; and Judith is almost sure it will last this time."

Miss Scope broke off, and looked away again from Boyne. Her "almost" wrung his heart, and he wanted to put his hand out, and clasp the large gray cotton glove clenched on her knee. But instead he only said: "If anything can make it last, you and Judith will"; and the governess answered: "Oh, it's all Judith. And she has all the children behind her. They say they refuse to be separated again. Even the little ones say so. They're much more attached to each other than you'd think, to hear them bickering and wrangling. And they all worship Judith. Even the two foreigners do."

IV

THE children, at first, had been unanimously and immovably opposed to going to Monreale.

Long before the steamer headed for Palermo the question was debated by them with a searching thoroughness. Judith, who had never been to Sicily, had consulted Boyne as to the most profitable way of employing the one day allotted to them, and after inclining to Segesta, Boyne, on finding that everybody, including Chip, was to be of the party, suggested Monreale as more accessible.

"And awfully beautiful too?" Judith was looking at him with hungry ignorant eyes.

"One of the most beautiful things in the world. The mosaics alone. . ."

She clasped ecstatic hands. "We must go there! I've seen so little—"

"Why, I thought you'd travelled from one end of Europe to the other."

"That doesn't show you anything but sleeping-cars and Palace Hotels, does it? Mother and father never even have a guide-book; they just ask the hall-porter where to go. And then something always seems to prevent their going. You must show me everything, everything."

"Well, we'll begin with Monreale."

But the children took a different view. Miss Scope, unluckily, had found an old Baedeker on the steamer, and refreshing her mind with hazy reminiscences gleaned from former pupils, had rediscovered the name of a wonderful ducal garden containing ever so many acres of orange-trees always full of flowers and fruit. Her old pupils had gone there, she recalled, and been allowed by the gardeners to pick up from the ground as many oranges as they could carry away.

At this the children, a close self-governing body, instantly voted as one man for the Giardino Aumale. Boyne had already observed that, in spite of Judith's strong influence, there were moments when she became helpless against their serried opposition, and in the present case argument and persuasion entirely failed. At length Terry, evidently wishing, as the man of the party, to set the example of reasonableness, remarked that Judith, who had all the bother of looking after them, ought to go wherever she chose. Bun hereupon squared his mouth for a howl, and Blanca observed tartly that by always pretending to give up you generally got what you wanted. "Well, you'd better try then," Terry retorted severely, and the blood rose under his sister's delicate skin as if he had struck her.

"Terry! What a beast you are! I didn't mean—"

Meanwhile Beechy, melting into tears at the sight of Bun's distress, was hugging his tumbled head against her breast with murmurs of: *"Zitto, zitto, carissimo! Cuor mio!"* and glaring angrily at Judith and Terry.

"Well, I want to go where there's zoranges to eat," said Zinnie, in her sharp metallic American voice, with which she might almost have peeled the fruit. "—'r if I don't, I want something a lot better'nstead, n' I mean to have it!"

Boyne laughed, and Judith murmured despairingly: "We'd better go to their orange-garden."

"Look here," Terry interposed, "the little ones are

mad to hear the end of that story of the old old times, about the two children who'd never seen a motor. They're all so fed up with airships and machinery and X rays and wireless; and you know you promised to go on with that story some day. Why couldn't we go to the place you want to see, and you'll promise and swear to finish the story there, and to have chocolates for tea?"

"Oh—and oranges; I'll supply the oranges," Boyne interposed. "There's a jolly garden next to the cloister, and I'll persuade the guardian to let us in, and we'll have a picnic tea there."

"An'masses of zoranges?" Zinnie stipulated, with a calculating air, while Beechy surreptitiously dried Bun's tears on her crumpled pinafore, and Bun, heartlessly forsaking her to turn handsprings on the deck, shrieked out: "Noranges! Noranges! NORANGES!"

"Oh, very well; I knew—" Blanca murmured, shooting her gray glance toward Boyne; and Judith, lifting up Chip, triumphantly declared: "He says he wants to go to Monreale."

"That settles it, of course," said Blanca, with resigned eyelids.

A wordy wrangle having arisen between Zinnie, Beechy and Bun as to whether the fruit for which they clamoured should be called zoranges or noranges, Judith and Miss Scope took advantage of the diversion to settle the details of the expedition with Boyne, and the next morning, when the steamer lay to off Palermo, the little party, equipped and eager, headed the line of passengers for the tug.

Boyne, stretched out at length on a stone bench in the sun, lay listening with half-closed eyes to Judith's eager plaintive voice. He had bribed the custodian to let them pass out of the cloister into the lavender-scented cathedral garden drowsing on its warm terrace above the orange-orchards. Far off across the plain the mountains descended in faint sapphire gradations to the denser sapphire of the sea, along which the domed and towered city gleamed uncertainly. And here, close by, sat Judith Wheater in the sun, the children heaped at her knee, and Scopy and Nanny, at a discreet distance, knitting, and nursing the tea-basket. Judith's voice went on: "But when Polycarp and Lullaby drove home in the victoria with the white horse to their mamma's palace they found that the zebra door-mat had got up and was eating all the flowers in the drawing-room vases, and the big yellow birds on the wall-paper were all flying about, and making the most dreadful mess scattering seeds about the rooms. But the most wonderful thing was that the cuckoo from the nursery clock was gone too, so that the nurses couldn't tell what time it was, and when the children ought to be put to bed and to get up again. . ."

"Oh, how perfectly lovely," chanted Bun, and Beechy chorused: "Lovelly, lovelly. . ."

"Not at all," said Judith severely. "It was the worst thing that had happened to them yet, for the cook didn't know what time it was either, and nobody in the house could tell her, so there was no breakfast ready; and the cook just went off for a ride on the zebra, because she had no carriage of her own, and she said there was nothing else to do."

"Why didn't they tell their father'n'mother?" Zinnie queried in a practical tone.

"Because they'd got new ones, who didn't know about the cuckoo either, I guess," said Bun with authority.

"Then why didn't the children go with their old fathers an' mothers?" Zinnie inserted.

"Because their old mother's friend, Sally Money, wasn't big enough . . . big enough . . . big enough . . . for her to take them all with her. . ." Bun broke off, visibly puzzled as to what was likely to follow.

"Big enough to take them all on her back and carry them away with her. But I daresay the new father and mother would have been all right," Judith pursued, "if only the children had been patient and known how to treat them; only just at first they didn't; and besides, at the time I am telling you about, they happened to be away travelling—"

"Then why didn't the children telephone to them to come back?"

"Because there weren't any telephones in those days."

"No telephones? Does it say so in the hist'ry books?" snapped Zinnie, sceptical.

"Course it does, you silly. Why, when Scopy was little," Terry reminded them, "she lived in a house where there wasn't any telephone."

Beechy, ever tender-hearted, immediately prepared to cry at the thought of Scopy's privation; but Scopy interpolated severely: "Now, Beatrice, don't be *foreign—*" and the story-teller went on: "So there was no way whatever for them to get any breakfast, and—"

"Oh, I know, I know! They starved to death, *poverini!*" Beechy lamented, promptly transferring her grief to another object, and flinging her little brown arms heavenward in an agony of participation.

"Not just yet. For they met on the edge of the wood—"

("What wood? There wasn't any wood before," said Zinnie sharply.)

"No, but there was one now; for all the trees and flowers from the wall-papers had come off the wall, and gone out into the garden to grow, so that the big yellow birds should have a wood to build their nests in, and the zebras should—"

"Zebras! There was only one zebra." This, sardonically, from a grown-up looking, indifferent Blanca.

"Stupid! He'd been married already and had a lot of perfectly lovely norphans and three dear little steps like us, and Mrs. Zebra she had a big family too, no, she had two big families," Zinnie announced, enumerating the successive groups on her small dimpled fingers.

"Oh, how lovely for the zebra! Then all the little zebras stayed together always afterward—f'rever and ever. Say they did—oh, Judith, *say* it!" Beechy clamoured.

"Of course they did. (Zinnie, you mustn't call Blanca stupid.) But all this time Polycarp and Lullaby were starving, because the clock had stopped and the cook had gone out on the zebra. . ."

"And they were starving—slowly starving to death . . ." Zinnie gloated.

"Yes; but on the edge of the wood whom did they meet but a great big tall gentleman with a mot—no, I mean a pony-carriage. . ."

"What's a pony?"

"A little horse about as big as Bun—"

("Oh, oh—I'm a pony!" shouted Bun, kicking and neighing.)

"And the pony-carriage was full—absolutely brim full

of—what do you think?" Judith concluded, her question drowned in a general cry of "Oranges! No, noranges—zoranges!!!" from the leaping scrambling group before whom, at the dramatic moment, Boyne had obligingly uncorded his golden bales, while Miss Scope and Nanny murmured: "Now, children, children—now—"

"And this is our chance," said Boyne, "to make a dash for the cathedral."

He slipped his hand through Judith's arm, and drew her across the cloister and into the great echoing basilica. At first, after their long session on the sun-drenched terrace, the place seemed veiled in an impenetrable twilight. But gradually the tremendous walls and spandrils began to glow with their own supernatural radiance, the solid sunlight of gold and umber and flame-coloured mosaics, against which figures of saints, prophets, kings and sages stood out in pale solemn hues. Boyne led the girl toward one of the shafts of the nave, and they sat down on its projecting base.

"Now from here you can see—"

But he presently perceived that she could see nothing. Her little profile was studiously addressed to the direction in which he pointed, and her head thrown back so that her lips were parted, and her long lashes drew an upward curve against her pale skin; but nothing was happening in the face which was usually the theatre of such varied emotions.

She sat thus for a long time, and he did not move or speak again. Finally she turned to him, and said in a shy voice (it was the first time he had noticed any shyness in her): "I suppose I'm much more ignorant than you could possibly have imagined."

"You mean that you don't particularly care for all this?"

She lowered her voice to answer: "I believe all those big people up there frighten me a little." And she added: "I'm glad I didn't bring Chip."

"Child!" He let his hand fall on hers with a faint laugh. What a child she became as soon as she was away from the other children!

"But I do want to admire it, you know," she went on earnestly, "because you do, and Scopy says you know such a lot about everything."

"It's not a question of knowing—" he began; and then broke off. For wasn't it, after all, exactly that? How many thousand threads of association, strung with stored images of the eye and brain, memories of books, of pictures, of great names and deeds, ran between him and those superhuman images, tracing a way from his world to theirs? Yes; it had been stupid of him to expect that a child of fifteen or sixteen, brought up in complete ignorance of the past, and with no more comprehension than a savage of the subtle and allusive symbolism of art, should feel anything in Monreale but the oppression of its awful unreality. And yet he was disappointed, for he was already busy at the masculine task of endowing the woman of the moment with every quality which made life interesting to himself.

"Woman—but she's not a woman! She's a child." His thinking of her as anything else was the crowning absurdity of the whole business. Obscurely irritated with himself and her, he stood up, turning his back impatiently on the golden abyss of the apse. "Come along; it's chilly here after our sun-bath. Gardens are best, after all."

In the doorway she paused a moment and sent her gaze a little wistfully down the mighty perspective they were leaving. "Some day, I know, I shall want to come back here," she said.

"Oh, well, we'll come back together," he replied perfunctorily.

But outside in the sunlight, with the children leaping about her, and guiding her with joyful cries toward the outspread tea-things, she was instantly woman again—gay, competent, composed, and wholly mistress of the situation. . .

Yes; decidedly, the more Boyne saw of her the more she perplexed him, the more difficult he found it to situate her in time and space. He did not even know how old she was—somewhere between fifteen and seventeen, he conjectured—nor had he as yet made up his mind if she were pretty. In the cathedral, just now, he had thought her almost plain, with the dull droop of her mouth, her pale complexion which looked dead when unlit by gaiety, her thick brown hair, just thick and just brown, without the magic which makes some women's hair as alive as their lips, and her small impersonal nose, a nose neither perfectly drawn like Blanca's nor impudently droll like Zinnie's. The act of thus cataloguing her seemed to reduce her to a bundle of negatives; yet here in the sunshine, her hat thrown off her rumpled hair, and all the children scrambling over her, her mouth became a flame, her eyes fountains of laughter, her thin frail body a quiver of light—he didn't know how else to put it. Whatever she was, she was only intermittently; as if her body were the mere vehicle of her moods, the projection of successive fears, hopes, ardours, with hardly any material identity of its own. Strange, he mused, that such an imponderable and elusive creature should be the offspring of the two solid facts he recalled the Cliffe Wheaters as being. For a reminder of Joyce Mervin as he had known her, tall, vigorous and substantial, one must turn to Blanca, not Judith. If Blanca had not had to spare a part of herself for the making of Terry she would have been the reproduction of her mother. But Judith was like a thought, a vision, an aspiration—all attributes to which Mrs. Cliffe Wheater could never have laid claim. And Boyne, when the tired and sleepy party were piled once more into the motor, had not yet decided what Judith looked like, and still less if he really thought her pretty.

He fell asleep that night composing a letter to the lady in the Dolomites. ". . . what you would think. A strange little creature who changes every hour, hardly seems to have any personality of her own except when she's mothering her flock. Then she's extraordinary: playmate, mother and governess all in one; and the best of each in its way. As for her very self, when she's not with them, you grope for her identity and find an instrument the wind plays on, a looking-glass that reflects the clouds, a queer little sensitive plate, very little and very sensitive—" and with a last flash of caution, just as sleep overcame him, he added: "Unluckily not in the least pretty."

V

"I'M so much interested in your picturesque description of the little-girl-mother (sounds almost as nauseating as 'child-wife,' doesn't it?) who is conducting that heterogeneous family across Europe, while the parents are jazzing at Venice. What an instance of modern manners; no, not manners—there are none left—but customs! I'm sure if I saw the little creature I should fall in love with her—as you are obviously doing. Luckily you'll be parting soon, or I should expect to see you arrive here with the girl-bride of the movies and a tribe of six (or is it seven?) adopted children. Don't imagine, though, that in that case I should accept the post of governess." And then, p.s: "Of course she's awfully pretty, or you wouldn't have taken so much pains to say that she's not."

One of Rose Sellars's jolly letters: clever, understanding and humorous. Why did Boyne feel a sudden flatness in it? Something just a trifle mincing, self-conscious—prepared? Yes; if Mrs. Sellars excelled in one special art it was undoubtedly that of preparation. She led up to things—the simplest things—with the skill of a clever rider putting a horse at a five-barred gate. All her life had been a series of adaptations, arrangements, shifting of lights, lowering of veils, pulling about of screens and curtains. No one could arrange a room half so well; and she had arranged herself and her life just as skilfully. The material she had had to deal with was poor enough; in every way unworthy of her; but, as her clever hands could twist a scarf into a divan-cover, and ruffle a bit of paper into a lamp-shade, so she had managed, out of mediocre means, a mediocre husband, an ugly New York house, and a dull New York set, to make something distinguished, personal, almost exciting—so that, in her little world, people were accustomed to say "Rose Sellars" as a synonym for cleverness and originality.

Yes; she had had the art to do that, and to do it quietly, unobtrusively, by a touch here, a hint there, without ever reaching out beyond her domestic and social frame-work. Her originality, in the present day, lay in this consistency and continuity. It was what had drawn Boyne to her in the days of his big wanderings, when, returning from an arduous engineering job in Rumania or Brazil or Australia, he would find, in his ever-shifting New York, the one fixed pole of Mrs. Sellars's front door, always the same front door at the same number of the same street, with the same Whistler etchings and Sargent water-colours on the drawing-room walls, and the same quiet welcome to the same fireside.

In his homeless years that sense of her stability had appealed to him peculiarly: the way, each time he returned, she had simply added a little more to herself, like a rose unfurling another petal. A rose in full sun would have burst into quicker bloom; it was part of Mrs. Sellars's case that she had always, as Heine put it, been like a canary in a window facing north. Not due north, however, but a few points north by west; so that she caught, not the sun's first glow, but its rich decline. He could never think of her as having been really young, immaturely young, like this girl about whom they were exchanging humorous letters, and who, in certain other ways, had a precocity of experience so far beyond Mrs.

Sellars's. But the question of a woman's age was almost always beside the point. When a man loved a woman she was always the age he wanted her to be; when he had ceased to, she was either too old for witchery or too young for technique. "And five years is too long a time," he summed it up again, with a faint return of the apprehension he always felt when he thought of his next meeting with Mrs. Sellars.

Five years was too long; and these five, in particular, had transformed the situation, and perhaps its heroine. It was a new Rose Sellars whom he was to meet. When they had parted she was still a wife—resigned, exemplary, and faithful in spite of his pleadings; now she was a widow. The word was full of disturbing implications, and Boyne had already begun to wonder how much of her attraction had been due to the fact that she was unattainable. It was all very well to say that he "wasn't that kind of man"—the kind to tire of a woman as soon as she could be had. That was all just words; in matters of sex and sentiment, as he knew, a man was a different kind of man in every case that presented itself. Only by going to the Dolomites to see her could he really discover what it was that he had found so haunting in Rose Sellars. So he was going.

"Mr. Boyne—could we have a quiet talk, do you think?"

Boyne, driven from the deck by the heat and glare, and the activities of the other passengers, was lying on his bed, book in hand, in a state of after-luncheon apathy. His small visitor leaned in the doorway, slender and gray-clad: Terry Wheater, with the faint pinkness on his cheek-bones, the brilliance in his long-lashed eyes, that made his honest boy's face at times so painfully beautiful.

"Why, of course, old man. Come in. You'll be better off here than on deck till it gets cooler."

Terry tossed aside his cap and dropped into the chair at Boyne's bedside. They had shared a cabin for nearly a fortnight, and reached the state of intimacy induced by such nearness when it does not result in hate; but Boyne had had very few chances to talk with the boy. Terry was always asleep when the older man turned in, and Boyne himself was up and out long before Terry, kept in bed by the vigilant Miss Scope, had begun his leisurely toilet. Boyne, by now, had formed a fairly clear idea of the characteristics of the various young Wheaters, but Terry was perhaps the one with whom he had spent the least time; and the boy's rather solemn tone, and grown-up phraseology, made him lay aside his book with a touch of curiosity.

"What can I do for you, Terry?"

"Persuade them that I ought to have a tutor."

"Them?"

"I mean the Wheaters—father and mother," Terry corrected himself. The children, Boyne knew, frequently referred to their parents by their surname. The habit of doing so, Miss Scope had explained, rose from the fact that, in the case of most of the playmates of their wandering life, the names "father" and "mother" had to be applied, successively or simultaneously, to so many different persons; indeed one surprising little girl with black curls and large pearl earrings, whom they had met the year before at Biarritz, had the habit of handing to each new playmate a typed table of her parents' various marriages and her own successive adoptions. "So they all do it now; that is, speak of their different sets of parents by their names. And my children have picked up the habit from the others, though in their own case, luckily, it's no longer necessary, now that their papa and mamma have come together again."

"I mean father and mother," Terry repeated. "Make them understand that I must be educated. There's no time to lose. And *you* could." His eyes were fixed feverishly—alas, too feverishly—on Boyne's, and his face had the air of precocious anxiety which sometimes made Judith look so uncannily mature.

"My dear chap—of course I'll do anything I can for you. But I don't believe I shall be seeing your people this time. I'm going to jump into the train the minute we get to Venice."

The boy's face fell. "You are? I'm sorry. And Judy will be awfully sold."

"That's very good of her—and of you. But you see—"

"Oh, I can see that a solid fortnight of the lot of us is a good deal for anybody," Terry acquiesced. "All the same, Judy and I did hope you'd stay in Venice for a day or two. We thought, you see, there were a good many things you could do for us."

Boyne continued to consider him thoughtfully. "I should be very glad if I could. But I'm afraid you overrate my influence. I haven't seen your parents for years. They'd hardly remember me."

"That's just it: you'd be a novelty," said Terry astutely.

"Well—if that's an inducement. . . Anyhow, you may be sure I'll do what I can . . . if I find I can alter my plans. . . "

"Oh, if you could! You see I've really never had anybody to speak for me. Scopy cuts no ice with them, and of course they think Judy's too young to know about education—specially as she's never had any herself. She can't even spell, you know. She writes stomach with a *k*. And they've let me go on like this, just with nurses and nursery-governesses (that's really all Scopy is), as if I wasn't any older than Bun, when I'm at an age when most fellows are leaving their preparatory schools." The boy's face coloured with the passion of his appeal, and the flush remained in two sharp patches on his cheeks.

"Of course," he went on, "Judy says I'm not fair to them—that I don't remember what a lot they've had to spend for me on doctors and climate, and all that. And they did send me to school once, and I had to be taken away because of my beastly temperature. . . I know all that. But it *was* a sell, when I left school, just to come back again to Scopy and Nanny, and nobody a fellow could put a question to, or get a tip from about what other fellows are learning. Last summer, at St. Moritz, I met a boy not much older than I am who was rather delicate too, and he'd just got a new father who was a great reader, and who had helped him no end, and got a tutor for him; and he'd started Cæsar, and was getting up his Greek verbs—with a temperature every evening too. And I said to Judy: 'Now, look at that.' And she said, yes, it would be splendid for me to have a tutor. And for two weeks the other fellow's father let me work a little with him. But then we had to go away—one of our troubles," Terry interrupted himself, "is that we're so everlastingly going away. But I suppose it's always so with children—isn't it?—with all the different parents they're divided up among, and all the parents living in different places, and fighting so about when the children are to go to which, and the lawyers always changing things just as you think they're arranged. . . Of course a chap must expect to be moving about when he's young. But Scopy says that later parents settle down." He added this on a note of interrogation, and Boyne, feeling that an answer was expected, declared with conviction: "Oh, but they do—by Jove, they do!"

Inwardly he was recalling the warm cocoon of habit in which his own nursery and school years had been enveloped, giving time for a screen of familiar scenes and faces to form itself about him before he was thrust upon the world. What had struck Boyne first about the little tribe generically known as the Wheaters was that they were so exposed, so bared to the blast—as if they had missed some stage of hidden growth for which Palace Hotels and Riviera Expresses afforded no sufficient shelter. He found his gaze unable to bear the too-eager questioning of the boy's, and understood why Miss Scope looked away when she talked of Terry.

"Settle down? Rather! People naturally tend to as they get older. Aren't your own parents proving it already? Haven't you all got together again, so to speak?" Boyne winced at his own exaggerated tone of optimism. It was a delicate matter, in such cases, to catch exactly the right note.

"Yes," Terry assented. "You'd think so. But I know children who've thought so too, and been jolly well sold. The trouble is you can never be sure when parents will really begin to feel old. Especially with all these new ways the doctors have of making them young again. But anyhow," he went on more hopefully, "if you would put in a word I'm sure it would count a lot. And Judy is sure it would too."

"Then of course I will. I'll stop over a day or two, and do all I can," Boyne assured him, casting plans and dates to the winds.

He was not certain that the appeal had not anticipated a secret yearning of his own; a yearning not so much to postpone his arrival at Cortina (to that he would not confess) as to defer the parting from his new friends, and especially from Judith. The Monreale picnic had been successfully repeated in several other scenes of classic association, and during the gay and clamorous expeditions ashore, and the long blue days on deck, he had been gradually penetrated by the warm animal life which proceeds from a troop of happy healthy children. Everything about the little Wheaters and their "steps" excited his interest and sympathy, and not least the frailness of the tie uniting them, and their determination that it should not be broken. There was something tragic, to Boyne, in the mere fact of this determination—it implied a range of experience and a power of forethought so far beyond a child's natural imagining. To the ordinary child, Boyne's memories told him, separation means something too vague to fret about beforehand, and too pleasantly tempered, when it comes, by the excitement of novelty, and the joy of release from routine, to be anything but a jolly adventure. Boyne could not recall that he had ever minded being sent from home (to the seashore, to a summer camp, or to an aunt's, when a new baby was expected) as long as he was allowed to take his mechanical toys with him. Any place that had a floor on which you could build cranes and bridges and railways was all right: if there was a beach with sand that could be trenched and tunnelled, and water that could be dammed, then it was heaven, even if the porridge wasn't as good as it was at home, and there was no mother to read stories aloud after supper.

He could only conjecture that what he called change would have seemed permanence to the little Wheaters, and that what change signified to them was something as radical and soul-destroying as it would have been to Boyne to see his mechanical toys smashed, or his white mice left to die of hunger. That it should imply a lasting separation from the warm cluster of people, pets and things called home, would have been no more thinkable to the infant Boyne than permanence was to the infant Wheaters.

Judith had explained that almost all their little friends (usually acquaintances made in the world of Palace Hotels) were in the same case as themselves. As Terry had put it, when you were young you couldn't expect not to move about; and when Judith proceeded to give Boyne some of the reasons which had leagued her little tribe against the recurrence of such moves he had the sick feeling with which a powerless looker-on sees the torture of an animal. The case of poor Doll Westway, for instance, who was barely a year older than Judith, and whom they had played with for a summer at Deauville; and now—!

Well, it was all a damned rotten business—that was what it was. And Judith's resolve that her children should never again be exposed to these hazards thrilled Boyne like the gesture of a Joan of Arc. As the character of each became more definite to him, as he measured the distance between Blanca's cool self-absorption, tempered only by a nervous craving for her twin brother's approval, and the prodigal self-abandonment of Beechy, as he compared the detached and downright Zinnie to the sinuous and selfish Bun, and watched the interplay of all these youthful characters, he marvelled that the bond of Judith Wheater's love for them should be stronger than the sum of such heredities. But so it was. He had seen how they could hang together against their sister when some childish whim united them, and now he could imagine what an impenetrable front they would present under her leadership. Of course the Cliffe Wheaters would stay together if their children were determined that they should; and of course they would give Terry a tutor if he wanted one. How was it possible for any one to look at Terry and not give him what he wanted, Boyne wondered? At any rate, he, Boyne, meant to accompany the party to Venice and see the meeting. Incidentally, he was beginning to be curious about seeing the Wheaters themselves.

VI

THERE was no doubt about the Wheaters' welcome. When Boyne entered the big hall of their hotel on the Grand Canal he instantly recognized Cliffe Wheater in the florid figure which seemed to fill the half-empty resonant place with its own exuberance. Cliffe Wheater had been just like that at Harvard. The only difference was that he and his cigar had both grown bigger. And he seemed to have as little difficulty in identifying Boyne.

"Hul*lo!*" he shouted, so that the hall rocked with his greeting, and the extremely slim young lady in a Quaker gray frock and endless pearls to whom he was talking turned her head toward the newcomer with a little pout of disdain. The pout lingered as her eyes rested on Boyne, but he perceived that it was not personally addressed to him. She had a smooth egg-shaped face as sweetly vacuous as that of the wooden bust on which Boyne's grandmother's caps used to be done up, with carmine lips of the same glossy texture, and blue-gray eyes with long lashes that curved backward (like the bust's) as though they were painted on her lids; and Boyne had the impression that her extreme repose of manner was due to the fear of disturbing this facial harmony.

"Why, Martin dear!" she presently breathed in a low level voice, putting out a hand heavy with rings; and Boyne understood that he was in the presence of the once-redundant Joyce Wheater, and that in her new fashion she was as glad to see him as ever.

"I've grown so old that you didn't recognise me; but I should have known *you* anywhere!" she reproached him in the same smooth silvery voice.

"Old—you?" he found himself stammering; but the insipidities she evidently awaited were interrupted by her husband.

"Know him? I should say so! Not an ounce more flesh on him than there used to be, after all these years: how d'yer do it, I wonder? Great old times we used to have in the groves of John Harvard, eh, Martin, my boy? 'Member that Cambridge girl you used to read poetry to? *Poetry!* She was a looker, too! 'Come into the garden, Maud'. . . *Garden* they used to call it in those days! And now I hear you're a pal of my son's. . . Well, no, I don't mean Chipstone—" he smiled largely— "but poor old Terry. . . Hullo, why here's the caravan! Joyce, I say—you've told them they're to be parked out at the *Pension Grimani?* All but Chip, that is. Can't part with Chipstone, can we? Here they all come, Judy in the lead as usual. Hullo, Judy girl! Chippo, old man, how goes it? Give us your fist, my son." He caught his last-born out of Judith's arms, and the others had to wait, a little crestfallen, yet obviously unsurprised, till the proud father had filled his eyes with the beauty of his last achievement. "Catch on to him, will you, Joyce? Look at old man Chippo! Must have put on another five pounds since our last meeting—I swear he has . . . you just feel this calf of his! Hard as a tennis ball, it is. . . Does you no end of credit, Judy. Here, pass him on to the room next to your mother's. . . Wish you'd develop that kind of calf, Terry boy. . ."

"Look at *my* calfs, too! I can show them upside down!" shouted Bun, bursting in with a handspring upon these endearments; while Blanca, wide-eyed and silent, fastened her absorbed gaze on the golden thatch of her mother's intricately rippled head, and Joyce clasped the children, one after another, to her pearls.

Give Terry a tutor? Boy's own idea, was it? Good old chap—always poking around with books. Wheater would have thought that Terry knew enough to be his own tutor by this time. . . Funny, wasn't it, for a son of *his?* Cut out to be a Doctor of Divinity; or President of a University, maybe! Talk of heredity—for him and Joyce to have turned out such a phenomenon! Hoped Chipstone wouldn't turn into a Doctor of Divinity too. But of course they'd give Terry a tutor—wouldn't they, Joyce? The boy was dead right; he couldn't be loafing about any longer with the women. . . Did Boyne happen to know of a tutor, by any chance? Wheater'd never before had anything of the sort to bother about. Right up on schools, of course—always meant to send Terry to Groton; but his rotten temperature had knocked that out, so now. . .

The three were sitting after dinner on the balcony of the Wheaters' apartment, watching the Grand Canal, gondola-laden, lamp-flecked, furrowed with darting motor-boats, drift beneath them in rich coils and glassy volutes. There was nothing doing in Venice, Wheater had explained, so early in the season; it was as dead as the grave. Just a handy place to meet the children in, and look them over before they were packed off to the Engadine or Leysin. And besides, the Wheaters had come there to pick up their new steam-yacht; the "Fancy

Girl," a real beauty. They were going on a short cruise in her before they left for Cowes, and Venice was a handy place to try her out. By-and-by, if Boyne liked, he and Joyce and Wheater might drift out to the Piazza, and take an ice at Florian's, and a turn on the Canal—not very exciting, but the best Wheater could suggest in the circumstances. But Boyne said: why not stay where they were? And Joyce, with a shrug that just sufficiently displaced the jet strap attaching her dress to her white shoulder, remarked that Cliffe never *could* stay where he was, but that nobody objected to his painting Venice red if he wanted to. . .

"Where'd I get the paint, at this time of year? Nobody here but guys with guide-books, and old maids being photo'd feeding the pigeons. . . Hotels cram full of 'em. . . Well, look here; about that tutor? You haven't come across anybody on your travels that would do, Martin? University chap, and that sort of thing?"

Martin didn't believe he had; but Mrs. Wheater, lifting a white arm to flick her cigarette into the Canal, said: "*I* know a tutor."

"Hell—you *do?*" her husband laughed incredulously. " 'Nother cigar, old chap? These Coronas ain't bad—specially made for me." He loosed the golden sheathings from a cigar and held his lighter to it.

"I know a tutor," Mrs. Wheater repeated. "Exactly the right person, if only we can persuade him to take the job."

"Well—I'll be blowed! Where'd you excavate him?"

She was silent for a moment; then she said: "I've been going to the galleries with him. It's the first time I've ever *seen* Venice. Fanny Tradeschi got him out from England to tutor her boys, and then she was bored here, and rushed back to Paris, and left him stranded. His name is Ormerod—Gerald Ormerod. It would be the greatest privilege for Terry if he could be persuaded. . ."

"Oh, I guess I can persuade him all right. I don't believe Fanny remembered to settle with him before she left."

"No, she didn't; but he's awfully proud. You'd better not take that tone with him, Cliffe."

"What; the tone of asking him what his screw is?"

"Shouting like that at the top of your lungs—as if everybody less rich than yourself was deaf," said his wife, with a slight steel edge in her silver voice.

"Hul*lo!* That the size of it? Well, fix it up with him any old way you like. I'm off for a round of the town. . . Not coming along, Martin? Well, so long. . . Can't for the life of me see why you've stuck yourself down at that frowsy *pension* with the children; I'm sure I could have bullied the manager here into giving you a room. . . Have it your own way, though. And you and Joyce can map out a tour for to-morrow: only no galleries for me, thank you! Look here—d'ye think I'd disturb Chipstone Wheater Esqre if I was just to poke my head in and take a look at him on my way out? Listen—my shoes don't creak the least bit. . . Oh, hang it, I don't care, I'm going to, anyway. . ."

Of the Joyce Mervin of Boyne's youth, the young Joyce Wheater of her early married days, nothing, apparently, was left in the slim figure leaning over the balcony at Boyne's elbow. Then she had been large, firm and rosy, with a core of artless sensibility; now she seemed to have gone through some process of dematerialization (no doubt there were specialists for this too) which had left a translucent and imponderable body about a hard little kernel of spirit.

"It's impossible to make Cliffe feel *nuances*," she murmured to her cigarette after Wheater had gone; then, turning to Boyne: "But now we can have a good talk—just like old times, can't we?" She settled down in her armchair, and exchanged her measured syllables for a sort of steely volubility which rattled about Boyne's head like a hail of *confetti*. She was awfully glad to see him, really she was, she declared; he *did* believe her when she said that, didn't he? He'd always been such a perfect friend, in the silly old days when she herself was just a stupid baby, years younger in experience than Judy was now. . . What did Martin think of Judy, by the way? Did he appreciate what a miracle the child was? Positively, she was older and wiser than any of them; and the only human being who had any influence whatever with Cliffe. . .

Oh, well: Cliffe . . . yes. . . It was awfully dear and sweet of Martin to say that he was glad she and Cliffe had come together again, and she was glad too, and she was ever so proud of Chip, and she *did* recognize poor Cliffe's qualities, she always had, even when things were at their worst . . . but, there, it was no use pretending with Martin, it never had been; and there was no denying that Cliffe had got into dreadfully bad hands when she left him . . . utterly demoralized and cowed by that beastly Lacrosse woman . . . and the money pouring out like water. . . Yes, she, Joyce, had seen it was her duty to take him back; and so she had. Because she still believed in the sanctity of marriage, in spite of everything. She hoped Martin did too? For if you didn't, what was there left to hold society together? But all the same, if one came to feel that by living with a man, even if he *was* one's husband, one was denying one's Ideal: that was awful too, wasn't it? Didn't Martin think it was awful?

Yes, Martin supposed it was; but he rather thought a bunch of jolly children were a pretty good substitute for any old Ideal he'd ever met. Mrs. Wheater laughed, with somewhat more of the old resonance, and said she thought so too, and that was what Judy had argued—no, Martin would never know how wonderful Judy had been during the ghastly days when Buondelmonte was dragging her, Joyce, through the mire, literally through the mire! "Why, there were things I couldn't tell even *you*, Martin—"

Martin felt his gorge rise. "Things I hope that Judy wasn't told, then?"

Mrs. Wheater's shoulder again slipped its light trammels in a careless shrug. "Bless you, you don't have to tell the modern child things! They seem to be born knowing them. Haven't you found that out, you dear old Rip van Winkle? Why, Judy's like a mother to me, I assure you."

"She's got a pretty big family to mother, hasn't she?" Boyne rejoined, and Mrs. Wheater sighed contentedly: "Oh, but she loves it, you know! It's her hobby. Why, she tried to be a mother to Zinnia Lacrosse. . . Fancy a child of Judy's age attempting to keep a movie star straight! She used to give good advice to Buondelmonte. . . But that nightmare's over now, and we're all together again, and there's only Terry, poor darling, to worry about. I *do* worry about him, you know, Martin. And isn't it sweet of him to want to be properly educated? For Cliffe, of course, education has always just been college sports and racing-motors. That's one reason why I've missed so much . . . but I am determined that Terry shall have all the opportunities I haven't had. This tutor I was speaking about, Gerald Ormerod—I wonder if you'd see him for me to-morrow, Martin? It's no use asking Cliffe—he'd just shout and brag, and spoil the whole thing. Gerald—I've got to calling him Gerald because Fanny Tradeschi always did—he comes of very good people, you see, and he's almost too sensitive . . . too much of an idealist. . . I can't tell you what it's been to me, these last weeks, to see Venice through the eyes of some one who really cares for beauty. . . You'll have a talk with him about Terry, Martin dear? I'm sure Cliffe would give any salary you advise—and it would be the saving of our poor Terry to be with some one really sensitive and cultivated . . . and Bun, too . . . he might put some sort of reason into Bun, who's beginning to get quite out of hand with Scopy. . . And, Martin, don't forget: you can fix the salary as high as you like."

VII

TWO days later Boyne sat taking his morning coffee with Judith Wheater at a rickety iron table in the mouldy garden of the *Pension Grimani*. He had bribed a maid to carry out their breakfast, so that they might escape the stuffiness of the low-ceilinged dining-room, full of yesterday's dinner smells, of subdued groups of old maids and giggling bands of school-girls, and of the too-pervasive clatter of the corner table about which Scopy and Nanny had gathered their flock. It was Boyne's last day in Venice, and he wanted a clear hour of it with Judith. Presently the family would surge up like a spring tide, every one of them—from Mr. and Mrs. Wheater, with the "Fancy Girl" lying idle off San Giorgio, and a string of unemployed motors at Fusina, to Beechy and Zinnie squabbling over their new necklaces from the Merceria, and Miss Scope with a fresh set of problems for the summer—all wanting Boyne's advice or sympathy or consolation, or at least his passive presence at their debates. All this was rather trying, and the eager proximity of the little Wheaters made privacy impossible. Yet Boyne was more than ever glad that he had resisted the persuasions of their parents, and carried his luggage to the *Pension Grimani* instead of to the Palace Hotel. The mere existence of Palace Hotels was an open wound to him. Not that he was indifferent to the material advantages they offered. Nobody appreciated hot baths and white tiles, electric bed-lamps and prompt service, more than he whose lot was usually cast in places so remote from them. He loved Palace Hotels; but he loathed the mere thought of the people who frequented them.

Judy, he discovered, was of the same mind. Boyne had felt a little resentful of the fact that only the Wheaters' youngest-born was to share the luxury of their hotel; it seemed rather beastly to banish the others to frowsy lodgings around the corner. At the moment he had avoided Judy's eye, fearing to catch in it the reflection of his thought: most of Judy's feelings were beginning to reverberate in him. But now, in the leisure of their first talk since landing, he learned that no such feeling had marred the meeting of the little Wheaters with their parents.

Blanca, Judith owned, probably had minded a little, just at first. Silly Blanca—she was always rather jealous of the fuss that Joyce and father made about Chip. Besides, she loved smartness, and picking up new ideas about clothes from the *chic* women in hotel restaurants; and she liked to be seen about with Joyce, who was so smart herself, and to have other smart ladies say: "Is this your dear little girl? We should have known her anywhere from the likeness."

But it was precisely because of Blanca that Judith most disliked going to "Palaces." "Ever since she got engaged to the lift-boy at Biarritz. . ."

"Engaged?" Boyne gasped. "But, Judy . . . but Blanca's barely eleven. . ."

"Oh, I was engaged myself at Blanca's age—to a page at a skating-rink." Judith's small face, as she made the admission, had the wistful air of middle-age looking back on the sweet follies of youth. "But that was different. He was a very nice little Swiss boy; and I only gave him one of my hair-ribbons, and he gave me one of his livery buttons; and when he went home for his holiday he sent me dried edelweiss, and forget-me-nots pasted on cards. But these modern children are different. Blanca's boy wanted a ring with a real stone in it; and he was a horrid big thing with a fat nose that wriggled. Terry and I could hardly bear it. And when Scopy found out about it she made an awful row, and threatened to write to mother . . . so altogether we're better off here. In fact I wrote to father that we'd better put up at a place like this, where the children can rush about and make a noise, and nobody bothers. I think it's rather jolly here, don't you, Martin?"

She had called him Martin, as a matter of course, since the second day out from Algiers; and he could never hear his name in her fresh young trill without a stir of pleasure.

He said he thought the *Pension Grimani* awfully jolly, and was glad it suited the rest of them as well as it did him. Then she asked if it was all right about Terry's tutor, and what he thought of the young man. The answer to this was more difficult. Boyne was not sure what he thought. He had had an interview with Mr. Ormerod on the previous day; an interview somewhat halting and embarrassed on his own part, perfectly firm and self-possessed on the tutor's. Mr. Ormerod was a good-looking young Englishman with the University stamp upon him. He had very fair hair, somewhat long and rumpled, lazy ironic gray eyes, and a discontented mouth. He looked clever, moody and uncertain; but he was cultivated and intelligent, and it seemed certain that Terry would learn more, and be more usefully occupied, in his care than in Miss Scope's. Boyne's embarrassment proceeded not only from the sense of his unfitness to choose a tutor for anybody, but from the absurdity of having to do so with the pupil's parents on the spot. Mr. Ormerod, however, seemed neither surprised nor disturbed. He had seen Terry, and was sure he was an awfully good little chap; his only hesitation was as to the salary. Boyne, who had fixed it to the best of his judgment, saw at once that, though it exceeded the usual terms, it was below Mr. Ormerod's mark. The young man explained that the Princess Tradeschi had let him down rather badly, and that it was a beastly nuisance, but he really couldn't give in about his screw. Boyne remembered Mrs. Wheater's parting injunction, and to get over the difficulty suggested throwing in Bun. "There's the little Buondelmonte boy—a sort of step-son; he's rather a handful for the governess, and perhaps you would take him on for part of the time. In that case—"

This closed the transaction to Mr. Ormerod's advantage, and enabled Boyne to report to the Wheaters that their eldest son's education would begin the next day. And now he had to answer Judith's question.

"He strikes me as clever; but I don't know how hard he'll make Terry work."

"Oh, Terry will make *him* work. And as long as Joyce wants it I'm glad it's settled. If she hadn't, father might have kicked at the price. Not that he isn't awfully generous to us; but he can't see why people should want to be educated when they don't have to. What does it ever *lead* to, he says." She wrinkled her young brows pensively. "I don't know; do you? I can't explain. But if Terry wants it I'm sure it's right. You've read a lot yourself, haven't you? I don't suppose I shall ever care much about reading . . . but what's the use of bothering, when I should never have a minute's time, no matter how much I cared to do it?"

He reminded her that she might have time later, and added that, now that her parents were in an educational mood, he wondered she didn't take advantage of it to get herself sent to a good school, if only to be able to keep up with Terry. At this she smiled a little wistfully; it was the same shy doubtful smile with which she had looked about her in the cathedral at Monreale, trying to puzzle out what he saw in it. But her frown of responsibility returned. "Go to school? Me? But when, I'd like to know? There'll always be some of the children left to look after. Why, I shall be too old for school before Chip is anywhere near Terry's age. And besides, I never mean to leave the children—*never!*" She brought the word out with the shrill emphasis he had already heard in her voice when her flock had to be protected or reproved. "We've all sworn that," she added. "We took an awful oath one day at Biskra that we'd never be separated again, no matter what happened. Even Chip had to hold up his fist and say: 'I swear.' We did it on Scopy's 'Cyclopædia of Nursery Remedies.' And if things went wrong again, and I was off at one of your schools, who'd see to it that the oath was kept?"

"But now that all the children are safely with your own people, couldn't you let the oath take care of itself, and think a little of what's best for you?"

She raised her eyes with a puzzled stare which made them seem as young as Zinnie's. "You'd like me to go to school?"

He returned the look with one of equal gravity. "Most awfully."

Her colour rose a little. "Then I should like to."

"Well, then—"

She shook her head and her flush faded. "I don't suppose you'll ever understand—you or anybody. How could I leave the children now? I've got to get them off to Switzerland in another fortnight; this is no place for Terry. And suppose Mr. Ormerod decides he won't come with us—"

"Won't come with you? But it's precisely what he's been engaged to do!"

She gave an impatient shrug like her mother's, and turned on Boyne a little face sharp with interrogation. "Well, then, suppose it was mother who didn't want him to?"

"Your mother? Why, child, it was she who found him. She knows all about him; she—"

"She jolly well likes doing Venice with him," Judy completed his sentence with a hideous promptness. It was Boyne's turn to redden. He averted his eyes from her with one of Miss Scope's abrupt twists, and pushed his chair back as if to get up. Judy leant across the table and touched his sleeve timidly.

"I've said something you don't like, Martin?"

"You've said something exceedingly silly. Something I should hate to hear if you were grown up. But at your age it's merely silly, and doesn't matter."

She was on her feet in a flash, quivering with anger. "My age? My age? What do you know about my age? I'm as old as your grandmother. I'm as old as the hills. I suppose you think I oughtn't to say things like that about mother—but what am I to do, when they're true, and there's no one but you that I can say them to?"

He never quite knew, when she took that tone, if he was most moved or offended by it. There were moments when she frightened him; when he would have given the world to believe either that she was five years older than she said, or else that she did not know the meaning of the words she used. At such moments it was always the vision of Rose Sellars which took possession of him, and he found himself breathlessly explaining this strange child to her, and feeling that what was so clear to him would become incomprehensible as soon as he tried to make it clear to others, and especially to Mrs. Sellars. "There's nothing to be done about it," he thought despairingly. Aloud he remarked, in an impatient tone: "You're very foolish not to go to school."

She made no reply, but simply said, with a return of her wistful look: "Perhaps if you were going to stay here you'd lend me some books."

"But I'm not going to stay here; I'm off to-morrow morning," he answered angrily, keeping his head turned away with an irritated sense that if he should meet her eyes he would see tears in them.

Her own anger had dropped—he knew it without looking at her, and he had the sense that she was standing near him, very small and pale. "Martin, if you'd only stay! There are so many things left undecided. . . Father and mother can't make up their minds where to go next, and it's always when they've got nothing particular to do that they quarrel. They can't get anybody to go on the yacht with them—not till Cowes. And if they have to chuck the cruise father wants to go to Paris, and mother wants to go motoring in the hill-towns of Italy (where are they, do you know?) And if they get wrangling again what in the world is to become of us children?"

He turned back then, and put his hand on her arm. There was an old bench, as shaky as the table, under a sort of ragged sounding-board of oleanders. "Sit down, my dear." He sat beside her, smiling a little, lighting a cigarette to prove his ease and impartiality. "You're taking all this much too hard, you know. You've too much on your shoulders, and you're over-tired: that's all. I've been with your father and mother for two days now, and I see no signs of anything going wrong. The only trouble with them is that they're too rich. That makes them fretful: it's like teething. Every time your father hears he's made another million it's like cutting a new tooth. They hurt to bite on when one has so many. But he'll find people soon to go off for a cruise with him, and then he'll have to decide about your summer. Your people must see that this place is not bracing enough for Terry; and they'll want him to settle down somewhere in the mountains, and get to work as soon as possible."

The tone of his voice seemed to quiet her, though he suspected that at first she was too agitated to follow what he said. "But what sort of people?" she brought out at length, disconsolately.

"What sort of people?"

"To go on the yacht. That's another thing. When mother is away from father, and I'm with her, it's easier in some ways—except that then I fret about the other children. When Joyce and father are together they do all sorts of crazy things, just to be in opposition to each other. Take up with horrid people, I mean, people who drink and have rows. And then they get squabbling again, as they did when Buondelmonte sent father the bill for his Rolls-Royce. . ."

"Buondelmonte?"

"Yes; but Joyce said we were never to talk about that—she forbade us all."

"She was quite right."

"Yes; only it's true. And they do get into all sorts of rows and muddles about the people they pick up—"

At this moment Boyne, hearing a shuffle on the gravel, looked around and saw the maid approaching with a card. The maid glanced doubtfully at the two, and finally handed the card to Boyne, as the person most likely to represent law and order in the effervescent party to which he seemed to belong. It was a very large and stiff piece of paste-board, bearing the name: *Marchioness of Wrench,* and underneath, in a sprawling untaught hand: "To see my daughter Zinnie Wheater," the "my" being scratched out and "her" substituted for it. Boyne, after staring at this document perplexedly, passed it on to Judith, who sprang up with an astonished exclamation.

"Why, it must be Zinnia Lacrosse! Why, she's married again! It's true, then, what Blanca saw in the papers. . ." She looked inquiringly at Boyne. "Do you suppose she's really here?"

"Of course I'm here!" cried a sharp gay voice from the doorway; and through the unkempt shrubbery an apparition sparkling with youth and paint and jewels swept toward them on a wave of perfume.

"Hullo, Judy—why, it's *you!*" But the newcomer was not looking at Judith. She stood still and scrutinised Boyne with great eyes set like jewels in a raying-out of enamelled lashes. She had a perfectly oval face, a small exquisitely curved mouth, and an air of innocent corruption which gave Boyne a slightly squeamish feeling as she turned and flung her arms about Judy.

"Well, old Judy, I'm glad to see you again. . . Who's your friend?" she added, darting a glance at Boyne through slanting lids. All her gestures had something smooth and automatic, and a little larger than life.

"He's Mr. Boyne. He's father's friend too. This is Zinnia Lacrosse, Martin."

"No, it isn't, either! It's the Marchioness of Wrench. Only I'm just called Lady Wrench, except on visiting-cards, and when they put me in the newspapers, or I talk to the servants. And of course you'll call me Zinnia just the same, Judy. How d'ye do, Mr. Boyne?" murmured the star, with an accession of elegance and a languidly extended hand. But she had already mustered Boyne, and was looking over his shoulder as she addressed him. "What I'm after is Zinnie, you know," she smiled. "Wrenny's waiting in the gondola—Wrenny's my husband—and I've promised to take her out and show her to him."

She cast an ingratiating glance at Judith, but the latter, quietly facing her, seemed to Boyne to have grown suddenly tall and authoritative, as she did when she had to cope with a nursery mutiny.

"Now, Zinnia," she began, in the shrill voice which always gave Boyne a sense of uneasiness, "you know perfectly well—"

"Know what?"

"You know what the agreement is; and you know Scopy and I aren't going to listen to anything—"

"Fudge, child! What d'you suppose I'd want to break the agreement for? Not that I care such an awful lot for Cliffe's old alimony, you know. It don't hardly keep me in silk stockings. If I wanted to carry Zinnie off, that wouldn't stop me half a second. But I only want to show Wrenny that I can have a baby if I choose. Men are so funny about such things; he doesn't believe I've ever had one. And of course I can see he's got to have an heir. Look here, Judy, ain't I always dealt with you white? Let me see her right away, won't you? I've got a lovely present for her here, and one for you too—a real beauty. . . Can't you understand a mother's feelings?"

Judy still kept her adamantine erectness. Her lips, colourless and pressed together, barely parted to reply to the film star, whose last advance she appeared not to have noticed.

"Of course you can see Zinnie. You needn't get excited about that. Only you'll see her here, with me and Mr. Boyne. All your husband has got to do is to get out of the gondola and come into the house."

"If you'd been brought up like a lady you'd call him Lord Wrench, Judy."

Judith burst out laughing. "Mercy! Then you'd better call me Miss Wheater. But if you want to see Zinnie you haven't got any time to lose, because father's going to send for the children in a minute or two, and take them all off on the yacht."

"Oh, Judy—but he can't prevent my seeing Zinnie!"

"Nobody wants to prevent you, if you'll do what I say."

The Marchioness of Wrench pondered this ultimatum for a moment, staring down at her highly polished oval nails. Then she said sullenly: "I'll try; but I don't believe he'll get out of the gondola. He's dead lazy. And we wanted to take Zinnie for a row." Judith made no reply, and finally Lady Wrench moved back toward the vestibule door with a reluctant step.

"I'll go and fetch Zinnie," Judith announced to Boyne, advancing to the house by another path; but as she did so a small figure, bedizened and glass-beaded, hurled itself across the garden and into her arms.

"Judy! That was Zinnia, wasn't it? I saw her from my window! Nanny said it wasn't, but I knew it was. She hasn't gone away without seeing her own little Zinnie, has she? I'll never forgive you if she has. Did she bring a present for me? She always does. Blanca's crazy to come down and see her clothes, but Scopy won't let her. She's locked her up."

Judith gave one of her contemptuous shrugs. "Oh, Scopy needn't have done that. It won't hurt Blanca to see your mother. There, stop pinching me, Zinnie, and don't worry. Your mother's coming back. She's only gone to get her husband to introduce him to you."

"Her new husband? What's his name? Nobody ever told me she had a new husband. 'Cos they always say: 'You're too little to understand.' Zif I wasn't Zinnia's own little daughter! Judy, hasn't she got a present for me, don't you think? If it's nothing but choc'lates, course I'll divvy with the others; but if it's jewelry I needn't, need I?" Zinnie's ruddy curls spiralled upward and her face flamed with cupidity and eagerness. With a flash of her dimpled fists she snatched the new Merceria beads from her neck and thrust them into the pocket of her frock. "There's no use her seeing I've had presents already—you don't mind, Martin, do you?" she queried over her shoulder, addressing Boyne, who had given her the necklace that morning. He burst out laughing; but Judith, before he could intervene, caught hold of the delinquent and gave her a wrathful shake. "You nasty false ungrateful little viper you—"

"Oo-oo-oo," wailed Zinnie, hunching up her shoulders in a burst of sobs.

"There—now, Wrenny, you just look at that. I wish I had my lawyers here! That's the way those Wheater people treat my child—" Lady Wrench stood in the garden door and pointed with a denunciatory arm toward her weeping infant. Over her shoulder appeared the fair hair and puzzled eyes of a very tall young man with a sickly cast of countenance, a wide tremulous mouth and a bald forehead. "Oh, Lord, my dear," he said.

VIII

LADY WRENCH had snatched up her daughter and stood, in an approved film attitude, pressing Zinnie's damp cheek against her own, while the child's orange-coloured curls mixed with the red gold of hers. "What's that nasty beast been doing to momma's darling?" she demanded, glaring over Zinnie's head at Judith. "Whipping you for wanting to see your own mother, I suppose? You just tell momma what it was and she'll. . ."

But Zinnie's face had cleared, and she was obviously far too much absorbed in her mother's appearance to heed the unimportant questions which were being put to her. She slid her fat fingers through the pearls flowing in cataracts down Lady Wrench's bosom. "Oh, Zinnia, are they real? Blanca says they can't be—she knows they can't, 'cos they're twice as big as Joyce's."

"Blanca? Why, is Blanca here? Where is she?"

"Scopy's got her locked up, so's she can't come down and stare at you, but she found Martin's op'ra glasses in his room'n she's looking at you through them'n she says they're so pow'ful she can count the pearls, and can't she come down, please, Zinnia, 'cos she wants to see f'you've got the same Callot model's Joyce's jess ordered, 'cos it'll make Joyce wild'n she'll want to get another one instead as quick as she can. Please, Zinnia!"

Lady Wrench's brow had cleared as quickly as her daughter's. She burst out laughing and pressed her lips to Zinnie's cheek. "There, Wrenny, what d'you think of that, I'd like to know? Isn't she my really truly little girl?"

Lord Wrench had shambled slowly forward in her wake. He stood, lax-jointed, irresolute, in his light loose flannels, a faded Homburg hat tilted back from his perplexed brow, gazing down on the group from the immense height to which his long limbs and endless neck uplifted him.

"Yes, I'll take my oath she's that," he replied, in a voice which seemed to come from somewhere even higher than his hat; and he gave a cackle that rose and overreached his voice, and went tinkling away to the housetops.

His wife's laugh joined and outsoared his, and she dropped down on the bench, still hugging Zinnie. "Judy thought we wanted to *steal* her, Wrenny—think of that! Oh, I forgot you didn't know each other—Lord Wrench, Judy Wheater. And this is Mr. Boyne, a friend of Cliffe's—aren't you a friend of Cliffe's, Mr. Boyne? My present husband, the Marqu—no; that's wrong, I know—just my husband. But where's Blanca, Judy? Do let her come down, and Terry too; that's a darling! After all, I'm their step-mother, ain't I? Or I was, anyhow. . . Is Blanca as much of a beauty as ever, Mr. Boyne? If that girl had more pep I wouldn't wonder but what I could do something with her on the screen. Judy, now, would never be any good to us—would she, Wrenny? Too much of a lady, I always used to tell her. . ."

"Shut up: here she is," Lord Wrench interpolated. As he spoke Judith reappeared with her younger sister. Blanca's eyes were stretched to their widest at the sight of her former step-mother, though her erect spine and measured tread betrayed nothing of her eagerness to appraise Lady Wrench's dress and jewels. Behind them walked Miss Scope, helmeted as if for a fray, her hands mailed in gray cotton, and clutching her umbrella like a spear.

"Well, Blanca! How are you? How you've grown! And what a looker you're going to be! Only you're so fearfully grand—always was, wasn't she, Judy? You're a lady yourself, but you ain't *such* a lady. Well, Blanca, shake hands, and let me introduce you to my new husband. Wrenny, this is Blanca, who used to come and stay, with Terry and Judy, when Cliffe and me were married. Where's Terry, Blanca? Why didn't he come down too? I'd love to see him."

"Terry's with his tutor at present," said Blanca distantly, though her eyes never for a second detached themselves from Lady Wrench's luminous presence.

"But he said he wouldn't have come down even if he hadn't of been," chimed in Zinnie, peering up maliciously into her mother's face. "He says he isn't 'quisitive like Blanca, and he can't be bothered every time somebody comes round to see the steps."

Lord Wrench, at this, joined Boyne in a fresh burst of laughter, but his bride looked distinctly displeased. "Well, I see Terry's tutor hasn't taught him manners anyhow," she snapped, while Miss Scope admonished her youngest charge: "*In*quisitive, Zinnie; you're really old enough to begin to speak correctly."

"No, I'm not, 'less Bun and Beechy do too," Zinnie retorted.

"Beatrice and Astorre are foreigners," Miss Scope rejoined severely.

"Well, so are you, you old flamingo! You're not a real true Merrican like us!"

"Zinnie," cried Blanca, intervening in her brother's

behalf in her grandest manner, "Terry never said any such thing"; but Zinnie, secure in her mother's embrace, laughed scorn at her rebukers, until Judith remarked: "I'm very sorry, but children who are rude are not to be taken on the yacht today. Father particularly told me to tell you so. Zinnie, if you don't apologise at once to Miss Scope I'm afraid you'll have to stay behind alone with Nanny."

"No, she won't, either, my Zinnie pet won't! She'll go out in the gond'la with her own momma and her new father," Lady Wrench triumphantly declared. But Zinnie's expressive countenance had undergone a sudden change. She detached herself from the maternal embrace, and sliding to the ground slipped across to Miss Scope and endearingly caught her by a gray cotton hand. "Scopy, I'm not a really naughty Zinnie, say I'm not—'cos I don't want to go out in a bally old gond'la, I want to go'n father's steam-yacht, I do!"

Fresh squeals of approval from Lord Wrench greeted this hasty retractation. "Jove—she's jolly well right, the kid is! No doubt about her being yours, Zinnia," he declared; whereat the lady rejoined, with an effort at lightness: "Zif I couldn't have a yacht of my own any day I like that'd steam all round that old hulk of Cliffe's! And I will too—you'll see," she added, sweeping a circular glance about the company.

"Righto. Come along now, and we'll pick one out," her husband suggested with amiable irony.

"Well, maybe I will," she menaced, rising to her feet with the air of throwing back an ermine train. But Blanca had advanced and was lifting shy eyes to hers. "Your dress is so perfectly lovely, Zinnia; I think it's the prettiest one I ever saw you in. Isn't it from that

Russian place mother's always talking about, where it's so hard to get them to take new customers?"

The star cast a mollified smile upon her. "You bright child, you! Well, yes; it is. But even if your mother could persuade them to take her on she wouldn't be able to get this model, because the Grand Duke Anastase designed it expressly for me, and I've got a signed paper saying it's the only one of the kind they'll ever make. See the way it's cut across the shoulders?"

Blanca contemplated this detail with ecstatic appreciation, and Lady Wrench, gathering up her sable scarf, glanced victoriously about her. "I guess anybody that wants to can buy a steam-yacht; but you can count on one hand with two fingers missing the women that Anastase'll take the trouble to design a dress for."

"Oh, I say, come on, old girl," her husband protested, shifting his weight wearily from one long leg to another; and Lady Wrench turned to follow him.

"Well, goodbye, Zinnie child. Next time I'll call for you on my two thousand ton oil-burner. Oh, look here—seen my bag, Wrenny? I believe I brought some caramels for the child—" She turned back, and began to fumble in a bejewelled bag, while the two little girls' faces fell at the mention of caramels. But presently a gold chain strung with small but lustrous pearls emerged from a tangle of cigarettes and bank-notes. "Here, Zinnie, you put that on, and ask Blanca to look at the pearls under the microscope, and then tell you if they're false, like your momma's."

Blanca paled at the allusion. "Oh, Zinnia, I never said yours were false! Is that what that little brute told you? I only said, I couldn't be sure they weren't, at that distance—"

Lady Wrench laughed imperturbably. "Well, I should think you'd have been sure they *were*, being so accustomed to your mother's. But movie queens don't have to wear fake pearls, my pet, 'cos if the real ones get stolen they can always replace 'em. You tell that to Mrs. Cliffe Wheater number three. And you needn't look so scared —I bear no malice." She drew a small packet from the bag. "See, here's a ring I brought you: I guess that'll bear testing too," she added, flinging the little box into Blanca's hand.

Blanca, white with excitement, snapped open the lid, which revealed to her swift appraising eye a little ruby set in brilliants. She drew it forth with a rapturous "Oh, Zinnia," and slipped it onto her hand, hastily thrusting the box into a fold of her jumper.

"When I give presents I don't go to the ten-cent store for them," remarked Lady Wrench, with a farewell wave of her hand. "So long, everybody! Shouldn't wonder if we met again soon by the sad sea waves. Wrenny and I are honeymooning out at the Lido, and maybe you'll all be over for the bathing. It's getting to be as gay as it is in August. All the smart people are snapping up the bathing tents. The Duke of Mendip's got the one next to ours. He's Wrenny's best friend, you know. By-bye, Judy. Mr. Boyne, hope you'll dine with us some night at the Lido Palace to meet the Duke. Ask for the Marchioness of Wrench—you'll remember?"

She vanished in a dazzle of pearls and laughter, leaving Blanca and Zinnie in absorbed contemplation of their trinkets till Miss Scope marshalled them into the house to prepare for the arrival of the "Fancy Girl" 's launch.

After the children were gone, Judy lingered for a moment in the garden with Boyne. Her features, so tense and grown-up looking during the film star's visit, had melted into the small round face of a pouting child.

"Well—that's over," Boyne said, flinging away his cigarette as though the gesture symbolised the act of casting out the Wrenches.

"Yes," she assented, in a tone of indifference. "Zinnia doesn't really matter, you know," she added, as if noticing his surprise. "She screams a lot; but she doesn't mean anything by it."

"Well, I should think you'd be glad she didn't, for whatever she meant would be insufferable."

Judith raised her eyebrows with a faint smile. "We're more used to fusses than you are. When there are seven children, and a lot of parents, there's always somebody fighting about something. But Zinnia's nothing like as bad as she looks." She paused a moment, and then, irrepressibly, as if to rid her heart of an intolerable weight: "But Blanca got away with my present. Did you see that? I knew she would! That's what she came down for—to wangle it out of Zinnia. Pretending she thought that old Callot model was one of Anastase's! There's nothing mean enough for Blanca!" Her eyes had filled with large childish tears, and one of them rolled down her cheek before she had time to throw back her head and add proudly: "Not that I care a straw, of course. I'm too grown up to mind about such rubbish. But I know Blanca must have noticed my 'nitials on the box. Didn't you see how quick she was about hiding it?"

BOOK II

IX

THE next day, during the journey through the hot Veneto and up into the mountains, the Wheater children and their problems were still so present to Boyne that he was hardly conscious of where he was going, or why.

His last hours with his friends had ended on a note of happiness and security. The new yacht, filled and animated by that troop of irrepressible children, whom it took all Miss Scope's energy and ubiquity to keep from falling overboard or clambering to the mast-head, seemed suddenly to have acquired a reason for existing. Cliffe Wheater, in his speckless yachting cap and blue serge, moved about among his family like a beneficent giant, and Mrs. Wheater, looking younger than ever in her white yachting skirt and jersey, with her golden thatch tossed by the breeze, fell into the prettiest maternal poses as her own progeny and the "steps" scrambled over her in the course of a rough-and-tumble game organised by Boyne and the young tutor.

The excursion had not begun auspiciously. Before the start from the *pension,* Bun and Beechy, imprisoned above stairs during Lady Wrench's irruption, had managed to inflict condign punishment on Zinnie for not having them fetched down with Blanca, and thus making them miss an exciting visit and probable presents. Terry's indifference to the whole affair produced no effect on the irascible Italians; and as Zinnie, when roused, was a fighter, and now had a gold necklace with real pearls to defend, all Judith's influence, and some cuffing into the bargain, were needed to reduce the trio to order; after which Boyne had to plead that they should not be deprived of their holiday. But once on the deck of the "Fancy Girl" all disagreements were forgotten. It was a day of wind and sparkle, with a lagoon full of racing waves which made the yacht appear to be actually moving; and after Beechy had drenched her new frock with tears of joy at being reunited to Chipstone, and Blanca and Zinnie had shown Lady Wrench's presents to every one, from the captain to the youngest cook-boy, harmony once more reigned among the little Wheaters.

Mr. Ormerod, with whom Terry was already at ease, soon broke down the reserve of the others. He proved unexpectedly good at games which involved scampering, hiding and pouncing, especially when Joyce and Judith took part, and could be caught and wrestled with; and Cliffe Wheater, parading the deck with Chip, whom he had adorned with a miniature yachting cap with "Fancy Girl" on the ribbon, was the model of a happy father. He pressed Boyne to chuck his other engagements and come off down the Adriatic as far as Corfu and Athens; and Boyne, lounging there in the bright air, the children's laughter encircling him, and Judith perched on the arm of his chair, asked himself why he didn't, and what better life could have to offer. "Uncle Edward would certainly have accepted," he thought, while his host, pouring himself another cocktail from the deck-table at his elbow, went on persuasively: "We'll round up a jolly crowd for you, see if we don't. Somebody's sure to turn up who'll jump at the chance. Judy, can't we hustle around and find him a girl?"

"Here's all the girl I want," Boyne laughed, laying his

hand on hers; and a blush of pleasure rose to her face. "Oh, Martin—if you would—oh, can't you?" But even that he had resisted—even the ebb of her colour when he shook his head. The wandering man's determination to stick to his decisions was strong in him. Too many impulses had solicited him in too many lands: it was because, despite a lively imagination, he had so often managed to resist them, that a successful professional career lay behind him, and ahead—he hoped—comparative leisure, and the haven he wanted.

He had tried to find a farewell present for Judith—some little thing which, in quality if not costliness, should make up for her disappointment at being done out of Lady Wrench's. Judith's frank avowal of that disappointment had been a shock to him; but he reflected again what a child she was, and called himself a prig for expecting her standards to be other than those of the world she lived in. After all he had had no time to search for anything rare, and could only push into her hand, at the last moment, a commonplace trinket from the Merceria; but her childish joy in it, and her way of showing that she valued it doubly because it came from him, made the parting from her harder. And now, alone in the dusty train, he was asking himself why he had not stayed in Venice.

As a matter of fact there were several reasons; among them the old-fashioned one that, months before, he had promised to meet Mrs. Sellars in the Dolomites. In a world grown clockless and conscienceless, Boyne was still punctual and conscientious; and in this case he had schooled himself to think that what he most wanted was to see Rose Sellars again. Deep within him he knew it was not so; at least, not certainly so. Life had since given him hints of other things he might want equally, want even more; his reluctance to leave Venice and his newly-acquired friends showed that his inclinations were divided. But he belonged to a generation which could not bear to admit that naught may abide but mutability. He wanted the moral support of believing that the woman who had once seemed to fill his needs could do so still. She belonged to a world so much nearer to his than the Wheaters and their flock that he could not imagine how he could waver between the two. Rose Sellars's world had always been the pole-star of his whirling skies, the fixed point on which his need for permanence could build. He could only conclude, now, that he combined with the wanderer's desire for rest the wanderer's dread of immobility. "Hang it all, you can't have it both ways," he rebuked himself; but secretly he knew that that was how the heart of man had always craved it. . .

Had all that happened only forty-eight hours ago? Now, as he sat on the balcony of the *châlet*, over against the mighty silver and crimson flanks of the Cristallo group, the episode had grown incredibly remote, and Boyne saw his problems float away from him like a last curl of mist swallowed up in the blue behind the peaks. Simply change of air, he wondered? The sudden rise into this pure ether that was like a shouting of silver trumpets? Partly, perhaps—and all that had chanced to go with it, in this wonderful resurrection of a life he had secretly thought dead.

"Bethesda is what you ought to call this," he murmured to himself. It was so like Rose Sellars, the live Rose Sellars who had already replaced his delicately embalmed mummy of her, to have found this *châlet* on the slope above the big hotels, a place so isolated and hidden that he and she were alone in it with each other and the mountains. How could he have so underrated his old friend's sense of the wonder of the place, and of what she owed to it, as to suppose that, even for two or three weeks, she would consent to be a number in a red-carpeted passage, and feed with the rest of the numbers in a blare of jazz and electricity? The *châlet* was only just big enough for herself and her maid, and the cook who prepared their rustic meals; had there been a corner for Boyne, she assured him that he should have had it. But perhaps it added to the mystery and enchantment that to see her he had to climb from the dull promiscuity of his hotel into a clear green solitude alive with the tremor of water under meadow-grasses, and guarded by the great wings of the mountains.

"You do really like it?" she had asked, as they sat, the first evening, on the balcony smelling of fir-wood, and watched the cliffs across the valley slowly decompose from flame to ashes.

"I like it most of all for being so like you," he answered.

She laughed, and turned an amused ironic face on him—a face more than ever like one of those light three-crayon drawings of which she had always reminded him. "Like me? Which—the *châlet* or the Cristallo group?"

"Well, both; that's the funny part of it."

"It must make me seem a trifle out of drawing."

"No; first aloof and aloft, and then again small and sunny and near."

She sighed faintly, and then smiled. "Well, I prefer the last part of the picture. I'd a good deal rather be a sunny balcony than a crystal peak. But I enjoy looking out on the peak."

"There you are—that's what I meant! It's the view from *you* that I've missed so, all these years."

She received this in a silence softened by another little laugh. The silence seemed to say: "That will do for our first evening," the laugh: "But I like it, you know!"

Aloud she remarked: "I'm glad you came up here after Venice and the millionaires. It's all to the good for the mountains—and for me."

Their first direct talk about themselves had ended there, drifting away afterward into reminiscences, questions, allusions, the picking up of threads—a gradual leisurely reconstruction of their five years apart. Now, on this second evening, he felt that he had situated her once more in his own life, and established himself in hers. So far he had made no allusion to his unsatisfied passion. In the past, by her own choice, her sternly imposed will, their relation had been maintained in the strict limits of friendship, and for the present he found it easier, more natural, to continue on the same lines. It was neither doubt nor pride that held him back, nor any uncertainty as to her feeling; but simply his sense of the well-being of things as they were. In the course of his life so much easy love had come his way, he had grown so weary of nights without a morrow, that he needed to feel there was one woman in the world whom he was half-afraid to make love to. Rose Sellars had chosen that he should know her only as the perfect friend; just at first, he thought, he would not disturb that carefully built-up picture. If he had suspected a rival influence he would not have tolerated delay; but as they travelled together over her past he grew more and more sure that it was for him the cold empty years of her marriage had kept her. Manlike, he was calmed rather than stimulated by this, though he would have repudiated more indignantly than ever the idea that she was less desirable because she was to be had. As a matter of fact, he found her prettier and younger than when they had parted. Every change in her was to her advantage, and he had instantly discarded his sentimental remembrance of her—dense coils of silvery-auburn hair, and draperies falling to the ankles—in favour of the new woman which her hair, dressed to look short, and her brief skirts, had made of her. Freedom of spirit and of body had mysteriously rejuvenated her, and he found her far more intelligent and adaptable than he had guessed when their relation had been obscured by his passion and her resistance. Now there was no resistance —and his passion lay with folded wings. It was perfect.

Every day they went off on an excursion. Sometimes they hired a motor, leaving it, far afield, for a long climb; but neither could afford such luxuries often, nor did they much care for them. Usually they started on foot, with stick and rucksack, getting back only as the great cliffs hung their last lustre above the valley. Mrs. Sellars was a tireless walker, proud of her light foot and firm muscles. She loved all the delicate detail revealed only to walkers: the thrust of orchis or colchicum through pine-needles, the stir of brooks, the uncurling of perfumed fronds, the whirr of wings in the path, and that continual pulsation of water and wind and grasses which is the heart-beat of the forest. Boyne, always alive to great landscape, had hitherto been too busy or preoccupied to note its particulars. It was years since he had rambled among mountains without having to look at them with an engineering eye, and calculate their relation to a projected railway or aqueduct; and these walks opened his eyes to unheeded beauties. It was like being led through the flowered borders of an illuminated missal of which he had hitherto noticed only the central pictures.

Better still were the evenings. When he first came a full moon held them late on the balcony, listening and musing, and sent him down dizzy with beauty through the black fir-shadows to his hotel. When the moon had waned, and the nights were fresh or cloudy, they sat by the fire, and talked and talked, or turned over new books and reviews. Boyne, with his bones and his brain so full of hard journeys and restless memories, thought he would have liked to look forward to an eternity of such evenings, in just such a hushed lamplit room, with a little sparkle of fire, reviews and papers everywhere, and that quiet silvery-auburn head with its mass of closely woven braids bending over a book across the hearth. Rose Sellars's way of being silently occupied without seeming absorbed was deeply restful. And then her books! She always managed to have just the ones he wanted to get hold of—to a homeless wandering man it was not the least of her attractions. Once, taking up a volume they had been talking of, Boyne recalled Judith Wheater's wistful: "Perhaps you might lend me some books." From what fold of memory had the question—and the very sound of the girl's voice—come back to him? He was abruptly reminded that it was a long time since he had given a thought to the little Wheaters.

There had been so many years to cover in the exchange of reminiscences that he had not yet touched on his encounter with them; and Mrs. Sellars seemed to have forgotten the description of the little band which had amused her in his letters. But now he was reminded, with a pang, of the contrast between her ordered and harmonious life (she always reminded him of Milton's "How charming is divine philosophy!") and the chaotic experiences of the poor little girl who for a moment had displaced her image. Inconceivably vulgar and tawdry, sordid and inarticulate, under all the shouting and the tinsel, seemed that other life and those who led it. Boyne would have brushed the vision away with contempt but for the voice which had called to him out of the blur. With a sigh he put down the book he had opened. Mrs. Sellars, who sat at the table writing, looked up, and their eyes met. "What were you thinking of?"

He had a start of distrust—the first since he had been with her. Would she understand if he tried to explain; if she did, would she sympathize? He shrank from the risk, and evaded it. "Seeing you so hard at work reminds me of all the letters I haven't written since I've been here."

She arched her eyebrows interrogatively, and he was sure she was thinking: "Why doesn't he tell me that he's no one to write to when he's with me?" Aloud she said: "You know I'm burdened with any number of fond relations who are consumed with the desire to know how I'm spending my first holiday."

"You're a wonderful correspondent."

As if scenting irony she rejoined: "So are you."

"I haven't been since I came here."

"Well, come and share the inkpot." She made the gesture of pushing it over to him, but he shook his head and stood up. "The night's too lovely. Put on your cloak and come out on the balcony."

She held her pen suspended, her eyes following his. "On the balcony? But there's no moon—"

"*Because* there's no moon," he insisted, smiling.

At that, smiling too, she drifted out to him.

X

"DARLING MARTIN,

"It's lovely here and very warm. Weve been baithing at the Lido and weve been out on the yaht again. Buondelmontes wife the lion taimer is dead and he has maried a rich American airess and Beechy and Bun are very much exited they think theyle get lots of presents now like Zinnie got from her mother and the one I was to get but Blanca took it, but I do like yours a hundred times better Martin dear, because you gave it to me and besides its much more orriginal.

"Ime worried because Buondelmonte mite want Bun back now hese rich and it would kill Beechy if Bun went away but I made him sware again on Scopys book he wont go whatever hapens.

"Mother and father had a grate big row because Mother wanted Zinnia and Lord Rench invited on the yatch and father said he woudnt it was too low, so she said why did he mind when she didnt. She wants to know the Duke of Mendip whose with them and Zinnia invites Gerald every day to lunch and dine and that makes Joyce fureaous. You will say I ought not to tell you this dear Martin then what can I do if there is a Row between them about Gerald Terry will loose his tutor and its too bad so I want to get away with the children as quick as we can.

"Terry said he must see this before I send it to you because I spell so badly but I wont let him because hed stop me sending it.

"Please Martin dear I do imploar you write and tell father to send us off quickly. Terry's temprature has gone up and Ime worried about everything. How I wish you were here then theyde do what you say.

"Your Judith who misses you."

"P.S. Please dont tell the Wheaters that Ive written."

Boyne's first thought, as he put the letter down, was that he was glad it had come after what had happened that very evening on the balcony. There had happened, simply, that the barriers created by a long habit of reticence had fallen, and he had taken Rose Sellars into his arms. It was a quiet embrace, the hushed surface of something deep and still. She had not spoken; he thanked his gods for that. Almost any word might have marred the moment, tied a tag to it, and fitted it with others into some dusty pigeon-hole of memory. She had known how to be different—and that was exquisite. Their quiet communion had silently flowered, and she had let it. There was neither haste nor reluctance in her, but an acquiescence so complete that what was deepest in both of them had flowed together through their hands and lips.

"It will be so much easier now to consult her—she'll understand so much better."

He didn't quite know why he felt that; perhaps because the merging of their two selves seemed to include every claim that others could have on either of them. Only yesterday he might have felt a doubt as to how Mrs. Sellars would view the Wheater problem, what she could possibly have in common with any of the Wheaters, or their world; now it was enough that she had him in common, and must share the burden because it was his.

He went over Judith's letter again slowly, imagining how Mrs. Sellars's beautiful eyes would deepen as she read it. The very spelling was enough to wring her heart. He would take the letter to her the next day. . . But the next day was here already. He pushed back his window, and leaned out. In the cold colourless air a few stars were slowly whitening, while behind the blackness of the hillside facing him the interstellar pallor flowed imperceptibly into morning gold. His happiness, he thought, was like that passing of colourless radiance into glow. It was joy enough to lean there and watch the transmutation. Was it a sign of middle-age, he wondered, to take beatitude so quietly? Well, Rose, for all her buoyancy, was middle-aged too. Then he remembered their kiss, and laughed the word away as the sun rushed up over the mountains.

All that day there was too much to do and to say; there were too many plans to make; too many memories to retrace. Boyne did not forget Judith Wheater's letter; her problem lay like a vague oppression in the background of his thoughts; but he found no way of fitting it into the new pattern of his life. Just yet—

It was decided that he and Mrs. Sellars should linger on in the mountains for another month—a month of mighty rambles, long hours of summer sunlight, and nights illuminated by a waxing moon. After that, Boyne's idea had been that they should push on at once to Paris, and there be married as quickly as legal formalities allowed. It was at this hint of an immediate marriage that he first noticed, in Mrs. Sellars, the recoil of the orderly deliberate woman whose life has been too vacant for hurry, too hopeless for impatience. Theoretically, she told him with a smile, she hated delay and fuss as much as he did—and how could he question her eagerness to begin their new life? But practically, she reminded him, there were difficulties, there might even be obstacles. Oh, not real ones, of course! She laughed that away, remarking with a happy blush that she was of age, and her own mistress. ("Well, then—?" he interjected.) Well, there were people who had to be considered; who might be offended by too great haste: her husband's family, for instance. She had never hit it off with them particularly well, as Boyne knew; but that was the very reason, she insisted, why she must do nothing that might give them cause. . . ("Cause for what?") Well, to say unpleasant things. She couldn't possibly marry within a year of her husband's death without seriously offending them—and latterly, she had to admit, they had been very decent, especially about straightening out Charles's will, which had been difficult to interpret, Mr. Dobree said.

"Mr. Dobree?"

"He's been such a friend to me through everything, you know," she reminded him, a shade reproachfully; and he remembered then that Mr. Dobree was the New York lawyer who had unravelled, as much as possible to her advantage, the tangle of Charles Sellars's will—the will of a snubbed secretive man whose only vindictiveness had been posthumous. Mr. Dobree had figured a good deal of late in Mrs. Sellars's letters, and she had given Boyne to understand that it was he who had brought the Sellars family to terms about the will. Boyne vaguely remembered him as a shy self-important man with dark-gray clothes that were always too new and too well-cut—the kind of man whose Christian name one never knew, but had to look up in the "Social Register," and then was amused to find it was Jason or Junius, only to forget it again at once—so fatally did Mr. Dobree tend always to become Mr. Dobree once more. A man, in short, who would have been called common in the New York of Boyne's youth, but now figured as "a gentleman of the old school," and conscientiously lived, and dressed, up to the character. Boyne suspected him of being in love with Mrs. Sellars, and Mrs. Sellars of feeling, though she could not return the sentiment, that it was not ungratifying to have inspired it. But Boyne's mind lingered on Mr. Dobree only long enough to smile at him as the rejected suitor, and then came back to his own grievances.

"You don't mean to say you expect me to wait a whole year from now?"

She laughed again. "You goose. A year from Charles's death. It's only seven months since he died."

"What of that? You were notoriously unhappy—"

"Oh, *notoriously*—"

He met her protest with a smile. "I admit the term is inappropriate. But I don't suppose anybody thinks your marriage was unmitigated bliss."

"Don't you see, dear? That's the very reason."

"Oh, hang reasons—especially unreasonable ones! Why have you got to be unhappy now because you were unhappy then?"

"I'm not unhappy now. I don't think I could be, ever again, if I tried."

"Dear!" he rejoined. She excelled at saying nice things like that (and was aware of it); but her doing so now was like putting kickshaws before a hungry man. "It's awfully sweet of you," he continued; "but I shall be miserable if you insist on things dragging on for another five months. To begin with, I'm naturally anxious to get home and settle my plans. I want some sort of a job as soon as I can get it; and I want *you,*" he concluded, putting his arm about her.

Obviously, what struck her first in this appeal was not his allusion to wanting her but to the need of settling his plans. All her idle married years, he knew, had been packed with settling things, adjusting things, adapting things, disguising things. She did see his point, she agreed at once, and she wanted as much as he did to fix a date; but why shouldn't it be a later one? There were her own aunts too, who had always been so kind. Aunt Julia, in particular, would be as horrified as the Sellarses at her marrying before her year of mourning was over; and she particularly wanted to consider Aunt Julia.

"Why do you particularly want to consider Aunt Julia? I seem to remember her as a peculiarly stupid old lady."

"Yes, dear," she agreed. "But it's just because she *is* peculiarly stupid—"

"If you call that a sufficient reason, we shall never get married. In a family as large as yours there'll always be somebody stupid left to consider."

"Thanks for your estimate of my family. But it's not the only reason." Her colour rose a little. "You see, I'm supposed to be Aunt Julia's heir. I found it out because, as it happens, Mr. Dobree drew up her will; and the doctors say any one of these attacks of gout—"

"Oh—."

He couldn't keep the disenchanted note out of his voice. The announcement acted like a cold douche. It ought, in reason, to have sent a pleasant glow through him, for he knew that, in spite of Mr. Dobree's efforts, Mrs. Sellars had been left with unexpectedly small means, and the earnings of his own twenty years of hard work in hard climates had been partly lost in unlucky investments. The kind of post he meant to try for in New York—as consulting engineer to some large firm of contractors—was not likely to bring in as much as his big jobs in the past; and the appearance of a gouty aunt with benevolent testamentary designs ought to have been an unmixed satisfaction. But trimming his course to suit the whims of rich relations had never been his way—perhaps because he had never had any rich relations. Anyhow, he was not going to be dictated to by his wife's; and it gave him a feeling of manliness to tell her so.

"Of course, if it's a case of choosing between Aunt Julia and me—" he began severely.

She raised her eyebrows with that soft mockery he enjoyed so much when it was not turned against himself. "In that case, dear, I should almost certainly choose you."

"Well, then, pack up, and let's go straight off to Paris and get married."

"Martin, you ought to understand. I can't be married before my year of mourning's out. For my own sake I can't; and for yours."

"Damn mine!"

"Very well; I have my personal reasons that I must stick to even if I can't make you understand them." Her eyes filled, and she looked incredibly young and wistful. "I don't suppose I ought to expect you to," she added.

"You ought to expect me to understand anything that's even remotely reasonable."

"I had hoped so."

"Oh, dash it—" he began; and then broke off. With a secret dismay he felt their lovers' talk degenerating for the first time into a sort of domestic squabble; if indeed so ungraceful a term could be applied to anything as sweetly resilient as Rose's way of gaining her end. Was marriage always like that? Was the haven Boyne had finally made to be only a stagnant backwater, like other people's? Or was it because he had been wandering and homeless for so long that the least restraint chafed him, and arguments based on social considerations made him fume? He was certainly in no position to quarrel with Mrs. Sellars for wishing to better her fortunes, and the discussion ended by his lifting her hand to his lips and saying: "You know I want only what you want." The coward's way out—and he knew it. But since he had parted with the substance of his independence, why cling to the form? He felt her eyes following his inner debate, and knew that the sweetness of her smile was distilled out of satisfaction at his defeat. "Damn it," he thought, "what cannibals marriage makes of people." He suddenly felt as if they were already married—as if they had been married a long time. . .

During their first fortnight not a cloud had shadowed their comradeship; but now that love and marriage had intervened the cloud was there, no bigger than the Scriptural one, but menacing as that proverbial vapour. She was kinder than ever because she had gained her point; and he knew it was because she had gained her point. But was it not his fault if he had begun thus early to distinguish among her different qualities as if they belonged to different vintage years, and to speculate whether the quality of her friendship might not prove more exquisite than her love could ever be? He was willing to assume the blame, since the joy of holding her fast, of plunging into her enchanted eyes, and finding his own enchantment there, was still stronger than any disappointment. If love couldn't be friendship too, as he had once dreamed it might, the only thing to do was to make the most of what it was. . .

Judith Wheater's letter had been for over a week in Boyne's pocket when he pulled it out, crumpled and smelling of tobacco.

He and Mrs. Sellars were reclining at ease on a high red ledge of rock, with a view plunging down by pine-clad precipices, pastures and forests to illimitable distances of blue Dolomite. The air sang with light, the smell of crushed herbs rose like incense, and the hearts of the lovers were glad with sun and wind, and the glow of a long climb followed by such food as only a rucksack can provide.

"And now for a pipe," Boyne said, in sleepy beatitude, stretching himself out on the turf at Mrs. Sellars's elbow. He fumbled for his tobacco pouch, and drew out with it the forgotten letter.

"Oh, dash it—"

"What?"

"Poor little thing! I forgot this; I meant to show it to you days ago."

"Who's the poor little thing?"

For a moment he wavered. His old dread of her misunderstanding returned; and he felt he could not bear to have her misunderstand that letter. What was the use of showing it, after all? But she was holding out her hand, and he had no alternative. She raised herself on her elbow, and bent her lustrous head above the page. From where he lay he watched her profile, and the subtle curves of the line from ear to throat. "How lovely she still is," he thought.

She read attentively, frowning a little in the attempt to decipher Judith's spelling, and her mouth melting into amusement or compassion. Then she handed back the letter. "I suppose it's from the little Wheater girl you wrote about? Poor little thing indeed! It's too dreadful. I didn't know there really *were* such people. But who are the Wheaters she speaks of in the postscript, who are not to be told?"

Boyne replied that those were her parents.

"Her parents? Why does she speak of them in that way?"

He explained that in the Wheater circles it was the custom among the children to do so, the cross-tangle of divorces having usually given them so many parents that it was more convenient to differentiate the latter by their surnames.

"Oh, Martin, it's too horrible! Are you serious? Did the poor child really tell you that?"

"The governess did—as a matter of course."

She made a little grimace. "The sort of governesses they must have, in a world where the parents are like that!"

"Well, this particular one is a regular old Puritan brick. She and Judith keep the whole show together." And he told her about the juvenile oath on Scopy's "Cyclopædia of Nursery Remedies."

"She doesn't appear to have grounded her pupils very thoroughly in spelling," Mrs. Sellars commented; but her eyes were soft, and she took the letter back, and began to read it over again.

"There's a lot I don't begin to understand. Who are these people that Mrs. Wheater wants to invite on the yacht because they know a Duke, and Mr. Wheater won't because it's too low?"

"They're Lord and Lady Wrench. Wasn't there a lot in the papers a month or two ago about Lord Wrench's marrying a movie star? He has a racing-stable; I believe he's very rich. Her name was Zinnia Lacrosse."

"A perfect name. But why, in the Wheater world, are movie stars regarded as too low? Too low for what—or for whom?" Her mouth narrowed disdainfully on the question.

"Well, this one happens to have been Wheater's wife—for a time."

"His *wife?*"

"Not for long, though. They've been divorced for much longer than they were married. So I suppose Mrs. Wheater doesn't see the use of making a retrospective fuss about it."

"Practical woman! And who's the Gerald that she and the other lady are fighting for?"

"Oh, he's the boy's tutor; Terry's tutor. Or was to have been. I'm afraid he's a rotter too. But Terry, poor chap, is the best fellow you ever saw. I back him and Judith and Scopy to keep the ship on her course, whatever happens. If only Terry's health holds out."

"And they get him another tutor."

"As things go, he's lucky if he has any."

Mrs. Sellars again sighed out her contempt and amazement, and let the letter fall. For a long time she sat without moving, her chin on her hand, looking out over the great billowing landscape which rolled away at their feet as if driven on an invisible gale. When she turned to Boyne he saw that her eyes were full of a puzzled sadness. "Don't the Wheaters *care* in the least about their children?"

In old days, in their melancholy inconclusive talks, she had often confessed her grief at being childless; and now he heard in her voice the lonely woman's indignation at the unworthiness of those who had been given what she was denied. "Don't they *care?*" she repeated.

"Oddly enough, I believe they do. I'm afraid that's going to be our difficulty. Why should they have taken on the steps if they hadn't cared? They certainly seem very fond of the children, whenever they're with them. But it's one thing to be fond of children, and another to know how to look after them. My impression is that they realised their incapacity long ago, and that's why they dumped the whole problem on Judy."

"Long ago? But how old is Judy? This is the writing of a child of ten."

"She's had no time to learn any other, with six children to look after. But I suppose she's fifteen or sixteen."

"Fifteen or sixteen!" Mrs. Sellars gave a little sigh. "Young enough to be my daughter."

It was on the tip of his tongue to say: "I wish she had been!" But he had an idea it might sound queerly, and instead he stretched out his hand and took back the letter. The gesture seemed to rouse her to a practical view of the question. "What are you going to do about it, dearest?"

"That's what I want you to tell me."

This stimulated her to action, as he had known it would. He was glad that he had consulted her: she had been full of sympathy, and might now be of good counsel. How stupid it was ever to mistrust her!

"Of course you must write to her father."

"Well—perhaps. But doing that won't get us much forrarder."

"Not if you appeal to him—point out that the children oughtn't to be kept in Venice any longer? Didn't you say he knew the climate was bad for the boy?"

"Yes; and Wheater will respond at once—in words! He'll say: 'Damn it, Joyce, Boyne's right. What are the children doing here? We'll pack them off to the Engadine to-morrow.' Then he'll cram my letter into his pocket, and no one will ever see it again, except the valet when he brushes his coat."

"But the mother—Joyce, or whatever her name is? If he tells *her*—"

"Well, there's the hitch."

"What hitch?"

"Supposing she wants to keep the children in Venice on account of Gerald?"

"Gerald? Oh, the tutor! Oh, Martin—" A shiver of disgust ran over her. "And you dare to tell me she's fond of her children!"

"So she is; awfully fond. But everything rushes past her in a whirl. Life's a perpetual film to those people. You can't get up out of your seat in the audience and change the current of a film."

"What *can* you do about it?"

He lay back on the grass, frowning up into the heavens. "Can't think. Unless I were to drop down to Venice for a day or two, and try talking to them." To his surprise, he found that the idea opened out before him rather pleasantly. "Writing to that kind of people's never any sort of good," he concluded.

Mrs. Sellars was sitting erect beside him, her eyes bent

on his. They had darkened a little, and the delicate bend of her lips narrowed as it had when she asked what there could be in the Wheater world that movie stars were too low for.

"Go back to Venice?" He felt the edge of resistance in her voice. "I don't see of what use that would be. It's a good deal to ask you to take that stifling journey again. And if you don't know what to write, how would you know any better what to say?"

"Perhaps I shouldn't. But at any rate I could feel my way. And I might comfort Judith a little."

"Poor child! I wish you could." She was all sweetness again. "But I should try writing first. Don't you think so? Write to her too, of course. Whatever you decide, you'd better begin by feeling your way. It's always awkward to interfere in family matters, and if you turned up again suddenly the Wheaters might think it rather odd."

He was inclined to tell her that nothing would seem odd to the Wheaters except what seemed inevitable and fore-ordained to her. But he felt an irritated weariness of the whole subject. "I daresay you're right," he agreed, pocketing his pipe and getting to his feet. It was not his idea of a holiday that it should be interfered with by other people's bothers, and he put Judith's letter back into his pocket with an impatient thrust. After all, what business was it of his? He would write the child a nice letter, of course; but Rose was right—the idea of going down to Venice was absurd. Besides, Judith's letter was more than a week old, and ten to one the party had scattered by this time, and the children were safe somewhere in the mountains. "Poor little thing, she's always rather overwrought, and very likely she just had a passing panic when she wrote. Hang it, I wish she hadn't written," he concluded, relieved to find a distant object for his irritation.

Arm in arm, he and his love wandered down the mountain.

XI

"OF course I've written to her—I wrote last night," Boyne assured Mrs. Sellars the next evening. He was conscious of a vague annoyance at being called to account in the matter—as if he couldn't deal with his own correspondence without such reminders. But Mrs. Sellars's next word disarmed him. "I'm so glad, dear. I should have hated to feel that our being so happy here had made you neglect your little friend."

That was generous, he thought—and like her. He adored her when she said things like that. It proved that, in spite of her little air of staidness, she was essentially human and comprehending. He had persuaded her that night—for fun, for a change, after her months of seclusion—to come down and dine with him, not at his own modest hotel, but at the towering "Palace" among the pines below the *châlet*, where he thought the crowd and gaiety of the big restaurant might amuse her, and would at any rate make their evenings at the *châlet* more delicious by contrast.

They had finished dining, and were seated over their coffee in a corner of the big panelled hall to which the other diners were slowly drifting back. Boyne, seeing Mrs. Sellars, for the first time since his arrival, in the company of women as graceful and well-dressed as herself, noted with satisfaction that not one of them had exactly her quality. But the groups about the other tables were amusing to study and speculate about, and he sat listening to her concise and faintly ironic comments with an enjoyment mellowed by the flavour of the excellent cigar he had acquired from the head-waiter.

"The girl in peach-colour, over there by the column—lovely, isn't she? Only one has seen her a thousand times, in all the 'Vogues' and 'Tatlers.' Oh, Martin, won't it be too awful if beauty ends by being standardised too?"

Boyne rather thought it had been already, in the new generation, and secretly reflected that Mrs. Sellars's deepest attraction lay in her belonging to a day when women still wore their charm with a difference.

"I'm sure if I owned one of these new beauties I shouldn't always be able to pick her out in a crowd," he agreed.

She laughed her satisfaction, and then, sweeping the hall with lifted eye-glass: "That one you would. . ."

"A new beauty? Where?"

"Beauty—no. Hardly pretty . . . but different. The girl who's just come in. Where's she vanished to? Oh, she's speaking to the porter. Now she's looking this way—but you can't see her from where you're sitting. She's hardly more than a child; but the face is interesting."

He barely caught the last words. The porter had come up with a message. "Young lady asking for you, sir." Boyne got to his feet, staring in the direction indicated. He had not been mistaken. It was Judith Wheater who stood there, frail and straight in her scant travelling dress, her hat pulled down over her anxious eyes, so small and dun-coloured that she was hardly visible among those showy bare-armed women. Yet Mrs. Sellars had picked her out at once! Yes, there was something undeniably "different"; just as there was about Mrs. Sellars herself. But this was no time for such considerations. Where on earth had the child come from, and what on earth had brought her?

"Wait a minute, will you? It's some one I know." He followed the porter between the tables to where Judith stood in the shadow of the stairway.

"Child! Where in the world have you dropped from?"

"Oh, Martin, Martin! I was so afraid you'd gone!"

He caught her by both hands, and she lifted a drawn little face to his. Well, why not? He had kissed her goodbye in Venice; now he touched his lips to her cheek. "Judy, how in the world did you get here? Have the heads of the clan come too?"

"Oh, Martin, Martin!" She kept fast hold of him, and he felt that she was trembling. She paid no attention to his question, but turned and glanced about her. "Isn't there a writing-room somewhere that we could go to? There's never anybody in them after dinner."

He guided her, still clinging to him, to one of the handsomely appointed rooms opening off the corridor beyond the hall. As she had predicted, its desks were deserted, its divans unoccupied. She dropped down by Boyne, and threw her arms about his neck.

"Oh, Martin, say you're glad! I must hear you say it!"

"Glad, child? Of course I'm glad." Very gently he released himself. "But you look dead-beat, Judy. What's the matter? Has anything gone wrong? Are your people here?"

She drew back a little and turned full on him her most undaunted face. "If you mean father and mother, they're in Venice. They don't know we're here. You mustn't be angry, Martin: we've run away."

"Run away? Who's run away?"

"All of us; with Scopy and Nanny. I always said we'd

have to, some day. Scopy and Terry and I managed it. We're at the *Pension Rosenglüh,* down the hill. Father and mother will never guess we're here. They think we've gone to America on the Cunarder that touched at Venice yesterday. I left a letter to say we had. Terry was splendid; he invented it all. We hired motors at Padua to come here. But I'm afraid he's dreadfully done up. This air will put him right though, won't it?" She poured it all out in the same tone of eager but impartial narrative, as if no one statement in her tale were more surprising or important than the others—except, of course, the matter of Terry's health. "The air here is something wonderful, Martin, isn't it?" she pleaded; and he found himself answering with conviction: "There's simply nothing like it."

Her face instantly grew less agitated. "I knew I was right to come," she sighed in a tired voice; and he felt as if she were indeed an overwrought child, and the next moment might fall asleep on his shoulder.

"Judy, you're dreadfully done up yourself, and you look famished. It's after ten. Have you had anything to eat since you got here?"

"I don't believe I have. There wasn't time. I had to see the children settled first, and then make sure you were here."

"Of course I'm here. But before we do any more talking you've got to be fed."

"Well, it would be nice to have a bite," she confessed, recovering her usual confident tone.

"Wait here, and I'll go and forage." Boyne walked down the corridor and back into the hall, where people were beginning to group themselves about the bridge-tables. The fact of finding himself there roused him to the recollection of having left Mrs. Sellars alone with his empty coffee-cup. Till that moment he had forgotten her existence. He made his way back to their corner, but it was deserted. In the so-called "salon," against a background of sham tapestries and gilt wall-lights, other parties were forming about more bridge-tables; but there also there was no sign of Mrs. Sellars.

"Oh, well, she's got bored and gone home," he thought, a little irritably. Surely it would have been simpler and more friendly to wait . . . but that was just a part of her ceremoniousness. Probably she had thought it more tactful to disappear. Damn tact! That was all he had to say. . . The important thing now was to give Judy something to eat, and get her back to her *pension*. After that he would run up to the *châlet* and explain.

He found a waiter, learned that it was too late to resuscitate dinner, and ordered ham sandwiches and cocktails to be brought at once to the writing-room. On the whole, he found it simplified things to have Mrs. Sellars out of the way. Perhaps there was something to be said for tact after all.

The first sip of her cocktail brought the glow back to Judith's eyes and lips, the next made her preternaturally vivid and alert. She must eat, he told her—eat at once, before she began to talk; and he pushed his own sandwiches on to her plate, and watched her devouring them, and emptying first her glass and then his. She sparkled at him across its brim, but kept silence, obediently; then she asked for a cigarette, and leaned back at ease against the cushions.

"Well, we're all here," she declared with satisfaction.

"Not Chip?" he questioned, incredulous.

"Chip? I should think so! Do you suppose I'd have stirred an inch without Chip?"

"But what the deuce is it all about, child? Have you gone crazy, all of you?"

"Father and mother have. They do, you know. I warned father we'd run away if it happened again."

"What happened?"

"Why, what I told you would. But I don't suppose you ever got my letter? I was sure you'd have answered it if you had." She turned her eyes on him with a look of such unshaken trust that he stammered uncomfortably: "Tell me all about it now."

"Well, everything went to smash. I knew it would. And then all the old shouting began—about detectives, and lawyers, and mother's alimony. You know that's what the children mean when they talk about mother's old friend Sally Money. They've heard about her ever since they can remember. They think mother sends for her whenever anything goes wrong. . ."

"And things have gone thoroughly wrong?"

"Worse than ever. They were dividing us up already. Bun and Beechy back to Buondelmonte, because he's married a rich American. And Zinnia is ready to take Zinnie. Lord Wrench thinks she's so awfully funny. And father would have had Chip, of course, and we three older ones would have begun to be sent back and forth again as we used to be, like the shabby old books Scopy used to get out of the lending library at Biarritz. You could keep the stupid ones as long as you liked, but the jolly ones only a week." She turned her burning face to his. "Now, Martin, didn't I *have* to get them all away from it?"

The food and wine had sent such a flame through her

that he began to wonder if she had fever, or if it were only the glow of fatigue. He took her hand and it was burning, like her face.

"Child, you're too tired. All the rest will keep till to-morrow. Put on your hat now, and I'll take you down the hill to your *pension*."

"But, Martin, you'll promise and swear to see us through?"

"Through everything, bless you. On Scopy's book. And now come along, or you'll fall asleep in your tracks."

In reality he had never seen her so acutely wakeful; but she submitted in silence to being bundled into her hat and coat, and linked her arm confidingly in his as they threaded their way among the bridge-players and out into the great emptiness of the night. The moon hung low above the western peaks, and the village clock below them in the valley chimed out the three quarters after eleven as they walked down the road between blanched fields and sleeping houses. On the edge of the village a few lights still twinkled; but the *Pension Rosenglüh*, demurely withdrawn behind its white palings, showed a shuttered front to the moon. Boyne opened the garden gate, and started to go up the doorstep ahead of Judith. "Oh, you needn't ring, Martin. It would wake everybody. I don't believe the door's locked. I told Scopy to see that I wasn't shut out." She tried the door-knob, which yielded hospitably, and then turned and flung her arms about her companion.

"Martin, darling, I don't believe I'd ever have dared if I hadn't known you'd see us through," she declared with a resounding kiss.

"The devil you wouldn't!" he murmured; but he

pushed her gently in, thinking: "I ought never to have given her that second cocktail." From the threshold he whispered: "Go upstairs as quietly as you can. I'll be down in the morning to see how you're all getting on." Then he shut the door on her, and slipped out of the gate.

Midnight from the village clock! What would his friend say if he knocked up the *châlet* at that hour? Half way to the hotel he left the road and branched upward through the fir-wood, by a path he knew. But there were no lights in the *châlet*.

XII

BEFORE mounting to Mrs. Sellars's the next morning Boyne went down to the *Pension Rosenglüh* to gather what farther details he could of the strange flight of the little Wheaters.

As he reached the *pension* gate he was met by Miss Scope, looking more than commonly gaunt and ravaged, but as brightly resolute as her fellow-conspirator. Her gray cotton glove enfolded Boyne's hand in an unflinching grasp, and she exclaimed at once how providential it was that they should have caught him still at Cortina. She added that she had been on the look-out for him, as both Judith and Terry were still asleep, and she was sure he'd agree that they had better not be disturbed, after all they'd been through; especially as Terry was still feverish. The other children, he gathered, had already breakfasted, and been shepherded out by Nanny and the nursemaid to the downs above the valley; and meanwhile perhaps Mr. Boyne would come in and have a chat.

The word seemed light for the heavy news he was prepared to hear; but he suspected that Miss Scope, like the Witch of Atlas, was used to racing on the platforms of the wind, and laughed to hear the fire-balls roar behind. At any rate, her sturdy composure restored his own balance, and made him glad of the opportunity to hear her version of the adventure before his next encounter with Judith.

Miss Scope was composed, as she always was—he was

soon to learn—in real emergencies. She had been through so many that they seemed to her as natural and inevitable as thunder-storms or chicken-pox—as troublesome, but no more to be fussed about. Nevertheless, she did not underrate the gravity of the situation: to do so, he suspected, would have robbed it of its savour. There had been cataclysms before—times when Judy had threatened to go off and disappear with all the children—but till now she had never even attempted to put her threats into execution. "And now she's carried it off with a master hand," Miss Scope declared in a tone of grim triumph.

But carried it where to? That was the question Boyne could not help putting. He was sure Judith had been masterly—but where was it all going to lead? Had any of them taken that into account, he asked?

Well, Miss Scope had to own that their departure had been too precipitate for much taking into account. It had to be then or never—she had seen that as clearly as Judy and Terry. The fact that Terry was with them showed how desperate the situation was—

"Desperate? Really desperate?"

"Oh, Mr. Boyne! If you'd been through it twice before, as my poor children have. . ."

Listening to the details of her story, he agreed that it must indeed have been awful, and ended by declaring that he did not question Judith's reasons; but now that the first step in the mutiny was taken, how did Miss Scope imagine that they were going to keep it up? In short, what did they mean to do when they were found out?

"I think Judith counts very much on your intervention. That's the reason she was so anxious to find you still here. And of course she hopes there'll be time—time to consider, to choose a course of action. She believes it will be some days before we're found out, as you put it. I daresay she's told you that she left a letter . . . Mr. Boyne," said Miss Scope, interrupting herself with her sternest accent, "I hope you don't think that, in ordinary circumstances, I should ever condone the least deceit. The children will tell you that on that point I'm inexorable. But these were not ordinary circumstances." She cleared her throat, and brought out: "Judith said in the letter that we'd sailed for America. She thinks her father will hurry there to find them, and in that way we shall gain a little time, for the steamer they're supposed to be on is not due in New York for ten days."

The plan seemed puerile, even for so immature a mind as Judith's; but Boyne did not raise that point. He merely said: "I hope so. But meanwhile what are you all going to live on? It costs something to feed such an army."

Miss Scope's countenance turned from sallow to white. Her eyes forsook his face, as they did when she talked of Terry, and she brought out, hesitatingly: "Judith, I understand, has means. . ."

"Poor woman!" Boyne thought. "I believe she's plumped in all her savings.—I see," he said. He was filled with a sudden loathing of all the wasteful luxury, the vanity and selfishness and greed, out of which this poor pale flower of compassion had sprung. "I see," he repeated. He stood up, and held out his hand. "You're their real mother. If there's anything on earth I can do—to the limit of my small capacity—." A tear ran down the furrows of Miss Scope's averted cheek. He knew it by the hasty dab of her cotton hand. "I know—

I know—. Oh, Mr. Boyne, it's providential, our finding you."

He pressed her wet glove hard, and assured her that she could count on him. He would go off now, he added, to reflect further on the problem, and come back later, when Judy and Terry were awake.

It was after eleven when he reached the *châlet;* but luckily no long excursion had been planned for that morning. Mrs. Sellars had told him the night before that she had letters to write, and should not expect him early. When he approached the little house in its clearing of emerald turf he saw her on the balcony, her writing-materials on a table at her elbow. But she was leaning on the rail, looking down the path by which he always came. He waved his hand, and she answered with a welcoming gesture. "Come up—I'm deep in papers," she called down cheerily.

"I came last night, but your lights were out, and I was afraid of the cook," he laughed, taking her in his arms as she went to meet him. The day was warm, and she had put on a thin white dress which gave her a springlike look. Her complexion too had a morning freshness, through which the blood ran up to his kiss. "But not afraid of me?" she questioned.

"Of you? I like that! You deserted me; it's you who ought to be afraid. I've come to make a row, you know."

"You ought to have come to thank me for my tact. I saw you'd run across old friends, and slipped out of the way."

"I'd run across one young friend—Judith Wheater. When I came back to tell you about it you'd gone."

Her eyes lit up with curiosity and interest. "Your famous little Judith? Really? Why, you always speak of her as such a child—I shouldn't have guessed. . ."

"You said yourself last night how young she looked—"

"Yes; awfully young; but still—grown up."

"Well, she's not grown up. She's a child—a child tremendously to be pitied. I want to tell you all about it. I want your help and your advice. You don't know what a quandary I'm in."

She had gone back to her seat on the balcony, and he dropped into the chair beside her. As he spoke her colour flickered up again, and she smiled a little uncertainly. "A quandary—about that child?" The smile faded, and her colour with it. "Martin, you don't mean . . . you can't . . ?"

He stared, perplexed, and then burst out laughing. "That the quandary's *mine*—about little Judith? Bless you, what an idea! Why, she's hardly out of the nursery." He laughed again, partly to bridge over his surprise and her constraint. It was incredible, what far-fetched delusions the most sensible women took up with, at the very moment when one wanted them to look at a question like a man! "This is a very different business," he went on. "Not in the least sentimental, but merely squalid. The Wheater *ménage* has gone to smash again, and Judy's bolted with all the children, to try to prevent their being separated, as they are whenever there's a new deal."

Mrs. Sellars sat looking at him with wide eyes and parted lips. The situation was evidently too new to her to be at once intelligible, and she repeated vaguely: "Bolted—bolted from whom?"

"From Joyce and Wheater. Gone clean away, without any warning."

She was again silent, her eyes as it were fixed on this

statement, which seemed to carry her no farther toward comprehension.

"But bolted with whom? They can't have gone away all by themselves?"

"The governess is with them, and the two nurses. In a crisis like this they all stand by Judith. I've just been talking with the governess, and she entirely approves. You see, they've been through this kind of thing before."

"Through the running away?"

"No, but through what led up to it. The last time, it appears, Judith told her parents that if they were divorced again she meant to go off with all the children, rather than have them separated from each other as they were before. You see, whenever a smash comes the children are divided up among the ex-parents, and some of them are pretty rotten, I imagine—a blackmailing Italian prince, a rather notorious movie star, and Lord knows who besides. Not to speak of the new elements to be introduced, if Joyce and Wheater both marry again, as I've no doubt they will, in no time."

Mrs. Sellars, her chin resting on her hand, sat listening in a silence still visibly compounded of bewilderment and disgust. For a minute after Boyne had ceased speaking she did not move or look up. At last she said, in a low voice: "It's all too vile for belief."

"Exactly," he agreed. "And it's all true."

"The horrors those children must know about—"

"It's to save them from more horrors that Judith has carried them away."

"I see—I see. Poor child!" Her face melted into pity. "Just at first it was all too new to me. But now I'm beginning to understand. And I suppose she came here hoping you would help her?"

"I suppose she didn't have much time to think or choose, but vaguely remembered I was here, as her letter showed."

"But the money? Where in the world did they get the money? You can't transport a nursery-full of children from one place to another without paying for it."

Boyne hesitated a moment; but he felt he must not betray Miss Scope, and merely answered that he hadn't had time to go into all that yet, but supposed that in an easy-going extravagant household like the Wheaters' there were always some funds available, the more so as preparations were already being made to send the children off to the mountains.

"Well, it's all hideous and touching and crazy. Where are the poor little things—at your hotel?" Mrs. Sellars had gone indoors, and was picking up her hat and sunshade. "I should like you to take me down at once to see them."

Boyne was touched by the suggestion, but secretly alarmed at what might happen if Mrs. Sellars were exposed unprepared to the simultaneous assault of all the little Wheaters. He explained that Judith had taken her flock to an inexpensive *pension* in the village, and that the younger children, when he had called there, were already away on the downs, and Judith and Terry still sleeping off their emotions. Should he go down again, he asked, and bring Judith back alone to the *châlet?* "You'd better see her first without the others. You might find the seven of them rather overwhelming."

Seven? Mrs. Sellars confessed she hadn't realised that there were actually seven. She agreed that it would be perhaps better that she should first see Judith without her brothers and sisters, and proposed that Boyne should invite her to come back with him to the *châlet* to lunch. "If you think she won't be too frightened of a strange old woman?" The idea of Judith's being frightened of anything or anybody amused Boyne, but he thought it charming of Mrs. Sellars to suggest it, and was glad, after all, that she was there to support and advise him. When she had had a quiet talk with Judith he felt sure she would be on the children's side; and perhaps her practical vision might penetrate farther than his into the riddle of what was to be done for them.

"If only," he said to himself, "Judith doesn't begin by saying something that will startle her"; and he thought of warning Mrs. Sellars not to expect a too great ingenuousness in his young friend. Then he reflected that such a warning might unconsciously prejudice her against the girl, and decided that it would be wiser to trust to Judith's natural charm to overcome anything odd in her conversation. If there were hints to be given, he concluded, there would be less risk in giving them to Judith.

But the utility of giving hints in that quarter became equally dubious at first sight of her. Refreshed and radiant after her night's rest, and unusually pretty in her light linen frock, and a spreading hat with a rosy lining, Judith received him at the gate of the *pension* in an embrace which sent her hat flying among the currant-bushes, and exposed her rumpled head and laughing eyes to his close inspection. "You look like a pansy this morning," he said, struck by the resemblance of her short pointed oval and velvet-brown eyes to the eager inquisitive face of the mountain flower. But Judith was no gardener, and rejected the comparison with a grimace. "How horrid of you! Nasty wired things in wreaths at funerals! I don't feel a bit as if I were at a funeral. It's so jolly to be here, and to have found you. You've come to say you'll lunch with us, haven't you? The children will be mad with joy. It was partly because I promised them we'd find you here that they agreed to come. Blanca and Zinnie unsettled them at first—they're always afraid of missing some excitement if they have a row with mother. But I told them we'd have lots more excitement with you." She was hanging on his arm, and drawing him up the path to the house.

"I must tell the landlady you're coming to lunch. Scopy's upstairs with Terry, and she told me to be sure not to forget, so that the cook could give us something extra." By this time they were in the little sitting-room, which smelt of varnish and dried edelweiss, and had a stuffed eagle perched above the stove. Judith sat down on the slippery sofa, and dragged Boyne to a seat at her side. "And first, I was to ask you what pudding you'd particularly like."

"Oh, bless you, any pudding. But about lunch—"

She drew herself up, and tossed him an arch smile. "Or perhaps you're here incog., with a lady, and would rather not come? I told Scopy I shouldn't wonder—"

"Nonsense, Judith; how absurd—"

"Why absurd? Why shouldn't you be here with a lady? *Vous êtes encore très bien, mon cher. . .*" She drew her deep lids half shut, and slanted an insinuating glance at him.

"Don't talk like a manicure, child. As a matter of fact, I have an old friend here who wants very much to see you, and who kindly suggested—"

"An old lady-friend?"

"Yes."

"As old as Scopy?"

"No; probably not as old as your mother, even. I only meant—"

"But if she's younger than mother, how can you say she's old? Is she prettier, too?" Judith broke in searchingly.

"I don't know, really; I haven't thought—"

"Well, I don't believe she's as well-dressed. Unless, perhaps, you think Joyce's clothes are sometimes just a shade *too*—"

"I haven't thought about that either. What I mean by 'old' is that Mrs. Sellars and I have been friends for years. She's living in a *châlet* on the hill above the hotels; and she wants me to bring you up to lunch with her today."

"Me—only me?" Judith questioned, visibly surprised.

Boyne smiled. "Well, my dear, I'm sure she would have liked to invite you all, Chip included; but her house is tiny and couldn't possibly take in the whole party. So, to avoid invidious distinctions, why not come by yourself and make her acquaintance? I want you awfully to know her, for no one can give you better advice than she can."

Judith drew herself up stiffly and her face became a blank. "I don't want anybody's advice but yours, Martin. But of course I'll go if you want me to."

"It's not a question of what I want. But you may be sure if my advice is any good it will be because I've consulted Mrs. Sellars. Two's not too many to get you out of this predicament. I sometimes think you don't realise what an awful row you're all in for."

"If she's not as old as mother, and you've never noticed how she's dressed, you must be in love with her,"

Judith went on, as if his last words had not made the least impression on her.

"I don't see what difference it makes if I am or not," he retorted, beginning to lose his temper. "The point is that she happens to be one of the kindest and most sensible women I know—"

"That's what men always think," said Judith thoughtfully. She drew back to study him again through half-closed lids. "It's a wonderful thing to be in love," she murmured; and then continued with a teasing smile: "Blanca's ever so much sharper than I am. She said: 'Why's Martin in such an awful hurry to rush away from Venice, if he isn't slipping off on the quiet to meet a friend?' I suppose," she added, with a fall in her voice, and a corresponding droop of the lips, "it was awfully stupid of me to blunder in on you like this, and you're racking your brains to think how you can get rid of us all, and keep out of a row with father and mother."

Boyne, half-exasperated and half-touched, as he so often was in his talks with her, and especially when he knew she wished to give him pain, laid his hand reproachfully on hers. "Look here, Judith, I could shake you when you talk such drivel. The only thing I'm racking my brains about is how to help you to get what you want. To keep you all together, as you are now, and yet not let your father and mother think that I've had anything to do with this performance. You're quite right; I do want to stay on good terms with them, because if I do I may succeed in persuading them that, whatever happens, they've no right to separate you children again. If I do that I shall have done my best for you. But I don't see my way to it yet, and that's why I want you to come and make friends with Mrs. Sellars."

To his surprise she listened in an attentive silence, and, when he had ended, lifted to his the face of an obedient child. "Of course I'll do what you want, Martin. But don't you think your friend would perhaps understand better if I had Nanny bring up Chip to see her after lunch?"

"Bless you—of course she would," he agreed enthusiastically; and she thereupon proposed that before they started he should come upstairs and see Terry.

XIII

SEEING Terry, Boyne had to admit, was the surest way of attaching one, body and soul, to the cause of the little Wheaters. Whatever Mrs. Sellars thought of Judith —a question of obvious uncertainty—there could be no doubt as to what she would think of Terry.

There had been moments during the morning when Boyne did not see how any good will on either part could bridge the distance between Mrs. Sellars's conception of life, and Judith Wheater's experience of it; but between Mrs. Sellars and Terry there would be nothing to explain or bridge over. Their minds would meet as soon as their eyes did. "I'll bring her down to see him after lunch," Boyne decided.

There was no hope of Terry's being up that day. The excitement of the flight, and the heat and fatigue of the journey, had used up his small surplus of strength, and he could only lie staring at Boyne with eager eyes, and protest that he knew the air of Cortina would put him all right before long. Scopy had already had the doctor in, and administered suitable remedies, and the patient's temperature had dropped to nearly normal. "If only father and mother will let us stay here I'm sure I shall be patched up this time. And you'll be here for a bit to look after the children, won't you, Martin?"

Boyne said he would stay as long as he could, and at any rate not leave till the little Wheaters' difficulty with their parents was on the way to adjustment. He pointed out that negotiations would no doubt be necessary, and

Terry promptly rejoined: "That's just why Judy and I decided to come here. We knew that if we could get hold of you, you'd back us up, and help us to make some kind of terms with father and mother." His eyes fixed his friend's with a passionate insistence. "You see, Martin, it won't do, separating us again—it really won't. We're not going to get any sort of education at this rate. And as for manners! The children have all been completely demoralised since Zinnia's visit. Now they've heard of Buondelmonte's marriage, and the steps have gone off their base too; and as for Blanca she thinks of nothing but dressing-up and flirtation. . . As soon as things go wrong between father and mother the children seem to feel it in the air; even before the actual fighting begins, they all get out of hand. Zinnie gave Bun a black eye the other day because he said he was going to be a Prince again, and live in his father's palace in Rome, and have his own Rolls . . . a child who hardly knows his letters!" Terry concluded with a gesture of contempt.

"I know, old man. It's all wrong," Boyne agreed, "and something's got to be done, and done soon. That's what I'm going to try to make your father and mother see. Meanwhile you must make the most of this respite to get a good rest. I promise I'll do what I can when the time comes."

"Oh, you needn't promise," Terry said, letting his head sink back contentedly on the pillows.

On the way up the hill with Judith, Boyne was able to gather some of the details she had been too tired and excited to impart the night before. Miss Scope's confidences were always in the nature of sombre generalizations. When it came to particulars, she retreated behind professional secrecy; and Boyne had not liked to force her defences. Besides, he knew that no such scruples would hamper Judith, who saw life only in particulars. But, after all, there was nothing very unexpected in Judith's story. As she said, it was always the same old row over again. As soon as Zinnia Lacrosse had cast a covetous eye on Gerald Ormerod, Joyce had decided that she could not live without him. The thought of his dining every night at the Lido with the Wrenches and the Duke of Mendip, while she and Wheater sat alone on the deck of the "Fancy Girl," or made the most of such mediocre guests as they could collect, was too much for a high-spirited woman; and Joyce had suddenly requested her husband to sack the tutor. Wheater, surprised, had protested that Terry liked him (and Terry did—he was very jolly, and a good teacher, Judith impartially admitted); whereupon Joyce had declared that if Ormerod wasn't sent away at once she intended to divorce Wheater and marry him. Wheater, of course, was furious, and there had been, in Judith's language, an all-round circus, complicated by the fact that what Gerald really wanted was to marry *her*—

"What—what? Marry *you?* Have you all of you gone crazy?" Boyne found himself indignantly repeating.

Judith smiled. "I'm not crazy. And I'm nearly sixteen. And I suppose I'm a nairess." (She pronounced the word as she wrote it.) "But you don't imagine I'd leave the children, do you? Besides, Terry says it would be ridiculous to marry till I can learn how to spell."

"My God—I should say it would," cried Boyne furiously. What on earth would come of it, he asked himself, if she opened the conversation with Mrs. Sellars on this note? "Judith, look here—."

"But I don't know, after all," she went on, in a reflective tone. "Gerald says some of the greatest people never *could* spell. Napoleon couldn't—or Madame de Sévigné—and Shakespeare signed his name differently every time."

"I see you've taken a course in history since I left," Boyne sneered; to which she responded with simplicity: "No; but he told me that one day when he found me crying because of my awful spelling."

"Well, you're quite right to cry about your spelling. And Terry's quite right to say that the first thing you want is to have some sort of an education, all of you."

"Perhaps, then, it would have been better for me to marry Gerald," she rejoined, with a return of her uncanny impartiality. "But no," she interrupted herself; "I never could have kept the children if I had; so what's the use?"

"Well, here we are," Boyne broke in nervously.

"Why, you poor child, how young you are, after all!" Mrs. Sellars exclaimed, swaying forward to drop an impulsive kiss on Judith's cheek. Boyne's first thought was, how young she looked herself, in her thin black dress, her auburn head bent like an elder sister's above Judith's; then how much too young Judith was to be conciliated by that form of greeting.

Judith looked at her hostess with a smile. "Young for what?" she asked, with an ominous simplicity.

"Why—for all your responsibilities," the other answered, checked in her premeditated spontaneity.

Judith was still smiling: a small quiet smile from which the watchful Boyne augured no good.

"I suppose I ought to be flattered," she said. "I know that at your age and mother's it's thought awfully flattering to be called young. But, you see, I'm not sixteen yet, so it's nothing extraordinary to me."

"Your being so young makes it extraordinarily kind of you to come and see an old lady like me," Mrs. Sellars smiled back, taking nervous refuge in platitudes.

Judith considered her with calm velvety eyes. "Oh, but I wanted to come. Martin says you'll be a friend; and we need friends badly."

Mrs. Sellars's eyes at once softened. "Martin's quite right. I'll be as good a friend as you'll let me. I'm so glad you've come to share my picnic lunch. And Martin will have told you how sorry I was not to have room for the whole party in this tiny house."

"Well," said Judith, "he thought you'd find us rather overwhelming—"; but Mrs. Sellars laughed this away as an unauthorized impertinence of her old friend's.

On the whole, things were beginning better than the old friend had expected. He only hoped Rose wouldn't mind Judith's chucking down her hat on the sitting-room sofa, and turning to the glass above the mantelpiece to run her fingers through her tossed hair. Once at table, Mrs. Sellars led the talk to the subject of the little Wheaters, whose names she had cleverly managed to master, and whose acquaintance she expressed the wish to make at the earliest opportunity, "steps" and all. "For I assure you," she added, "I'm not as easily overwhelmed as Martin seems to think."

Judith was always at her best when she was talking of the children, and especially of Terry, whose name Mrs. Sellars had spoken with a sympathy which brought a glow to the girl's cheek. "Oh, Terry's far and away the best of us; you'll love Terry. If only he could have half a chance. I don't mean about his health; father and mother have really done all they could about that. But he's never had any proper education, and he isn't strong enough yet to go to school." She went on, forgetting herself and her habit of being on the defensive, carried away by the need to explain Terry, to put him in the handsomest possible light before this friend of Martin's, who was so evidently a person of standards and principles—like Terry himself. It was just another bit of poor Terry's bad luck, she pursued; for ever so long he'd been begging and imploring their parents to let him have a good tutor, like other boys of his age who weren't strong enough for school; and finally they had understood, and agreed that he couldn't be left any longer to Scopy and the nurses; and then, when the tutor was finally found, and everything working so well, Joyce had to take it into her head to marry him. Didn't Mrs. Sellars agree that it was a particularly rotten piece of luck?

Yes; Mrs. Sellars did agree. Only, Boyne saw from the curve of her lips, "luck" was not precisely the noun she would have used, nor "rotten" the adjective.

"But surely it's just a passing whim of—of your mother's. When it comes to the point, she won't break up everything in order to marry this young man."

Judith's eyes widened. "Well, what can mother do—if she's in love with him?"

Mrs. Sellars lowered her lids softly, as if she were closing the eyes of a dead self. "Why, she could . . . she could . . . think of all of you, my dear."

"Oh, she'll do that," Judith rejoined. "She has already. She and father are fighting over us now. That's why we bolted. Hasn't Martin told you?"

"I think Martin felt he'd rather have you tell me about

it yourself—that is, as much as you care to," said Mrs. Sellars, with tactful evasiveness.

Judith pondered, her brows gathering in a puzzled frown. "I don't know that there's anything more to tell. I brought the children away so that we shouldn't be separated again. If children don't look after each other, who's going to do it for them? You can't expect parents to, when they don't know how to look after themselves."

"Ah, my dear," murmured Mrs. Sellars. With an impulsive movement she put her hand on Judith's. "Just say that to your mother as you've said it to me, and she'll never give you up for anybody."

Judith's frown relaxed, and her eyebrows ran up incredulously. "She has before, you know. What are you to do when you fall in love? That's one thing I never mean to do," she announced, in a decisive tone. "Besides, you know," she went on, "one does get used to children. I suppose you've never had any, have you?" Mrs. Sellars made a faint sign of negation. "Oh, well," Judith continued encouragingly, "I daresay it's not too late. But if you'd had all of us on your hands, and the three steps besides, you'd probably take us for granted by this time. Not that mother isn't fond of us—only she has these heart-storms. That's what poor Doll Westway used to call them. And *she* knew—"

Mrs. Sellars laid down the spoon with which she was absently stirring her coffee. "Doll Westway—?"

Judith's face lit up. "You knew her?"

"No," said Mrs. Sellars, in a tone of rejection acutely familiar to Boyne, but obviously unremarked by the girl.

"She was my very best friend," Judith went on. "You never saw anybody so lovely to look at. In tea-rose bathing tights—"

"My dear," Mrs. Sellars interrupted, "don't you think it seems a pity to sit indoors in such weather? If you've finished your coffee, shall we move out on the balcony? Martin, do find the cigarettes." Her sweetness suffused them like a silvery icing. Judith, obviously puzzled, rose to follow her, and Boyne distributed cigarettes with a savage energy. Oh, damn it, what had gone wrong again now?

But whatever had gone wrong was, for the moment at any rate, set right by the appearance of a blue-veiled nurse who was conducting a rosy little boy up the slope beneath the balcony. "Hullo! This way—here I am!" Judith joyously signalled to the pair; and Mrs. Sellars, leaning over the railing at her side, instantly declared: "Here's somebody too beautiful not to be the celebrated Chip."

Yes; it was clever of Judith to have arranged that Chipstone should appear at that moment. To a childless woman the sight of that armful of health and good humour must be at once a pang and a balm. Mrs. Sellars's eyes met Boyne's, smiling, trembling, and his signalled back: "Damn Aunt Julia." Chipstone had already filled the air with his immovable serenity. They had gone back into the sitting-room to greet him, and he settled himself Buddha-like on Mrs. Sellars's knee, and laughed with satisfaction at the sight of Judy and Martin and Nanny grouped admiringly before him. Whatever came Chip's way seemed to turn into something as fresh as new milk with the bubbles on it.

"Oh, Chip's a good enough fellow," said Judith, fondly disparaging. "But wait till you see Terry. . ."

"Terry couldn't come; but the rest of us have," announced a sharp little voice outside the door.

"Good gracious! If it isn't Zinnie!" Judith jumped up in a rush of indignation; but before she could reach the door it had opened on the self-possessed figure of her little step-sister, behind whose fiery mop appeared the dark bobbing heads of Bun and Beechy.

"Well, if ever—I never did! Susan swore to me she'd never let 'em out of her sight while we was away," Nanny ejaculated, paling under Judith's wrathful glance.

"She never did, neither," said Zinnie composedly. "She watched us almost all the way; but we could run faster than her, 'cos she's got a shoe't hurts her, 'n' so after a while she had to give up chasing us. Didn't she?" This was flung back to the "steps" for corroboration.

But a masterly somersault had already introduced Bun to the centre front, where he remained head down, bare legs and sandal-soles in air; and Beechy had rushed up to Mrs. Sellars and flung her passionate arms about Chipstone. "Oh, my Cheepo, we thought we'd losted you, and you were dead," she joyfully wailed; and Chip received her pæan with a rosy grin.

"Yes, 'n' Judy hadn't ought to of sneaked away and left us all like that, 'n' not said anything 'bout coming here, but only 'ranged for Chip to come and see you, when he's the youngest of the bunch—ought she of?" Zinnie appealed indignantly to Mrs. Sellars; who replied that it evidently didn't seem fair, but she must take the blame to herself for living in such a small house that she hadn't been able to invite them all to lunch because the dining-room wouldn't have held them. "And I suppose," she concluded diplomatically, "Chipstone was chosen to represent you because he takes up the least room."

"No, he doesn't, either; I do!" shouted Bun, swiftly reversing himself and facing Mrs. Sellars in a challenging attitude. "I can crawl through a croky hoop, and I can—"

"You can't hold your tongue, and Chip can, and that's why I brought him, and not the rest of you," cried Judith, administering a shake to Bun, while Nanny seized upon Beechy to stifle her incipient howl of sympathy.

"Oh, these dreadful children—." It was another voice at the door, this time so discreetly pitched, so sweetly deprecating, that Mrs. Sellars instinctively rose to receive a visitor who seemed as little used as herself to noisy company.

"I *am* so sorry—." Blanca was in the room now, slim, white-frocked, imperturbable, with an air of mundane maturity which made Judith seem like her younger sister.

"Poor Susan told me they'd run away from her when they found Nanny was coming here with Chip, and I rushed after them, but couldn't catch them. I'm sorry, but it wasn't my fault." Prettily breathless, she excused herself to Judith; but her long lashes were busy drawing Mrs. Sellars and Boyne into their net. "Darling Martin!" She bestowed on him one of her mother's most studied intonations. "I'm Terry's twin," she explained to Mrs. Sellars.

The latter, at ease with graces so like her own, replied with a smile that, since Terry could not come, she appreciated his sending such a charming delegate. Judith shot a grimace at Boyne, but Blanca, with a sudden rush of sincerity, declared: "Oh, but when you've seen Terry you won't care for any of the rest of us."

"Yes, she will; she'll care for Beechy and me because we're Roman Princes!" Bun shouted, threatening another handspring which a gesture from Judith curtailed.

Zinnie pushed him aside and planted herself firmly in front of their hostess. "My mother could buy 'em all out if she wanted to, 'cos she's a movie star," she affirmed in her thin penetrating voice. "But I'd never let her, 'cos we all love each other very much, 'n' Judy's made us all swear on Scopy's book we'd stay together till we got married. I'm probably going to marry Bun."

At this announcement signs of damp despair revealed themselves on Beechy's features; but Bun, regardless of the emotions he excited, interposed to say: "My *real* mother was a lion-tamer; but that don't matter, 'cos she's dead."

Mrs. Sellars had risen to the occasion on one of her quick wing-beats. Games, tea and more games had been improvised with the promptness and skill which always distinguished her in social emergencies; and the afternoon was nearly over when a band of replete and sleepy children took their way home to the *Pension Rosenglüh*. On the threshold of the *châlet* Zinnie paused to call up to the balcony: "I s'pose 'f you'd known we were coming you'd have had some presents ready for us—." A cuff from Judith nipped the suggestion, and the flock was hurried off down the hill, but not too quickly to catch Mrs. Sellars's response: "Come up to-morrow and you'll see!"

Mrs. Sellars, however, did not wait till the next day to return the little Wheaters' visit. Soon after their departure she gathered up an armful of books, selected for Terry's special delectation, and walked down to the *pension* with Boyne. The younger children were by this time at supper; but the visitor was introduced to Miss Scope, and conducted by her to Terry's bedside. Neither

Judith nor Boyne accompanied her, since the doctor did not want his patient to see many people till he had recovered from his fatigue. Mrs. Sellars, for this reason, remained only for a few minutes with the little boy, and when she rejoined Boyne, who was waiting for her at the gate, she said simply: "I'm glad I came." Boyne liked her for knowing that he would guess the rest. He had never had any doubts about this meeting.

When he got back to his hotel he found the telegram which he had been expecting since the morning. "For God's sake wire at once if children with you and Chipstone all right worried to death cannot understand insane performance police traced them to Padua where they hired motors for Botzen please ship them all back immediately will wire you funds. Wheater."

"Damn it—well, I'll have to go and see him myself," Boyne muttered, crumpling up the paper and jamming it into his pocket. The message had shattered his dream-paradise of a day, and now the sooner the business ahead of him was over the better for everybody. But with a certain satisfaction he concluded, after a glance at the clock: "Too late to wire tonight, anyhow."

XIV

"HERE—how was I to answer this?" Boyne challenged Mrs. Sellars that evening, pushing the telegram across the dinner-table, where they had lingered over their wood-strawberries and cream.

She had been charming about the Wheater children after their departure; appreciative of Judith—with a shade of reserve—discerning and tender about Terry, and warmly motherly about the others. It was heart-breaking, the whole business . . . and so touching, the way they all turned to Martin for help . . . regarding him apparently as their only friend (how well she understood that!) . . . But what on earth was he going to do about it? What possible issue did he see?

All through dinner they went in and out of the question, till Boyne, feeling that, thanks to Terry, her sympathy was permanently secured, drew the Wheater telegram from his pocket. Mrs. Sellars scrutinised it thoughtfully.

"When did this come?"

"Just now. I found it when I went back to the hotel."

She sighed. "Of course the Wheaters were bound to find out within twenty-four hours where they'd gone. Poor little conspirators! I wish we could have kept them a day or two longer . . . especially with that boy so overdone. . ."

"Well, perhaps we can."

Her eyebrows queried: "How?" But instead of taking

this up he said: "You haven't told me yet what I'm to answer."

Her mobile brow sketched another query. "What *can* you answer? Their father'll come and fetch them if you don't send them back."

"I certainly shan't do that."

"Shan't—? Then what?" Her eyes darkened, and she took up the telegram and studied it again; then she lifted a faintly mocking smile to Boyne. "I confess I'm curious to hear your alternative."

He considered this with a frown of perplexity. "Why should I answer at all?"

"If you don't, Wheater has only to telephone to your hotel, and find out if you're still here, and if you've been seen about with a party of children."

"I shan't be here. I'll pack off at once—to Pieve di Cadore, or somewhere."

"And the children?"

"I'll take them with me."

"Are you serious?"

"Absolutely."

She received this with a little silken laugh. "Then you're a child yourself, dear. How long do you suppose it will be before you're run down? You'll only be making things worse for the children—and for yourself."

"Hang myself! But for them—." He frowned and pondered again. "Well, damn it; perhaps. But what have you got to suggest?"

"That you should persuade Judith to take them straight back, of course. I'm awfully sorry for them all—and Terry especially. But as far as I can see there's nothing else to do."

He stood up and began to pace the floor. "I'll never do that."

She leaned her white arms on the table and her smile followed his impatient pacings. "Then what?"

"I don't know. Not yet. Anyhow, I've got the night to think it over."

"All the thinking in the world won't get you any farther."

He met her smile with a grin which was almost antagonistic. "I've got out of one or two tighter places in my life before now."

"I've no doubt you have," she returned in her tone of slightly humorous admiration.

There they had dropped the discussion, both too experienced in debate not to feel its uselessness. And the next morning had, after all, told Boyne, without any one's help, what he intended to do. He decided that his first step was to see Judith; and he was down at the *pension* before the shutters of her room were unlatched. Miss Scope was summoned to the sitting-room, and he told her that Judith must come down immediately to see him.

"Bad news, Mr. Boyne—oh, I hope not?"

"Well, you didn't seriously suppose it was going to take Wheater much longer than this to run you down, did you?"

Miss Scope whitened. "Are the police after us?"

"The police?" He burst out laughing. "To arrest you for abduction? If they do, it shall be over my dead body."

She turned to go, and then paused to face him from the threshold. "Whatever Judith did was done with my knowledge and consent—consent; I don't say approval," she declared in an emphatic whisper.

"Of course, of course. But send her down at once, will you please?"

A moment later Judith was there, huddled into a scant poppy-coloured dressing-gown, her hair tumbling thickly over childish eyes still misty with sleep. "What is it, Martin? The police?"

He laughed again, this time more impatiently. "Don't be ridiculous, child. You're as bad as Scopy. You didn't really believe your father would have you arrested, did you?"

She met this with another question. "What *is* he going to do?"

Boyne handed her the telegram, and she flashed back: "You haven't answered it?"

"Not yet."

"Well, we'll have to start at once, I suppose."

Boyne stared at her, so unprepared for this prompt abdication that the feeling uppermost in him was a sudden sense of flatness. He had come there ready to put up a fight, valiant if unresourceful, and now—

"Couldn't we catch a steamer at Trieste?" she continued, apparently pursuing some inward train of thought. The unexpected question jerked him back out of his supineness.

"Trieste? Why Trieste?" He stared at her, puzzled. "Where to?"

"Oh, almost anywhere where they can't reach us too quickly." As if unconscious of his presence, she continued to brood upon her problem. "Perhaps, do you know, after all, we'd better go to America. Don't you think so? There's Grandma Mervin—Joyce's mother.

We might go to her. And meanwhile you can make the Wheaters think we're still here, and so they won't be worried, and we shall have time to slip away."

In spite of himself, Boyne's first feeling was one of relief that she meant to keep up the struggle. To begin with, it was more like her; and he had reached the point of wanting her at all costs to be like herself. But he kept his wits sufficiently to reply on a note of sarcasm: "Thank you for the part for which I'm cast. But, my poor child, even if you could get away to America without your parents' knowing it, such journeys cost money, and I don't suppose—"

"Oh, I've oceans of money," she answered with a startling composure.

"What do you call oceans of money? Scopy's savings?" he taunted her.

Judith flushed up. "She told you?"

"She told me nothing. I guessed."

Her head drooped for a moment; then she raised it with a confident smile. "Well, of course I shall pay her back. She's sure of that. She knows I'm a nairess."

"Heroic woman! But how far do you expect to go on what she's contributed?"

This also Judith faced with composure. "Not very—poor dear Scopy! But, you see, I've got a lot besides."

"A lot of money?"

She leaned her rumpled head back against the hard sofa, apparently determined to enjoy his bewilderment for a moment longer before enlightening him. "Don't you call five thousand dollars a lot of money?" she asked.

Boyne gave a whistle of astonishment, and she nodded softly in corroboration.

"You had five thousand dollars—of your own?"

"No. But I knew where father had them."

Boyne jumped to his feet, and stood glaring down at her incredulously. "You knew—?"

"Don't gape at me, Martin. If you like to call it so, I stole the money. He always has a lot about, because it bores him so to write cheques."

"And you helped yourself—to what you wanted?"

"It was awfully easy. I knew where the key was." She seemed anxious to disclaim any undeserved credit in the matter. "And, anyhow, I knew part of it was intended for our expenses in the Engadine this summer. So it really wasn't exactly like stealing—was it?"

Boyne sat down again, this time in a chair on the farther side of the room. There seemed to be something almost maleficent in the proximity of the small scarlet figure with rumpled hair and sleep-misted eyes, curled up defiantly in the sofa corner. "You told your father this, I suppose, in the letter you left for him?"

"Told him I'd taken the money?" She laughed. "If I had, there wouldn't have been much use in taking it—would there?"

He groaned, and sat silent, his eyes fixed on the carefully scrubbed boards of the floor. For a while he concentrated his whole attention on one of their resinous knots; then, with limbs of lead, he slowly stood up again. "Well, I wash my hands of you—all of you."

Judith rose also, and went quickly up to him. "Martin," she said in a frightened voice, "what are you going to do?"

"Do? Nothing. You'd better answer that telegram yourself," he retorted roughly, shaking off the hand she had put out. He walked across the room, blinked unseeingly at his hat and stick, which he had thrown down on the table, and turned to go out of the door without remembering to pick them up. On the threshold he was checked by Judith's passionate clutch on his arm. Her lifted face was wet and frightened. "Martin—why don't you say you think I'm a thief, and have done with it?"

He swung round on her. "I think you're an unutterable fool. I think the average Andaman islander has a more highly developed moral sense than you."

"I don't know who they are. But Doll Westway always used to—"

"Used to what?"

"Go to her mother's drawer. There wasn't any other way. They all hate the bother of paying bills—parents do." She clung to him, her lips still trembling.

"Miss Scope knows about this, I suppose?"

She nodded. "I persuaded her. She hated it awfully—but she saw there was no other way. She's saved so little herself—because she has a brother who drinks. . ."

"And Terry? Does Terry know?"

"Oh, Martin! Terry? How could you think it? But you don't really, do you? You just said that to frighten me. Oh, Martin . . . you'll never tell Terry, will you? I shall die if you do. It doesn't matter about anybody else. . ."

He stood silent, suffering her clasp of desperate entreaty, as if a numbness had crept into the arm she held, and yet as if every nerve in it were fire. Something of the same duality was in his brain as he listened. It struck him dumb with the sense of his incapacity. All the forces of pity—and of something closer to the soul than pity—were fighting in him for her. But opposed to them was the old habit of relentless unconditional probity; the working man's faith in a standard to be kept up, and imposed on others, at no matter what cost of individual suffering. "I can't let her drift," was as near as he could come to it. . .

"Martin, tell me what you want me to do," she whispered, her lips trembling. His own hardened.

"Sit down at that table and write to your father that you took the money—and why you took it."

For a while she considered this painfully. "If I don't," she finally brought out, "shall you tell Terry?"

He gave her an indignant look. "Of course I shan't tell Terry!"

"Very well. Then I will."

Boyne flushed with the suddenness of his triumph, and most of all at the reason for it. "That's my Judy!"

She coloured too, as if surprised, but her face remained drawn and joyless. "But if I do, the game's up—isn't it?"

"The game's up anyhow, my dear."

Her colour faded. "You mean you're really going to give us away?"

He paused, and then said with deliberation: "I'm going to Venice at once to see your father."

"To tell him we're here?"

"Of course."

Her hand fell from his arm, and she stood drooping before him, all the youth drained out of her face. He was frightened at the effect of his words. Her boundless capacity for suffering struck him as the strangest element in her tragic plight.

"Then you give us up altogether? You don't care any longer what becomes of us?"

He paused a moment, and then turned back into the room, and took her two cold hands in his.

"Judith, look at me." She obeyed.

"Can't you understand that I care for only one thing at this moment? That you should realise what you've done—"

"About the money?" she breathed.

"Of course. About the money."

"You really think that matters more than anything else?"

The unexpectedness of the question suddenly cut him adrift from his argument. It seemed to come out of some other plane of experience, to be thrust at him from depths of pain and disillusionment that he had not yet begun to sound.

"You see," she pressed on, snatching at her opportunity, "if we could only get to Grandma Mervin's, I believe she'd keep us. At any rate, she'd try to make mother see that we mustn't be separated. I know she would, because in her letters to mother she always calls us 'those poor children.' She's awfully old-fashioned, Grandma Mervin. . . And the money, Martin—father won't find out for ever so long that it's gone. There was a lot more where I took it from. He always has such heaps with him; and he never knows how much he's spent. Once he had a valet who stole a lot, and he didn't discover it for months. . . And without that money we can't possibly get to America. . ."

Boyne pulled himself together with an effort, averting his eyes from the perilous mirage. "And you're gambling on being as lucky as the other thief?" There—saying that had cleared his conscience, and he could go on more humanely: "Don't you see, child, that this business of the money spoils the whole thing? You've got to give it back to me; and I've got to take it to your father. Then I'll put up the best fight I can for you."

Of this appeal she seemed to hear only the last words. "You will—oh, Martin, darling, you really will?"

In an instant her arms were about his neck, her wet face pressed against his lips. ("Now . . . now . . . now . . ." he grumbled.) "I knew it, Martin! I knew in my soul you'd never chuck us," she exulted in the sudden ecstasy of her relief. Waves of buoyancy seemed to be springing beneath her feet. "Martin, I know you'll know just what to say to them," she chanted.

"Go upstairs, Judith, and get that money," he admonished her severely.

She turned and left the room. While she was gone he stood gazing out of the window. Of all the world of light and freedom before him, its spreading mountain slopes, its spires of granite reared into a cloud-pillared sky, and the giant blue shadows racing each other across the valleys, he saw nothing but the narrow thread of railway winding down to Venice and the Wheaters. He had still to make Judith write the letter to her father. He had still to deliver her—this child who trusted him—bound and helpless into the hands of the enemy.

XV

"DAMN—damn, damn—oh, *damn!*" It seemed to be the only expletive at Cliffe Wheater's command, and Boyne felt that he had used it so often that it was as worn out as an old elastic band, and no longer held his scattered ideas together.

He plunged down into an armchair of the Lido Palace lounge—the Wheaters had moved out to the Lido—and sat there, embraced by a cluster of huge leather bolsters, his good-humoured lips tinged with an uneasy purple, the veins in his blond temples swollen with a helpless exasperation. "Damn!" he ejaculated again.

The place was empty. It was the hour of the afternoon sun-bath on the sands below the hotel, and no one shared with them the cool twilight of the hall but a knot of white-jacketed boys languishing near the lift, and a gold-braided porter dozing behind his desk.

Boyne sat opposite to Wheater, in another vast slippery armchair to which only a continual muscular effort could anchor his spare frame. He sat and watched Cliffe Wheater with the narrow-lipped attention he might have given to the last stages of a debate with a native potentate on whom he was trying to impose some big engineering scheme which would necessitate crossing the ruler's territory.

But with the potentate it would have been only a question of matching values; of convincing him of the material worth of what was offered. In such negotiations the language spoken, when interpreted, usually turned out to be the same. But in his talk with Wheater, Boyne had the sense of using an idiom for which the other had no equivalents. Superficially their vocabularies were the same; below the surface each lost its meaning for the other. Wheater continued to toss uneasily on a sea of incomprehension.

"What in hell can I do about it?" he demanded.

It was almost unintelligible that anything should have happened to him against which his wealth and his health could not prevail. His first idea seemed to be that it must be all a mistake—or somebody else's damned negligence. As if they had forgotten to set the burglar alarm, or to order the motor, or to pay the fire-insurance, or to choke off a bore at the telephone, or, by some other unstopped fissure in the tight armour of his wellbeing, had suddenly let tribulation in on him. If he could get at the offender—if he only could! But it was the crux of his misery that apparently he couldn't—

"Not that I blame the child," he said suddenly, looking down with an interrogative stare at his heavy blond-haired hands, with their glossy nails and one broad gold ring with an uncut sapphire. He raised his eyes and examined Boyne, who instantly felt himself leaping to the guard of his own face.

"That business of the money—you understand, Judith didn't in the least realise. . ." Boyne began.

"Oh, damn the money." That question was swept away with a brush of the hand: Boyne had noticed that the poor little letter of confession he had extracted from Judith had received hardly a glance from her father, who had pocketed the bank-notes as carelessly as if they were a gambling debt. Evidently the Lido Palace values were different. It was the hideous inconvenience of it all that was gnawing at Wheater—and also, to be fair to him, a vague muddled distress about his children. "I didn't know the poor little chaps cared so much," was all this emotion wrung from him; none the less, Boyne felt, it was sincere.

"They care most awfully for each other—and very much for you and Joyce. What they need beyond everything is a home: a home with you two at its head."

"Oh, damn," Wheater groaned again. It was as if Boyne had proposed to him to ascend the throne of England. What was the use of dealing in impossibles? There were things which even his money couldn't buy—and when you stripped him of the sense of its omnipotence he squirmed like a snail out of its shell.

"Why can't there not be rows?" he began again, perspiring with the oppression of his helplessness.

"There wouldn't be, if you and Joyce would only come to an understanding."

The aggrieved husband met this derisively. "Joyce—and an understanding!"

"Well—she's awfully fond of the children; and so are you. And they're devoted to both of you, all of them. Why can't you and she agree to bury your differences, and arrange your lives so that you can keep the children together, and give them something that looks like a home, while you both . . . well, do whatever you like . . . privately. . ." Boyne felt his lips drying as they framed this arid proposal.

Wheater leaned his elbows on his knees and gazed at the picture presented. "Joyce doesn't care to do what she likes privately," he replied, without irony.

"But the children—I'm sure she doesn't want to part with them."

"No; and no more do I. And what's more, I won't!" He brought down a clenched fist on the leather protuberance at his elbow. It sank in soggily, as if the Lido armchair had been the symbol of Joyce's sullen opposition. "By God, I can dictate my terms," Wheater pursued, sonorously but without conviction.

Boyne stood up with a sense of weariness. His bones felt as stiff as if he had been trying to hang on to a jagged rock above a precipice; his mind participated in their ache.

"Look here, Cliffe, what's the use of threats? Of course you're all-powerful. Between you, Joyce and you can easily destroy these children's lives. . ."

"Oh, see here!" Wheater protested.

"Destroy their lives. Look at that poor Doll Westway, who was kicked about from pillar to post. . . Judith told me her miserable story. . ."

"I don't see the resemblance. And what's more I strongly object to being classed with a down-and-outer like Charlie Westway. Why, man, no law-court in the world would have given a blackguard like that the custody of his children. Whereas mine will always be perfectly safe in my hands, and Joyce knows it; and so do her lawyers."

"I daresay; but the trouble is that the children need Joyce at least as much as they do you. And they need something that neither one of you can give them separately. They need you and Joyce together: that's what a home is made of—togetherness . . . the mysterious atmosphere. . ." Boyne broke off, nervously swallowing his own eloquence.

Wheater gave him a helpless look. "Have a drink?" he suggested. He waved his hand to the white-coated guardians of the lift. Far off across the empty reaches of the hall a waiter appeared with napkin and tray—sail and raft of a desert ocean. "Hi!" Wheater called out feverishly. Boyne wondered that he did not brandish his handkerchief at the end of a stick. The two men drank in a desperate silence.

Capturing Joyce's attention was less easy. It was difficult even to secure her presence. Not that she avoided her husband—on the contrary, she devoted all the time she could spare to arguing with him about their future arrangements. And she had flung herself on Boyne in an agony of apprehension about the children. But once assured of their safety she remarked that their going off like that had served Cliffe right, and she hoped it would be a lesson to him; and thereupon hurried away to a pressing engagement on the beach, promising Boyne to see him when she came up to dress for dinner—anywhere between eight and nine. She supposed Cliffe would look after him in the interval?

It was nearer nine than eight when Boyne finally waylaid her in an upper corridor, on the way back to her room. She relegated him to her sitting-room while she got out of her bathing tights, and presently reappeared swathed in perfumed draperies, with vivid eyes, tossed hair as young as Judith's, and the animating glow imparted by a new love-affair. Boyne remembered Terry's phrase: "With all the new ways the doctors have of making parents young again," and reflected that this oldest one of all was still the most effective. She threw herself down on a lounge, clasped her arms behind her head, and declared: "It was too clever of Judith to give her father that scare. Now perhaps he'll come to his senses." Yes,

Boyne thought—she was going to be more difficult to convince than Wheater.

"What do you call coming to his senses?"

"Why, giving all the children to me, of course—to me and Gerald." Her lids closed softly on the name. Boyne was frightened by a reminder of Judith's way of caressing certain thoughts and images with her lashes. He hated anything in the mother that recalled what he most loved in her daughter. . .

"The trouble is, Joyce, that what they want—what they need—is not you and . . . and anybody else . . . but just you and Cliffe: their parents."

"Me and Cliffe! An edifying spectacle!"

"Oh, well, they've discounted all that—at least Judith and Terry have. And they're incurably fond of you both. What the younger ones require, of course, is just the even warmth of a home—like any other young animals."

She considered her shining nails, as if glassing her indolent beauty in them.

"You see," Boyne pressed on, "it's all these changes of temperature that are killing them."

"What changes of temperature?"

"Well, every time there's a new deal—I mean a new step-parent—there's necessarily a new atmosphere, isn't there? Young things, you know, need sameness—it's their vital element."

Joyce, at this point, surprised him by abounding in his own sense. It was never she who wanted to change, she assured him. Hadn't she come back of her own accord to Cliffe, and loyally made the attempt all over again—just on account of the children? And what had been the result, as far as they were concerned? Simply their being compelled to assist, with older and more enlightened eyes, at the same old rows and scandals (for Cliffe *was* scandalous) which had already edified their infancy. Could Boyne possibly advise the renewal of such conditions as a "vital element" in their welfare, the poor darlings? It would be the most disastrous experiment that could be made with them. Whereas, if they would just firmly declare their determination to remain with Joyce, and only with Joyce, Cliffe would soon come to his senses —and, anyhow, as soon as another woman got hold of him, he wouldn't know what to do with the children, and would be only too thankful to know they were in safe hands. And had Boyne considered what a boon it would be to dear Terry to have Gerald always with him, not as a salaried tutor, but, better still, as friend, companion, guardian—as everything his own father had failed to be? Boyne must have seen what a fancy Terry had taken to Gerald. And Gerald simply loved the boy. That consideration, Joyce owned, had influenced her not a little in her determination to break with Wheater.

Joyce was much more articulate than her husband, and, paradoxical as it seemed, proportionately harder to deal with. She swept away all Boyne's arguments on a torrent of sentimental verbiage; and she had the immense advantage over Wheater of believing that the children would be perfectly happy with her, whereas Wheater merely believed in his right to keep them, whether his doing so made them happy or not.

But these considerations were interrupted by Joyce's abrupt exclamation that it was past nine already, and the Wrenches and the Duke of Mendip were waiting for her . . . of course dear Martin would join them at dinner? . . . No; Martin thought he wouldn't, thanks; in fact, he'd already promised Cliffe. . .

"But Cliffe's coming too. Oh, you didn't know? My dear, he's infatuated with Sybil Lullmer. She came here to try and catch Mendip, and failing that she's quietly annexed Cliffe instead. Rather funny, isn't it? But of course that kind of woman sticks at nothing. With her record, why should she? And Cliffe has had to make up with Zinnia Wrench because it was the easiest way of being with Sybil. . . So you will dine with us, Martin, won't you? And do tell me—you're sure Chip's perfectly contented? And you think Cortina will do Terry good?"

Half an hour later, Boyne, who had sternly told himself that this also was part of the game, sat at a table in the crowded Lido Palace restaurant, overhanging the starlit whisper of the Adriatic. His seat was between Zinnia Lacrosse and Joyce Wheater, and opposite him was a small sleek creature, who reminded him, when she first entered, of Judith—who had the same puzzled craving eyes, the same soft shadowy look amid the surrounding glare. But when he faced her across the table, saw her smile, heard her voice, he was furious with himself for the comparison.

"Do you mean to say you don't know Syb Lullmer?" Joyce whispered to him under cover of the saxophones. "But you must have heard of her as Mrs. Charlie Westway? She always manages to be in the spot-light. Her daughter Doll committed suicide last year at Deauville. It was all pretty beastly. Syb herself is always chock full of drugs. Doesn't look it, does she? She might be Judy's age . . . in this light. What do you think of her?"

"I think she's hideous."

Mrs. Wheater stared. "Well, the dress-makers don't.

They dress her for nothing. Look at her ogling Gerald! That's what makes Cliffe so frantic," Cliffe's wife smilingly noted. After a moment she added: "A nice stepmother for my children! Do you wonder I'm putting up a fight to keep them?"

From across the table Mrs. Lullmer was speaking in a low piercing whine. When she spoke her large eyes became as empty as a medium's, and her lips moved just enough to let out a flat knife-edge of voice. "I told Anastase I'd never speak to him again, or set foot in his place, if ever I caught him selling one of the dresses he'd designed for me to a respectable woman; and he said: 'Why, I never saw one in my establishment: did you?' And I said to him: 'Now you've insulted me, and I'll sue you for libel if you don't take fifty per cent off my bill.' I'm poor, you see," Mrs. Lullmer concluded plaintively, sweeping the table with her disarming gaze. The Duke, Zinnia, Lord Wrench and Cliffe Wheater received the anecdote with uproarious approval. Gerald Ormerod looked at the ceiling, and Joyce looked tenderly at Gerald. "I got off twenty-five per cent anyhow," Mrs. Lullmer whined, spreading her fluid gaze over Boyne. . .

All about them, at other tables exactly like theirs, sat other men exactly like Lord Wrench and Wheater, the Duke of Mendip and Gerald Ormerod, other women exactly like Joyce and Zinnia and Mrs. Lullmer. Boyne remembered Mrs. Sellars's wail at the approach of a standardised beauty. Here it was, in all its mechanical terror—endless and meaningless as the repetitions of a nightmare. Every one of the women in the vast crowded restaurant seemed to be of the same age, to be dressed by the same dress-makers, loved by the same lovers, adorned by the same jewellers, and massaged and manipulated by the same Beauty doctors. The only difference was that the few whose greater age was no longer disguisable had shorter skirts, and exposed a wider expanse of shoulder-blade. A double jazz-band drowned their conversation, but from the movement of their lips, and the accompanying gestures, Boyne surmised that they were all saying exactly the same things as Joyce and Zinnie and Mrs. Lullmer. It would have been unfashionable to be different; and once more Boyne marvelled at the incurable simplicity of the corrupt. "Blessed are the pure in heart," he thought, "for they have so many more things to talk about. . ."

Out in the offing the lights of the "Fancy Girl" drew an unheeded triangle of stars, cruising up and down against the dusk. A breeze, rising as darkness fell, carried the reflection toward the shore on a multitude of little waves; but the sea no longer interested the diners, for it was not the hour when they used it.

"I say—why shouldn't we go and finish our cigars on board?" Cliffe Wheater proposed, yearning, as always, to have his new toy noticed. The night was languid, the guests were weary of their usual routine of amusements, and the party, following the line of least resistance, drifted down to the pier, where the "Fancy Girl" 's launch lay mingling the glitter of its brasses with the glow of constellations in the ripples.

"To-morrow morning, old man," Wheater said, his arm in Boyne's, "we'll have it all out about the children . . ."

XVI

BOYNE knew that "morning," in the vocabulary of the Lido, could not possibly be construed as meaning anything earlier than the languid interval between cocktails and lunch, or the still more torpid stretch of time separating the process of digestion from the first afternoon bath. All his energies were bent on getting the Wheaters to fix on one or the other of these parentheses as the most suitable in which to examine the question of their children's future; and he accounted himself lucky when they finally agreed to meet him in a quiet corner of the hotel lounge before luncheon.

Unfortunately for this plan, no corner of the lounge —or of its adjacent terraces—could be described as quiet at that particular hour. The whole population of the "Palace" was thronging back through its portals in quest of food and drink. Hardly had Boyne settled Mr. and Mrs. Wheater in their fathomless armchairs (his only hope of keeping them there lay in the difficulty of getting up in a hurry) when Lady Wrench drifted by, polishing her nails with a small tortoiseshell implement, and humming a Negro Spiritual in her hoarse falsetto.

"Goodness—what you people doing over here, plotting together in a corner? Look as if you were rehearsing for a film. . ." She stopped, wide-eyed, impudent, fundamentally indifferent to everything less successful than her own success.

"I don't know what we *are* doing," Joyce returned with a touch of irritability. "Martin seems to think he ought to tell us how to bring up the children." It obviously seemed preposterous to her that Zinnia Wrench should be idling about, polishing her nails and humming tunes, while this severe mental effort was exacted of one who, the night before, had been up as late, and danced as hard, as the other.

"Something's *got* to be decided," Wheater growled uncertainly.

"Oh, well—so long," smiled Lady Wrench. "I'm off to see Mendip's new tent; the one he's just got over from: where is it? Morocco, I guess he said. But isn't that a sort of leather? Somewhere in South Africa, anyhow. . . They're just rigging it up. It's a wonder."

"A new tent?" Joyce's face lit up with curiosity, and the scattered desire to participate in everything that was going.

"Yes; absolutely different from anything you've ever seen. The very last thing. Sort of black Cubist designs on it. Might give Anastase ideas for a bath-wrap. Hullo, Gerald—that you? I've been looking for you everywhere; thought you'd got drowned. Come along and see Mendip's tent."

Joyce raised a detaining hand. "Gerald—Mr. Ormerod! Please. I want you to stay here. We're discussing something about which I may need your advice."

"Oh, look here, Joyce, I say—" her husband interrupted.

His wife gave him a glance of aggrieved dignity. "You don't want me to be without advice, I suppose? You've got Martin's."

Wheater groaned: "This isn't going to be a prize fight, is it?"

"I don't know. It might. Sit down, please, Gerald."

Mrs. Wheater indicated an armchair beside her own, and Ormerod reluctantly buried his long limbs in it. "In this heat—" he murmured.

"Oh, well, s'long," cried Lady Wrench, evaporating.

"Joyce—Cliffe! Look here: have you seen Mendip's new tent?" Mrs. Lullmer, exquisite, fadeless, her scant bathing tights inadequately supplemented by a transparent orange scarf, paused in a plastic attitude before the besieged couple. "Do let's rush down and take a look at it before cocktails. Come on, Cliffe."

Mrs. Wheater drew her lips together, and a slow wave of crimson rose to her husband's perspiring temples.

"See here, Syb; we're talking business."

"Business?" Instantly Mrs. Lullmer's vaporous face became as sharp-edged as a cameo, and her eyes narrowed into two observation-slits. "Been put on to something good, have you? I'm everlastingly broke. For God's sake tell me!" she implored.

Wheater laughed. "No. We're only trying to settle about the children."

"The children? Do you mean to say you're talking about them still? That reminds me—where's my own child? Pixie, pet! Ah, there she is. Darling, nip up to my room, will you, and get mummy one of those new lipsticks: no, not *Baiser Défendu,* sweet, but *Nouveau Péché*—you know, the one that fits into the gold bag the Duke gave me yesterday."

An ethereal sprite, with a pre-Raphaelite bush of fair hair, and a tiny sunburnt body, detached herself from a romp with a lift-boy to spring away at her mother's behest.

"Pixie's such a darling—always does just as I tell her. If only my poor Doll had listened to me!" Mrs. Lullmer observed to Boyne, with a retrospective sigh which implied that the unhappy fate of her eldest daughter had been the direct result of resistance to the maternal counsels.

"Well—as I was saying—" Boyne began again, nervously. . .

But a fresh stream of bathers, reinforced by a troop of arrivals from Venice who had steamed over to the Lido for lunch, closed in vociferously about the Wheaters, and at the same instant the big clock on the wall rang out the stroke of one.

"See here, old Martin—this is no time for business, is it? I believe Joyce has asked half of these people to lunch," Wheater confessed to his friend with a shamefaced shrug. "But afterward—"

"All right. Afterward."

Lunch was over; the Duke's tent had been visited; and one by one the crowd in restaurant and grill-room had dispersed for bathing or bridge.

"Why not here?" Boyne suggested patiently to Mrs. Wheater.

"Here?" She paused under the lifted flap of the stately Moroccan tent, her astonishingly youthful figure outlined against the glitter of the sands.

"Why not?" Boyne persisted. "It's cool and quiet, and nobody is likely to bother us. Why shouldn't you and Cliffe go into this question with me now?"

She wavered, irresolute. "Where's Cliffe, to begin with? Oh, out there—under Syb's umbrella, of course. *I'm* perfectly willing, naturally—"

"Very well; I'll go and recruit him."

Boyne threaded his way between the prone groups on

the beach to where Mrs. Lullmer lay, under the shadow of a huge orange-coloured umbrella, with Cliffe Wheater outspread beside her like a raised map of a mountainous country.

"I say, Cliffe, Joyce is waiting for you in the Duke's tent—for our talk."

Wheater raised a portion of his great bulk on a languid elbow. "What talk? . . . Oh, all right." His tone implied that, at the moment, it was distinctly all wrong; but he got slowly to his feet, gave himself a shake, lit a cigarette, and shambled away after Boyne. At the tent door Mrs. Lullmer swiftly overtook them. "I suppose you don't mind—" she smiled at Joyce; and Wheater muttered, half to his wife and half to Boyne: "She's had so much experience with children."

"All I want is what is best for mine," said Mrs. Wheater coldly; adding, as they re-entered the tent: "Martin, you'll find Gerald somewhere about. Won't you please tell him to come?"

Wheater gave an angry shrug, and then settled down resignedly on one of the heaps of embroidered Moroccan cushions disposed about the interior of the tent. Boyne's first inclination was to come back empty-handed from a simulated quest for Ormerod; but, reflecting that if he did so Joyce would seize on this as another pretext for postponement, he presently returned accompanied by the tutor, in whose wake Lady Wrench trailed her perfumed elegance. "See here, folks, I guess if anybody's got a right to be here I have," she announced with a regal suavity. "That is, if you're proposing to make plans about my child."

This argument seemed—even to Boyne—incontrovertible; and Lady Wrench sank down upon her cushions with a smile of triumph.

"Pity Buondelmonte's not here," Wheater growled under his breath to Boyne; and Lady Wrench, catching the name, instantly exclaimed: "But Wrenny is—I left him this minute at the bar; and I don't see why I shouldn't have my own husband's advice about my own child."

It was finally conceded that the benefit of Lord Wrench's judgment could not properly be denied to his wife; and, as Lord Wrench and the Duke of Mendip were too inseparable to be detached from one another on so trivial a pretext, and as the conference was taking place in the shelter of the Duke's own tent, it surprised no one—not even Boyne—when the two gentlemen strolled in together, and accommodated themselves on another pile of cushions. "Mendip wants to see how these things are done in America," Lord Wrench explained, before composing himself into a repose which seemed suspiciously like slumber; while the small dry-lipped Duke mumbled under his brief moustache: "Might come in useful—you never know."

"I'm sure *I* don't know exactly what we're supposed to be talking about," Joyce Wheater began. "I've said a hundred times that all I care for is what's best for the children. Everybody knows I've sacrificed everything for that once before. And what earthly use has it been?"

"Ah, that's what I say," Lady Wrench agreed with sudden sympathy. "You might cut yourself in pieces for a man, and his dirty lawyers would come and take your child away from you the next day, and haggle over every cent of alimony. But if it comes to money, I'll spend as much as anybody—"

"Oh, shut up, Zinnia," her husband softly intervened, and redisposed himself to rest.

"I don't think you ought any of you to look at the matter from a legal stand-point," Boyne interrupted. "My friends here are awfully fond of their children, and we all know they want what's best for them. The only question is how that best is to be arrived at. It seems to me perfectly simple—"

("Solomon," said the Duke, with his dry smile.)

"No. Exactly the reverse. Division is what I'm here to fight against—no; not fight but plead." Boyne turned to Cliffe Wheater. "For God's sake, old man, let the lot of them stay together."

"Why, they *were* together; they would have been, as long as they'd stayed with me," Wheater grumbled helplessly.

His wife reared her golden crest with a toss of defiance. "You don't suppose for a minute I'm going to abandon my children to the kind of future Cliffe Wheater's likely to provide for them? Gerald and I are prepared—"

"So are Cliffe and I," murmured Mrs. Lullmer, with a glance at the Duke under her studied lashes. The Duke threw back his head, and became lost in an inspection of the roof of the tent. "Cliffe and I," repeated Mrs. Lullmer, more incisively.

"Well, and what about me and Wrenny, I'd like to know?" Lady Wrench broke in. "I guess I can afford the best lawyers in the country—"

"I don't see that the law concerns these children," Boyne intervened. "What they need is not to be fought over, but just to be left alone. Judith and Terry understand that perfectly. They know there is probably going to be another change in their parents' lives, but they want to remain together, and not be affected by that change. I'm not here to theorise or criticise—I'm simply here as the children's spokesman. They're devoted to each other, and they want to stay together. Between you all, can't it be managed somehow—for a time, at any rate?"

"But my Pixie would be such a perfect little companion for Terry and Blanca. She knows all the very nicest children everywhere. That's one of the great advantages of hotel life, isn't it? And, after all, Judith may be marrying soon, and then what will become of the others?" Mrs. Lullmer turned a meaning smile on Boyne. "Haven't *you* perhaps thought of Judith's marrying soon, Mr. Boyne?"

Boyne curtly replied that he hadn't; and Lady Wrench intervened: "I want my Zinnie to have a lovely simple home life, out on our ranch in California. This kicking about in hotels is too horribly demoralising for children." She bent her great eyes gently on Mrs. Lullmer. "You know something about that, Mrs. Lullmer."

Mrs. Lullmer returned a look as gentle. "Oh, no; my children were never on a ranch at Hollywood," she said.

"Hollywood—Hollywood!" gasped Lady Wrench, paling with rage.

Mrs. Lullmer arched her delicate brows interrogatively. "Isn't Hollywood in California? Stupid of me! I was never in the West myself."

Joyce Wheater raised herself on her elbow. "I'm sure I don't see the use of this. Four of the children are mine and Cliffe's. I've always tried to make them all happy. I've treated Zinnie, and Buondelmonte's children, exactly like my own; and this is all the thanks I get for it! No one could be more competent than Gerald to direct Terry's education; which is something his father never happens to have thought of. But of course everybody here is trying to put me in the wrong. . ."

Mrs. Lullmer looked her soft surprise. "Oh, no. Don't say that, Joyce. All I feel is that perhaps the poor babies haven't been quite loved enough. You don't mind my suggesting it, do you? If they were mine, I don't think I should care so awfully much about making them into high-brows. What I should want would be just to see them all healthy and rosy and happy, and romping about all day like my little Pixie. . ."

"With lift-boys and barmen. Yes; I guess that *is* about the best preparation for life in the smart set," said Lady Wrench parenthetically.

Mrs. Lullmer smiled. "Yes; Pixie's little friends are all in what I believe you call the 'smart set.' I confess I think that even more important for a child than learning that Morocco is not in South Africa."

"Not in South Africa? Where is it, then, I'd like to know? Wrenny, you told me—"

"Well," said the Duke, getting up, "I'm off for a swim."

This announcement instantly disorganised the whole group. Nothing—as Boyne had already had occasion to remark—chilled their interest in whatever they were doing as rapidly as the discovery that one of the party had had enough of it, and was moving on to the next item of the day's programme. And no one could dislocate a social assemblage as quickly as the Duke of Mendip. The shared sense that wherever he was, there the greatest amount of excitement was obtainable, dominated any divergence of view among his companions. Even Lord Wrench roused himself from his slumbers and gathered up his long limbs for instant departure, and his wife and Mrs. Lullmer followed his example.

"Mercy, what time is it? Why, there's that diving match off Ella Muncy's raft!" Lady Wrench exclaimed. "I've got fifty pounds on the Grand Duke; and directly afterward there's the mannequin show for the smartest bathing-dresses; I've given a prize for that myself."

Mrs. Lullmer had taken a stick of rouge from her mesh-bag, and was critically redecorating her small pensive face. "Coming, Cliffe?" she negligently asked. "You're one of the judges of the diving match, aren't you?"

Cliffe Wheater had scrambled heavily to his feet, and stood casting perplexed glances about him. "I did say I'd be, I believe. Damn it all—I'd no idea it was so late. . ."

"It's always late in this place. I don't see how we any of us stand it," murmured Mrs. Lullmer. "I always say we're the real labouring classes."

Joyce Wheater still sat negligently reclined. "Very well, then; I suppose we may consider the matter settled."

"Settled—settled? Why, what do you mean?" Wheater stammered uneasily from the threshold.

"We came here to decide about the children, I believe. I assume that you agree that I'm to keep my own."

"Keep them? Keep them? I agree to no such thing. Martin, here, knows what my conditions are. I've never agreed to any others, and never shall—"

"Ormerod! Ormerod! Where the deuce is Gerald Ormerod? He's next on the diving programme, and Mrs. Muncy's just sent word to say that everything's being held up—oh, here you are, Gerald! Come along, for God's sake, or I shall catch it. . ."

A bronzed young amphibian, dripping and sputtering from the sea, had snatched back the tent flap, singled out Gerald Ormerod, still supine in his corner, and dragged him to his feet. "Dash it, wake up, old man, or there'll be no end of a rumpus."

Joyce Wheater sprang into sudden activity. "Gerald, Gerald—but of course you mustn't miss your turn! Cliffe, is the launch there to take us out to the raft? How can I have forgotten all about it?" She addressed herself plaintively to Boyne. "That's what always happens—whenever there's any question of the children, I forget about everything else. . ."

Wheater laid a persuasive hand on Boyne's shoulder. "You see how it is, old man. In this hell of a place there's never any time for anything. See here—come along with us to this diving match, won't you? The sea's so calm I've had the launch lying to out there ever since lunch; we'll be out at the raft in no time. . . No? You won't? Well—sorry . . . it's a pretty sight. To-morrow then. . . Oh, you're really off to-morrow morning, are you? Can't see why you don't stay on a day or two, now you're here. Of course the children are all right where they are for the present—we all know that. And if you stayed on for a day or two we could go into the whole thing quietly. . . No? Well, then—why, yes, tonight, of course. Tell you what, old man: you and Joyce and I will go out to the 'Fancy Girl' after dinner, and talk the whole thing out by ourselves. That suit you?"

BOOK III

XVII

ON the afternoon of the fourth day Boyne stood again in the sitting-room of the *châlet* facing the Cristallo group.

He had wired to Judith Wheater: "All right, don't worry"; but to Mrs. Sellars he had made no sign. He knew she did not wholly approve of his journey, though she had made no unfavourable comment, and had even offered of her own accord to keep an eye on the *Pension Rosenglüh* in his absence. It was not necessary for Rose Sellars to formulate objections; they were latent everywhere in her delicate person, in the movements of her slim apprehensive fingers, the guarded stir of her lashes. But the sense of their lurking there, vigilant guardians of the threshold, gave a peculiar quality to every token of her approval. Boyne told himself that she was not a denier, but that rarer being, a chooser; and he was almost certain where her choice would lie when all the facts were before her.

She was out when he reached the *châlet,* and his conviction strengthened as he sat awaiting her. It drew its strength from the very atmosphere of the place—its self-sufficing harmony. *"Willkommen, suesser Daemmerschein!"* His apostrophe took in the mighty landscape which overhung him; the sense of peace flowed in on him from those great fastnesses of sun and solitude, with which the little low-ceilinged room, its books and flowers, the bit of needle-work in the armchair, the half-written letter on the desk, had the humble kinship of quietness and continuity. "I'd forgotten that anything had any meaning," he thought to himself as he let the spell of the place weave its noiseless net about him.

"Martin—but how tired you look!" She was on the threshold, their hands and lips together. He remembered that kiss afterward. . . She lingered close, her arms on his shoulders. "I didn't even know you'd got back." There was the faintest shadow of reproach in her tone.

"I didn't know till the last minute when I could get away—I just jumped into the first train," he explained. He was conscious of the weariness in his voice. He passed his hand over his eyes as though to see if it would brush away her image, or if there were still women like her in the world, all made of light and reason. "Dear!" he said, more to himself than her.

"You've failed?" Her eyes were full of an unmixed sympathy; there was nothing in them to remind him that they had foreseen his failure.

"No," he exclaimed, "I've succeeded!"

"Oh—." He fancied he detected a hint of flatness in the rejoinder; there are occasions, he knew, when one has to resign oneself to the hearing of good news. But no; he was unfair. It was not that, it was only the echo of his own fatigue. For, as she said, he was tired—thoroughly tired. . .

She continued, with a faint smile: "You don't look like somebody who has succeeded."

"I daresay not. I feel rather like one of the fellows they let down into a disused well, and haul up half-asphyxiated. . ."

"It was—asphyxiating?"

"Some of it; most of it. But I'm coming to. And I've

got what I wanted." He returned her smile, and sat down beside her.

"How wonderful! You mean to say you've reconciled the Wheaters?"

"I've reconciled them to the idea of not separating the children—for the present, at any rate."

"Oh, Martin—splendid!" She was really warming to the subject now. Her face glowed with a delicate appreciation. "It will do Terry more good than all the Alps and Dolomites piled on top of one another."

"Yes; and Judith too, incidentally." He had no intention of not including Judith in his victory.

"Of course; but Judith's a young lady who is eminently capable of fighting her own battles," Mrs. Sellars smoothly rejoined.

"She ought to be—she's had to fight everybody else's."

He leaned his head against the back of his armchair, and wondered what had become of the glow with which he had entered the room. It had vanished instantly under the cool touch of Mrs. Sellars's allusion to Judith. He had succeeded, it was true: there could be no doubt that he had succeeded. The mere fact of gaining time was nine tenths of the battle; and that he had already achieved. But already, too, he was beginning to wonder how he was to fit Rose Sellars into the picture of his success. It was curious: when they were apart it was always her courage and her ardour that he felt; as soon as they came together again she seemed hemmed in by little restrictions and inhibitions.

"Do tell me just what happened," she said.

"Well—at the very last minute they decided to make me, informally, into the children's guardian: a sort of trial-guardian, you might call it."

"A trial-guardian?" Her intonation, and the laugh that followed it, lifted the term into the region of the absurd. "What a jolly thing to be a trial-guardian!"

"Well, I'm not so sure." Boyne faced her irritably. "It's not a joke, you know."

"I shan't know what it is till you explain."

Explain—explain! Yes; he knew now that the explaining was just what he was dodging away from. To Judith and Terry no explanations would be necessary. He would only have to say: "It's all right," and be smothered in hugs and jubilations. Those two would never think of asking for reasons—life had not accustomed them to expect any. But here sat lovely Logic, her long hands clasped attentively—

"Oh, by Jove!" Boyne exclaimed, clapping his own hands first on one pocket, then on another. "Here's something I got for you in Venice."

He drew forth a small parcel, stringless and shapeless, as parcels generally seemed to be when they emerged from his pockets, unwrapped the paper, and pressed the catch of a morocco box. The lid flew open, and revealed a curious crystal pendant in a network of worn enamel.

"Oh, the lovely thing! For me?"

"Oh, no; not that," he stammered. He jerked the trinket back, wrapped the box up, and pushed it into his pocket with the exasperated sense of blushing like a boy over his blunder.

"But, Martin—"

"Here—." He delved deeper, pulled out another parcel, in wrappings equally untidy, and took up one of the long hands lying on her knee. "This is for you." He slipped on her fourth finger a sapphire set in diamonds. She lowered her lids on it in gentle admiration. "It's much too beautiful," her lips protested. Then her mockery sparkled up at him. "Only, you've put it on the wrong hand—at least, if it's meant for our engagement."

"Looks as if it were, doesn't it?" he bantered back; but inwardly he was thinking: "Yes, that's just the trouble—it looks like the engagement ring any other fellow would have given to any other woman. Nothing in the world to do with her and me." Aloud he said: "I hadn't time to find what I wanted—" and then realised that this was hardly a way of bettering his case. "I wanted something so awfully different for you," he blundered on.

"Well, your wanting that makes it different—to me," she said; and added, more tepidly: "Besides, it's lovely." She held out her left hand, and he slipped the jewel on the proper finger. "It's rotten," he grumbled. The ring had cost him more than he could afford, it had failed to please her, he saw himself that it was utterly commonplace—and saw also that she would never forgive him for pocketing the trinket he had first produced, which was nothing in itself, but had struck her fancy as soon as she knew it was not meant for her. Should he pull it out again, and ask her to accept it? No; after what had passed that was impossible. Judith Wheater, if he had been trying an engagement ring on her finger (preposterous fancy!) would have blurted out at once that she preferred the trinket he had shoved back into his pocket. But such tactlessness was unthinkable in Mrs. Sellars. Not for the world, he knew, would she have let him guess that she had given the other ornament a thought.

She sat turning her hand from side to side and diligently admiring the ring. "And now—do tell me just what happened."

"Well—first, of course, a lot of talk."

He settled himself in his chair, and tried to take up the narrative. But wherever he grasped it, the awkward thing seemed to tumble out of his hold, as if, in that respect too, he were always taking the wrong parcel out of his pocket. To begin with, it was so difficult to explain to Mrs. Sellars that, after the Wheaters had been reassured as to the safety and wellbeing of the children, the negotiations had been carried on piecemeal, desultorily, parenthetically, between swims and sun-baths, cocktails and fox-trots, poker and baccara—and, as a rule, in the presence of all the conflicting interests.

To make Mrs. Sellars understand that Lady Wrench, her husband and Gerald Ormerod had assisted at the debates as a matter of course was in itself a laborious business; to convey to her that Mrs. Lullmer—still notorious as the former Mrs. Westway—had likewise been called upon to participate, as Joyce's possible successor, was to place too heavy a strain on her imagination. Her exquisite aloofness had kept her in genuine ignorance of the compromises and promiscuities of modern life, and left on her hands the picture of a vanished world wherein you didn't speak to people who were discredited, or admit rivals or enemies to your confidence; and she punctuated Boyne's narrative with murmurs of dismay and incredulity.

"But in that crowd," Boyne explained, "no man is another man's enemy for more than a few minutes, and no woman is any other woman's rival. Either they forget they've quarrelled, or some social necessity—usually a party that none of them can bear to miss—forces them together, and makes it easier to bury their differences. But generally it's a simple case of forgetting. Their memories are as short as a savage's, and the feuds that savages remember have dropped out. They recall only the other primitive needs—food, finery, dancing. I suppose we *are* relapsing into a kind of bloodless savagery," Boyne concluded.

Besides, he went on, in the Wheater set they could deal with things only collectively; alone, they became helpless and inarticulate. They lived so perpetually in the lime-light that they required an audience—an audience made up of their own kind. Before each other they shouted and struck attitudes; again like savages. But the chief point was that nobody could stay angry—not however much they tried. It was too much trouble, and might involve too many inconveniences, interfere with too many social arrangements. When all was said and done, all they asked was not to be bothered—and it was by gambling on that requirement that he had finally gained his point.

"And your point is, exactly—"

Well, as he got closer to it, Boyne was not even sure that it could be defined as a point. It was too shapeless and undecided; but he hoped it would serve for a time—and time was everything; especially for Terry. . .

"They've agreed to leave the children together, and to leave them here, for the next three or four months. The longest to bring round was Lady Wrench. Her husband has taken a fancy to Zinnie, and he's so mortally bored by life in general that his wife clutches at anything that may amuse him. Luckily, according to the terms of the divorce—"

"Which divorce?" Mrs. Sellars interpolated, as though genuinely anxious to keep her hand on all the clues.

"Wheater *versus* Zinnia Lacrosse. It was Wheater who got the divorce from the present Lady Wrench.

Legally he has the final say about Zinnie, so the mother had to give in, though she has a right to see the child at stated intervals. But of course my battle royal was over Chipstone; if the Wheaters had insisted on keeping Chipstone till their own affairs were settled in court the whole combination would have been broken up."

"And how did you contrive to rescue Chipstone?"

Boyne sank down more deeply into his armchair, and looked up at the low ceiling. Then he straightened himself, and brought his gaze to the level of Mrs. Sellars's. "By promising to stay here and keep an eye on the children myself. That's my trial-guardianship." He gave a slight laugh, which she failed to echo.

"Martin!"

His eyes continued to challenge hers. "Well—?"

She turned the sapphire hesitatingly on her finger. "But these children—you'd never even heard of them till you met them on board your steamer a few weeks ago. . ."

"No; that's true."

"You've taken over a pretty big responsibility."

"I like responsibilities."

Mrs. Sellars was still brooding over her newly imprisoned finger. "It's very generous of you to assume this one in such a hurry. Usually one doesn't have to go out of one's way to find rather more of them than one can manage. But in this case, I wonder—"

"You wonder?"

"Well, I had understood from Terry—and also from your friend Judith—that what all the children really want is to go to America: to Mrs. Wheater's mother, isn't it?"

"Yes; that's it; and I hope they'll pull it off by-and-by. But at present the Wheaters won't hear of it. I never for a moment supposed they'd consent to putting the ocean between themselves and Chip. My only chance was to persuade them that, now Terry's in the mountains, they'd better leave him here, and the others with him, till the hot weather's over. With those people it's always a question of the least resistance—of temporizing and postponing. My plan saved everybody a certain amount of mental effort; so they all ended by agreeing to it. But of course it's merely provisional."

"Happily," Mrs. Sellars smiled; and added, as if to correct the slight acerbity of the comment: "For you must see, dear, that you're taking a considerable risk for the future—"

"What future?"

"Why—suppose anything goes wrong during these next few months? You'll be answerable for whatever may happen. With seven children—and one of them already grown up!"

Boyne frowned, and stirred uneasily in his chair. "If you mean Judith, in some ways she's as much of a child as the youngest of them."

Mrs. Sellars smiled confidentially at her ring. "So a man would think, I suppose. But you forget that I've had four days alone with her. . . She's a young lady with very definite views."

"I should hope so!"

"I agree with you that it makes her more interesting—but conceivably it might lead to complications."

"What sort of complications?"

"You ought to know better than I do—since you tell me you've been frequenting the late Mrs. Westway at the Lido. Judith doesn't pretend to hide the fact that she lived for a summer in the bosom of that edifying family. . ."

"She doesn't know it's anything to hide. That's what's so touching—"

"And so terrifying. But I won't sit here preaching prudence; you'd only hate me for it. And all this time those poor infants are waiting." She stood up with one of her sudden changes of look and tone; as if a cloud had parted, shedding a ray of her lost youth on her. He noticed for the first time that she was all in white, a rose on her breast, and a shady hat hanging from her arm. "Do go down and see them at once, dear. It's getting late. I'll walk with you to the foot of the hill; then I must come back and write some letters. . ." He smiled at the familiar formula, and she took up his smile. "Yes; really important letters—one of them to Aunt Julia," she bantered back. "And besides, the children will want to have you all to themselves." Magnanimously she added: "I must say they all behaved beautifully while you were away. They seemed to feel that they must do you credit. And as for Terry—I wish he were mine! When the break-up comes, as of course it will, why shouldn't you and I adopt him?"

She put on her hat, and linked her arm in Boyne's for the walk down the hill; but at the fringe of the wood, where the path dipped to the high road, she left him.

"You'll come back and dine? I've got some news for you too," she said as he turned down to the village.

XVIII

RECENT memories of Armistice Day—remote ones of Mafeking Night, which he had chanced to experience in London—paled for Boyne in the uproar raised by the little Wheaters when, entering their *pension* dining-room, he told them that everything was all right.

He had not imagined that seven could be so many. The miracle of the loaves and fishes seemed as nothing to the sudden multiplication of arms, legs and lungs about that rural supper-table. At one end of the expanse of coarse linen and stout crockery, Miss Scope, rigid and spectacled, sat dispensing jam without fear or favour; at the other Judith was cutting bread and butter in complete unawareness of her immortal model. Between the two surged a sea of small heads, dusky, ruddy, silver-pale, all tossing and mixing about the golden crest of Chipstone, throned in his umpire's chair. For a moment, as usual, Bun and Zinnie dominated the scene; then Terry, still pale, but with new life in his eyes, caught his cap from the rack with a call for three cheers to which the others improvised a piercing echo. ("Luckily we're the only boarders just now," Miss Scope remarked to Boyne as he pressed her hand.)

In this wonderful world nobody asked any questions; nobody seemed to care for any particulars; their one thought was to bestow on their ambassador the readiest token of their gratitude, from Blanca's cool kiss to the damp and strangulating endearments of Beechy. To Boyne it was literally like a dip into a quick sea, with waves that burnt his eyes, choked his throat and ears, but stung him, body and brain, to fresh activity. "And now let's kiss him all over again—and it's my turn first!" Zinnie rapturously proposed; and as he abandoned himself once more to the battering of the breakers he caught a small voice piping: "We suppose you've brought some presents for us, Martin."

The law which makes men progressively repeople the world with persons of their own age and experience had led Boyne, as he grew older, to regard human relations as more and more ruled by reason; but whenever he dipped into the universe of the infant Wheaters, where all perspective ceased, and it was far more urgent to know what presents he had brought than what fate had been meted out to them by their respective parents, he felt the joy of plunging back into reality.

The presents were there, and nobody had been forgotten, as the rapid unpacking of a small suit-case showed —nobody, that is, but Judith, who stood slightly apart, affecting an air of grown-up amusement, while Blanca and the little girls were hung with trinkets, and Bun made jubilant by an electric lamp. Even Miss Scope had an appropriate reticule, Nanny a lavishly garnished needle-case; and the bottom of the box was crammed with books for Terry.

The distributing took so long, and the ensuing disputes and counter-claims were so difficult of adjustment, that twilight was slipping down the valley when Boyne said to Judith: "Come and take a turn, and I'll tell you all about it."

They walked along the road to a path which led up the hillside opposite to the hotels, and from there began to mount slowly toward the receding sunlight. Judith, unasked, had slipped her arm through Boyne's, and the nearness of her light young body was like wings to him. "What a pity it's getting dark—I believe I could climb to one of those ruby peaks!" he said, throwing his head back with a deep breath; and she instantly rejoined: "Let's run back and get Bun's lamp; then we could."

Boyne laughed, and went on, in a voice of leisurely satisfaction: "Oh, Bun wouldn't part with that lamp—not yet. Besides, we're very well as we are; and there'll be lots of other opportunities."

"There will? Oh, Martin—they're really going to let us stay?" Her strong young hands imprisoned him in a passionate grasp.

"Well, for a time. I made them see it was Terry's best chance."

"Of course it is! And, Martin—they'll leave us all together? Chip and all?"

"Every man of you—for the summer, at any rate." They had stopped in the fern-fringed path, and he stood above her, smiling down into her blissful incredulous eyes. "There's one condition, though—" Her gaze darkened, and he added: "You're all to be accountable to me. I've promised your people to keep an eye on you."

"You mean you're going to stay here with us?" Her lips trembled with the tears she was struggling to keep back, and he thought to himself: "It's too much for a child's face to express—." Aloud he said: "Let's sit down and watch the sunset. This tree-trunk is a pretty good proscenium box."

They sat down, and he set forth at length the history of his negotiations. Complicated as the narrative was, it was easier to relate to his present hearer than to Mrs.

Sellars, not only because fewer elucidations were necessary, but because none of the details he gave shocked or astonished Judith. The tale he told evidently seemed to her a mere bald statement of a matter-of-course affair, and she was too much occupied with its practical results to give a thought to its remoter bearings. She listened attentively to Boyne's report of the final agreement, and when he had ended, said only: "I suppose father's made some arrangement about paying our bills?"

"Your father's opened an account for me: Miss Scope and I are to be your ministers of finance."

She received this in silence; for the first time since his return he felt that the news he brought was still overshadowed for her. At last she asked: "Was father awfully angry . . . you know . . . about that money?"

The question roused Boyne with a start. He perceived that in his struggle to adjust conflicting interests he too had lost sight of the moral issue. And how confess to Judith that, as for her father, he had hardly been aware of it? He felt that it was a moment for prevarication. "Of course your father was angry—thoroughly angry—about the whole thing. Anybody would have been."

She lowered her voice to insist: "But I mean about my taking his money?"

"Well, he's forgiven you for that, at any rate."

"Has he—really and truly?" Her voice lifted again joyfully. "Terry was sure he never would."

Boyne turned about on her in surprise. "Terry—then you told him after all?"

She made a mute sign of assent. "I had to."

"Well, I understand that." He gave her hand a little squeeze. "I'm glad you did."

"He was frightfully upset, you know. And furious with me. I was afraid I'd made him more ill. He wouldn't believe me at first. He said if I had no more moral sense than that, the first thing I knew I'd land in prison."

"Oh—." Boyne could not restrain a faint laugh.

"That didn't worry me very much, though," Judith confessed in a more cheerful tone, "because I've seen a good deal more of life than Terry, and I've known other girls who've done what I did, and none of them ever went to prison."

This did not seem as reassuring to Boyne as it did to the speaker; but the hour for severity was over, the words of rebuke died on his lips. At last he said: "The worst of it was hurting Terry, wasn't it?" and she nodded: "Yes."

For a while after that they sat without speaking, till she asked him if he thought the Wheaters had already started divorce proceedings. To this he could only answer that it looked so, but he still hoped they might calm down and think better of it. She received this with a gesture of incredulity, and merely remarked: "There might have been a chance if Syb Lullmer hadn't been mixed up in it."

"I do wish you wouldn't call that woman by her Christian name," Boyne interrupted.

Judith looked at him with a gentle wonder. "She wouldn't mind. Everybody else does." She clearly assumed that he was reproving her for failing in respect to Mrs. Lullmer.

"That's not what I meant. But she's such a beast."

"Oh, well—." Judith's shrug implied that the epithet was too familiar to her to have kept more than a tinge of obloquy. "I rather hope she won't marry father, though."

"I hope to God she won't. What I'm gambling on is that he and your mother will get so homesick for you children that they'll patch things up on your account."

Her smile kept its soft incredulity. "They don't often, you know; parents don't."

"Well, anyhow, you've got a reprieve, and you must make the most of it."

"I wish you'd say 'we,' not 'you,' Martin."

"Why of course it's 'we,' my dear—that is, as long as you all behave yourselves."

They both laughed at this, and then fell silent, facing the sunset, and immersed, in their different ways, in the overwhelming glory of the spectacle. Judith, Boyne knew, did not feel sunsets as Rose Sellars did—they appealed to a different order of associations, and she would probably have been put to it to distinguish the quality of their splendour from that of fireworks at the Lido, or a brilliant *finale* at the Russian ballet. But something of the celestial radiance seemed to reach her, remote yet enfolding as a guardian wing. "It's lovely here," she breathed, her hand in Boyne's.

He remembered, at a similar moment, Rose Sellars's quoting:

All the peaks soar, but one the rest excels;
Clouds overcome it;
No, yonder sparkle is the citadel's
Circling its summit—

and he murmured the words half aloud.

Judith's pressure tightened ardently on his hand.

"Oh, Martin, how beautifully you do describe things! The words you find are not like anybody else's. Terry says you ought to be a writer."

"Well, in this case, unluckily, somebody found the words before me."

"Oh—." Her enthusiasm flagged. She hazarded: "Mrs. Sellars?"

He gave a little chuckle at her sharpness. "In a way, yes—but, as a matter of fact, Robert Browning got ahead of both of us."

This seemed to give her a certain satisfaction. "Then she just cribbed it from him? Is he another friend of hers?"

"Yes; and will be of yours some day, I hope. He died long before you were born; but you'll find some of the best of him in one of the books I brought to Terry."

"Oh, he's just an author, you mean," she murmured, as if the state were a strictly posthumous one. Her attention always had a tendency to wander at the mention of books, and he thought she was probably a little vexed at having been betrayed into a conversational slip; but presently, with a return of her habitual buoyancy: "I'd rather hear you talk than anybody who's dead," she declared.

"All right; I'll make it a rule to give you only my own vintage," he agreed, gazing out past her into the light. They continued to sit there in silence, the sea of night creeping softly up to them, till at length they were caught in its chill touch. Boyne got reluctantly to his feet. "Come along, child. Time to go down," he said.

"Oh, not down yet—up, up, up!" She caught his arm again, pulling him with all her young strength along the pine-scented steep to where the mystery of the forest drew down to meet them. "I want to climb and climb—don't you? I want to stay up all night, as if we were coming home at sunrise from a ball. It's like a great ball-room over there, isn't it," she cried, pointing to the west, "with the lights pouring out of a million windows?"

Boyne laughed, and suffered himself to be led onward. The air on that height was as fresh as youth, and all about them were the secret scents that dew and twilight waken into life. He knew that he and Judith ought to be turning homeward; but, even if she had released his captive arm, it was growing too dark to consult his watch. Besides, the wandering man in him, the man used to mountains, to long lonely tramps, to the hush and mystery of nights in the open, felt himself in the toils of the old magic. It was no longer Judith drawing him on, but the night itself beckoning him to fresh heights. The child at his side had travelled with him into the beauty as far as she could go, and now he needed nothing from her but the warmth of her nearness. His highest moments had always been solitary. . .

She seemed to guess that there was nothing else to say, and they continued to mount the hill in silence. As they rose the air turned colder, the fires faded, and above them arched a steel-blue heaven starred with ruddy points which grew keen and white as darkness deepened. It was not till they passed out of the fringes of the forest to an open crag above the valley, and saw the village lights sprinkling the black fields far below, that Boyne unwillingly woke to the sense of time and place.

"Oh, by Jove—you must come!" he exclaimed, swinging round to guide his companion down the ledge.

She made no answer, but turned and followed him

along the descending path. He could feel that she was too tired and peaceful for reluctance. She moved beside him like a sleepy child bringing back an apronful of flowers from a happy holiday; and the fact of having reassured her so quickly awed Boyne a little, as if he had meddled with destiny. But it was pleasant, for once, to play the god, and he let himself drift away into visions of a vague millennium where all the grown people knew what they wanted, and if ever it happened that they didn't, the children had the casting vote.

By the time they reached the *pension,* and Judith had loosed her hold of Boyne's arm, he was afraid to look at his watch, but pushed her through the gate with a quick goodnight—and then, a moment later, called to her in an imperious whisper. "Judith!" She hurried back to the summons.

"Did you really think I hadn't brought you any present?"

She gave an excited little laugh. "N—no; I really thought perhaps you had; only—"

"Only what?"

"I thought you'd forgotten some one else's, and had imagined I shouldn't much mind your taking mine, because I'm so much older than the others. . ."

"Well, of course I should have imagined that; but here it is."

He pulled out the parcel he had inadvertently produced in Mrs. Sellars's sitting-room, and Judith caught it to her with a gasp of pleasure.

"Oh, Martin—"

"There; own up that you'd have been fearfully sold if I'd forgotten you."

She answered solemnly: "If you'd forgotten me I should have died of it."

"Well—run off with you; we're hours late," he admonished her.

"Mayn't I look at it before you go?"

"You baby, how could you see in the dark? Besides, I tell you there's no time."

"Not even time to kiss you for it, Martin?"

"No," he cried, slamming the gate shut, and starting up the hill toward his hotel at a run.

When they started on their walk nothing had been farther from Boyne's mind than this disposal of the crystal pendant, though it was for Judith that the trinket had been chosen. Since Mrs. Sellars, owing to his blunder, had seen and coveted it, he felt a certain awkwardness about letting it appear on Judith's neck, and decided that his little friend must again be left out in the general distribution of presents. But during their walk in the mountain dusk, while she hung on his arm, pressed close by the intruding fir-branches, he needed more and more to think of her as a child, and, thinking thus, to treat her as one. He knew how the child in her must have ached at being left out when he unpacked his gifts; and when the time came to say goodnight it was irresistible to heal that ache. There was no way of doing it but to take the pendant from his pocket—the pendant which he had meant for her, and which it had taken so long to unearth at the Venetian antiquary's that there was no time for much thought of Mrs. Sellars's—the pendant which was Judith's by right because, like her, it was odd and exquisite and unaccountable.

"If only she doesn't parade it up at the *châlet!*" the coward in him thought, as he climbed the hill. But all the while he knew it was exactly what she would do.

"Oh, well, damn—after all, I chose it for her," he grumbled, as if that justified them both.

In the *châlet* sitting-room Mrs. Sellars, in her cool evening dress, looked up from the table at which she sat, not writing a letter but reading one. She laid it down thoughtfully as he entered.

"I'm afraid it's awfully late—I hadn't time to go to the hotel and brush up; you don't mind?" he said, blinking a little in the lamplight, and passing his hand through his rumpled hair. As he bent to kiss her his glance fell on the admonishing needles of the little travelling clock at her elbow. "You don't mean to say it's after nine?"

"What does it matter? As a matter of fact, it's after half-past. I was only afraid something had gone wrong about the children."

He tossed his hat down with a laugh. "Bless you, no! Everything's as right as right. But I had to get the Lido out of my lungs; and a long tramp was the only way."

Her smile told him how much she loved him for hating the Lido. "And what do you think my news is? You know I said I had something to tell you. Mr. Dobree is coming here to see me—he arrives next week." She announced the fact as if it were not only important, but even exciting.

"Oh, damn Mr. Dobree!" Boyne rejoined with a careless benevolence. The door had opened on the candlelight of their little dinner-table, on its sparkle of white wine and smell of wild strawberries and village bread. "Well, this is good enough for me," Boyne said, as he dropped into the seat opposite Mrs. Sellars with a sense of proprietorship which made Mr. Dobree's movements seem wholly negligible.

XIX

THE next day there occurred, with a fatal punctuality, exactly what Boyne had foreseen. Mrs. Sellars had invited Judith, Terry and Blanca to lunch; and when they appeared Mrs. Sellars's eye instantly lit on the crystal pendant, Judith's on the sapphire ring. The mutual reconnaissance was swift and silent as the crossing of search-lights in a night sky. Judith said nothing; but Blanca, as Mrs. Sellars bent to kiss her, raised her hostess's hand with an admiring exclamation. "A new ring! What a beauty! I never saw you wear it before."

Mrs. Sellars smiled, and tapped Blanca's cheek with her free hand. "What sharp eyes! But everybody seems to have had a present from Venice—so why shouldn't I?"

Blanca returned the smile, lifting her own wrist to display a hoop of pink crystal. "Isn't mine sweet? Nobody finds presents like Martin."

"So I thought when he showed me Judith's last night."

Mrs. Sellars turned to the older girl, but not to kiss her. She reserved her endearments for the younger children, and merely laid a friendly touch on Judith's shoulder. "Such a wonder, that pendant—I never saw one like it. Decidedly, not Venetian; seventeenth century Spanish, perhaps? It's a puzzle. You're lucky, my dear, to have a *connaisseur* to choose your presents."

That was all—and then a jolly lunch, simple, easy, full of chaff and laughter, Mrs. Sellars, always a perfect hostess, was at her best with Terry and Blanca. The boy touched and interested her, the little girl (Boyne divined) subtly flattered her by a wide-eyed but tactful admiration. Boyne wondered if Mrs. Sellars had noticed how Blanca's clear gray eyes darkened with envy at the praise of the crystal pendant. What a fool he had been not to give the crystal to Blanca, and the tuppenny bracelet to Judith, who would have liked it best because it came from him! Decidedly, he was doomed to blunder in his dealings with women, even when they were no more than little girls. Meanwhile Terry was telling Mrs. Sellars about the books Boyne had brought him, and how he and Judith had already hunted down Boyne's quotation from "The Grammarian's Funeral"— "You know, that splendid one he told Judith yesterday, about 'all the peaks soar'; she came home last night saying it over and over for fear she'd forget it, and woke me up to hunt for it before she went to bed."

"It was so splendid, hearing it up there on the mountain, in the dark, with the stars coming out," Judith glowed, taking up the tale, while Blanca ingenuously added: "It was so late when Judy got home that we were all asleep, and Scopy had to go down and let her in. Did you see Scopy in her crimping-pins, Martin; or had you gone when she opened the door?"

"Yes—the coming of twilight up on the heights is something to remember," Mrs. Sellars intervened, letting her eyes rest attentively on Boyne's before she turned them again to Terry. "But there are better things than that in Browning, you know. Bring me your book tomorrow, and I'll show you. . ."

It all went off perfectly—and Boyne, when he started the children homeward after lunch, was wondering whether tact were as soothing as a summer breeze, or as terrible as an army with banners.

He was to drop the young Wheaters at their *pension*, and afterward meet Mrs. Sellars at the post-office for a climb in the direction of Misurina. At the corner of the highroad descending to Cortina he signalled the hotel omnibus, packed in the twins, and walked on with Judith. At the moment he would rather have escaped from the whole party; but Judith had declared her intention of walking, and he could not do otherwise than go with her. They waited under the trees for the omnibus to sweep on with its load of dust and passengers, and almost at once Judith said: "I suppose you're engaged to Mrs. Sellars, aren't you, Martin?"

The suddenness of the question struck him like a blow, and he realised for the first time that he had never spoken to Rose Sellars about making their engagement known. He had never even asked her if she had broken the news to her formidable aunt, or to the galaxy of minor relatives with whom she maintained her incessant exchange of letters. Her insistence that their marriage should be put off for nearly half a year seemed to make the whole question too remote for immediate decisions. "I suppose I ought to have asked her if she wanted it announced," he thought, reflecting remorsefully that his long exile had made him too careless of the social observances. He turned an irritated eye on Judith. "What in the world put such an idea into your head?"

"Why, your bringing her a ring from Venice, and her putting it on the finger where engagement rings are worn," Judith replied with a smiling promptness.

"Oh, that's the finger, is it?" Boyne said, temporising; and then, with an abrupt clutch at simplification:

"Yes; I am engaged to Mrs. Sellars. But I don't think she wants it spoken of at present."

He turned his gaze away to the long white road glinting through the trees under which he and Judith were withdrawn. Things happened so suddenly and overwhelmingly in Judith's face that he did not feel equal to what might be going on there till he had steadied his gaze by a protracted study of the landscape. When he looked at her again he received the shock of smiling lips and eyes, and two arms thrown filially about him.

"You darling old Martin, I'm so glad! At least I am if you are—really and truly?"

Her hug was almost as suffocating as Zinnie's, and given—he divined it instantly—with the same whole-hearted candour. "So Blanca was right after all! How lovely it must be to be in love! For I suppose that's the reason why you're marrying? I know you're awfully romantic, though you sometimes put on such a gruff manner; I'm sure you wouldn't marry just for position, or for money, or to regularise an old *liaison;* would you?"

"An old *liaison?*" Boyne laughed, but with a touch of vexation. "The ideas you've picked up—and the lingo! You absurd child—why, 'regularise' isn't even English. . . And can't you see, can't you imagine, that a man's first need is to—to respect the woman he hopes to marry?"

Judith received this with a puzzled frown. "Oh, I can *see* it; I have, often—in books, and at the movies. But I can't imagine it, exactly. I should have thought wanting to give her a good hug came before anything."

Boyne shrugged impatiently. Things that seemed funny, and utterly guileless, when she said them to others, shocked him when she commented on his private concerns in the vocabulary of her tribe. "What's the use? You're only a baby, and you repeat things like a parrot, as all children do. Mrs. Sellars is the most perfect, the most exquisite. . ." He broke off, feeling that such asseverations led nowhere in particular, and continued at a tangent: "I can tell you one thing—I should never have dared to take on the job of looking after you children if she hadn't been here—"

Judith's face fell. "Oh, is she going to stay all summer, then?"

"I devoutly hope so! Being with somebody like her is so exactly what. . ." This, again, seemed to land him in a sort of rhetorical blind alley, and he stepped down from it into the dust of the highroad. "Come along; we mustn't dawdle. I'm due at the post-office." He was aware that a settled anger was possessing him, he hardly knew why. Hardly—yet just under the surface of his mind there stirred the uneasy sense that he was perhaps disappointed by Judith's prompt congratulations. Half an hour earlier, he would have said that her approval would add the final touch to his happiness; that there was nothing he wanted more than to have her show herself in fact the child he was perpetually calling her. "The youngest of them all"—that was how he had described her to Mrs. Sellars. Was it possible he had not meant what he said?

He was roused by Judith's squeeze on his arm. "I don't know why you're so cross with me, old Martin. I do really want anything you want. . ."

"That's a good Judy . . . and what rot, dear, thinking I'm cross. Only, remember, it's your secret and mine, and not another soul's." After all, he tried to tell himself, Judith's knowing of his engagement was already a relief. It would do away with no end of hedging and prevaricating. And he was sure he could trust to Judith's discretion; sure of it without her added pressure on his arm, and the solemn: "On Scopy's book!" which had become the tribal oath of the little Wheaters. Boyne had sometimes winced at Judith's precocious discretion, as another proof of what she had been exposed to; now he hailed in it a guaranty of peace. "Perhaps there's something to be said for not keeping children in cotton wool—for she *is* only a child!" he repeated to himself, insistently.

That very evening, while he and Mrs. Sellars were talking over the likelihood of picking up some kind of a tutor for Terry, she asked irrelevantly: "By the way, do the children know of our engagement?"

Contradictory answers rose to Boyne's lips, and he gulped them down to mumble: "I didn't suppose I was authorized to tell anybody."

"But hasn't anybody guessed?"

"Well—as a matter of fact, Judith has. Today. I can't imagine—"

Mrs. Sellars smiled. "My ring, of course. Trust Blanca, too! It was stupid of me not to think of it. But perhaps it's better—"

"Much better."

She pondered. "Only I'd rather no one else knew—at least for the present. Out of regard for Aunt Julia—till I've heard from her." Boyne, relieved, expressed his complete agreement. "Besides," she continued, "I like it's being our secret, don't you? We won't even tell Mr. Dobree."

"Oh, particularly not Mr. Dobree," Boyne replied emphatically.

Two days later Mr. Dobree arrived; and Boyne learned

that an event which seems negligible before it happens may fill the picture when it becomes a fact. The prospect of Mr. Dobree's arrival had now become the fact of Mr. Dobree's presence; and Mr. Dobree, though still spare and nimble for a man approaching sixty (he was ready, and glad, to tell you to what exercises he owed it), took up a surprising amount of room. He was like somebody who travels with a lot of unwieldy luggage—his luggage being, as it were, the very absence of it, being his tact, his self-effacingness, his general neatness and compactness. Wherever you turned, you were in the aura of Mr. Dobree's retractility, his earnest and insistent dodging out of your way, which seemed to leave behind it a presence more oppressive than any mere physical bulk—so that a dull fat man rooted in your best armchair might have been less in the way than the slim and disappearing Mr. Dobree. Mr. Dobree's tact seemed to Boyne like a parody of Mrs. Sellars's; like one of those monstrous blooms into which hybridizers transform a delicate flower. It was a "show" tact, a huge, unique, disbudded tact grown under glass, and destined to be labelled, exhibited, given a prize and a name, and a page to itself in the florists' catalogues. Such at least was Boyne's distorted vision of the new guest at the *châlet*.

Mr. Dobree (as became a man with such impedimenta) was lodged, not at Boyne's inn, but at the "Palace" where Boyne and Mrs. Sellars had once dined. From there a brisk five minutes carried him to the *châlet;* except when his urgent hospitality drew Mrs. Sellars and Boyne to the big hotel. The prompt returning of invitations was a fundamental part of Mr. Dobree's code. He seemed to think that hospitality was something a gentleman might borrow, like money, but never, in any circumstances, receive as a gift; and this obliged Mrs. Sellars to accept his repeated invitations, before, in the battle of their tacts, hers came off victorious, and she made him see that it may be more blessed to receive than to be invited out. The sapphire had vanished from her finger before Mr. Dobree's arrival; and this precaution, for which Boyne blessed her, made him, for Mr. Dobree, simply an old friend, a guest of the Sellars's in New York days, whom one could be suitably pleased to meet again.

Boyne was less pleased to meet Mr. Dobree. His coming was natural enough; and so was Mrs. Sellars's pleasure at seeing him, since he brought not only the latest news of Aunt Julia but papers which settled satisfactorily the matter of Mr. Sellars's will. Boyne had resented what promised to be a tiresome interruption of pleasant habits; but before long he discovered that Mr. Dobree's presence left him free to spend much more time with his young friends of the *Pension Rosenglüh.* This made him aware that during the last weeks he had forfeited a certain amount of his liberty, and he found himself perilously pleased to recover it. He assured Mrs. Sellars that it would look very odd to Mr. Dobree, who had come to discuss family matters with his client, if a third person were present at these discussions; and armed with this argument he proceeded to dispose of his time as he pleased.

His liberation gave a new savour to the hours spent with the little Wheaters; and as for Mr. Dobree (with whom the children had had only one brief and awe-inspiring encounter), he came in very handily as the theme of the games they were always calling on Boyne to invent. To ascertain Mr. Dobree's Christian name (Boyne told them) had long been his secret ambition; but hitherto he had not even been able to learn its first letter. A chance glimpse of Mr. Dobree's glossy suit-cases showed his initials to be A.D., and the letter A was one calculated, as Boyne said, to give them a good gallop. Indeed, he found the puzzle so absorbing that one day, when Judith remarked on his unusual absent-mindedness, he had to own that he had not been listening to what she said because all his faculties were still absorbed in the task of guessing Mr. Dobree's Christian name.

"But Mrs. Sellars must know—why don't you ask her?"

"Must know? Do you think so? I doubt it."

"But she talks of him as an old friend—as old as you."

"Even that doesn't convince me. I doubt if anybody knows Mr. Dobree's Christian name. How should they? Can you imagine anybody's ever having called him by it, or dared to ask him what it was?"

"Well, you might ask her," suggested Judith, from whose make-up a taste for abstract speculation was absent.

"Ask her? Not for the world! Suppose she did know? All our fun would be over."

"Of course it would," cried Terry, plunging into the sport. "If she knows, she mustn't be asked till we've exhausted every other possibility; must she, Martin?"

"Certainly not. I see you grasp the rules of the game. And now let's proceed by elimination. Abel—Abel's the first name in A, isn't it, Terry?"

"No! There's a Prince Aage of Denmark, or something; I saw him in 'The Tatler,'" exulted Terry.

"All right. Let's begin with Aage. Do any of you *see* Mr. Dobree as Aage?" This was dismissed with a general shout of incredulity.

"Well, then: as Abel—Abel Dobree? Don't be in a hurry: try to deal with this thing in a mood of deliberateness and impartiality."

"No, no, no—not Abel!" the assistance chorused.

"Oh, I'm going to sleep," Judith grumbled, stretching out at full length on the sunburnt grass-bank on which the party were encamped.

"Let her—for all the use she is!" Boyne jeered. "Now then—Adam?"

"Adam's a Polish name, isn't it? Who *was* Adam?" Judith opened her eyes to ask.

"A national hero, I think," said Blanca, with a diligent frown.

Miss Scope, perched higher up the bank, cut through these conjectures with a groan. "Children—children! One would think I'd brought you up like savages. Adam—"

"Oh, Scopy means the Adam in the Bible: but Mr. Dobree's parents wouldn't have called him after anybody as far away as that," Blanca shrugged; while Zinnie interposed: "Who was already dead, and couldn't have given him a lovely cup for his christening." Beechy, her face wrinkling up in sympathy at such a privation, wailed out: "Oh, poor little Mr. Dobree—"; and Boyne, recognizing the difficulty, pursued: "Aeneas, then; but he's almost as far away as Adam, I'm afraid."

This drew him into a discussion with Terry regarding the relative seniority of the Biblical and Virgilian heroes, in the intervals of which Miss Scope continued to demand despairingly: "But what in the world are you all arguing about, when we know that Adam was the First Man?"

Judith lifted her head again from its grassy pillow. With half-closed eyes she murmured to the sky: "I don't believe Mr. Dobree would care a bit if his godfather was Adam or not. He could buy himself any christening cup he liked. I believe he's a very rich man."

"Oh, then, do you think he'll give us all some lovely presents when he goes?" Zinnie promptly inferred.

"What makes you think he'll ever go?" Judith retorted, closing her eyes.

"Annibal—Annibal! Annibal begins with an A! I know because he was a Prince, my ancestor," shouted Bun, leaping back into the game.

XX

MRS. SELLARS'S social discipline was too perfect to permit her, even in emergencies, to neglect one obligation for another; and after Mr. Dobree had been for a week at Cortina she said one day to Boyne: "But I've seen nothing lately of the little Wheaters. What's become of them?"

He assured her that they were all right, but had probably been too shy to present themselves at the *châlet* since Mr. Dobree's arrival; to which Mrs. Sellars replied, with the faintest hint of tartness, that she had never had occasion to suspect the little Wheaters of being shy, and that, furthermore, Mr. Dobree did not happen to be staying at the *châlet*.

Boyne smiled. "No; but they know he's with you a good deal, and he's a more impressive figure than they're used to."

He saw that she scented irony in this, and was not wholly pleased with it. "I don't know what you mean by impressive; I didn't know anything in the world could impress the modern hotel child. But Mr. Dobree is very sorry for them, poor dears, and I'm sure it would interest him to see something of them. Why shouldn't we take them all on a picnic to-morrow? I know Mr. Dobree would like to invite them."

Boyne felt that, for all the parties concerned, the undertaking might prove formidable. He pointed out that, if Zinnie and the two Buondelmonte children were included in an all-day expedition, Miss Scope's presence would be necessary, since otherwise all Judith's energies would be absorbed in keeping the party in order; and Mrs. Sellars acquiesced: "Yes, the poor little things are dreadfully spoilt."

Boyne was secretly beginning to be of the same mind; but Mrs. Sellars could no longer criticise his young friends without rousing his instinctive opposition. "They certainly haven't had much opportunity to become little Lord Fauntleroys, if that's what you mean," he said impatiently; and his betrothed rejoined: "What I mean is that Mr. Dobree feels sorry for them because of the kind of opportunity they have had. You see, he was one of the lawyers in the Westway divorce."

Boyne gave her a quick look, in which he was conscious that his resentment flamed. "I'm hanged if I see what there can be in Mr. Dobree's mind to make him connect the Westway divorce with the Wheater children."

"Why, simply his knowledge of Judith's intimacy with that wretched drug-soaked Doll Westway, and his familiarity with the horrible details that led up to the girl's suicide. She and Judith were together at Deauville the very summer that she killed herself. Both their mothers had gone off heaven knows where. Judith proclaims the fact to every one, as you know."

Boyne had removed his eyes from Mrs. Sellars's face, and was staring out at the familiar outline of the great crimson mountains beyond the balcony. A phrase of Stevenson's about "the lovely and detested scene" (from "The Ebb-tide," he thought?) strayed through his mind as he gazed. It was hateful to him to think that he might hereafter come to associate those archangelic summits with Mrs. Lullmer's smooth impervious face, and Mr.

Dobree's knowledge of the inner history of the Westway divorce.

He turned back to Mrs. Sellars. "Aren't you getting rather sick of this place?" he asked abruptly.

She gave back his irritated stare with one of genuine surprise. "Sick of what? You mean of Cortina?"

"Of the whole show." His sweeping gesture gathered up in one contemptuous handful the vast panorama of mountain, vale and forest. "I always feel that when scenery gets mixed up with our personal bothers all the virtue goes out of it—as if our worries were so many locusts, eating everything bare."

Mrs. Sellars was silent for a moment; then her hand fell on his. "I've always been afraid, dear, that this queer responsibility you've assumed was going to end by getting on your nerves—"

Boyne jumped up, drawing abruptly away from her. "Responsibility? What responsibility?" He walked across the room, turned back, and awkwardly laid an answering caress on her hair. "Gammon! It's Mr. Dobree who gets on my nerves—just a little." ("Hypocrite!" he cursed himself inwardly.) "Fact is, I liked Cortina a damned sight better when you and I and the children had it all to ourselves." He saw the light of reassurance in her averted cheek. "Just my beastly selfishness, I know—I needn't tell you that men *are* beastly selfish, need I?" He laughed, and her faint laugh echoed his.

"Mr. Dobree is going soon, I believe," she volunteered.

Boyne pulled himself together. "Well, that makes it a good deal easier to be unselfish while he s here, and I take it upon myself to accept his picnic for to-morrow. I'll drop down and announce it to the children." He flattered himself that his simulation of buoyancy had produced the desired effect, and that his parting from Mrs. Sellars was unclouded. But half way down the hill he stood suddenly still in the path, and exclaimed aloud: "But after he's gone; what then?"

The picnic was beautifully successful—one of those smooth creaseless well-oiled successes as to which one feels that at any moment it may slip from one's hold and reveal the face of failure. A very Janus of a picnic, Boyne thought. . .

To the chief actors, however, it presented no such duality, but was the perfect image of what constitutes A Good Time For The Young People, when made out of the happy union of tact and money. To Mr. Dobree it was certainly that, and he was justified in feeling that if you order the two roomiest and most balloon-tired motors obtainable, and fill enough hampers with the most succulent delicacies of a "Palace" restaurant, and are actuated throughout by the kindliest desire to give pleasure, happiness will automatically follow.

As regards the younger members of the party, it undoubtedly did. Terry was strong enough to enjoy the long day on the heights without fear of Miss Scope's thermometer; Blanca was impressed by the lavish fare which replaced their habitual bread and chocolate; and the small children were in the state of effervescence induced by freedom from lessons and the sense of being the central figures of the day.

And Judith—?

After lunch the younger members of the party trailed away with Miss Scope to hunt for wild strawberries while the others sat pillowed in moss beside a silver waterfall.

Boyne, supine against his boulder, studied the scene and meditated from behind a screen of pipe smoke. Judith, a little way off, leaned luxuriously against her mossy cushion, her hat tossed aside, her head resting in the curve of an immature arm. Her profile looked small and clear against the auburn tremor of bracken turned inward by the rush of the water. A live rose burned in her cheeks, darkening her eyebrows and lashes, and putting a velvet shadow under her closed lids. She had fallen asleep, and sleep surrendered her unguarded to her watchers.

"She looks almost grown up—she looks kissable. Why should she, all of a sudden?" Boyne asked himself, suddenly disturbed, not by her increased prettiness (the measure of that varied from hour to hour) but by some new quality in it. He turned his eyes away, and they fell on Mr. Dobree, who sat facing him in the studied *abandon* of a picnicker unused to picnics. Mr. Dobree's inexhaustible wardrobe had supplied him with just the slightly shabby homespun suit and slightly faded hat adapted to the occasion; and Boyne wondered whether it were this change of dress which made him also seem different. But no: the difference was deeper. Despite his country clothes, Mr. Dobree did not look easier or less urban; he merely looked more excited and off his guard. His clear cautious eyes had grown blurred and furtive; one could almost see a faint line stretching from them to the recumbent Judith. Along that line it was manifest that Mr. Dobree's thoughts were racing; and Boyne knew they were the same thoughts as his own. The discovery shocked him indescribably. But he remembered that the levelling tendencies of modern life have levelled differences of age with the rest; and that Mr. Dobree was, to all intents and purposes, but little older than himself. Moreover, he was still brisk and muscular; his glance was habitually alert; in spite of his silver hair there seemed no reason why he should not share with Boyne the contemplation of Judith's defenceless beauty.

But if this was Boyne's conclusion it was apparently not Mr. Dobree's. As Boyne continued to observe him, Mr. Dobree's habitual pinkness turned to a red which suffused even his temples and eyelids, so that his carefully brushed white hair looked like a sunlit cloud against an angry sky. But with whom was Mr. Dobree angry? Why, with himself, manifestly. His eyes still rested on the dreaming Judith; but the rest of his face looked as if every muscle were tightened in the effort to pull the eyes away. "He's frightened—he's frightened at himself," Boyne thought, calling to mind—with a faint recoil from the reminder—that he also, once or twice, had been vaguely afraid of himself when he had looked too long at Judith. Had his eyes been like that, he wondered? And the muscles of his face been stretched in the effort to detach the eyes? The thing was not pleasant to visualise; and he disliked Mr. Dobree the more for serving as his mirror. . .

But suddenly Mr. Dobree was on his feet, his whole attention given to Mrs. Sellars. Again Boyne followed his change of direction with a start. Mrs. Sellars—but then she had been there all the time! Shadowed by her spreading hat, her light body bedded in the turf, she looked almost as young and sylvan as Judith. But somehow she had been merged in the landscape, all broken up into a dapple of sun and shade, of murmurs and soughings: her way of fitting into things sometimes had this effect of effacing her. She lifted her head, and in the shade of the hat-brim Boyne caught a delicate watchfulness of brows and lips, as of tiny live things under a protecting leaf.

Mr. Dobree was challenging her jauntily. "Do you see why those young cannibals should monopolise all the wild strawberries? Suppose we leave Mr. Boyne to mount guard over the sleeping beauty, and try to bag our share before it's too late?"

The words said clearly enough: "Take me away—it's high time," and Mrs. Sellars's gay little answer: "Come on—I'll show you a patch they'll never find," seemed to declare as clearly: "I know; but I'll see that you don't come to any mischief."

She was on her feet before his hands could help her up; something light and bounding in her seemed to spring to his call. "This way, this way," she cried, starting ahead of him up the boulder-strewn way. Boyne heard their voices mounting the streamside, mingling with the noise of the water, fading and flashing out again like the glimpses of her dress through the beech-leaves. He lay without moving, watching the smoke of his pipe rise in wavering spirals, twisted out of shape by puffs of air from the waterfall. With Mr. Dobree's withdrawal the ideas suggested by his presence had gone too; Judith Wheater seemed once more a little girl. Though perplexities and uncertainties still lingered on the verge of Boyne's mind his central self was anchored in a deep circle of peace. Every fibre of him was alive to the exquisite moment; but he had no need to fly from it, no fear of its flying from him. Judith's sleep was a calm pool in which he rested.

He fancied he must have been watching her for a long time, his thoughts enclosing her in a sort of calm fraternal vigilance, when she opened her eyes and turned them on him, still dewy with sleep.

"Martin!" she hailed him drowsily; then, fully awake, she sat up and exclaimed: "Darling, when are you going to be married? I've positively got to know at once."

She was always startling Boyne, but she had perhaps never startled him more than by this question; for even as she spoke he had been half unconsciously putting it to himself. He remembered, as something already far off, picturesque and unreal as a youthful folly, his resentment of Mrs. Sellars's delay in fixing a date for their marriage. Was it only two or three weeks ago that he had sent her, with a basket of gentians picked on a lofty upland, a quotation from Marvell's "Coy Mistress"? Now all that seemed an undergraduate's impatience. She had taught him that they were very well as they were, and if he still asked himself when they were to be married, the question had imperceptibly taken another form. "What in God's name will become of the children after we're married?" was the way he now instinctively put it.

He too sat up, and gazed into Judith's sleepy eyes. As he did so he was aware that an uncomfortable redness (which did not, he hoped, resemble Mr. Dobree's) was creeping up to his temples.

"When I'm going to be married? Why? What's the odds? I don't know that it's anybody's business, anyhow," he grumbled in an ill-assured voice.

Judith brushed the rebuff aside. "Oh, but it is—it's mine. For a very particular reason," she continued, as if affectionately resolved to break down the barrier of his reserve.

"A reason? Nonsense! What has a chit like you got to do with reasons?"

"You mean I'm so unreasonable?" A quick shadow crossed her face. "You didn't really mean that?"

"I didn't mean anything at all—any more than you do. I only meant: why aren't we very well as we are?"

Her eyes grew wide at this, and continued to fix him with a half mocking gravity, while her lips rounded into a smile. "Oh, but, Martin dear, it's Mrs. Sellars who ought to say that—not you!"

Boyne burst out laughing. How could one ever keep serious for two minutes with any of these preposterous children? And once more he told himself that Judith was as preposterous, and as much of a child, as the youngest of them.

"You know, darling, you ought to be *empressé,* impatient, passionate," she adjured him, as if his very life depended on his following her advice.

He leaned on his elbow and examined her with deliberation. "Well, of all the cheek—!"

She shook her head, still smiling. "I'm not cheeky; I'm really not, Martin. But sometimes you strike me as having so little experience—"

("Thank you," Boyne interjected.)

"Oh, I mean in those sorts of ways. As if you'd lived all your life so far away from the world."

"From your world? So I have, thank heaven." After a moment he added with severity: "So has Mrs. Sellars—thank heaven too."

The girl stood up, and crossing the mossy space between them, dropped down beside him and laid her hand on his arm. "Now I've offended you. Doll Westway always said I had no tact. And all I wanted was to explain why I have to know as soon as possible when you're to be married."

"Well, you certainly haven't explained that," Boyne answered, turning away from her to relight his pipe.

"No; but I'm going to. And you'll be pleased. It's because we've all clubbed together—even the steps and Scopy have—to give you a really jolly wedding present; and I think you'll like what we've found. We unearthed it the other day at Toblach, at the *antiquaire*'s. And we want to know exactly the right moment to give it to you. You do love presents, don't you, Martin?" she urged, as if straining her utmost to reach some human chord in him. He met the question with another laugh.

"Love presents? I should think I did! Almost as much as you do." She coloured a little at the insinuation; and perceiving this, he hastened on: "It's awfully dear of you all, and I'm ever so grateful. But there was no need to be in such a devil of a hurry."

Her face became all sympathy and interrogation. "Oh, Martin, you don't mean—things haven't gone wrong, have they?" Her look and intonation showed that she would have been genuinely distressed if they had. A pang like neuralgia shot through Boyne—yet a pang that was not all bitter. He took her hand, and laid what she had once called a "grown up kiss" on it. "Of course not, dear. And thank you—thank you for everything. . . Whatever you've all chosen for me, I shall love. . . Only, you know, there's really no sort of hurry."

She met this in silence, as something manifestly final. Folding her arms behind her, she let her head droop back on them, and her gaze wandered lazily skyward through the flicker of boughs.

Boyne had got his pipe going again. Gradually the tumult in his mind subsided. He sank back lazily at her side, tilting his hat over his brows, and saying to himself:

"What on earth's the use of thinking ahead, anyhow?"

Directly in the line of his vision, Judith's sandalled feet lay in a bed of bracken, crossed like a resting Mercury's. He could almost see the little tufted wings at the heels. For the moment his imagination was imprisoned in a circle close about them.

XXI

THAT evening, when the children, weary but still jubilant, had been dropped at the *Pension Rosenglüh,* and Boyne had joined Mrs. Sellars for a late dinner at the *châlet,* the first thing that struck him was that his sapphire had reappeared on her hand.

He wondered afterward how it was that he, in general so unobservant of such details, had noticed that she had resumed the modest stone; and concluded that it was because of Judith's ridiculous cross-examination about the date of his marriage. He almost suspected that, baffled by his evasiveness, the pertinacious child had ended by addressing herself to Mrs. Sellars, and that the latter, thus challenged, had put on her ring. But no—though Judith was sometimes lacking in tact (as she herself acknowledged) this indiscretion could not be imputed to her, for the reason that Mrs. Sellars—Boyne remembered it only now—had not reappeared on the scene till it was time to pack the sleepy picnickers into the motors. She and Mr. Dobree had been a long time away. They had apparently prolonged their walk, and, incidentally, had failed to find the promised strawberries—or else had consumed them on the spot. And on the way home Judith and Mrs. Sellars had not been in the same car. Why, then, had Mrs. Sellars suddenly put on her ring? Boyne would only suppose that she had decided, for reasons unknown to him, to announce their engagement that night to Mr. Dobree, who was no doubt going to join them at dinner.

The idea obscurely irritated Boyne; he felt bored in advance by the neat and obvious things Mr. Dobree would consider it becoming to say. Boyne's whole view of Mrs. Sellars's friend had been changed by his sudden glimpse of the man who had looked out of Mr. Dobree's eyes at Judith. Before that, Boyne had pigeon-holed him as the successful lawyer, able in his profession, third-rate in other capacities, with a methodically planned existence of which professional affairs filled the larger part, and the rest was divided up like a carefully-weighed vitamin diet (Mr. Dobree was strong on vitamins) between exercise, society, philanthropy and travel. Now, a long way off down this fair perspective, a small, an almost invisible Dobree, lurked and prowled, staring as he had stared at Judith. A sudden irritation filled Boyne at the thought of what, unknown to Mrs. Sellars, peered and grimaced behind her legal counsellor. It was as if Mr. Dobree had unconsciously evoked for him some tragic allegory of Judith's future. . .

"Where's your friend? Are we waiting for him?" Boyne's question sounded abrupt in his own ears, but was received by Mrs. Sellars with her usual equanimity.

"Mr. Dobree? No, we're not waiting for him. He's not coming."

Boyne felt relieved, yet vaguely baffled. If Dobree wasn't coming (he immediately thought), why the devil wasn't he? And what was he up to instead?

"Chucked you for a party at the 'Palace,' I suppose? I'm glad he didn't drag you up there to dine with him."

"No; I don't think he's giving a party—or going to one. He had letters to write; and he said he was tired."

This seemed to dispose of the matter, and Boyne, still faintly disturbed, followed his betrothed to the dining-table, at which of late he had so seldom sat alone with her.

"Don't you like it better like this?" she asked, smiling at him across the bowl of wild roses which stood between them.

It was indeed uncommonly pleasant to be alone with her again. She gratified him, at the outset, by praising the behaviour of the children on the picnic; and as they talked he began to think that his growing irritability, and his odd reluctance to look forward to their future together, had been caused only by the intrusion of irrelevant problems and people. "When we're alone together everything's always all right," he thought, reassured.

Dinner over, they drifted out onto the balcony in the old way, and he lit his cigar, and yielded to the sense of immediate wellbeing. He saw that Rose Sellars knew he was glad to be alone with her, and that the knowledge put her at her ease, and made her want to say and do whatever would maintain that mood in him. There was something pathetic in the proud creature's eagerness to be exactly what he wished her to be.

"Judith was looking her very prettiest today, wasn't she? Mr. Dobree was so much struck by her," she said softly, after a silence.

It was as if she had flung a boulder into the very middle of the garden-plot she had just been at such pains to lay out. Boyne met the remark with an exasperated laugh.

"I should say he *was* struck. That was fairly obvious."

"Well—she is striking, at times," Mrs. Sellars conceded, still more gently.

"As any lovely child is. That's what she is—a lovely

child. Dobree looks at her like a dog licking his jaws over a bone."

"Martin—!"

"Sorry. I never could stand your elderly men who look at little girls. If your friend is so dotty about Judith, he'd better ask her to marry him. He's rich, isn't he? His money might be an inducement—who knows?"

"Marry her? Marry Judith? Mr. Dobree?" Mrs. Sellars gave way to a mild mirth. His words certainly sounded absurd enough when she echoed them; but Boyne, for the moment, was beyond heeding anything but the tumult in his own veins.

"Why not?" he continued. "As the poor child is situated, money is a big consideration. What's the use of being a hypocrite about it? If she's to fight her parents, and keep the children together, she'll need cash, and a big pile of it; and a clever lawyer to manœuvre for her, too. I call it an ideal arrangement."

Mrs. Sellars waited a little before answering; then she said: "I don't see how the biggest fortune, and the cleverest lawyer in the world, could keep the Wheaters from ordering their children home the day they choose to. But I'm sure that if Judith wanted help and advice no one would be more happy to give it to her than Mr. Dobree."

"Ah, there you're right," Boyne agreed with an ironic shrug.

"Well, and don't you think perhaps it might be a good thing if she did consult him—or at least if you did, for her?"

"If I intervened in any way between Dobree and Judith I don't think he'd thank you for putting me up to it."

"Why—what do you mean?"

"If you don't know what I mean I can only suppose you didn't notice how he was looking at the child this afternoon, before you carried him off for a walk."

Mrs. Sellars fell silent again. He saw the faint lines of perplexity weaving their net over her face, and reflected that when a woman is no longer young she can preserve her air of freshness only in the intervals of feeling. "It's too bad," he thought, vexed with himself for having upset the delicate balance of her serenity. But now she was smiling again, a little painfully.

"Looking at her—looking at her how?"

"Well—as I've told you."

The smile persisted. "I certainly didn't see anything like that. And neither did I carry him off for a walk; as it happens, it was he who carried *me*—"

"Oh, well," Boyne murmured at this touch of feminine vanity.

Mrs. Sellars continued: "And I don't think he's thinking of Judith in the way you imagine—or that he can have looked at her in that way. I hope he didn't; because, as it happens, he took me off on that walk to ask me to marry him."

The words dropped from her with a serene detachment, as if they had been her luminous little smile made audible. "I don't know that it's quite fair to him to tell you," she added, with one of her old-fashioned impulses of reserve.

It was Boyne's turn to find no answer. For some time he sat gazing into the summer darkness without speaking. "Marry him? Marry Dobree—you?"

"You see you were right: he does want to get married," she softly bantered. "It was what he came for—to ask me. I'd no idea. . . And now he's going away . . . he leaves to-morrow," she added, with a faint sigh in which deprecation and satisfaction were perceptibly mingled. If it was her little triumph she took it meekly, even generously—but nevertheless, he saw, with a complete consciousness of what it meant.

Boyne laughed again, this time at himself.

"I don't know what you see in it that is so absurd," Mrs. Sellars murmured, a faint note of vexation in her voice. Again he found no reply, and she continued, with the distant air she assumed when echoing axioms current in her youth: "After all, it's the highest honour a man can—"

"Oh, quite," Boyne agreed good-humouredly. He rubbed his hand across his forehead, as if to brush away some inner confusion. But it was no use; he couldn't straighten his thoughts out. He couldn't shake off the fact that his surprise and derision had not concerned Rose Sellars at all—that his laugh had simply mocked his own power of self-deception, and uttered his relief at finding himself so deceived. "So *that* was all!" The words escaped him unawares. In the dusk he felt the shadowy figure at his side stiffen and withdraw from him.

"Shall we go in? It's getting chilly," said Mrs. Sellars, turning back toward the lamplight.

Boyne, still in the bewilderment of his own thoughts, followed her into the room. He noticed that she had grown unusually pale. She sat down beside the table, and began turning over the letters and papers which the evening post had brought. Boyne stood in front of the fireplace, his hands in his pockets, watching her movements as one letter after another slipped through her fingers. But all he could see was the sapphire ring, re-established, enthroned, proclaiming his own destiny to all concerned and unconcerned.

"So you told him you were already engaged?"

She looked up at him. "It was only fair, wasn't it?"

"Certainly—that is, if being engaged was the only obstacle."

"The only obstacle?"

"If you were prepared to marry Dobree, supposing you'd still been free."

She weighed this, and then laughed a little, but without much gaiety. "How do I know what I should have done if I'd been free?"

He continued to look at her. "Do you want to try?"

The colour rose to her forehead. She dropped the letters, and composed her hands on them as if in the effort to control a secret agitation. "Is this a way of telling me you're vexed because I announced our engagement to Mr. Dobree?"

He hesitated, feeling (and now he hated himself for feeling) that it was a moment for going warily. "Not vexed; that's not the word. Only I did agree with you that, as long as—as nothing about our future was definitely settled—it was ever so much pleasanter keeping our private affairs to ourselves. It was your own idea, you know; you proposed it," he reminded her, as she remained silent.

"Yes; it was my idea." She pondered. "But you needn't be afraid that Mr. Dobree will betray us."

"It's not a question of betraying. It's just the feeling—"

"The feeling that some one else is in our secret? But all the Wheater children have been—for a long time." She spoke the words ever so lightly, as if she had barely pencilled them on a smooth page.

Boyne was startled. He could see no analogy, but did not know how to explain that there was none. "Oh, the children; but the children don't count. Besides, that wasn't my fault. Judith guessed." He smiled a little at the reminiscence. "But perhaps Mr. Dobree guessed," he added, with a return of ease. After all, he was carrying it off very well, he thought—though what he meant by "it" he would have been put to it to say.

Mrs. Sellars gave another little laugh. "Oh, no; Mr. Dobree didn't guess. I had to dot the *i*'s for him. The fact is"—she paused a moment—"he was convinced that you were in love with Judith Wheater."

Instantly all the resentments and suspicions which Boyne had dismissed rushed back on him. He had been right, then—he had not mistaken the signs and portents. As if they were ever mistakable! "How rotten," he said in a low voice.

Mrs. Sellars dropped one of the letters which she had absently taken up again.

"Martin—"

"Rotten. The mere thinking of such a thing—much less insinuating it to any one else. But it just shows—" He broke off, and then began again, on a fresh wave of indignation: "Shows what kind of a mind he must have. Thinking in that way about a child—a mere child—and about any man, any *decent* man; regarding it as possible, perhaps as natural . . . worst of all, suggesting it of some one standing in my position toward these children; as if I might take advantage of my opportunities to—to fall in love with a child in the schoolroom!"

Boyne's words sounded in his own ears as if they were being megaphoned at him across the width of the room. He dropped down into the nearest chair, hot, angry, ashamed, with a throat as dry as if he had been haranguing an open-air meeting on a dusty day.

Opposite him, Mrs. Sellars remained with her hands suspended above the letters. The sapphire burned at him across the interval. "Martin . . . but you *are* in love with her!" she exclaimed. She paused a moment, and then added in a quieter voice: "I believe I've always known it." They sat and looked at each other without speaking.

At length Boyne rose, and started to move around the table to where she was sitting.

"This is ridiculous—" he began.

She held up her hand, and the gesture, though evidently meant only to check the words on his lips, had the effect also of arresting his advance. He felt self-conscious and clumsy, and dimly resented her making him feel so. He was sure it was she who had been ridiculous, not he; yet, curiously enough, the conviction brought him no solace. Again they faced each other, guardedly, apprehensively, as if something fragile and precious, which they had been carrying together, had slipped between their fingers and been broken. He felt that, if he glanced at the floor, he might see the glittering fragments. . .

Mrs. Sellars was the first to recover her self-possession. She rose in her turn, and going up to Boyne laid her hand on his arm.

"I wonder why we're trying to hurt each other?" She looked at him through moist lashes, and he felt himself a brute for not instantly taking her in his arms and obliterating their discussion with a kiss. But there lay the glittering fragments, and he could not seem to reach to her across them.

"Now I know what she thinks of Judith," he reflected savagely.

"It's all my fault, Martin; I know I'm nervous and stupid." She was clasping his arm, pleading with lifted eyes and lips. Her self-abasement humiliated him. "If she really thinks what she says, why doesn't she kick me out?" he wondered.

"I suppose I walked too far today, and got over-tired; and what Mr. Dobree said startled me, upset me. . ."

He smiled. "His asking you to marry him?"

She smiled back a little wearily. "No. But what he said about—about your interest in Judith. You must understand, dear, that sometimes your attitude about those children is a little surprising to people who don't know all the circumstances."

Boyne felt himself hardening again. "What business is it of people who don't know all the circumstances? *You* do; that's enough."

She seized at this with a distressing humility. "Of course I do, dearest; of course it is. And you'll try to forget my stupid nerves, won't you? Try to think of me as I am when there's nobody in the world but you and me?" Her arms stole up to his shoulders, her hands met behind his neck, and she drew his head down softly. "If only it could always be like that!"

As their lips touched he shut his eyes, and tried, with a violent effort of the will, to recall what her kiss would have meant to him on the far-off day when the news of Sellars's death had overtaken him somewhere in the Nubian desert, and in the middle of the night he had started awake, still clutching the letter, and crying out to himself: "At last. . ."

XXII

NEXT day, when Boyne thought over the scene of the previous night, he found for it all the excuses which occur to a sensible man in the glow of his morning bath.

It was all the result of idling and lack of hard exercise; when a working man has had too long a holiday, and resting has become dawdling, Satan proverbially intervenes. But though at first Boyne assumed all the blame, by the time he began to shave he had handed over a part to Mrs. Sellars. After all, it was because of her old-fashioned scruples, her unwillingness to marry him at once, and let him get back to work, that they were still loitering in the Dolomites. It probably wasn't safe for middle-aged people to have too much leisure in which to weigh each other's faults and merits.

But then, again, suddenly he thought: "If we'd been married, and gone home when I wanted to, what would have become of the children?" It was undoubtedly because Mrs. Sellars had insisted on prolonging their engagement that Boyne had become involved in the Wheater problem; but when he reached this point in his retrospect he found he could not preserve his impartiality. It was impossible to face the thought of what might have happened to the little Wheaters if chance had not put him in their way. . .

After all, then, everything was for the best. All he had to do was to persuade Mrs. Sellars of it (which ought not to be difficult, since it was a "best" of her own devising), and to banish from his mind the disturbing figure of Mr. Dobree. Perhaps—on second thoughts—his irritability of the previous evening had been partly due to the suspicion that Mrs. Sellars, for all her affected indifference, was flattered by Mr. Dobree's proposal. "You never can tell—" Boyne concluded, and shrugged that possibility away too. The thought that he might have had to desert his young friends in their hour of distress, and had been able, instead, to stay and help them, effaced all other considerations. So successfully did he talk himself over to this view that only one cloud remained on his horizon. Mrs. Sellars had said: "I don't see how the biggest fortune, and the cleverest lawyer in the world, could keep the Wheaters from ordering their children home the day they choose to"; and in saying it she had put her finger on Boyne's inmost apprehension. He had told himself the same thing a hundred times; but to hear it from any one else made the danger seem more pressing. It reminded him that the little Wheaters' hold on him was not half as frail as his own on them, and that it was folly to indulge the illusion that he could really direct or control their fate.

And meanwhile—?

Well, he could only mark time; thank heaven it was still his to mark! The Lido season had not yet reached its climax, and till it declined and fell he was free to suppose that its devotees would linger on, hypnotized. As between taking steps for an immediate divorce, and figuring to the last in the daily round of entertainment, Boyne felt sure that not one of the persons concerned would hesitate. They could settle questions of business afterward; and it was purely as business that they regarded a matter in which the extent of the alimony was always the chief point of debate. And what could replace the excitement of a Longhi ball at the Fenice, or of a Marriage of the Doge to the Adriatic, mimed in a reconstituted Bucentaur by the rank and fashion of half Europe? No one would be leaving Venice yet.

But, all the same, the days were flying. The increasing number of arrivals at Cortina, the growing throng of motors on all the mountain ways, showed that before long fashion would be moving from the seashore to the mountains; and when the Lido broke up, what might not break up with it? Boyne felt that the question must at last be faced; that he must have a talk about it that very day with Judith.

It was more than a month since Judith and her flock had appeared at Cortina; and the various parents concerned had promised Boyne that the children should be left in the Dolomites till the summer was over. But what was such a promise worth, and what did the phrase mean on lips so regardless of the seasons? Nothing—Boyne knew it. He was conscious now that, during the last four weeks, he had never gone down to the *Pension Rosenglüh* without expecting to be told that a summons or a command had come from the Lido. But so far there had been none. The children were protected by the fact that there was no telephone at the *pension,* and that none of their parents was capable—except under the most extreme pressure—of writing a letter.

When it was impossible to telephone they could, indeed, telegraph; but even the inditing of a telegram required a concentration of mind which, Boyne knew, would become increasingly difficult as the Lido season culminated. Telegrams did, of course, come, especially in the first days, both to Boyne and to Judith: long messages from Joyce about clothes and diet, rambling communications from Lady Wrench, setting forth her rights and grievances in terms which, by the time they had passed through two Italian telegraph-offices, were as confused as the thoughts in her own mind; and lastly, a curt wire from Cliffe Wheater to Boyne: "Wish it definitely understood relinquish no rights whatever how is Chipstone reply paid."

To all these communications Boyne returned a comprehensive "All right," and, acting on his advice, Judith did the same, merely adding particulars as to the children's health and happiness. "On the whole, you know," she explained to Boyne, "it's a relief to them all, now the thing's settled—I always knew it would be." She and Terry still cherished the hope that in the autumn she would be permitted to take the children out to Grandma Mervin, in America; or that, failing permission, she would be encouraged by Boyne to carry them off secretly. With this in view, she and Miss Scope saved up every penny they could of the allowance which Cliffe Wheater had agreed to make, and which Boyne dealt out to them once a week. But all these arrangements were so precarious, so dependent on the moods of unreasonable and uncertain people, that it seemed a miracle that the little party at the *Pension Rosenglüh* was still undisturbed. Certainly, if it had been possible to reach them by telephone they would have been scattered long ago. "As soon as they break up at the Lido they'll be after you," Boyne had warned Judith from the first; but she had always answered hopefully: "Oh, no: not till after Cowes, if they still go there; and if they don't, after Venice there's Biarritz. You'll see. And before Biarritz there's a fortnight in Paris for autumn clothes."

Cowes, in due course, had been relinquished, the Lido exerting too strong a counter-attraction; but after a few more weeks that show also would be packed away in the lumber-room of spent follies.

The fact of having these questions always on his mind kept Boyne from being unduly disturbed by his discussion of the previous evening with Mrs. Sellars. In the wholesome light of morning a sentimental flurry between two sensible people who were deeply attached to each other seemed as nothing compared to the ugly reality perpetually hanging over the little Wheaters; and he felt sure that Mrs. Sellars would take the same view.

She did not disappoint him. When he presented himself at the luncheon hour the very air of the little sitting-room breathed a new serenity; it was as if she had been out early to fill it with flowers. Boyne was not used to delicate readjustments in his sentimental relations. For so many years now his feeling for Rose Sellars had been something apart, like a beautiful picture on the wall of a quiet room; and his other amorous episodes had been too brief and simple for any great amount of manœuvring. He was therefore completely reassured by the gaiety and simplicity of her welcome, and thought to himself once again that there was everything to be said in favour of a long social acquiescence. "A stupid woman, now, would insist on going over the whole thing again, like a blue-bottle that starts in banging about the room after you're sure you've driven it out of the window."

There was nothing of the blue-bottle about Mrs. Sellars; and she was timorously anxious that Boyne should know it. But her timidity was not base; if she submitted, she submitted proudly. The only sign she gave of a latent embarrassment was in her too great ease, her too blithe determination to deny it. But even this was minimised by the happy fact that she had a piece of news for him.

She did not tell him what it was till lunch was over, and they were finishing their coffee in the sitting-room: she knew the importance of not disturbing a man's train of thought—even agreeably—while he is in the act of enjoying good food. Boyne had lit his cigar, and was meditating on the uniform excellence of the coffee she managed to give him, when she said, with a little laugh: "Only imagine—Aunt Julia's on the Atlantic! I had a radio this morning. She says she's coming over to Paris to see you."

Boyne had pictured Aunt Julia—when he could spare the time for such an evocation—as something solid, ponderous, essentially immovable. She represented for him the obstinate stability of old New York in the flux of new experiments. It was like being told that Trinity Church, for instance, was taking a Loretto-flight across the Atlantic to see him.

Mrs. Sellars laughed at his incredulous stare. "Are you surprised? I'm not. You see, Aunt Julia was always the delicate sister, the one who had to be nursed. Aunt Gertrude, the strong one, who did the nursing, died last winter—and since then Aunt Julia's been perfectly well."

They agreed that such resurrections were not uncommon, and Mrs. Sellars went so far as to declare that, if she didn't get to Paris in time to meet Aunt Julia, she was prepare to have the latter charter an aeroplane and descend on Cortina. "Indeed we're only protected by the fact that I don't believe there's any landing-field in the Dolomites."

She went on to say that she would have to leave in a

day or two, as Aunt Julia, who was accustomed to having her path smoothed for her, had requested that hotel rooms fulfilling all her somewhat complicated requirements should be made ready for her arrival, a six-cylinder motor with balloon tires and an irreproachable chauffeur engaged to meet her at the station, and a doctor and a masseuse be found in attendance when she arrived—as a result of which precautions she hoped, after an interval of repose, to be well enough to occupy herself with her niece's plans.

Boyne gasped. "Good Lord—what that cable must have cost her!"

"Oh, it's not the cost that ever bothers Aunt Julia," said Aunt Julia's niece with a certain deference.

Boyne laughed, and agreed that Mrs. Sellars could not prudently refuse such a summons. Somehow it no longer offended him that she should obey it from motives so obviously interested. He could not have said why, but it now seemed to him natural enough that she should hold herself at the disposal of a rich old aunt. He wondered whether it was because her departure would serve to relieve a passing tension; but he dismissed this as a bit of idle casuistry. "The point is that she's going—and that she and I will probably be awfully glad to see each other when she gets back."

Mrs. Sellars cast a wistful look about her. After a pause she said: "You don't know how I hate to think that our good evenings in this dear little room are so nearly over," in a tone suggesting that she had rather expected Boyne to say it for her, and that he had somehow missed a cue.

"But why over? Not for more than a week, I hope?

You're not going to let yourself be permanently annexed by Aunt Julia?"

She smiled a little perplexedly: evidently other plans were in her mind, plans she had pictured him as instinctively divining. "Not permanently; but I don't quite know when I shall be able to leave her—"

"Oh, I say, my dear!"

The perplexity lifted from her smile: it seemed to reach out to him like a promise. "But then I expect you to join me very soon. As soon as Aunt Julia's blood-pressure has been taken, and the doctor and the masseuse and the chauffeur have been tested and passed upon."

Boyne listened in astonishment. It had never seriously occurred to him that he was to be involved in the ceremony of establishing Aunt Julia on European soil. "Oh, but look here—what earthly use should I be? Why should I be butchered to make Aunt Julia's holiday?"

"You won't be. It will be—almost the other way round. I'm going to do everything I possibly can for Aunt Julia; everything to start her successfully on her European adventure. And then I'm going to present the bill."

"The bill?"

She nodded gaily. "You're the bill. I'm going to present you, and say: 'Now you've seen him, can you wonder that I mean to marry him at once, whether you like it or not?' "

The words fell on a silence which Boyne, for the moment, found it impossible to break. Mrs. Sellars stood by her writing-table, her slender body leaning to him, her face lit with one of those gleams of lost youth which he had once found so exquisite and poignant. He found it so now, but with another poignancy.

"You mean—you mean—you've changed your mind about the date?" He broke off, the words "of our marriage" choking on his lips. Through a mist of bewilderment he saw the tender mockery of her smile, and knew how much courage it disguised. ("I stand here like a stock—what a brute she'll think me!")

"Did you imagine I was one of the dreadful women who never change their minds?" She came close, clasped her hands about his arm, lifted her delicate face, still alight with expectation. The face said: "Here I am: to be cherished or shattered—" and he thought again of the glittering fragments he had seen at his feet the night before. He detached her hands, and lifted them, one after another, to his kiss. If only some word—if only the right word—would come to him!

"Martin—don't you *want* me to change my mind?" she suddenly challenged him. He held her hands against his breast, caressing them.

"Dear, first of all, I don't want to be the cause of you doing anything that might offend your aunt . . . that might interfere . . . in any way . . . with her views. . ." No; he couldn't go on; the words strangled him. He was too sure that she was aware they did not express what he was thinking, were spoken only to gain time.

But with a gentle tenacity she pursued: "It's awfully generous of you to think of that. But don't you suppose, dear, I've been miserable at asking you to linger on here when I've always known that what you wanted was to be married at once, and get back to work? I've been imprisoned in my past—I see it now; I had become the slave of all those years of conformity you used to reproach me with. For a long time I couldn't get out of their shadow. But you've opened my eyes—you've set me free. How monstrous to have waited so long for happiness, and then to be afraid to seize it when it comes!" Her arms stole up and drew him. "I'm not afraid now, Martin. You've taught me not to be. Henceforth I mean to think of you first, not of Aunt Julia. I mean to marry you as soon as it can be done. I don't suppose the formalities take very long in Paris, do they? Then, as soon as we're married, we'll sail for home."

He listened in a kind of stupor, saying inwardly: "It's not that I love her less; it can't be that I love her less. It's only that everything that happens between us always seems to happen at the wrong time."

The silence prolonged itself, on her side stretched and straining, on his built up like a wall, opaque, impenetrable. From beyond it came her little far-off laugh. "Dear, I'm utterly in your hands, you see!"

Evidently there had to be an answer to that. "Rose—" he began. Pretty as her name was, he hardly ever called her by it; he had always felt her too close to him to need a name. She looked up in surprise.

He made a fresh start. "But you see, darling, how things are—"

A little tremor ran across her face. "What things?"

"You know that, after you'd refused to consider the possibility of our getting married at once, I pledged myself. . ."

The tremor ceased, and her face once more became smooth and impenetrable. He found himself repeating to vacancy: "I pledged myself. . ."

She drew quietly away, and sat down at a little distance from him. "You're talking about your odd experiment with the Wheater children?"

"It's more than an experiment. When I saw the parents in Venice I told them, as you know, that I'd be responsible for the welfare of the children as long as they were left with me."

"As long as they were left with you! For life, perhaps, then?" She leaned forward, her face drawn with the valiant effort of her smile. "Martin! Is all this serious? It can't be! You can't really be asking me to understand that all our plans—our whole future, yours and mine—are to depend, for an indefinite length of time, on the whim of two or three chance acquaintances of yours who are too heartless and self-engrossed to look after their own children!"

Boyne paused a moment; then he said: "We had no plans—I mean, no immediate plans—when I entered into the arrangement. It was by your own choice that—"

"My own choice! Well, then, my own choice, now, is that we should have plans, immediately." She stood up, trembling a little. She was very pale, and her thin eyebrows drew a straight black bar across her forehead. "Martin—I ask you to come with me at once to Paris."

"At once? But just now you said in a week or two—"

"And now I say at once: to-morrow."

He stood leaning against the chimney, as far from her as the little room allowed. A tide of resistance rose in him. "I can't come to-morrow."

He was conscious that she was making an intense effort to steady her quivering nerves. "Martin . . . I don't want to be unreasonable. . ."

"You're never unreasonable," he said patiently.

"You mean it might have been better if I were!" she flashed back, crimsoning.

"Don't be—now," he pleaded.

"No." She paused. "Very well. Come to Paris in a few days, then."

"Look here, dear—all this is of no use. No earthly use. I can't come in a few days, any more than I can come to-morrow. I can't desert these children till their future is settled in one way or another. I've said I'd stick to them, and I mean to. If I turned my back on them now they'd lose their last chance of being able to stay together."

She received this with bent head and hands clasped stiffly across her knee; but suddenly her self-control broke down. "But, Martin, are you mad? What business is it of yours, anyhow, what becomes of these children?"

"I don't know," he said simply.

"You don't know—you don't know?"

"No; I only feel it's got to be. I'm pledged. I can't get round it."

"You can't get round it because you don't want to. You're pledged because you want to be. You want to be because Mr. Dobree was right . . . because. . ."

"Rose, take care," he interrupted, very low.

"Take care? At this hour? Of what? For whom? All I care for is to know the truth. . ."

"I'm telling you the truth."

"You may think you are. But the truth is something very different—something you're not conscious of yourself, perhaps . . . not clearly. . ."

"I believe I'm telling you the whole truth."

"That when I ask you to choose between me and the Wheater children, you choose the Wheater children—out of philanthropy?"

"I didn't say out of philanthropy. I said I didn't know. . ."

"If you don't know, I do. You're in love with Judith Wheater, and you're trying to persuade yourself that you're still in love with me."

He lifted his hands to his face, and covered his eyes, as if from some intolerable vision she had summoned to them. "Don't Rose, for the Lord's sake. . . Don't let's say stupid things—"

"But, dear, I must." She got up and came close to him again; he felt her hands on his arm. "Listen, Martin. I love you too much not to want to help you. Try to feel that about me, won't you? Then everything will be so much easier."

"Yes."

"Try to understand your own feelings—that's the best way of sparing mine. I want the truth, that's all. Try to see the truth, and face it with me—it's all I ask."

He dropped his hands, and turned his discouraged eyes on her. But he could only feel that he and she were farther apart than when he had last looked at her; all the rest was confusion and obscurity.

"I don't know what the truth, as you call it, is; I swear I don't; but I know it's not what you think. Judith's as much a child to me as the others—that I swear to you."

"Then, dear—"

"Then, I've got to stick to them all the same," he repeated doggedly.

For a time the two continued to stand in silence, with eyes averted, like people straining to catch some far-off sound which will signal relief from a pressing peril. Then, slowly, Boyne turned to Mrs. Sellars. His eyes rested on her profile, so thin, drawn, bloodless, that a fresh pang shot through him. He had often mocked at himself as a man who, in spite of all his wanderings, had never had a real adventure; but now he saw that he himself had been one, had been Rose Sellars's Great Adventure, the risk and the enchantment of her life. While she had continued, during the weary years of her marriage, to be blameless, exemplary, patient and heroically gay, the thought of Boyne was storing up treasures for her which she would one day put out her hand and take—no matter how long she might have to wait. Her patience, Boyne knew, was endless—it was as long as her hair. She had trained herself to go on waiting for happiness, day after day, month after month, year after year, with the same air of bright unruffled vigilance, like a tireless animal waiting for its prey. One day her prey, her happiness, would appear, and she would snap it up; and on that day there would be no escape from her. . .

It was terrible, it was hideous, to be picturing her distress as something grasping and predatory; it was more painful still to be entering so acutely into her feelings while a central numbness paralysed his own. All around this numbness there was a great margin of pity and of comprehension; but he knew this was not the region by way of which he could reach her. She who had always lived the life of reason would never forgive him if he called upon her reason now. . .

"Rose—" he appealed to her.

She turned and he saw her face, composed, remodelled, suffused with a brilliancy like winter starlight. Her lips formed a smiling: "Dear?"

"Rose—"

She took his hand with the lightest pressure. "Dearest,

what utter nonsense we've both been talking! Of course I don't mean that you're to desert the Wheater children for me—and of course you don't mean that you're to desert me for them; do you? I believe I understand all you feel; all your fondness for the poor little things. I should shiver at you if you hadn't grown to love them! But you and I have managed to get each other all on edge, I don't know how. Don't you feel what a mistake it would be to go in and out of this question any longer? I have an idea I could find a solution almost at once, if only I weren't trying to so hard. And so could you, no doubt." She paused, a little breathlessly, and then resumed her eager monologue. "Let's say goodbye till to-morrow, shall we?—and produce our respective plans of action when we meet again. And don't forget that the problem may solve itself without regard to us, and at any minute."

She had caught at the last splinter of the rock of Reason still visible above the flood; and there she clung, dauntless, unbeaten, uttering the right, the impartial word with lips that pined and withered for his kiss. . .

"Oh, my dear," he murmured.

"To-morrow?"

"Yes—to-morrow."

Before he could take her in his arms she had slipped out of reach, and softly, adroitly closed the door on him. Alone on the landing he was left with the sense that that deft gesture had shut him up with her forever.

XXIII

IT was growing more and more evident to Boyne that he could recover his old vision of Mrs. Sellars only when they were apart. He began to think this must be due to his having loved her so long from a distance, having somehow, in consequence of their separation, established with her an ideal relation to which her slightest misapprehension, her least failure to say just what he expected, was a recurring menace.

At first the surprise of finding her, after his long absence, so much younger and more vivid than his remembrance, the glow of long-imagined caresses, the whole enchanting harmony of her presence, had hushed the inner discord. But though she was dearer to him than ever, all free communication seemed to have ceased between them—he could regain it only during those imaginary conversations in which it was he who sustained both sides of the dialogue.

This was what happened when he had walked off the pain and bewilderment of their last talk. For two hours he tramped the heights, unhappy, confused, struggling between the sense of her unreasonableness and of his own predicament; then gradually there stole back on him the serenity always associated with the silent sessions of his thought and hers. On what seemed to him the fundamental issues—questions of fairness, kindness, human charity in the widest meaning—when had she ever failed him in these wordless talks? His position with regard to the Wheater children (hadn't he admitted it to her?) was unreasonable, indefensible, was whatever else she chose to call it; yes, but it was also human, and that would touch her in the end. He had no doubt that when they met the next day she would have her little solution ready, and be prepared to smile with him over their needless perturbation.

The thought of her deep submissive passion, which contrasted so sharply with his own uneasy self-assertiveness, was the only anxiety that remained with him. He knew now how much she loved him—but did he know how much he loved her? Supposing, for instance, that on getting back to his hotel, now, this very evening, he should find a line telling him that she had decided for both their sakes to break their engagement: well, could he honestly say that it would darken earth and heaven for him? Mortified, hurt, at a loose end—all this he would be; already the tender flesh of his vanity was shrinking, and under it he felt the thrust of wounded affection. But that was all—in the balance how little!

He got back late to the hotel, and walked unheedingly past the letter-rack toward which, at that hour, it was usual to glance for the evening mail. The porter called to him, waving a letter. The envelope bore the New York post-mark, and in the upper corner Boyne recognised the name of the big firm of contracting engineers to whom he had owed some of his most important jobs. They still wrote now and then to consult him: no doubt this letter, which had been forwarded by his London bankers, was of that nature. He pushed it into his pocket, deciding to read it after he had dined. And then he proceeded to dine, alone in a corner of the unfashionable restaurant of his hotel, of which the tables with their thick crockery and clumsy water-carafes seemed like homely fragments of a recently-disjoined *table d'hôte*, the long old-fashioned hotel table at which travellers used to be seated in his parents' day. A coarse roll lay by his plate, the table bore a bunch of half-faded purply-pink cosmos in an opaque blue vase: everything about him was ugly and impersonal, yet he hugged himself for not being at the *châlet* table, with its air of exquisite rusticity, its bowl of cunningly-disposed wild flowers, the shaded candles, the amusing food. Yes; and he was glad, too, not to be sharing the little Wheaters' pudding at the *Pension Rosenglüh;* he was suddenly aware of an intense unexpected satisfaction in being for once alone, his own master, with no one that he need be on his guard against or at his best before; no one to be tormented or enchanted by, no one to listen to and answer. "Decidedly, I'm a savage," he thought, emptying his plateful of savourless soup with an appetite he was almost ashamed of. The moral of it, obviously, was that he had been idle too long, that what he was thirsting for at this very moment was not more rest but more work, and that the idea of giving up his life of rough and toilsome activity for the security of an office in New York, as he had aspired to do a few short months ago, now seemed intolerable. Too old for the fatigue and hardships of an engineer's life? Why, it was the fatigues and the hardships which, physically speaking, had given the work its zest, just as the delicate mathematical calculations had provided its intellectual stimulus. The combination of two such sources of interest, so rare in other professions, was apparently what he needed to keep him straight, curb his excitable imagination, discipline his nerves, and make him wake up every morning to a steady imperturbable view of life. After dinner, sitting in the dreary little lounge, as he lit his pipe and pulled the letter from his pocket he thought: "I wish to God it was an order to start for Tierra del Fuego!"

It was nothing of the sort, of course: merely an inquiry for the address of a young engineer who had been Boyne's assistant a few years earlier, and whom the firm in question had lost sight of. They had been struck with Boyne's estimate of the young man's ability, and thought they might have an interesting piece of work for him, if he happened to be available, and was not scared by hardships and responsibility. Boyne put the letter into his pocket, leaned back in his chair, and thought: "God! I wish I was his age and just starting—for anywhere."

His mind turned round and round this thought for the rest of the evening. Perhaps he could make Mrs. Sellars understand that, after all, he had made a mistake in supposing he had reached the age for sedentary labours. Once they were married she would surely see that, for his soul's sake, and until the remainder of his youth was used up, she must let him go off on these remote exciting expeditions which seemed the only cure for—for what? Well, for the creeping grayness of age, no doubt. The fear of that must be what ailed him. At any rate he must get away; he must. As soon as the fate of the little Wheaters was decided, and he and Rose were married, and he had established her in New York, he must get back into the glorious soul-releasing world of girders and abutments, of working stresses, curvatures and grades.

She had talked of having her little plan ready for him the next day. Well, he would have one for her, at any rate; this big comprehensive one. First, the Wheater tribe transplanted (he didn't yet see how) to the safe shelter of Grandma Mervin's wing; then his own marriage; then—flight! He worked himself into a glow of eloquence, as he always did in these one-sided talks, which never failed to end in convincing Mrs. Sellars because he unconsciously eliminated from them all the objections she might possibly have raised. . . He went to bed with a sense of fresh air in his soul, as if the mere vision of escape had freed him. . .

Mrs. Sellars had not said at what hour she expected him the next day; so he decided to wait till lunch, and drop in on her then, as his habit was when they had no particular expedition in view. In the morning he usually strolled down to see how the *Rosenglüh* refugees were getting on; but on this occasion he left them to themselves, and did not go out till he made for the *châlet*. As he approached it he was startled by a queer sense of something impending. Oh, not another "scene"; Rose was much too intelligent for that. What he felt was just an uneasy qualm, as if the new air in his soul's lungs were being gradually pumped out of them again. He glanced up at the balcony, lifting his hand to signal to her; but she was not there. He pushed open the hall door and ran up the short flight of stairs. The little sitting-room was empty: it looked speckless and orderly as a tomb. He noticed at once that the littered writing-table was swept and garnished, and that no scent of viands greeted him through the dining-room door.

She had gone—he became suddenly sure that she had gone. But why? But when? Above all, why without a word? It was so unlike her to do anything abrupt and unaccountable that his vague sense of apprehension returned.

He sat down in the armchair he always occupied, as if the familiar act must re-evoke her, call her back into the seat opposite, in the spirit if not in the flesh. But the room remained disconcertingly, remained even spiritually empty. He had the sense that she had gone indeed, and had taken her soul with her; and the discovery made a queer unexpected void in him. "This is—absurd!" he heard himself exclaiming.

"Rose!" he called out; there was no answer. He stood up, and his wandering eye travelled from the table to the mantelpiece. On its shelf he saw a letter addressed to himself. He seized it and tore it open; and all at once the accents of the writer's reasonableness floated out into the jangled air of the little room.

"Dearest—After you left yesterday I had a radio from Aunt Julia, asking me to get to Paris as soon as I could, so I decided to motor over to Padua this morning, and catch the Orient Express. And I mean to slip off like this, without seeing you, or even letting you know that I'm going, because, on second thoughts, I believe my little plan (you know I promised you one) will be all the better for a day or two more of quiet thought; so I'll simply write it to you from Paris instead of talking it to you hurriedly this morning.

"Besides (I'll confess) I want to keep the picture of our happiness here intact, not frayed and rubbed by more discussion, even the friendliest. You'll understand, I know. This being together has been something so complete, so exquisite, that I want to carry it away with me in its perfection. . . I'll write in a few days. Till then, if you can, think of me as I think of you. No heart could ask more of another. Rose."

He sat down again, and read the letter over two or three times. It was sweet and reasonable—but it was also desperately sad. Yes; she had understood that for a time it was best for both that they should be apart. And this was her way of putting it to him. His eyes filled, and he wondered how he could have thought, the night before, that if he suddenly heard she was leaving it would be a relief. . .

But presently he began to visualise what the day would have been if he had found her there, and they had now been sitting over the lunch-table, "fraying and rubbing" their happiness, as she had put it, by more discussion—useless discussion. How intelligent of her to go—how merciful! Yes; he would think of her as she thought of him; he could now, without a shadow of reserve. He would bless her in all honesty for this respite. . .

He took a fading mountain-pink from one of the vases on the mantelpiece, put it in his pocket-book with her letter, and started to walk down to the village to send her a telegram. As he walked, he composed it, affectionately, lingeringly. He moved fast through the brisk air, and by the time he had reached the foot of the hill a pang of wholesome hunger reminded him that he had not lunched. Straight ahead, the *Pension Rosenglüh* lay in his path, and he knew that, even if the little Wheaters had finished their midday meal, Miss Scope would persuade the cook to conjure up an omelette for him. . .

Instantly he felt a sort of boyish excitement at the idea of surprising the party; and finding the front door unlatched, he crossed the hall and entered the private dining-room which had been assigned to them since the arrival of adult boarders less partial than himself to what Judith called the children's "dinner-roar."

His appearance was welcomed with a vocal vigour which must have made the crockery dance even in the grown-up *Speise-saal* across the hall. "Have the wild animals left a morsel for me?" he asked, and gaily wedged himself in between Judith and Blanca.

XXIV

UNINTERRUPTED communion with the little Wheaters always gave Boyne the same feeling of liberation. It was like getting back from a constrained bodily position into a natural one. This sense of being himself, being simply and utterly at his ease, which the children's companionship had given him during the Mediterranean voyage, but which he had enjoyed only in uncertain snatches since their arrival at Cortina, came back to him as soon as he had slipped his chair between Judith's and Blanca's at the lunch-table. He would not ascribe it to her having gone, but preferred to think it was because her going left him free to dispose of himself as he chose. And what he chose was, on the spot, to resume his half-fatherly attitude toward the group, and devote every moment of his time to them.

Being with them again was like getting home after a long and precarious journey during which he had been without news of the people he loved. A great many things must have happened in the interval, and not a moment must be lost in gathering up the threads. There were, in fact, many threads to be gathered. He got a general outline of the situation that very evening from Miss Scope—learned that Terry's health was steadily improving, that the young Swiss tutor whom Boyne had unearthed at Botzen was conscientious and kind, and got on well with Terry, but found Bun hopelessly unmanageable ("And nothing new in that," Miss Scope commented); that on the whole the three little girls, Blanca, Zinnie and Beechy, though trying at times, were behaving better than could have been hoped, considering the unusual length of their holiday; and lastly that Chipstone, even in the process of cutting a new tooth, retained his rosy serenity, and had added a pound or more to his weight.

All this was as absorbing to Boyne as if every one concerned had been of the highest interest and consequence. He had a long talk with the tutor, went carefully into the question of Terry's studies, suggested a few changes, and encouraged and counselled the young man. As to luring or coercing Bun up the steep way of knowledge, a stronger hand would be needed; and while Bun ranged unchecked there was not much to be done with the little girls. Even Blanca, though she felt herself so superior in age and culture, found the company of her juniors tolerable, and their bad example irresistible, when there was nothing better going. But, as against these drawbacks, there was the happy fact that the high air, which had done all the children good, had transformed Terry from a partial invalid into a joyous active boy who laughed at temperatures and clamoured for second helpings. And so far the Lido had refrained from interfering. On the whole, therefore, as the weeks passed, Boyne had more and more reason to be satisfied with his achievement. To give the children a couple of months of security, with the growing hope of keeping them all together under old Mrs. Mervin's roof, had assuredly been worth trying for. The evening after Mrs. Sellars's departure he wrote a long letter to Grandma Mervin.

Boyne, once more alone with the children, found that

his confused feeling about Judith had given way to the frank elder-brotherly affection he had felt for her on the cruise. Perhaps because she herself had become natural and simple, now that there were no older people to put her on the defensive, she seemed again the buoyant child who had first captivated him. Or perhaps his thinking so was just a part of his satisfaction at being with his flock again, unobserved and uncriticised by the grown up. He and they understood each other; he suspected that, even had their plight not roused his pity, his own restlessness and impulsiveness would have fraternized with theirs. "The fact is, we're none of us grown up," he reflected, hugging himself for being on the children's side of the eternal barrier.

His talks with Judith turned, as usual, on the future of the children. He sometimes tried to draw from her the expression of a personal preference; but she seemed to want nothing for herself; she could not detach herself, even in imagination, from the others. For them she had fabulous dreams and ambitions. If only they could keep together till they were grown up! She had a quaint vision of their all living in a house somewhere in the country (perhaps her father would buy them one when she came of age); a house which should be always full of pets and birds; and leading there a life in which the amusements of the nursery were delightfully combined with grown up pursuits. And for each of the children she had thought out a definite career. Blanca, of course, was to be "lovely": to Judith loveliness was a vocation. Terry was to be a great scholar, the guide and counsellor of the others—she had a savage reverence for the wisdom and authority to be acquired from books. Bun was manifestly meant to drive racing-motors, and carry off championships in games and athletics; Beechy would marry and have heaps of children, yet somehow be always able to look after Bun; and Zinnie—well, Zinnie was undoubtedly predestined to be "clever"; a fate of dubious import. But Judith hoped it would not be with the sharp cunning of little Pixie Lullmer, who seemed so childish and simple, and was really an abyss of precocious knowledge, initiated into all the secrets of hotel life; a toad of a child, Judith summed it up, whereas her poor half-sister, Doll Westway, had hated it all so much that she had taken the shortest way out by shooting herself. . .

Ah—and Chipstone! Well, there was no hurry about Chipstone, was there? But he was so large and calm, and so certain to get what he wanted, that Judith thought perhaps he would be a banker—and own a big yacht, and take them all on wonderful cruises. And Nanny and Susan would of course always stay with them, to look after Beechy's children. . .

Boyne had decided to write to old Mrs. Mervin without mentioning the fact to Judith. He had meant to consult her, had even intended to have a talk with her on the day when Mrs. Sellars's abrupt departure had momentarily unsettled his plans; but when the idea recurred to him Judith was already re-established in his mind as the blithe creature of their first encounter, and he had a superstitious dread of doing anything to change the harmony of their relation. After all, he could plead the children's cause with their grandmother as well as Judith could; and if his appeal were doomed to failure she need never know it had been made. He found himself insisting rather elaborately, in his own mind, on the childishness he was fond of ascribing to her when he talked of her to others; and now he feared lest anything should break through that necessary illusion. In his letter to Mrs. Mervin he tried to combine the maximum of conciseness and of eloquence, and ended by reminding her that the various parents might intervene at any moment, and begging her to cable at once if, as he earnestly hoped, she could give her assent to the plan. The sending off of the letter was like handing in an essay at school; with its completion he seemed entering with the children on a new holiday. "Two or three weeks' respite, anyhow; and then," he thought, "who knows? I may be able to carry them all back to New York with me." Incredible as it was, he clung to the hope with a faith as childish as Judith's.

Mrs. Sellars had said that she would write in a few days. Instead, she telegraphed to announce her arrival in Paris, and again, a little later, to inform Boyne of Aunt Julia's. To each message she added a few words of tender greeting; but ten days or more elapsed before the telegrams were followed by a letter.

Boyne found it one evening, on his return from a long expedition with the children. He had ceased, after a day or two, to speculate on Mrs. Sellars's silence, had gradually, as the days passed, become unconscious of their flight, and was almost surprised, when he saw her handwriting, that a letter from Paris should have reached Cortina so quickly. He waited till after dinner to read it, secretly wishing to keep the flavour of the present on his lips. Then, when the task could no longer be postponed, he withdrew to the melancholy lounge, and settled himself in the same slippery chair in which he had sat when he read the letter of the engineers asking if he could trace the whereabouts of the young man to whom they wanted to offer a job. "It's to say she's coming back," he muttered to himself as he broke the seal. But Mrs. Sellars did not say that.

The letter was one of her best—tender, gay and amusing. The description of Aunt Julia's arrival was a little masterpiece. The writer dwelt at length on the arts she had exercised—was still exercising—to persuade the family tyrant that he, Boyne, was justified in wishing for an immediate marriage, and she added, on a note of modest triumph, that success was already in sight. "But even if it were not, dear," the letter pursued, "I shouldn't allow that to alter my plans—our plans—and I'm prepared to have you carry me off under Aunt Julia's nose (formidable though that feature is), if she should refuse her sanction. But she won't; and the important question is what we intend to do, and not what she may think about it."

At this stage Boyne laid the letter aside, took out a cigar, cut it, and put it down without remembering to light it. He took up the letter again.

"But it's more important still that we should come to a clear understanding about our future—isn't it, dearest? I feel that I made such an understanding impossible the other day by my unreasonableness, my impatience, my apparent inability to see your point of view. But I did see it, even then; and I see it much more clearly now that I have studied the question at a sufficient distance to focus it properly. Of course we both know that, whatever decision we reach, some of the numerous papas and mammas of your little friends may upset it at a moment's notice; but meanwhile I have a plan to propose. What you want—isn't it?—is to guard these poor children as long as possible from the unsettling and demoralising influence of continual change. I quite see your idea; and it seems to me that those most exposed to such risks are the ones we ought to try to help. By your own showing, Mr. Wheater will never give up Chipstone for long; Zinnie, and Prince Buondelmonte's funny little pair, are bound to be claimed by their respective parents now that they have settled down to wealth and domesticity. As for the enchanting Judith, though you persist in not seeing it, she will be grown up and married in a year or two; and meanwhile, if the Wheaters do divorce, she will probably choose to remain with her mother, as she did before. The twins, in fact, seem to me the chief victims. They are old enough to understand what is going on, and not old enough to make themselves lives of their own; and above all they are at an age when disintegrating influences are likely to do the most harm. You have often told me that poor Terry's health has been an obstacle between him and his father (what a horrible idea that it should be so!), and that the bouncing Chip has cut him out. Terry needs care and sympathy more than any of them; and I am sure you will feel, as I do, that it would be unthinkable to separate dear little Blanca from the brother she adores. What I propose, then, is that you should ask Mr. and Mrs. Wheater to give up the twins—regarding us in any capacity you like, either as their friends, or as their legal guardians, if that is better—till they come of age. I will gladly take a share in looking after them, and I believe that between us we can turn them into happy useful members of society. If you agree, I am ready to—"

Boyne stopped reading, folded up the letter and thrust it into his pocket. There rushed over him a wave of disappointment and disgust. "Dear little Blanca indeed!" he muttered furiously. "Useful members of society!" That Mrs. Sellars should calmly propose to separate the children was bad enough; but that, of the lot, she should choose to foist on him the only one he could feel no affection for, and hardly any interest in—that to the woman he was going to marry Blanca should alone seem worthy of compassion among the four little girls who had been cast upon his mercy, this was to Boyne hatefully significant of the side of Mrs. Sellars's character to which, from the moment of their reunion, he had been trying to close his eyes. "She chooses her because she knows she need never be jealous of her," was his inmost thought.

Well, and supposing it were so—how womanly, how human, after all! Loving Boyne as she did, was it not natural that she should prefer to have under her roof the two children least likely to come between herself and him, to interfere in any way with their happiness? Yes—but was that loving him at all? If she had really loved him would she not have entered into his feeling about the little group, and recognised the cruelty of separating them? He paused a moment over this, and tried conscientiously to imagine what, in a similar case, his love for her would have inspired him to do. Would it, for instance, ever induce him to live with Aunt Julia as a dependent nephew-in-law? A million times no! But why propound such useless riddles? No one could pretend that the cases were similar. Rose Sellars would simply be asking him to gratify a whim; what he was asking of her was vital, inevitable. She knew that it lay with him, and with no one else, to save these children; she knew that, little by little, his whole heart had gone into the task. Yet coolly, deliberately, with that infernal air she had of thinking away whatever it was inconvenient to admit, she had affected to sympathise with his purpose while in reality her proposal ignored it. Send back the younger children to their parents—to such parents as Zinnia Lacrosse and Buondelmonte!—return Judith to her mother, to a mother about to marry Gerald Ormerod, who, by Judith's own showing, would have preferred herself? Boyne recoiled from the thought as from the sight of some physical cruelty he could not prevent. He got up, threw away his cigar, and went out hatless, indignant, into the night.

The air was warm, the sky full of clouds tunnelled by shifting vistas of a remote blue sprinkled with stars. Boyne groped his way down the obscure wood-path from his hotel, and walked across the fields to the slopes which Judith and he had climbed on the day of his return from the Lido. It was from that day—he recalled it now—that Rose Sellars's jealousy of Judith had dated; he had seen it flash across her fixed attentive face when, the next morning, Judith had blurted out an allusion to their ramble. Boyne—he also remembered—had given Mrs. Sellars to understand that on that occasion he had gone off for a walk by himself, "to get the Lido out of his lungs"; very likely his prevarication had first excited her suspicion. For why should he dissemble the fact that he had been with Judith, if Judith was only a child to him, as he said? Why indeed? It seemed as though, in concealing so significant a fact, he had simply, unconsciously, been on his guard against this long-suspected jealousy; as if he had always guessed that the most passionate and irrational of sentiments lurked under Mrs. Sellars's calm and reasonable exterior. If it were so, it certainly made her more interesting—but also less easy to deal with.

For jealousy, to excite sympathy, must be felt by some one who also inspires it. Shared, it was a part of love; unshared, it made love impossible. And Boyne, in his fatuous security, could not imagine feeling jealous of Mrs. Sellars. "Though of course I should hate it like anything, I suppose. . ." But the problem was one that he could only apprehend intellectually.

He tramped on through the summer night, his mind full of tormented thoughts; and as he groped upward among the pines he remembered that other night, not many weeks since, when he had climbed the same path, and his feet had seemed winged, and the air elixir, because a girl's shoulder brushed his own, and he listened to unpremeditated laughter.

It was so late when he got back to the hotel that the porter, unwillingly roused, looked at him with a sulky astonishment.

"There was a lady here—she left a parcel for you."

"A lady? Where's the parcel?"

"Up in your room. I had to help her to carry it up. It was awkward getting it round the turn of the stairs. She left a letter for you too."

Awkward round the turn of the stairs? What on earth could the object be, and who the lady? Boyne, without farther questions, sprang up to his room. Rose had come back—there could be no doubt of it. She had decided, adroitly enough, to follow up her letter by the persuasion of her presence. At the thought he felt flurried, unsettled, as if she had come too soon, before he had set his mind in order to receive her.

And what could she possibly have brought him that had to be manœuvred up the hotel stairs? Whatever it was, he could not, try as he would, figure her labouring up to his room with it, even with the assistance of the porter. Why, she had never even been to his room, the room with every chair and table of which Judith and the other childred were so carelessly familiar! It was utterly unlike Rose—and yet Rose of course it must be. . .

He flung open his door, and saw a large shrouded object in the middle of the floor; an object of odd uncertain shape, imperfectly wrapped in torn newspapers tied with string. The wrappings yielded to a pull, and an ancient walnut cradle with primitive carven ornaments revealed itself to his petrified gaze. A cradle! He threw himself into a chair and stared at it incredulously, as if he knew it must be an hallucination. At length he remembered the porter's having mentioned a letter, and his glance strayed to his chest of drawers. There, perched on the pincushion, was an envelope addressed in a precise familiar hand—the hand of Terry Wheater, always the scribe of the other children when their letters were to be subjected to grown up criticism. Boyne tore the envelope open and read:

"Darling Martin,

"We are all of us sending you this lovely cradle for your wedding present because we suppose you are going to be married very soon, as we think Mrs. Sellars has gone to Paris to order her trousseau. And because you have been like a father to us we hope and pray you will soon be a real father to a lot of lovely little children of your own, and they will all sleep in this cradle, and then you will think of

Your loving Judith, Terry, Blanca—"

Under the last of the rudimentary signatures, Chipstone had scrawled his mark; and below it was a scribbled postscript from Judith: "Darling, I open this while Terry's not looking to say he said we oughternt to call the craidle lovely, but it is lovely and we wanted you to know it was. Judith."

In the midnight silence Boyne sat and laughed and laughed until a nervous spinster in the next room banged on the wall and called out venomously: "I can hear every word you're both saying."

BOOK IV

XXV

BOYNE had been wrong in imagining that Mrs. Sellars might come back unannounced to assure herself of the effect of her letter. She did not do so; and after two days he decided that he could no longer put off sending some kind of answer.

Only, what could he say?

Being with the children all day and every day, sharing their meals, their games and scrambles, had gradually detached his thoughts from Mrs. Sellars, reducing her once more to the lovely shadow she had so long been; with the difference that she was now a shadow irrevocably, whereas before he had always believed she might become substantial. Finally he girt himself to the task; and at once his irritation, his impatience, seemed to materialise her again, as if she were fated to grow real only when she thwarted or opposed him. He wondered if that were another of the peculiarities of being in love. "People get too close to each other—they can't see each other for the nearness, I suppose," he reflected, not altogether satisfied with this explanation. He wrote: "And as to what you propose about the children, do please believe that I don't mean to be unreasonable—but, unless I'm a little mad, your suggestion apparently amounts to this: that I should shove them straight back into the hell I've temporarily got them out of. For them that hell, at least the worst of it, is being separated from each other; and you ask me to separate them, when to keep them together is the one thing that they and I have been fighting for. I make no comment on your proposal to hand over the younger ones to Lady Wrench and Buondelmonte; women like you are what they are at the price of not being able even to picture such people as those two. But I know what they are, and never, as long as I can help it, will I be a party to giving back into such hands these children who have trusted me. And when you say that Judith, thanks to whom the younger ones have developed a sense of solidarity and mutual trust in a world which is the very negation of such feelings—that Judith should be asked to see her work deliberately wrecked, and all the feelings she has cultivated in the others trampled on—" He broke off, flung down the pen, and sat hopelessly staring at what he had written. "Oh, hell—that's no use," he groaned.

The truth was that, even in his most rebellious moments, he could not trick himself into the idea that he had a grievance against Mrs. Sellars. In reality it was the other way round. When he had gone to Venice to negotiate with the Wheaters about the future of their mutinous family he had gone as an affianced man. In pledging himself to his strange guardianship he had virtually pledged Mrs. Sellars also, and without even making his promise depend on her consent. He had simply assumed that because she loved him she would approve of whatever he did, would accept any situation he chose to put her in. He had behaved, in short, like a romantic boy betrothed to a dreamer of his own age. All this was true, and it was true also that Mrs. Sellars had never reproached him with it. The sense of her magnanimity deprived his argument of all its force, and benumbed his angry pen. He pushed away the letter, pulled out another sheet, and scrawled on it: "Awfully sorry but cannot undo what I have done do try to understand me dearest."

Yes, a telegram was better: easier to write, at any rate. . . He tore up the letter, put on his hat, and walked down to the post-office with his message.

For its answer he had only twenty-four hours to wait; and when Mrs. Sellars's telegram came it merely said: "I do understand you letter follows. . ." Well, that was not unsatisfactory, as far as it went; but when two days more had elapsed, it was not a letter but a small registered packet which the postman put into Boyne's hands. Even in the act of signing the receipt, at his very first glance, he had guessed what the packet contained. He went up to his room, a little dizzy with the abruptness of the event, and angrily ripped off seal and string, revealing the morocco box he had expected to find there. For a minute or two he sat looking at the box, almost as unconscious of what he was feeling as a man in the first minute or two after being stabbed or shot. "So that's that," he said aloud. But what "that" was going to be he had as yet no notion. It was a wound, of course—but was it mortal? He didn't know. Suddenly, with a mumbled curse at his own plight, he snapped the box open and saw a thin slip of paper twisted about the sapphire ring. On the paper he read: "I shall always remember; I shall never resent; and that is why I want you to give this to some woman who can make you as happy as you have made me." He pitched the box and the paper aside, and hid his face in his hands. After all he must have loved her, he supposed—or at least the vision of her which their long separation had created. . .

He was roused by a knock, and looking up with dazed eyes saw Judith Wheater standing doubtfully on the threshold.

"Oh, Martin dear—were you asleep, or have you got one of those beastly headaches?" She came in and closed the door without waiting for his answer. "Have I disturbed you most awfully?" she questioned, passing her cool hand softly over his hair.

"Yes—no." He wondered whether her sharp eyes had already detected the open ring-box, and the paper signed with Rose's name. But to try to conceal them would only attract her attention. He put up his hand and pressed hers. "Yes—I believe I have got a beastly headache," he said.

"Then I'd better be off, perhaps?" she interrupted reluctantly. She was bending over him with the look she had when one of the children fell and scraped a knee, and Boyne could not help smiling up into her anxious eyes. "That depends on what you came for. What's up? Anything wrong at *Rosenglüh?*"

"Not particularly. But, you know, dear, we haven't seen you for two whole days. . ."

"You haven't?" In the struggle which had been going on in his mind since he had received Mrs. Sellars's letter he had completely forgotten the passage of time. "No more you have," he exclaimed. "I didn't realise I'd neglected you all so shamefully. Fact is, I've been tied up to a boring piece of business that I had to get off my chest. Sit down and have a cigarette." He fumbled for a box, and shoved it across the table to Judith, who had settled down comfortably into his only armchair. "Oh, Martin, how lovely to be here all alone with you!"

"Well, I don't believe you'll find me particularly good company," he rejoined, suddenly conscious of the ears of the acrimonious spinster next door, and wondering if he ought not to propose to Judith to finish her visit in the garden.

"Oh, yes, I shall, if you'll let me talk to you," she declared with her rich candour; and Boyne laughed in spite of himself.

"I've never been able to prevent your talking when you wanted to," he remarked, lighting a cigarette; and Judith thrust her thin shoulder-blades into the chair-back, crossed her legs, and sighed contentedly: "Few can."

"Well, then—what's your news?"

"A letter from mother, this morning."

The laugh died on Boyne's lips. The expected menace —here it was! He knew Joyce never wrote unless she had news of overwhelming importance, and usually of a disagreeable nature, to impart. "What does she say?" he asked apprehensively.

"Not much. I can't quite make out. She just says she's given up Gerald, and that she realises for the first time what a rotten rubbishy life she's been leading, and wants us all to forgive her for it."

"She *does?* But then—?"

Judith shrugged away his anticipations with a faint smile. "Oh, that's not particularly new. Mother always realises about the rottenness of her life when she's going to make a change."

"A change? What sort of a change?"

"Getting engaged to somebody else, generally."

"Oh, come, my dear! Why shouldn't it mean, this time, just what I've always hoped: that your father and mother see they can't get on without you—all of you—and that they're going to patch it up for good and all?"

Judith scanned him half-humorously through the veil

of her cigarette-smoke. "Like in the nicer kind of movies?"

"You young sceptic, you! Why not? Your mother's too intelligent not to be fed up with jazz some day—"

"That's what she says. She says she's met somebody who's opened her eyes to how wrong it all is—and that always means she's going to get engaged again." Boyne was silent, and Judith added: "Anyhow, she's leaving at once for Paris to start divorce proceedings, because she says it's too wicked to live any longer with a man like father."

The load dropped from Boyne's heart. If Mrs. Wheater was leaving for Paris without suggesting that the children should join her, it was at least a respite—how long a one he couldn't guess, but at any rate enough to provide an excuse for deferring action. That was as far as his hopes dared venture. But he met Judith's eyes, and was surprised at their untroubled serenity. "Aren't you afraid—?" he began; and she rejoined immediately: "With you here? Why should we be?"

Immediately the sense of his responsibility descended on him with a redoubled weight. To have taken the risks he had for these children was mad enough; but to find that his doing so had deified him in their imagination, made them regard him as a sort of human sanctuary, turned his apprehensions to dismay.

"But, my child—look here. We've been awfully lucky so far; but we mustn't forget that, any day, this arrangement of ours may go to smash. How can I prevent it?"

She gave him all her confidence in a radiant look. "You have till now, haven't you? And if there's another row, couldn't we all nip over quietly to America with you?" She paused, and then began again, with a shade of hesitation that was new in her: "I suppose you'll be married very soon now, won't you, Martin? And when I got mother's letter this morning we wondered—Terry and I wondered—whether, if Grandma Mervin is afraid to take us in, we couldn't all go and live with you in New York, if we children paid a part of the rent? You see, father and mother couldn't possibly object to that, and I know you and Mrs. Sellars are fond of Chip and the steps, and we big ones really wouldn't be any trouble. Scopy and I have saved up such a lot out of father's allowance that I daresay you could afford to take a biggish house; and we'd all be awfully decent in the morning about not keeping the bath a minute longer than we had a right to."

The abruptness of Judith's transitions from embittered shrewdness to nursery simplicity was always disconcerting. When ways and means had to be considered, the disenchanted maiden for whom life seemed to have no surprises became once more the helpless little girl in the hands of nurses and governesses. At such moments, Boyne thought, she was like a young Daphne, half emerging into reality, half caught in the foliage of fairyland.

"My dear child—"

She always responded to every change in his intonation; and as he spoke he saw the shadow in her eyes before it reached her lips. Trying to keep a smile on them, she interrupted: "Now I've said something stupid again."

"You've said something unexpected—that's all. Give me a little time—"

She sprang up, and moved toward him with one of her impulsive darts. "Martin! When people ask for time, it's always for time to say no. Yes has one more letter in it, but it doesn't take half as long to say. And now you'll hate me for asking you something that you've got to take time to answer."

"Not a bit of it. I want time because I've got several answers. And the first is: how do you know your Grandma Mervin won't take you all in?"

She shook her head. "Because I wrote to her a month ago, and she's taking time before she answers. And besides—really and truly—I've always known that if Grandma Mervin did take us in, she'd give us up again the minute father shouted loud enough. You see," Judith added, with a sudden spring back to her wistful maturity, "grandma gets a big allowance from father."

"All right; that brings me to my second answer. How do you know your father won't order you back at once to the Lido—or wherever he is—if your mother has definitely decided to leave him?"

"Because father's gone off to Constantinople on the yacht with Syb—Mrs. Lullmer, I mean—and a whole crowd of people."

In spite of himself, Boyne again drew a breath of relief. If Wheater was off on the "Fancy Girl" with a band of cronies, and his wife rushing to Paris to start divorce proceedings, there might indeed be no need for an immediate decision. Never had procrastination seemed so sweet.

"Well, my dear, in that case it would appear that they're both going to let you alone—for a while, at any rate. So why jump unnecessary ditches?"

Judith responded with a joyful laugh. "Who wants to, darling? I don't! As long as you're with us I always feel safe." Again a little shiver of apprehension ran over Boyne; but he dissembled it by joining in her laugh. The more precarious was the tie between himself and the little Wheaters, the more precious seemed the days he could still hope to spend with them; he would not cloud another with vain fears. "Right you are. Suppose we go and do something desperate to celebrate the occasion? What about a good tramp for you and me, and then supper with the little Wheaters?"

She stood looking at him with her happiest eyes. "Hurrah, Martin! I haven't seen you so jolly for days. Terry was afraid you were moping because Mrs. Sellars had gone—he thought that was why you hadn't been to see us, and we decided that I'd better come up and find out."

"Trust you to find out," he grinned; and added sardonically: "I'm bearing up, as you see. But come along. Don't let's waste any more sunshine."

She moved obediently toward the door, but stopped short half-way with an exclamation of surprise. Boyne, who was rummaging in a corner for his stick, turned about to see her standing before the ancient cradle.

"Oh, Martin, you—you keep your boots in it!" A reproachful flush rose to her face, and was momentarily reflected in his own. Hang it—why was he always such an untidy fellow? And why was a cradle so uncommonly handy to hold boots? "Jove—how stupid! Must have been that confounded chambermaid—" But he broke off in confusion as he caught Judith's incredulous eye. "Well, hang it, you know—I've nothing else to put in it just at present," he cried defiantly.

Her face softened, and she met his banter with the wistful tentative gaze that he called her Monreale look. "But very soon you will have, won't you? A baby of your own, I mean," she explained. "I suppose you and Mrs. Sellars are going to be married as soon as she gets back with her trousseau, aren't you? Blanca and I were wondering if perhaps she'd ask us to be bridesmaids. . ."

Boyne was flinging the boots out of the cradle with an angry hand, and made no answer to this suggestion. Judith stood and watched him for a few moments; then she went to his side and slipped her arm through his. "Why, Martin—I believe you're very unhappy!" she exclaimed.

"Unhappy? Unhappy?" He swung around on her, exasperated. "Well, yes; I suppose I am unhappy. It's a way people have, you know. But, for the Lord's sake, can't you ever let things be? Can't you ever keep from treading on people's toes? I—oh, damn it, Judy; look here, for God's sake don't cry! I didn't mean to say anything to hurt you. . . I swear I didn't. . . Only sometimes. . ."

"Oh, I know, I know—you mean I have no tact!" she wailed.

"Damn tact! I'm thankful you haven't. There's nothing I hate as much as tact. But here—don't look so scared, child. There's no harm done . . . only don't try meddling with grown up things. It'll just wreck everything if you do. . ."

"But how can I not meddle when I love you so, and when I see that things are going wrong for you? Martin," she flung out breathlessly, "you don't mean to say you're not going to be married after all?"

Temptation suddenly twitched through him. It was as if saying "Yes" to her question might be the magic formula of freedom. After all, there lay the ring; he *was* free, technically—had only to utter the words to make them true. But he thrust his hands into his pockets and stood sullenly planted before the corner of the table on which he had tossed the open ring-box. "Not in this way," he thought. Aloud he said: "I mean that I don't yet know when I'm going to be married. That's all."

"Positively all?" He nodded.

"Ah," she sighed, relieved. It was evident that she identified herself whole-heartedly with his sentimental troubles, of whatever nature and by whomsoever they were caused.

She was still looking up at him, her face full of compunction and perplexity, and suddenly he put his arm about her and bent his head to her lips. They looked round and glowing, as they did in laughter or emotion; they drew his irresistibly. But he turned his head aside, and his kiss fell harmlessly on her cheek, near the tear-hung lashes. "That's my old Judy. Come, cheerio. On with your hat, and we'll go up the mountain." He saw that she was still trembling, and took her by the arm in the old brotherly way. "Come," he repeated, "let's go out."

In the doorway she paused and flung a last tragic glance at the cradle. "You poor old Martin, you! I suppose it's because you're so unhappy that you put your boots in it?" she sighed.

XXVI

TO Boyne the calm of the next day brought no reassurance. Too many uncertainties hung close. After a night of pondering he had sent back the ring to Mrs. Sellars, with a brief line saying that she was of course free if she chose to be, but that he could not so regard himself till they had had a talk, and she had convinced him that she would be happier if their engagement ended.

He knew that he was merely using an old formula, the accepted one in such cases, and he longed to get away from it, to be spontaneous, honest, himself. But as he wrote it became clear to him that he was terribly sorry for Rose Sellars, terribly sorry for having disappointed her; and that such phrases—the kind he had been brought up on—were the devices of decent people who hated to give pain, and were even capable of self-sacrifice to avoid it. "After all, they were a lot better than we are," he thought; and the thought softened the close of his letter, and impelled him to add: "Do be patient with me, dear. As soon as I can get away I'll come."

This done, the whole problem vanished to the background of his mind. He was hardly aware that he was no longer thinking of it. His life of practical activities and swift decisions had given him the habit of easily dismissing matters once dealt with. He flattered himself that he could thus dispose of sentimental cares as easily as of professional problems; and to a certain extent it was true. Behind the close-knit foreground of his daily life there had hung for years the mirage of Rose Sellars;

but that mirage was now the phantom of a phantom, and he averted his eyes lest he should find that it had faded into nothing.

After Mrs. Wheater's letter to Judith there came no more alarms to the *Pension Rosenglüh;* and the days slipped by in a security which seemed satisfying to Judith, and even to Miss Scope. But summer was waning in the high valleys of the Dolomites; tourists were scattering, the big hotels preparing to close. By-and-by a cold sparkle began to fill the air in the early mornings, and at night the temperature fell to freezing. On the lower slopes the larches were turning to pale gold, and the bare cliffs burned with an intenser fire against a sky as hard as metal. The very magic of the hastening days warned Boyne that they could not last, and that the change in the landscape symbolized another, as imminent, in the fortunes of his party.

Mrs. Sellars had written again—sweetly and reasonably—saying that she intended to remain for the present with Aunt Julia, who was settled in Paris for two or three months. If Boyne really wished for another talk, she added, she hoped he would be able to come before long; but in any case he could count on her affectionate understanding. She closed her letter with a friendly message to the children.

Boyne had been afraid that Judith would revert again to the subject of his private anxieties; but she contrived, by a visible effort which made him feel for the first time that she was really growing up, to keep off the forbidden topic. His own return to a more equable mood no doubt helped her; and so did the presence of the younger children and their preceptors. Boyne half-unconsciously avoided being alone with Judith; and the shortening days and freshening temperature curtailed their expeditions, and gave more time for games and romps around the cheerful stove in the children's dining-room.

It was there that, one rainy afternoon, he found himself sitting with the younger children. Judith had gone with Miss Scope and Nanny to Toblach, to fit out the family with autumn underclothes, Terry was upstairs, working with his tutor, Chip asleep in Susan's care; and Blanca, in the corner nearest the stove, was brooding over a torn copy of "The Tatler" with the passionate frown she always bent on the study of fashion-plates. "Skirts *are* going to be fuller," she said. "I've been telling Judy so for a month. . ."

Zinnie lifted her head from the rapt contemplation of an electric engine which Bun was putting together under Boyne's directions. "The lady that was here today had her skirt longer; a lot longer than Judy's," she remarked.

Beechy, whose attention was also riveted on the motions of Bun's agile fingers, interrupted indignantly: "She wasn't pretty like our Judy."

"The lady? What lady?" Boyne interposed, vaguely apprehensive. "Have you got a new lodger here?"

Blanca re-entered the conversation with a sniff. "You wouldn't have taken her for one if you'd seen her. She's not the *Rosenglüh* kind. She would certainly have been at the 'Palace' if it hadn't been closed. Not exactly smart, you know—smartness has been so overdone, hasn't it? She was—what's that funny old word that Scopy loves?—distinguished. At least, I *think* that's what distinguished means . . . the way that lady looked. Her clothes awfully plain; but not the least 'sports.' Rather governessy, really . . . like Scopy young, if Chanel could have dressed her. . ." Blanca paused, reduced to silence by the hopelessness of the attempt to fit her words to her meaning.

Boyne looked up from the engine. "Perhaps when you've finished with her clothes you'll tell me what she came for."

"To see you—you—*you!*" cried Zinnie, executing a double handspring she had lately learned from Bun, to the despair of Beechy, who was so fat that she invariably collapsed midway of the same attempt. "I could have told you that," Zinnie added, "for I spoke to her."

"You did? What impertinence!" cried Blanca, bounding from her seat. Bun, flat on his stomach, his legs in the air, his curls mixed with the engine, chanted over his shoulder: "Girls are always butting in—butting in. . ."

"Nasty rotters, girls are!" sympathised Beechy, always ready to champion her brother, and not as yet very clear as to her own sex.

Zinnie's reprisals were checked by the discovery that the landlady's gold-fish aquarium, which usually stood in the larger and colder public dining-room, had been brought in and placed on a stand before the window. She tiptoed off to inspect this forbidden Paradise while Boyne got to his feet and picked up the electric wire. "Where's the battery? Are your rails straight? Now, then, Bun, are you ready?" He turned to Zinnie. "To see *me*, did you say? What on earth for? Did she tell you?"

"Tell Zinnie! So likely!" ejaculated Blanca with a shrug. She turned to Boyne, drawing her lids together with her pretty cat-like smile. *"Félicitations, cher ami. Elle était plutôt bien, la dame, vous savez."*

"Oh, shucks—zif we didn't all of us talk French!" commented Zinnie, still watchfully circling about the aquarium.

The door opened, and a maid came in with a card which she handed hesitatingly to Boyne. The name on it was: *Princess Buondelmonte,* and underneath was written: "begs Mr. Boyne to see her on important business." Boyne crammed the card into his pocket without speaking, conscious that the eyes of all the children were upon him.

"It's the lady, it's the lady, I know it is!" Zinnie piped. "I heard her say she was coming back to see Martin. She's come all the way from Rome to see him."

Blanca, at his side, had slid an insinuating hand in his. "From Rome? Oh, Martin, who is it? Mayn't I come with you, at any rate as far as the door? I do want to see if her dress is made of kasha or crepella . . . just to be able to tell Judy. . ."

Boyne checked her firmly. "You've got to stay here and mind the infants. It's nothing important—I'll be back in a few minutes." He thanked his stars that the lady had sent in her card instead of confiding her name to the maid. He could not imagine what his noble visitor wanted of him, but the very sight of the name had let loose all his fears. As he left the room he turned and sent a last glance toward the group sprawling around the engine, which had after all refused to start—orange curls mixed with brown and dusky, sunburnt legs kicking high, voices mixed in breathless controversy. How healthy and jolly they all looked! And how good they smelt, with that mixed smell of woollen garments, and soap, and the fruity fragance of young bodies tumbled about together. As Boyne looked back at them he thought how funny and dear they were, and how different the world might have been if Rose Sellars had freed herself when he and she were still young. . .

A lady with a slim straight back was standing in the sitting-room, attentively examining the stuffed eagle above the stove. She turned at Boyne's entrance and revealed a small oval face, somewhat pale, with excessively earnest gray eyes, and a well-modelled nose and brow. It puzzled him to discover why an assemblage of such agreeable features did not produce an effect of beauty; but a second glance suggested that it was because their owner had never thought about being beautiful. That she had graver preoccupations was immediately evident from the tone of her slow and carefully-modulated speech. "Mr. Boyne?" she asked, as though she feared he might deny his identity, and was immediately prepared, if he did, to disprove the denial; and on his saying that he was, she continued, with a touch of nervousness: "I have come all the way from Rome to see my children."

"Your children—?" Boyne echoed in astonishment; and she corrected herself with a slight blush. "I should say the Prince's. Or my step-children. But I hate the word, for I feel about them already as if they were my own."

Boyne pushed an armchair forward, and she sat down, crossing her feet neatly, and satisfying herself that the skirt which Zinnie described as long was so adjusted as not to reveal too much of the pretty legs above her slender ankles. "They *are* here—Astorre and Beatrice?"

Boyne heard her with dismay, but kept up a brave exterior. "Here? Oh, yes—certainly. Mr. and Mrs. Wheater sent all the children here a few weeks ago—for the climate."

Princess Buondelmonte met this with a smile of faint

incredulity. "In your charge, I understand? Yes. But of course you must know that Mr. and Mrs. Wheater have really no business whatever to send my husband's children here, or anywhere else." She paused a moment, and added: "And I have come to take them home."

"Oh, Princess—" Boyne exclaimed.

She raised her handsome eyebrows slightly, and said: "You seem surprised."

"Well—yes. At any rate, I'm awfully sorry."

"Sorry? Don't you think that children ought to be in their own home, with their own parents?"

"Well, that depends."

"Depends! How can it ever—?" She crimsoned suddenly, and then grew even paler than before. "I don't suppose you intend to insinuate—?" She broke off, and he saw that her eyes had filled with tears. "For, of course, that I won't tolerate for a single instant," she added a little breathlessly, as though throwing herself on his mercy in a conflict she felt to be unequal if it should turn on Prince Buondelmonte's merits as a father.

Boyne felt so sorry for her that he answered: "I wasn't thinking of insinuating anything. I only meant that this little group of children have always been together, and it has made them so fond of each other that they really regard themselves as one family. It seems a pity, it seems cruel. . ."

"Cruel?" she interrupted. "The real cruelty has been to deprive the poor little things for so long of a father's influence, to take advantage of . . . of Prince Buondelmonte's misfortunes, his undeserved misfortunes, to keep his children without a real home, without family associations, without . . . without any guiding principle. . ." She leaned forward, her grave almost terrified eyes on Boyne. "What guidance have they had? What moral training? What religious education? Have you or your friends ever thought that? It's a big responsibility you've assumed. Have you never thought you might some day be asked to account for the use you've made of it?"

Boyne heard her with a growing wonder. She spoke slowly but fluently, not as if repeating a lesson learned by rote, but as though she were sustaining a thesis with the ease of a practised orator. There was something didactic—perhaps forensic, rather—in her glib command of her subject. He saw that she was trembling with nervousness, yet that her nerves would never control her; and his heart sank.

"I'm afraid I can't answer all your questions," he said, "I've only been with the children for a few weeks. Mr. and Mrs. Wheater asked me to keep an eye on them during the . . . the settling of certain family matters; but I can assure you that since I've known them they've always been in an atmosphere of the greatest kindness and affection; and I'm inclined to think that's the most important thing of all."

Princess Buondelmonte listened attentively, her brows drawn together in a cautious frown. "Of course I'm not prepared to admit that unreservedly. I mean, the kindness of salaried assistants or . . . or of inexperienced persons may do as much harm as good. To any one who has gone at all deeply into the difficult and absorbing subject of child-psychology—" she paused, and added with an air of modest dignity: "I ought perhaps to explain that I took my degree *cum laude*, in Eugenics and Infant Psychology, at Lohengrin College, Texas. You may have heard that my grandfather, Dr. Judson Tring, was the founder of the college, and also its first President." She stopped again, glanced half proudly, half shyly at Boyne, as though to see how much this glimpse of her genealogy had impressed him, and then pursued: "Can you give me, for instance, any sort of assurance that Astorre and Beatrice have ever been properly psychoanalyzed, and that their studies and games have been selected with a view to their particular moral, alimentary, dental and glandular heredity? Games, for instance, should be quite as carefully supervised as studies . . . but I know how little importance Europe still attaches to these supremely vital questions." No adequate answer occurred to Boyne, and she rose from her seat with an impatient gesture. "I don't know that there is any use in continuing a discussion which would not, in any case, affect my final decision, or Prince Buondelmonte's—"

"Oh, don't say that!" Boyne exclaimed.

"Don't—?"

"Not if it means you won't listen to any plea—won't first consider what it's going to be to these children to be suddenly uprooted. . ."

She interrupted: "It was not Prince Buondelmonte who first uprooted them. It was through circumstances of which he was himself the victim—I may say, Mr. Boyne, the *chivalrous* victim—that he found himself obliged (or thought himself obliged) to trust Astorre and Beatrice for a while to Mrs. Wheater. He did it simply in order that no breath of calumny should touch her." The Princess paused, and added, with a genuine tremor in her voice: "Though Mrs. Wheater was not his children's mother my husband always remembers that for a time she bore his name."

If the Princess's aim had been to reduce her interlocutor to silence, she had at last succeeded. Boyne sat speechless, wondering how much the granddaughter of Dr. Judson Tring believed of what she was saying, and to what extent her astounding version of the case was the result of patient schooling on her husband's part. He concluded that she was incapable of deliberate deception, and fully convinced of the truth of her assertions; and he knew this would make it all the harder to reason with her. For a few moments the two faced each other without speaking; then Boyne said: "But surely the fact that Prince Buondelmonte did leave his children with Mrs. Wheater ought to be considered. If he was willing to have her keep them he must have thought she knew how to take care of them."

The Princess again interrupted him. "My husband left his children with Mrs. Wheater for the reasons I've told you; but also because, owing to unfortunate circumstances, he had at the time no home to give them, and they had no mother to care for them. Now all that is changed. Since our marriage we have fortunately been able to buy back the Buondelmonte palace in Rome, and I am as anxious as he is that his children should come and live with us there."

Boyne stood up impatiently. The talk was assuming more and more the tone of a legal debate; conducted on such lines there seemed no reason for its ever ending. If one accepted the Princess's premises—and Boyne had no way of disproving them—it was difficult to question her conclusions. All he could do was to plead his lack of authority. He reminded his visitor that Mrs. Wheater, to whom, for whatever reason, their father had confided Bun and Beechy, had, in her turn, passed them over to their present guardians, who were therefore answerable to her, and her only. The Princess's lips parted nervously on the first syllable of a new protest; but Boyne interrupted: "Princess! It's really so simple—I mean the legal part. If your husband has a right to his children, no one can prevent his getting them. The real issue seems to me quite different. It concerns only the children themselves. They're so desperately anxious not to be separated; they're so happy together. Of course none of that is my doing. It's their eldest step-sister—or whatever you like to call her—Mrs. Wheater's eldest daughter, Judith, who has kept the six of them together through all the ups and downs of their parents' matrimonial troubles. Before you decide—"

The Princess lifted an imperative hand. "Mr. Boyne —I'm sorry. I can see that you're very fond of the children. But fondness is not everything . . . it may even be a source of moral danger. I'm afraid we shouldn't altogether agree as to the choice of the persons Mrs. Wheater has left in charge of them—not even as to her own daughter. The soul of a child—"

"Yes," Boyne acquiesced; "that's the very thing I'm pleading for. If you could see them together . . . "

"Oh, but I intend to," she responded briskly.

Her promptness took him aback. "Now, you mean?"

She gave a smiling nod. "Certainly. You don't suppose I came from Rome for any other reason? But you needn't be afraid of my kidnapping them." Her eyes became severe again. "I hope it won't have to come to that; but of course I intend to see my husband's children."

"Oh, all right," Boyne agreed. He was beginning to divine, under her hard mechanical manner, something young and untried, something one might still reach and appeal to; and he reflected that the sight of the children would perhaps prove to be the simplest way of reaching it. "The children are playing in the other room," he said. "Shall I go and get Bun and Beechy, or do you prefer to see them first with the others?"

The Princess said, yes, she thought she would like to see them all together at their games. "Games have such a profound psychological significance," she explained with a smile.

"Well, I'm glad you're going to take them by surprise. It's always the best way with children. You'll see what jolly little beggars they are; how they all understand each other; how well they get on together. . . I'm counting on the sight to plead our cause."

He led her down the passage and threw open the door of the children's dining-room.

On the threshold they were met by a burst of angry voices. Everything in the room was noise and confusion, and the opening of the door remained unheeded. In all his experience of the little Wheaters, Boyne had never before seen them engaged in so fierce a conflict: it seemed incredible that the participants should be only four. Some were screaming, some vituperating, some doing both, and butting at each other, head down, at the same time. The floor was strewn with the wreckage of battle, but the agitated movements of the combatants made the origin of the dispute hard to discover. "God," Boyne ejaculated, stepping back.

Zinnie's voice rose furiously above the others. "It wasn't me't upset the 'quarium, I swear it wasn't, Blanca—and those two wops know it just as well as I do. . ."

Bun squealed back: "It was you that tried to bathe Chip's rabbit in it, you dirty little lying sneak, you!"

"No, I didn't, neither; but Nanny don't never give him

enough to drink, 'n so I just ran up and brought him down while Chip was asleep, 'n if Beechy hadn't gone and butted in—"

"You rotten little liar, you, you know you were trying to find out if rabbits can swim."

"No, I wasn't, either. And it was Beechy pushed me 'gainst the 'quarium, and you know it was. . ."

" 'Cos the rabbit was drownding, and Judy'd have killed you if you'd of let it," Beechy wailed.

"She'll kill you anyhow if you call us wops again," roared Bun.

Blanca, reluctantly torn from her study of "The Tatler," had risen from the stove-corner and was distributing slaps and shakes with a practised hand. As she turned to the door, and saw Boyne and his visitor on the threshold, her arms dropped to her sides, and she swept the shrieking children into a corner behind her. "Oh, Martin, I'm so sorry! Did you ever see such a pack of savages? They were playing some silly game, and I didn't realise. . ." She addressed herself to Boyne, but, as usual, it was the newcomer who fixed her attention. "What will your friend think?" she murmured with a deprecating glance.

Princess Buondelmonte, pale and erect, stood in the doorway and returned her gaze. "I shall think just what I expected to," she said coldly. She turned to Boyne, and continued in a trembling voice: "It is just as I was saying: nothing in a child's education should be left to chance. Games have to be directed even more carefully than studies. . . Telling a child that an older person will kill it seems to me so unspeakably wicked. . . This perpetuating of the old militarist instinct. . . 'Kill' is one of the words we have entirely eliminated at Lohengrin. . ." Still nervously, she addressed herself again to Blanca. "I do hope," she said, "that the particular little savage who made that threat doesn't happen to be mine—to be Prince Buondelmonte's, I mean?"

Blanca was looking at her with a captivated stare. "You don't mean to say you're his new wife? Are you the Princess Buondelmonte, really?"

"Yes, I'm the Princess Buondelmonte," the visitor assented, with a smile of girlish gratification which made her appear almost as young as Blanca. It was manifest that, however heavily the higher responsibilities weighed on her, she still enjoyed the sound of her new title.

But Bun, brushing aside the little girls, had flung himself impetuously upon her. "Are you really and truly my father's new wife? Then you must tell him he's got to send me a gun at once, to shoot everybody who calls me and Beechy a wop."

The visitor stooped down, laying a timid yet resolute hand on his dark head. "What I shall do, my dear, is to carry you off at once, you and little Beatrice, to your own home—to your own dear father, who's pining for you—to a place where nobody ever talks about shooting and killing. . ."

Bun's face fell perceptibly. "Won't my father give me a gun, don't you suppose? Then I don't believe Beechy 'n me 'd care such a lot about going."

The Princess's lips narrowed with the same air of resolution which had informed her hand. "Oh, but I'm afraid you've got to, Astorre. This is not your real home, you know, and I'm going to take you both away to the loveliest house . . . and your father'll give you lots of other things you'll like ever so much better. . ."

"Not than a gun, I won't," said Bun immovably.

XXVII

"TAKE away my children? Take them away from me?" Judith Wheater had pushed open the door, and stood there, small and pale, in her dripping mackintosh and bedraggled hat. She gave a little laugh, and her gray eyes measured the stranger with a deliberate and freezing scrutiny. "I don't in the least know who you are," she said, "but I know you don't know what you're talking about. . ." She glanced away to the ravaged scene, and the frightened excited faces of the children. "Heavens! What an unholy mess! What on earth has been happening? Oh, the poor drenched rabbit. . . Here, wrap it up in my scarf. . . Nanny, take the children upstairs, and send Susan at once to tidy up. Yes, Blanca; you must go too. If you can't keep the little ones in order you've got to be treated like one of them." She turned to the bewildered visitor. "I'm Miss Wheater. If you want to see me, will you please come into the sitting-room?" Her eye fell on Boyne, who had drawn back into the dusk of the passage, as if disclaiming any part in the impending drama. "Martin," she challenged him, "was it you who brought this lady here?"

"It's the Princess Buondelmonte, Judith."

Judith again scanned her with unrelenting eyes. "I'm afraid that won't make any difference," she said. The Princess stood drooping her high crest a little, as if unused to receiving instructions from one so much smaller and younger than herself. Boyne remembered how Judith had awed and baffled Mrs. Sellars on their first meeting, and his heart swelled with irrational hopes. "Judith," he cautioned her, below his breath.

"This way. You'll come too, please, Martin." She led them down the passage, and into the sitting-room. After she had closed the door she pushed forward a chair for the Princess Buondelmonte, and said with emphasis: "Perhaps you don't know that Mr. Boyne has been appointed the guardian of the children."

The Princess did not seat herself. She leaned on the back of the chair, and smiled down at the champion of the little Wheaters. "They seem to have a great many guardians. I hear you're one of them too."

"Me?" Judith's eyes widened in astonishment. "I'm only their eldest sister. All I do is just to try to look after them."

Something in her accent seemed to touch the Princess, who seated herself in the chair on which she had been leaning, made sure that her skirts did not expose more than a decent extent of ankle, and began to speak in a friendlier tone. "I'm sure you're perfectly devoted to them—that all you want is what's best for them."

Judith paused a moment. "That depends on what you mean by best. All I want is for us all to stay together."

The Princess made a sign of comprehension. "Yes. . . But supposing it was not what's best for the children?"

"Oh, but it is," said Judith decisively. The other hesitated, and she pressed on: "Because nobody can possibly love them as much as Martin and Miss Scope and me."

"I see. But you seem to have forgotten that they have parents. . ."

"No. It's the parents who've forgotten," Judith flashed back.

"Not all of them. Since I'm here," the Princess smiled.

"What? Because you've just married Prince Buondelmonte, and probably think he ought to have remembered to look after Bun and Beechy? Well, I think so too. Only he didn't, you see; not when they were little, and had to be wiped and changed and fed, and walked up and down when they were cutting their teeth. And now that they're big enough to cut up their own food and be good company, I suppose you and he think it would be fun to come and carry them off, the way you'd pick out a pair of Pekes at a dog-show . . . only you forget that in the meantime they've grown to love *us* and not you, and that they're devoted to all the other children, and that it would half kill them to be separated from each other. . ."

"Oh—devoted?" the Princess protested with her dry smile.

"Of course they are. Why do you ask? Because they were having a scrap when you came in? Did that tussle about a gold-fish frighten you? Have you never seen children bite and scratch before?" Judith gave a contemptuous shrug. "I pity you," she said, "the first time you try to give Bun castor-oil. . ."

. . . .

Was it victory or defeat? Boyne and Judith sat late in the little sitting-room, asking themselves that, after the Princess Buondelmonte had gone. It had been Boyne's idea—and almost his only contribution to the fiery dialogue between the two—that the Princess should be invited to return in the evening and share the children's supper. The proposal, seconded by Judith after a swift glance at Boyne, seemed to surprise their visitor, and to disarm her growing hostility. The encounter with Judith had not tended to soften her feelings, and for a moment it looked as if things were taking a dangerous turn; but Boyne had intervened with the suggestion that the Princess, having seen the children at their worst, should be given a chance to meet them in pleasanter circumstances. He added that he would be glad of another talk with her; and as she did not leave till the next day, and was staying at an hotel near his own, he asked if he might walk back there with her, and fetch her down again for supper. She accepted both suggestions, and after a mollified farewell to Judith, started up the hill with Boyne. He saw that she was still inwardly agitated, and clutching desperately at what remained of her resolution; and he put in a pacifying word in excuse of Judith's irritability, and assured the Princess that the Wheaters would make no difficulty in recognising the Prince's legal right to his children. The real question, he went on, was surely quite different; was one of delicacy, of good taste, if you chose to call it so. Mrs. Wheater had taken in Beechy and Bun when their father was not able to; she had given them the same advantages as her own children (the Princess, at this, sounded an ironic murmur), and had shown them the same affection; though all she had done, Boyne hastened to add, was as nothing to the patient unflagging devotion of their step-sister—who technically wasn't even a step-sister. On that theme Boyne did not have to choose his words. They poured out with a vehemence surprising even to himself. The Princess, he supposed —whatever her educational theories were—would agree that the first thing young children needed was to be loved enough; above all, children exposed as they were in the Wheater world, where every new divorce and remarriage thrust them again into unfamiliar surroundings. Through all these changes, Boyne pointed out, Judith had clung to her little flock, loving them, and teaching them to love each other; she had even inspired governesses and nurses with her own passionate fidelity, so that in a welter of change the group had remained together, protected and happy. If only, Boyne pleaded, they could be left as they were for a few years longer; perhaps if they could it would be found, when they finally rejoined their respective families, that under Judith's care they had been better prepared for life than if their parents had insisted on separating them.

The Princess listened attentively to his arguments, but said little in reply; Boyne suspected that she had been taught not to commit herself unless she was on familiar ground, and apparently she was unfamiliar with the kind of plea he made. The sentiments he appealed to seemed to have a sort of romantic interest for her, as feudal ruins might have for an intelligent traveller; but he saw that there were no words for them in her vocabulary.

When they went back to the *Pension Rosenglüh* for supper the children, headed by Terry and Blanca, presented a picture of such roseate harmony that the Princess was evidently struck. To complete the impression, Chip, who was always brought down at this hour to say goodnight, walked in led by Nanny, placed a confiding palm in the strange lady's, said "Howoodoo," and wound his fingers in her hair, which he pronounced to be "ike Oody's"—for Chip was beginning to generalise and to co-ordinate, though his educators could not have put a name to the process, any more than the Princess could to the instinctive motions of the heart.

Supper, on the whole, was a success. The children were unusually well-behaved; even Zinnie subdued herself to the prevailing tone. Bun and Beechy, seated one on each side of their new step-mother, and visibly awed by her proximity, demeaned themselves with a restraint which the Princess made several timid attempts to break down. It was evident that what she had said about the prohibition of fire-arms still rankled in Bun, and both children were prim and non-committal, as they always were—to a degree unknown to the others—once their distrust was aroused. The Princess, to conceal her embarrassment, discoursed volubly about the historic interest of the ancestral palace which her husband had succeeded in repurchasing, and promised Bun that one of its spacious apartments should be fitted up as a modern playroom, in which he would learn to replace his artless antics by the newest feats in scientific gymnastics. Bun's eyes glittered; but after a reflective silence he shook his head. "We couldn't," he said, "not 'f we wanted to the most awful way; 'cos we've all sworen a noath on Scopy's book that we wouldn't."

This solemn self-reminder caused Beechy's eyes to fill, and Zinnie to cry out: "We'd be damned black-hearted villains if we did!"

The Princess looked distressed. "What do you mean by swearing an oath, Astorre?" she asked, pronouncing the words as if they were explosives and must be handled with caution.

"I mean a nawful oath," Bun explained, with an effort at greater accuracy.

"But I can't bear to hear children talk about swearing—or about villains either," his step-mother continued, turning with a reproachful smile to Zinnie, who promptly rejoined: "Then you'd better not ever have any of your own"; which caused the Princess to blush and lower her grave eyes.

To hide her constraint she addressed a question to the company in general. "What is this book that you children speak of as Miss Scope's? The choice of books is so imp—"

None of the younger children could pronounce the name of the book, and they therefore preserved a respectful silence; but Terry interrupted with a laugh: "Oh, it's the book that Scopy cures us all out of. It's called the 'Cyclopædia of Nursery Remedies'."

The Princess received this with a dubious frown. "I don't remember a book of that name being used in our courses at Lohengrin; is it a recent publication?"

Miss Scope sat rigid and majestic at the opposite table-end. Thus directly challenged, she replied reassuringly: "Dear me, no; it's been thoroughly tested. My mother and all my aunts used it in their families. I believe even my grandmother—"

"Even your grandmother? But then the book must be completely obsolete—and probably very dangerous."

Miss Scope smiled undauntedly. "Oh, I think not. My mother always found it most reliable. We were fourteen in the family, ten miles from the railway, in Lancashire, and she brought us through all our illnesses on it. In a family of that size one couldn't always be sending for the doctor. . ."

This gave her interlocutor's dismay a new turn. "Fourteen in your family? You don't mean to say your mother had fourteen children?"

Miss Scope replied with undisguised pride that that was what she did mean; and the Princess laid down her fork with the air of one about to spring up and do battle against such deplorable abuses. "It's incredible . . ." she began; then broke off to add in a lower tone: "But

I suppose that at that time—" her glance at Miss Scope's white head seemed to say that the whole business was an old unhappy far-off thing, and she resumed more hopefully: "In the United States such matters will soon be regulated by legislation. . ."

She met Miss Scope's horrified stare, and glanced nervously about the table, as if realising that the subject, even at Lohengrin, might hardly be considered suitable for juvenile ears. To relieve her embarrassment she leaned across Bun and addressed herself once more to Zinnie.

"You must be Lady Wrench's little girl, aren't you, my dear? Only think, I saw your mother the other day in Venice," she said, in an affable attempt to change the conversation.

Zinnie's face sparkled with curiosity. "Oh, did you see her, truly? What did she have on, do you remember?"

"Have on—?" The Princess hesitated, with a puzzled look, and Judith intervened: "Zinnie has a passion for pretty clothes."

"I think *yours* are awfully pretty," Zinnie insidiously put in, addressing the Princess; and added: "Are you sure my mother didn't give you any presents to give us?"

"Zinnie!" came reprovingly from Miss Scope.

The Princess shook her head. "No; she didn't give me any presents. Perhaps she thinks you ought to come and get them. But she gave me a message for you when she heard that I was coming here—she told me to tell you how dreadfully she wanted to see her little girl again."

Zinnie grew scarlet with excitement and gratification; such notice lifted her at once above the other children. But an afterthought soon damped her pride. "If she really feels like that I'd of thought she'd of sent me a present," she objected doubtfully.

"Presents aren't everything. And it's not very nice to associate the people you love with the thought of what they may be going to give you. Besides," continued the Princess illogically, "if your mother is so generous, think how many presents you'd get if you were always with her."

This seemed to plunge Zinnie into fresh perplexity. "Always with her? How could I be? She doesn't want to 'dopt the lot of us, does she? 'Cos you see we've all sweared—"

"You mustn't say swear," said the Princess.

"Swore," Zinnie corrected herself.

"I mean, not use such words," the Princess explained.

"But we *did,*" said Zinnie, "on Scopy's book; so she'd have to 'dopt us all, with Judy. Do you s'pose she would?"

"I don't know about that; perhaps it might be difficult. But why shouldn't she want to have her own little daughter with her?" The Princess again leaned over, and laid a persuasive hand on Zinnie's. "Don't you want me to take you back to Venice, to your own real mother, when I go to-morrow?"

There was a pause of suspense. Boyne signed to Judith to keep silent, and the children, taking the cue, remained with spoons above their pudding, and eyes agape, while this perfidious proposal was submitted. Zinnie, from crimson, had grown almost pale; the orange spirals of her bushy head seemed to droop with her drooping lips. Her head sank on her neck, and she twisted about in its crease of plumpness the necklace her mother had given her.

"What kind of presents 'd you s'pose they'd be?" she questioned back with caution.

"Oh, I don't know, dear. But you oughtn't to think about that. You ought to think only of your mother, and her wanting so much to have you. You must give me an answer to take back to her. Shan't I tell her you want to go to her, Zinnie?"

Zinnie hung her head still lower. If it had been possible for a Wheater child to be shy, she would have appeared so; but in reality she was only struggling with a problem beyond her powers. At last she raised her head, and looked firmly at the Princess. "I should like to consult my lawyer first," she said.

Boyne burst out laughing, and the Princess nervously joined him, perhaps to cover the appearance of defeat. Having so obviously failed to inspire the children with confidence, she once more addressed herself to Miss Scope. "I should be so much interested in talking over your educational system with you. I suppose you've entirely eliminated enforced obedience, as we have at Lohengrin?"

"Enforced—?" Miss Scope gave an incredulous gasp, and her charges, evidently struck by the question, again remained with suspended spoons, and eyes eagerly fixed on the Princess. Miss Scope gave a curt laugh. "I've never known children to obey unless they were forced to. If you know a way to make them, I shall be glad to learn it," she said drily.

This seemed to cause the Princess more disappointment than surprise. "Ah, that's just what we won't do; *make them.* We leave them as free as air, and simply suggest to them to co-operate. At Lohengrin co-operation has superseded every other method. We teach even our little two-year-olds voluntary co-operation. We think the idea of obedience is debasing." She turned with a smile to her step-son. "When Astorre and Beatrice come to live with me the first thing I shall do is to make them both co-operate."

Bun received this unsmilingly, and Beechy burst into passionate weeping and flung her arms jealously about her brother. "No—no, you bad wicked woman, you mustn't! You shan't operate on Bun, only on me—if you *must!*" she added in a final wail, her desperate eyes entreating her step-mother.

"But, my dear, I don't understand," the Princess murmured; and Judith hurriedly explained that Blanca had been operated upon for appendicitis the previous year, and that the use of the word in connection with her illness had had an intimidating effect on the younger children, and especially on Beechy.

"But this is all wrong . . . dreadfully wrong . . ." the Princess said with a baffled sigh. No one found an answer, and supper being over, Judith proposed that they should return to the sitting-room. The children followed, marshalled by Miss Scope, and the Princess again tried to engage them in talk; but she could not break down the barrier of mistrust which had been set up. Finally she suggested that they should all play a game together—a quiet writing game she thought would be interesting. A table was cleared, and paper and pencils found with some difficulty, and distributed among the children, the youngest of whom were lifted up onto sofa-cushions to make their seats high enough for collaboration. The Princess explained that the game they were going to play was called "Ambition," and that it had been introduced into the Vocational Department of Juvenile Psychology at Lohengrin in order to direct children's minds as early as possible to the choice of a career. First of all, she continued, each was to write down what he or she would most like to be or to do; then they were to fold the papers, and Mr. Boyne was to shake them up in his hat, and read them out in turn, and as he read the children were to try to guess who had made each choice.

The game did not start with as much *élan* as its organiser had perhaps hoped. The children were still oppressed by her presence, and all of them but Terry hated writing, and were unused to abstract speculations on the future; moreover, they probably felt that if they were to state with sincerity what they wanted to be their aspirations would be received with the friendly ridicule which grown ups manifest when children express their real views.

All this made for delay and hesitation, and it was only Terry's persuasion, and the fear of disobeying the tall authoritative lady who had suddenly invaded their lives, which finally set their pencils going. Boyne received the papers, shook them up conscientiously, and began to read them out.

"Al If Boy—oh, a *lift-boy;* yes—." Zinnie's burning blush revealed her as the author of this ambition, and Boyne read on: "An Ambassadoress"—Blanca, of course; and the added vowel certainly gave the word a new stateliness. "A great Poet, or the best Writer of Detective Stories," in Terry's concise hand, showed him torn between a first plunge into Conan Doyle, and rapturous communion with "The Oxford Book of English Verse."

Boyne read on: "Never brush meye tethe," laboriously printed out by Beechy; "A Crow Bat"—an aspiration obviously to be ascribed to Bun: "A noble character" (bless Scopy! As if she wasn't one already—); and lastly, in Judith's rambling script: "An exploarer." At the reading of that, something darted through Boyne like a whirr of wings.

The ambitions expressed did not long serve to disguise the choosers, and there was a prompt chorus of attributions as Boyne read out one slip after the other. The Princess had apparently hoped that something more striking would result. She said the game usually promoted discussion, and she hoped the next stage in it would lead to freer self-expression. The children, she explained, were now to say in turn why—that is, on what grounds—they wanted to be this or that. But an awestruck silence met her invitation to debate, and Beechy again began to show signs of emotion. The Princess seemed much distressed, but was assured by Miss Scope that this breach of manners was due only to over-excitement, and the strain of sitting up later than usual—she hoped the Princess would excuse her, but really the children had better go to bed. At this suggestion all the faces round the table lit up except Zinnie's, which was clouded by a pout. She slipped down from her cushions with the others, but when her turn came to file by the Princess for goodnight, she held up the march-past to ask: "N'arn't there going to be any prizes after that game?"

She was swept off in Miss Scope's clutch, and the Princess, after a timid attempt at endearment, imperfectly responded to, when Bun and Beechy took leave, sat down for a talk with Boyne and Judith. Much as she had evidently seen to disapprove of in the bringing-up of the little Wheaters she was in a less aggressive mood than in the afternoon; something she had been unprepared for, and had only half understood, in the relation of the children to each other and to their elders, seemed imperceptіbly to have shaken her convictions. Though she continued to repeat the same phrases, it was with less emphasis; and she listened more patiently to Boyne's arguments, and to Judith's entreaties.

Judith was presently called away to say goodnight to the children, and as soon as the Princess and Boyne were alone, the former began abruptly: "But you must listen to me, Mr. Boyne; you must understand me. It's not only that I cannot conscientiously approve of the way in which Beatrice and Astorre are being brought up: it is that I need them myself—I need them for my husband." She coloured at the avowal, and went on hastily: "If he is to begin a new life—and he *has* begun it already—his first step ought to be to take back his children. You must see that. . . You must see how I am situated. . ." Her voice broke, and Boyne suddenly felt the same pity for her as when she had shown her fear that he might be hinting a criticism of Prince Buondelmonte's past.

"I'll do what I can—only trust me," he stammered.

Judith came back, and the Princess, still a little rigid from the effort at self-control, began at once to thank her for her kindness, and to say that she was afraid it was time to go. She would tell Prince Buondelmonte, she added, with an effort at cordiality, that the children seemed very well ("*physically* well," she explained), and she would give him the assurance—she hoped she might?—that some sort of understanding as to their future would soon be reached.

Victory or defeat? Judith and Boyne, sitting late, asked each other which it was, but found no answer.

XXVIII

ALL the next day the rain continued. It was one of those steady business-like rains which seem, in mountain places, not so much a caprice of the weather as the drop-curtain punctually let down by Nature between one season and the next. Behind its closely woven screen one had the sense of some tremendous annual scene-shifting, the upheaval and overturning of everything in sight, from the clouds bursting in snow on the cliff-tops to the mattresses and blankets being beaten and aired in the hotel windows.

These images were doubtless born of Boyne's own mood. When he opened his shutters on the morning after the Princess Buondelmonte's apparition it seemed to him as if she herself had hung that cold gray mist before the window. He was afraid of everything now—of what the post might bring, of what his own common-sense might dictate to him, above all, of seeing Judith again, and having his apprehensions doubled by hers.

The worst of it was that, even should all their tormentors agree to leave them in peace, they could not—more particularly on Terry's account—delay on that height through the coming weeks of storm and rain. Moreover, all the hotels and *pensions*, which would reopen later for the season of winter sports, were preparing to close for their yearly cleaning and renovating. After the middle of October there would be no demand for accommodation till the arrival of the Christmas lugers and ski-ers. If it proved possible to keep the little Wheaters together any longer the best plan would probably be to transport them to Riva or Meran till winter and fine weather were established together in the mountains.

Boyne turned over these things with the nervous minuteness with which one makes plans for some one who is dying, and will never survive to see them carried out. It seemed to give him faith in the future, a sense of factitious security, as it sometimes does, beside a deathbed, to think: "To-morrow I'll see what the doctor says about a warmer climate."

Judith and Miss Scope shared his idea about Meran or Riva, and for some time had been talking vaguely of going down to look for rooms. But the ever-recurring difficulty of persuading a boarding-house keeper to lodge seven children made them decide that it would be best to try to hire an inexpensive villa. The episode of the goldfish and the rabbit had not endeared them to their present landlady, and they felt the hopelessness of trying to ingratiate themselves with another, in a place where they were unknown, and where the autumn season would be at its height. It had therefore been decided that Judith, Miss Scope and Boyne should motor to Meran that very week to look over the ground. But on reflection Boyne hesitated to leave the children alone with their nurses, even for so short an absence. With Joyce in Paris, once more reorganising her life, and the Princess Buondelmonte returning to Rome unsatisfied, danger threatened on all sides. Any one of these cross-blasts might dash to earth the frail nest which had resisted the summer's breezes; and Boyne, heavy-hearted, set out to call another council at the *Pension Rosenglüh.*

As he left the hotel a telegram was handed to him. He glanced first at the signature—Sarah Mervin—then read what went before. "I will gladly receive own dear grandchildren subject to parents' final settlement of affairs fear cannot assume responsibility step-children letter follows" . . . "A lawyer's cable," Boyne growled as he pocketed it. "That's the reason it's taken so long to compose."

Fresh bitterness filled him as he saw one more prop withdrawn from under the crazy structure of his hopes. "These people," he reflected, "all act on impulse where their own wants are concerned, and call in a lawyer when it's a question of anybody else's." But in his heart he was not much surprised. Mrs. Mervin was no longer young, and it is natural for ageing people to shrink from responsibilities. Besides, she might well plead that it was no business of hers to take in children she had never seen, and whose parents were eager, and financially able, to care for them. On second thoughts, it really did not need Judith's bald hint as to the allowance her grandmother received from Cliffe Wheater to account for the poor lady's attitude. "I don't see what else she could have done," the impartial Boyne was obliged to admit in the course of his interminable argument with the other, the passionate and unreasonable one.

What a Utopia he and Judith had been dreaming! He wondered now how he could have lent himself to such pure folly. . . Well, the dream was over, and his was the grim business of making her see it. . . Heavily he went down the hill through the rain.

At the *pension* Judith was watching for him from the window. She opened the door and led him into the sitting-room, where a sulky fire smouldered, puffing out acrid smoke. The landlady said it was always like that—the stove always smoked on the first day of the autumn rains, unless there was a little wind to make a draught. And there was not a breath today; the only way was to leave a window open, Judith explained as she turned to Boyne. Her face was colourless and anxious; he could see that she had been treading the wheel of the same problems as himself. The sight made him resolve to try and hide his own apprehensions a little longer.

"Well, old Judy—here we are, after all; and not a breach in the walls yet!"

"You mean she's gone—the Princess?"

He nodded. "I saw her off to Rome an hour ago."

Her eyes brightened, as they always did at his challenge; but it was only a passing animation. "And you haven't had any telegram?" she questioned.

The question took him unprepared. "I—why, have you?"

"Yes. From mother. Here." She produced the paper and thrust it feverishly into his hand. Boyne's anger rose—evidently, he thought, old Mrs. Mervin had waited to communicate with her daughter before answering him. What cowardice, what treachery! He pictured all these grown up powers and principalities leagued together against the handful of babes he commanded, and the bitterness of surrender entered into him. It was not that any of these parents really wanted their children. If they had, the break-up of Judith's dream, though tragic, would have been too natural to struggle against. But it was simply that the poor little things had become a bone of contention, that the taking or keeping possession of them was a matter of pride or of expediency, like fighting for a goal in some exciting game, or clinging to all one's points in an acrimoniously-disputed law-suit. Boyne unfolded Mrs. Wheater's telegram, and read: "You must come to

Paris immediately bringing Chip I must see you at once do not disobey me stop telegraph Hotel Nouveau Luxe Mother."

The vague phrasing made it impossible to guess whether the message were the result of a cable from Mrs. Mervin, or simply embodied a new whim of Joyce's. Boyne, on the whole, inclined to the latter view, and felt half ready to exonerate Mrs. Mervin. After all, perhaps she had kept faith with him, and her message was only the result of her own scruples.

He tossed the telegram onto the table with a shrug. "Is that all? You've heard nothing else?"

Yes; it appeared she had. Nanny, the day before, had received a letter from Mrs. Wheater's maid Marguerite, an experienced person who wielded a facile but rambling pen. This letter Judith had coaxed from Nanny, unknown to Miss Scope; for Miss Scope, even in the extremest emergencies, would not admit the possibility of her charges using, as a means of information, what the Princess would have called "salaried assistants."

Marguerite's news, if vague, was ample. It appeared that Mrs. Wheater had met in Venice a gentleman a good deal older than herself, whose name the maid could not even approximately spell, but who was quite different from any of the other gentlemen in her mistress's circle.

"Different—different how?"

"She says he's made a different woman of mother," Judith explained. "He's made her chuck Gerald, to begin with."

"But, for God's sake, why? I thought she was chucking your father on account of Gerald."

Judith went into this with the lucid impartiality she always applied to the analysis of her parents' foibles. She reminded Boyne that Joyce never stuck long to one thing, and that she had decided to marry Gerald chiefly in order to annoy her husband, and to have an excuse for detaining the young tutor at the Lido when the children left. "He's rather a Lido man, Gerald is," Judith commented, "and it made all the other women so furious. That's always rather fun, you know."

But, after all, she pursued, her mother had much more sense than her poor father, who was always the prey of women like Zinnia Lacrosse or Sybil Lullmer. "She does pull herself together sometimes—especially since that awful time with Buondelmonte. And so, when she met this other gentleman, who is so much older, and very religious, and enormously rich, and who only wants to influence her for good, Marguerite says it made her feel how dreadfully she'd wasted her life, and what a different woman she might have been if she'd known him years before. You see, he doesn't want to marry her, but only to be her friend and adviser. He thinks she's been married often enough. And so, in order not to leave Gerald at a loose end, she's kept him on as secretary till he can get another job, and she and Gerald and the other gentleman have gone to Paris together to see what had better be done. And the gentleman says she ought to have us all with her; and he feels awfully fond of us already, and knows mother will be ever so much happier if we're with her. . ."

"Oh, my God—then it's all up with us," Boyne groaned.

Judith made no answer, and he went on: "It only remains now to hear from Lady Wrench and the Princess!"

"Or Grandma Mervin—there's still grandma," Judith rejoined, half hopefully.

Boyne hesitated a moment; then he said to himself that there was no use in any farther postponement. "No; I've heard from her," he said.

Judith's eyes were again illuminated. "You have? Oh, Martin! If she'd only take us all, perhaps it would satisfy mother and the new gentleman. Oh, Martin, she doesn't say no?"

Silently—for no words came to him—he gave her the cable, and walked away to the window to be out of sight of her face. For a while he stood watching the gray curtain of failure that hung there between him and his golden weeks; then he pulled himself together and turned back."

"Judy—"

She handed him the cable.

"After all, you expected it, didn't you?" he said.

She nodded. "It doesn't make so much difference, anyhow," he continued, in an unconvinced voice, "if Bun and Beechy have to go. . ."

She pondered on this for a few moments without answering. Then, with one of her sudden changes of tone: "Martin," she broke out impetuously, "do you suppose she was right, after all—I mean the Princess—about our being so dreadfully behind the times? Do you suppose, if we did all the things she suggested: if we got new teachers and new books, and somebody for Bun's gymnastics, it would make any difference—do you think it would?" Every line of her face, from lifted eyebrows to parted lips, was a passionate demand for his assent. "After all, you know—perhaps she was right about some things: that stupid old book of Scopy's, for instance. Of course we all know poor darling Scopy's a back number. And about Bun's gymnastics too. Do you suppose if we took a villa at Meran we could afford to fit up a room like the one she described, and get an instructor—didn't she call him an instructor? And then there's fencing and riding—I dare say she was right about that too! But after all—" she paused, and her eyes looked as the rain did when the sun was trying to break through it. "After all, Martin," she began again, "the main thing is that the children are so well, isn't it? Look at our record—see what the summer has done! You wouldn't know Terry, would you, if you were to see him now for the first time after meeting us on the boat at Algiers? And Chip—isn't Chip a miracle? Every one stops Nanny in the street to admire him, and they always think he must be three years old. He was just beginning to walk alone when he came here—now he runs like a hare! Nanny gets worn out chasing him. And the tricks he's learnt to do! He can imitate everybody; I believe he's going to be a movie star. Have you seen him do the lion, with Bun as lion-tamer? Or the old man at the market, all doubled up with sciatica, who leans on a stick, and holds one hand behind his back? But it's a wonder! Oh, Martin, wait, and I'll fetch him down now to do the old man for you—shall I?"

Once again her grown up cares had vanished in the childish pride of recounting Chip's achievements. Would it always be like this, Boyne wondered, or would life gradually close the gates of the fairyland which was still so close to her? He would have given most of his chances of happiness to help her keep open that communication with her childhood. And what if he were the one being who could do it? The question wound itself through his thoughts like a persuasive hand insinuating itself into his. This heart-break of separation that was upon her—

what if he alone had the power to ease it? He stood looking down at her perplexedly.

"Judy—Chip's a great man, and I'd love to see him do the old gentleman with the sciatica. But first. . ."

"Yes—first?" she palpitated. But under his gaze her radiance gradually faded, and her lips began to tremble a little. "Ah, then you don't think . . . there's any hope for us?"

"I think you've got to go to Paris and see your mother."

"And take Chip? I'll never take Chip! I won't!"

"But listen, dear—." He sat down, and drew her to the sofa beside him, speaking as he might have to a child on a holiday who was fighting the summons back to school.

"Listen, Judy. We've done our best; we all have. But the children are not yours or mine. They belong to their parents, after all." How dry and flat his phrases sounded, compared with the words he longed to say to her!

She drew back into the corner of the sofa. "That Buondelmonte woman's got at you—she's talked you over! I knew she would." She was grown up again now, measuring him with angry suspicious eyes, and flinging out her accusations in her mother's shrillest voice.

"Why, child, what nonsense! You said just now that perhaps the Princess was right. . ."

"I never did! I said, perhaps we ought to get a new Cyclopædia for Scopy, and have Bun taught scientific gymnastics; and now you say . . ."

"I say that fate's too much for us. It didn't need the Princess Buondelmonte to teach me that."

She made no answer, and they sat in silence in their respective corners of the sofa, each gazing desperately into a future of which nothing could be divined except that it was the end of their hopes. Suddenly Judith flung herself face down against the knobby cushions and broke into weeping. Boyne, for a few minutes, remained numb and helpless; then he moved closer, and bending over drew her into his arms. She seemed hardly aware of his nearness; she simply went on crying, with hard uneven sobs, pressing her face against his shoulder as if it were the sofa-cushion. He held her in silence, not venturing to speak, or even to brush back her tumbled hair, while he pictured, with the acuity of his older and less articulate grief, what must be passing before her as the fibres of her heart were torn away. "It's too cruel—it's too beastly cruel," he thought, wincing at the ugly details which must enter into her vision of the future, details he could only guess at, while she saw them with all the precision of experience. Yes, it was too cruel; but what could he or she do? He continued to hold her in silence, listening to the beat of the rain on the half-open window, and smelling the cold grave-yard smell of the autumn earth, while her sobs ran through him in shocks of anguish.

Gradually her weeping subsided, and Boyne took courage to lift his hand and pass it once or twice over her hair. She lay in his hold as quietly as a frightened bird, and presently he bent his head and whispered: "Judy—." Why not? he thought; his heart was beating with reckless bounds. He was free, after all, if it came to that; free to chuck his life away on any madness; and madness this was, he knew. Well, he'd had enough of reason for the rest of his days; and a man is only as old as he feels. . . He bent so close that his lips brushed her ear. "Judy, darling, listen. . . Perhaps after all there's a way—"

In a flash she was out of his arms, and ecstatically facing him. "A way—a way of keeping us all together?" Ah, how hard her questions were to answer!

Boyne drew her down again beside him. Crying was a laborious and disfiguring business to her, and her face was so drawn and tear-stained that she looked almost old; but its misery was shot through with hope. If he could have kept her there, not speaking, only answering her with endearments, how easy, how exquisite it would have been! But her face was tense with expectation, and he had to find words, for he knew that his silence would have no meaning for her.

"Judith—" he began; but she interrupted: "Call me Judy, or I shall think it's more bad news." He made no answer, and she flung herself against him with a cry of alarm. "Martin! Martin! You're not going to desert us too?"

He held her hands, but his own had begun to tremble. "Darling, I'll never desert you; I'll stay with you always if you'll have me; if things go wrong I'll always be there to look after you and defend you; no matter what happens, we'll never be separated any more. . ." He broke off, his voice failing before the sudden sunrise in her eyes.

"Oh, Martin—" She lifted his hands one by one to her wet cheeks, and held them there in silent bliss. "Then you don't belong any longer to Mrs. Sellars?"

"I don't belong to any one but you—for as long as ever you'll have me. . ."

Her eyes still bathed him in their radiance. "My darling, my darling." She leaned close as she said it, and he dared not move, in his new awe of her nearness—so subtly had she changed from the child of his familiar endearments to the woman he passionately longed for. . . "Darling," she said again; then, with a face in which the bridal light seemed already kindled, "Oh, Martin, do you really mean you're going to adopt us all, and we're all going to stay with you forever?"

XXIX

BOYNE felt like a man who has blundered along in the dark to the edge of a precipice. He trembled inwardly with the effort of recovery, and the shock of finding himself flung back into his old world. Judith, in a rush of gratitude, had thrown her arms about him; and he shrank from her touch, from the warm smell of her hair, from everything about her which he had to think back into terms of childhood and comradeship, while every vein in his body still ached for her. There was nothing he would have dreaded as much as her detecting the least trace of what he was feeling. His first care must be to hide the break in their perfect communion—the fact that for a moment she had been for him the woman she would some day be for another man, in a future he could never share. He undid her hands and walked away to the window.

When he turned to her again he had struggled back to some sort of composure. "Judy, child, I wish you wouldn't take such terrible life-leases on the future." He tried to smile as he said it. "I'm always afraid it will bring us bad luck. We'd much better live from hand to mouth. I'm ready to promise all that a reasonable man can—that I'll put up another big fight for you, and that I don't despair of winning it. At any rate, I'll be there; I'll stand by you; I won't desert you. . ." He broke off, reading in her unsatisfied eyes the hopelessness of piling up vague assurances. . .

"Yes," she assented, in a voice grown as small and colourless as her face.

He stood before her miserably. "You do understand, dear, don't you?"

"I'm not sure. . ." She hesitated. "A little while ago I thought I did."

His nerves began to twitch again. Could he bear to go into the question with her once more—and what would be the use if he did? The immediate future must somehow or other be dealt with; but the last few minutes had deprived him of all will and energy. He had the desolate sense of her knowing that he had failed her, and yet not being able to guess why.

"Of course I'll do what I can," he repeated.

She remained silent, constrained by his constraint; and he saw the disappointment in her eyes.

"You don't believe me?"

Still she looked at him perplexedly. "But you said. . . I thought you said just now that you'd found a way of keeping us all together. No matter what happened; you had a plan, you said."

His senseless irritation grew upon him. Could such total simplicity be unfeigned? Could she have such a power of awaking passion without any inkling of its meaning? He hated himself for doubting it. In time—a short time, perhaps—her rich nature would come to its ripeness; but as yet the only full-grown faculties in it were her love for her brothers and sisters, and her faith in the few people who had shown her kindness in a world unkindly.

"I'm sorry," she continued, after pausing for an answer which did not come. "I must have misunderstood you, I suppose."

Boyne gave a nervous laugh. "You did, most thoroughly."

"And—you won't tell me what you really meant?"

He stood motionless, his hands in his pockets, staring down at the knots in the wooden floor, as he had stared at them on the day when she had owned to having taken her father's money—but in a mental perturbation how much deeper! A few minutes before, it had seemed like profanation to brush her with the thought of his love; now, faced by her despair, by her sense of being left alone to fight her battles, he asked himself whether it might not be fairer, even kinder, to speak. At the thought his heart again began to beat excitedly. Perhaps he had been too impetuous, too inarticulate. What if, after all, a word from him could wake the sleeping music?

The difficulty was to find a beginning. What would have been so simple if kisses could have told it, seemed tortuous or brutal when put in words. He shrank not so much from the possibility of hurting her as from the sudden fear of her hurting him beyond endurance.

"Judith," he began, "how old are you?"

"I shall be sixteen in three months—no, in five months, really," she said, with an obvious effort at truthfulness.

"As near as that! Well, sixteen is an age," he laughed.

She continued to fix her bewildered eyes on him, as if seeking a clue. "But I look a lot older, don't I?" she added hopefully.

"Older? There are times when you look so old that you frighten me." He remembered then that she had spoken to him with perfect simplicity of Gerald Ormerod's desire to marry her, as of the most natural thing in the world; and his own scruples began to seem absurd. "I'm always forgetting what a liberal education she's had," he thought with a touch of self-derision.

He cleared his throat, and continued: "So grown up that I suppose you'll soon be thinking of getting married."

The word was out now; it went sounding on and on inside of his head while he awaited her answer. When she spoke it was with an air of indifference and disappointment.

"What's the use of saying that? How can I ever marry, with all the children to look after?" It was clear that she regarded the subject as irrelevant; her tone seemed to remind him that he and she had long since dealt with and disposed of it. "You might as well tell me that I ought to be educated," she grumbled.

He pressed on: "But it might turn out . . . you might find . . ." He had to pause to steady his voice. "If we can't prevent the children being taken away from you, you'll be awfully lonely. . ."

"Taken away from me?" At the word her listlessness vanished. "Do you suppose I'll let them be taken like that? Without fighting to the very last minute? Let Syb Lullmer get hold of Chip—and Bun and Beechy go to that Buondelmonte man?"

"I know. It's hateful. But supposing the very worst happens—oughtn't you to face that now?" He cleared his throat again. "If things went wrong, and you were very lonely, and a fellow asked you to marry him—"

"Who asked me?"

He laughed again. "If I did."

For a moment she looked at him perplexedly; then her eyes cleared, and for the first time she joined in his laugh. Hers seemed to bubble up, fresh and limpid, from the very depths of her little girlhood. "Well, that would be funny!" she said.

There was a bottomless silence.

"Yes—wouldn't it?" Boyne grinned. He stared at her without speaking; then, like a blind man feeling his way, he picked up his hat and mackintosh, said: "Where's my umbrella? Oh, outside—" and walked out stiffly into the passage. On the doorstep, still aware of her nearness, he added a little dizzily: "No, please—I want a long tramp alone first. . . I'll come in again this afternoon to settle what we'd better do about Paris. . ."

He felt her little disconsolate figure standing alone behind him in the rain, and hurried away as if to put himself out of its reach forever.

XXX

IT was still raining when the Wheater colony left Cortina; it was raining when the train in which Boyne and Judith were travelling reached Paris. During the days intervening between the receipt of Mrs. Wheater's telegram and the clattering halt of the express in the gare de Lyon, Boyne could not remember that the rain had ever stopped.

But he had not had time to do much remembering—not even of the havoc within himself. After the struggle necessary to convince Judith that she must go to Paris and take Chip with her—since disobedience to her mother's summons might put them irretrievably in the wrong—he had first had to help her decide what should be done with the other children. Once brought round to his view, she had immediately risen to the emergency, as she always did when practical matters were at stake. She and Boyne were agreed that it would be imprudent to leave the children at Cortina, where the Princess, or even Lady Wrench, might take advantage of their absence to effect a raid on the *pension*. It took a three days' hunt to find a villa in a remote suburb of Riva where they could be temporarily installed without much risk of being run down by an outraged parent. Boyne put the *Rosenglüh* landlady off the scent by giving her the address of Mrs. Wheater's Paris banker, and letting it be understood that Judith was off to Paris to prepare for the children's arrival; and Blanca and Terry, still deep in Conan Doyle, gleefully contributed misleading details.

The excitement of departure, and the business of establishing the little Wheaters in their new quarters, left no time, between Boyne and Judith, for less pressing questions; and Boyne saw that, once their plan was settled, Judith was almost as much amused as the twins by its secret and adventurous side. "It will take a Dr. Watson to nose them out, won't it?" she chuckled, as she and Boyne, with Chip and Susan, scrambled into the Paris express at Verona. It was not till they were in the train that Boyne saw the cloud of apprehension descend on her again. But then fatigue intervened, and she fell asleep against his shoulder as peacefully as Chip, who was curled up opposite with his head in Susan's lap. As they sat there, Boyne remembered how, on the day of Mr. Dobree's picnic, he had watched her sleeping by the waterfall, a red glow in her cheeks, velvet shadows under her lashes. Now her face was pinched and sallow, the lids were swollen with goodbye tears; she seemed farther from him than she had ever been, yet more in need of him; and at the thought something new and tranquillizing entered into him. He had caught a glimpse of a joy he would never reach, and he knew that his eyes would always dazzle with it; but the obligation of giving Judith the help she needed kept his pain in that deep part of the soul where the great renunciations lie.

In Paris he left his companions at the door of the *Nouveau Luxe,* where Mrs. Wheater was established, drove to his own modest hotel on the left bank, and turned in for a hard tussle of thinking. He could no longer put off dealing with his own case, for Mrs. Sellars was still in Paris. He had not meant to let her know of his arrival till the next day; he needed the interval to get the fatigue and confusion out of his brain. But meanwhile he must map out some kind of a working plan; must clear up his own mind, and consider how to make it clear to her. And after an unprofitable attempt at rest and sleep, and a weary tramp in the rain through the dusky glittering streets, he suddenly decided on immediate action, and turned into a telephone booth to call up Mrs. Sellars. She was at home and answered immediately. Aunt Julia was resting, she said; if he would come at once they could talk without fear of interruption.

He caught the tremor of joy in her voice when he spoke her name—but how like her, how perfect of her, to ask no questions, to waste no time in exclamations; just quietly and simply to say "Come"! The healing touch of her reasonableness again came to his rescue.

He would have liked to find her close at hand, on the very threshold of the telephone booth; at the rate at which his thoughts were spinning he knew he would have to go over the whole affair again in his transit to her hotel. But there was no remedy for that; he could only trust to her lucidity to help him out.

Aunt Julia's apartment was in a hotel of the rue de Rivoli, with a row of windows overhanging the silvery reaches of the Tuileries gardens and the vista of domes and towers beyond. The room was large, airy, full of flowers. A fire burned on the hearth; Rose Sellars's touch was everywhere. And a moment later she stood there before him, incredibly slim and young-looking in her dark dress and close little hat. Slightly paler, perhaps, and thinner—but as she moved forward with her easy step the impression vanished. He felt only her mastery of life and of herself, and thought how much less she needed him than did the dishevelled child he had just left. The thought widened the distance between them, and brought Judith abruptly closer.

"Well, here I am," he said—"and I've failed!"

He had prepared a dozen opening phrases—but the sudden intrusion of Judith's face dashed them all from his lips. He was returning to ask forgiveness of the woman to whom he still considered himself engaged, and his first word, after an absence prolonged and unaccountable, was to remind her of the cause of their breach. He saw the narrowing of her lips, and then her victorious smile.

"Dear! Tell me about it—I want to hear everything," she said, holding out her hand.

But he was still struggling in the coil of his blunder. "Oh, never mind—all that's really got nothing to do with it," he stammered.

She freed her hand, and turned on the electric switch of the nearest lamp. As she bent to it he saw that the locks escaping on each temple were streaked with gray. The sight seemed to lengthen the days of their separation into months and years. He felt like a stranger coming back to her. "You've forgiven me?" he began.

She looked at him gravely. "What is it I have to forgive?"

"A lot—you must think," he said confusedly.

She shook her head. "You're free, you know. We're just two old friends talking. Sit down over there—so." She pointed to an armchair, sat down herself, and took off her hat. In the lamplight, under the graying temples, her face looked changed and aged, like her hair. But it was varnished over by her undaunted smile.

"Let us go back to where you began. I want to hear all about the children." She leaned her head thoughtfully on her hand, in the attitude he had loved in the little sitting-room at Cortina.

"I feel like a ghost—" he said.

"No; for I should be a little afraid of you if you were a ghost; and now—"

"Well—now. . ." He looked about the pleasant firelit room, saw her work-basket in its usual place near the hearth, her books heaped up on a table, and a familiar litter of papers on a desk in the window. "A ghost," he repeated.

She waited a moment, and then said: "I wish you'd tell me exactly what's been happening."

"Oh, everything's collapsed. It was bound to. And now I—"

He got up, walked across the room, glanced half-curiously at the titles of some of the books, and came back and leaned against the mantelpiece. She sat looking up at him. "Yes?"

"No. I can't."

"You can't—what?"

"Account for anything. Explain anything—" He dropped back into his chair and threw his head back, staring at the ceiling. "I've been a fool—and I'm tired; tired."

"Then we'll drop explanations. Tell me only what you want," she said.

What he really wanted was not to tell her anything, but to get up again, and resume his inarticulate wanderings about the room. With an effort of the will he remained seated, and turned his eyes to hers. "You've been perfect—and I do want to tell you . . . to make you understand. . ." But no; that sort of talk was useless. He had better try to do what she had asked him. "About the children—well, the break-up was bound to come.

You were right about it, of course. But I was so sorry for the poor little devils that I tried to blind myself. . ."

His tongue was loosened, and he found it easier to go on. After all, Mrs. Sellars was right; the story of the children must be disposed of first. After that he might see more clearly into his own case and hers. He went on with his halting narrative, and she listened in silence—that rare silence of hers which was all alertness and sympathy. She smiled a little over the Princess Buondelmonte's invasion, and sighed and frowned when he mentioned that Lady Wrench was also impending. When he came to Mrs. Wheater's summons, and his own insistence that Judith and Chip should immediately obey it, she lifted her eyes, and said approvingly: "But of course you were perfectly right."

"Was I? I don't know. When I left them just now at the door of that Moloch of a hotel—"

She gave a little smile of reassurance. "No; I don't think you need fear even the *Nouveau Luxe.* I understand what you're feeling; but I think I can give you some encouragement."

"Encouragement—?"

"About the future, I mean. Perhaps Mrs. Wheater's news about herself is not altogether misleading. At any rate, I know she's taken the best legal advice; and I hear she may be able to keep all the children—her own, that is. For of course the poor little steps—"

Boyne listened with a sudden start of attention. He felt like some one shaken out of a lethargy. "You've seen her, then? I didn't know you knew her."

"No; I've not seen her, and I don't know her. But a friend of mine does. The fact is, she ran across Mr. Dobree at the Lido after he left Cortina—"

"Dobree?" He stared, incredulous, as if he must have heard the wrong name.

"Yes; hasn't she mentioned it to the children? Ah, no—I remember she never writes. Well, she had the good sense to ask him to take charge of things for her, and though he doesn't often accept new cases nowadays he was so sorry for the children—and for her too, he says—that he agreed to look after her interests. And he tells me that if she follows his advice, and keeps out of new entanglements, he thinks she can divorce Mr. Wheater on her own terms, and in that case of course the courts will give her all the children. Isn't that the very best news I could give you?"

He tried to answer, but again found himself benumbed. Her eyes continued to challenge him. "It's more than you hoped?" she smiled.

"It's not in the least what I expected."

She waited for him to continue, but he was silent again, and she questioned suddenly: "What *did* you expect?"

He looked at her with a confused stare, as if her face had become that of a stranger, as familiar faces do in a dream. "Dobree," he said—"this Dobree. . ."

She kindled. "You're very unfair to Mr. Dobree, Martin; you always have been. He's not only a great lawyer, whose advice Mrs. Wheater is lucky to have, but a kind and wise friend . . . and a good man," she added.

"Yes," he said, hardly hearing her. All the torture of his hour of madness about Mr. Dobree had returned to him. He would have liked to leap up on the instant, and go and find him, and fight it out with his fists. . .

"I can't think," she continued nervously, "what more you could have hoped. . ."

He made a weary gesture. "God knows! But what does it matter?"

"Matter? Doesn't it matter to you that the children should be safe—be provided for? That in this new crash they should remain with their mother, and not be tossed about again from pillar to post? If you didn't want that, what did you want?"

"I wanted—somehow—to get them all out of this hell."

"I believe you exaggerate. It's not going to be a hell if their mother keeps them, as Mr. Dobree thinks she'll be able to. You say yourself that she's fond of them."

"Yes; intermittently."

"And, after all, if the step-children are taken back by their own parents, that's only natural. You say the new Princess Buondelmonte seems well-meaning, and kind in her way; and as for Zinnie—I suppose Zinnie is the one of the party the best able to take care of herself."

"I suppose so," he acceded.

"Well, then—." She paused, and then repeated, with a sharper stress: "I don't yet see what you want."

He looked about him with the same estranged stare with which his eyes had rested on her face. Something clear and impenetrable as a pane of crystal seemed to cut him off from her, and from all that surrounded her. He had been to the country from which travellers return with another soul.

"What I want. . . ?" Ah, he knew that well enough! What he wanted, at the moment, was just some opiate to dull the dogged ache of body and soul—to close his ears against that laugh of Judith's, and all his senses to her nearness. He was caught body and soul—that was it; and real loving was not the delicate distraction, the food for dreams, he had imagined it when he thought himself in love with Rose Sellars; it was this perpetual obsession, this clinging nearness, this breaking on the rack of every bone, and tearing apart of every fibre. And his apprenticeship to it was just beginning. . .

Well, there was one thing certain; it was that he must get away, as soon as he could, from the friendly room and Rose's forgiving presence. He tried to blunder into some sort of explanation. "I don't suppose I've any business to be here," he began abruptly.

Mrs. Sellars was silent; but it was not one of her speaking silences. It was like a great emptiness slowly widening between them. For a moment he thought she meant to force on him the task of bridging it over; then he saw that she was struggling with a pain as benumbing as his own. She could not think of anything to say any more than he could, and her helplessness moved him, and brought her nearer. "She wants to end it decently, as I do," he thought; but his pity for her did not help him to find words.

At length he got up and held out his hand. "You're the best friend I've ever had—and the dearest. But I'm going off on a big job somewhere; I must. At the other end of the world. For a time—"

"Yes," she assented, very low. She did not take the hand he held out—perhaps did not even see it. When two people part who have loved each other it is as if what happens between them befell in a great emptiness—as if the tearing asunder of the flesh must turn at last into a disembodied anguish.

"You've forgotten your umbrella," she said, as he reached the door. He gave a little laugh as he came back to get it.

XXXI

THE next day Boyne lunched at the *Nouveau Luxe* alone with Mrs. Wheater and Judith. He had wondered if it would occur to Joyce that it might be preferable to lunch upstairs, in her own rooms; but it had not; and his mind was too dulled with pain for him to care much for his surroundings. No crowd could make him feel farther away from Judith than the unseeing look in her own eyes.

Mrs. Wheater was dressed with a Quaker-like austerity which made her look younger and handsomer than when he had last seen her, in the rakish apparel of the Lido. She had acquired another new voice, as she did with each new phase; this time it was subdued and somewhat melancholy, but less studied than the fluty tones she had affected in Venice. Altogether, Boyne had to admit that she had improved—that Mr. Dobree's influence had achieved what others had failed to do. After lunch they went upstairs, and Joyce proposed to Judith that, as the rain had stopped, she should take Chipstone and Susan to the Bois de Boulogne. She herself wanted to have a quiet talk with dear Martin—Judith could send the motor back to pick her up at four; no, at half-past three. She had promised to go to a wonderful loan exhibition of Incunabula with Mr. Dobree. . . Judith nodded and disappeared, with a faint smile at Boyne.

Mr. Dobree had opened her eyes to so many marvels, Joyce continued when they were alone. Incunabula, for instance—would Boyne believe that she had never before heard of their existence? Mr. Dobree had thought she must be joking when she asked him what they were. But Martin knew how much chance she had had of cultivating herself in Cliffe's society. . . Yes, and she was beginning to collect books—first editions—and to form a real library. Didn't he think it would be a splendid thing for the children—especially for Terry? She blushed to think that while the family travelled over Europe in steam-yachts and Blue Trains and Rolls-Royces, poor Terry had had to feed on the rubbish Scopy could pick up for him in hotel libraries, or the *cabinets de lecture* of frowsy watering-places. Mr. Dobree had been horrified when he found that Cliffe, with all his millions, had never owned a library! But then he didn't know Cliffe.

Joyce went on to unfold her plans for the future. She spoke, as usual, as if they were fixed and immutable in every detail. She had decided to buy a place in the country—near either Paris or Dinard, she wasn't sure which. Probably Dinard on account of Terry's health. The climate was mild; and it was said that there were educational advantages. If the sea was too strong for him she could find a house somewhere inland. But they must be near a town on account of the children's education, and yet not in it because of the demoralising influences, and the lack of good air. In a few days she was going down to look about her at Dinard. . .

Boyne knew, she supposed, that she had begun divorce proceedings? Of course she ought to have done it long ago—but in that *milieu* one's moral sense got absolutely blunted. Evidence—? Heavens! She already had more than enough to make her own terms. Horrors and horrors. . . There was no doubt, Mr. Dobree said, that the courts would give her the custody of all the children.

And from now on they would be the sole object of her life. Didn't Boyne agree that, at her age, there couldn't be a more perfect conclusion? Oh, yes, she knew—she looked younger than she really was . . . but there were gray streaks in her hair already; hadn't he noticed? And she wasn't going to dye it; not she! She was going to let herself turn frankly into an *old woman*. She didn't mind the idea a bit. Middle-age was so full of duties and interests of its own; she had a perfect horror of the women who are always dyeing and drugging themselves, in the hopeless attempt to keep young—like that pitiable Syb Lullmer, for instance. She had learned, thank heaven, that there were other things in life. And her first object, of course, was to get the children away from hotels and hotel contacts—from all the *Nouveaux Luxes* and the "Palaces." She was counting the minutes till she could create a real home for them, and make them so happy that they would never want to leave it. . . She knew Boyne would approve. . . The monologue ended by her expressing her gratitude for all he had done for the children, and her delight at being reunited to Judith and Chip—Chip, oh, he was a wonder, so fat and tall, and walking and talking like a boy of four. And Judith told her it was all thanks to Boyne. . .

Mrs. Wheater seemed genuinely sorry to think that Bun and Beechy would probably have to return to their father. But perhaps, she added, if the new Princess Buondelmonte was so full of good intentions, and so determined to have her own way, the two children might get a fairly decent bringing-up. Buondelmonte wasn't as young as he had been, and might be glad to settle down, if his wife made him comfortable, and let him have enough money to gamble at his club. And as for Zinnie

—Joyce shrugged, and doubted if either her mother or Cliffe would really take Zinnie on, when it came to the point. She was rather a handful, Zinnie was; no one but Judy could control her. Still, grieved as Joyce would be to give up the "steps," poor little souls, she was too much used to human ingratitude not to foresee that they might be taken from her at any moment. But her own children—no! Never again. Of that Boyne might be assured. She had learned her lesson, her eyes had been opened to her own folly and imprudence; and Mr. Dobree had absolutely promised her—oh, by the way, wasn't Martin going to stay and see Mr. Dobree, who would be turning up at any minute now to take her to see the Incunabula? She thought he and Martin had met at Cortina, hadn't they? Yes, she remembered; Mr. Dobree had been so struck by Martin's devotion to the children. She hoped so much they might meet again and make friends. . . Boyne thanked her, and thought perhaps another time . . . but he was leaving Paris, probably; he couldn't wait then. . . He got himself out of the room in a confusion of excuses. . .

All day he wandered through the streets, inconsolably. His will-power seemed paralysed. He was determined to get away from Paris at once, to go to New York first, in quest of a job, and then to whatever end of the world the job should call him. There was no object in his lingering where he was for another hour. He and Rose Sellars had said their last word to each other—and to Judith herself what more had he to say? Yet he could not submit his mind to the idea that his happy unreal life of the last weeks was over; that he would never again enter the *pension* at Cortina, and see the little Wheaters flocking about him in a tumult of welcome, begging for a romp, a game, a story, clamouring to have their quarrels arbitrated, demanding to be taken on a picnic—with Judith serene above the tumult, or laughing and twittering with the rest. . . When he grew too tired to walk farther he turned in at a post-office, and wrote a cable which he had been revolving for some hours. It was addressed to the New York contractors who had written to ask if he could trace the young engineer who had been his assistant. Luckily he had not been able to, and he cabled: "Should like for myself the job you wrote about. Can I have it? Can start at once. Cable bankers."

This message despatched, he turned to the telephone booth, rang up the *Nouveau Luxe*, and asked to speak to Miss Wheater. Interminable minutes passed after he had put in his call; Mrs. Wheater's maid was found first, who didn't know where Judith was, or how to find her; then Susan, who said Judith had come back, and gone out again, and that all she knew was that the ladies were going to dine out that evening with Mr. Dobree, and go to the theatre. Then, just as Boyne was turning away discouraged, Judith's own voice: "Hullo, Martin! Where are you? When can I see you?"

"Now, if you can come. I'm off tonight—to London." He suddenly found he had decided that without knowing it.

She exclaimed in astonishment, and asked where she was to meet him; and he acquiesced in her suggestion that it should be at a tea-room near her hotel, as it was so late that she would soon have to hurry back for dinner. He jumped into a taxi, secured a table in a remote corner of the tea-room, and met her on the threshold a moment later. It was already long after six, and the rooms were emptying; in a few minutes they would have the place to themselves.

Judith, a little flushed with the haste of her arrival, looked gracefully grown up in her dark coat edged with fur, a pretty antelope bag in her gloved hand. The bare-headed girl of the Dolomites, in sports' frock and russet shoes, had been replaced by a demure young woman who seemed to Boyne almost a stranger.

"Martin! You're not really going away tonight?" she began at once, not noticing his request that she should choose between tea-cakes and *éclairs*.

He said he was, for a few days at any rate; the mere sound of her voice, the look in her eyes, had nearly dissolved his plans again, and his own voice was unsteady.

The fact that it was only for a few days seemed to reassure Judith. He'd be back by the end of the week, she hoped, wouldn't he? Yes—oh, yes, he said—very probably.

"Because, you know, the children'll be here by that time," she announced; and, turning her attention to the trays presented: "Oh, both, I think—yes, I'll take both."

"The children?"

"Yes; mother's just settled it. Mr. Dobree wrote the wire for her. If Nanny gets it in time they're to start to-morrow. Mr. Dobree thinks we may be able to keep the steps too—he's going to write himself to Buondelmonte. And he doesn't believe the Wrenches will ever bother us about Zinnie . . . at least not at present. He's found out a lot of things about Lord Wrench, and he thinks Zinnia'll have her hands full with him, without tackling Zinnie too."

She spoke serenely, almost lightly, as if all her anxieties had been dispelled. Could it be that the mere change of scene, the few hours spent with her mother, had so completely reassured her? She, who had always measured Joyce with such precocious insight, was it possible that she was deluded by her now? Or had she too succumbed to Mr. Dobree's mysterious influence? Boyne looked at her careless face and wondered.

"But this Dobree—you didn't fancy him much at Cortina? What makes you believe in him now?"

She seemed a little puzzled, and wrinkled her brows in the effort to find a reason. "I don't know. He's funny looking, of course; and rather pompous. And I do like you heaps better, Martin. But he's been most awfully good about the children, and he can make mother do whatever he tells her. And she says he's a great lawyer, and his clients almost always win their cases. Oh, Martin, wouldn't it be heavenly if he could really keep us together, steps and all? He's sworn to me that he will." She turned her radiant eyes on Boyne. "Anyhow, the children will be here the day after to-morrow, and that will be splendid, won't it? You must get back from London as soon as ever you can, and take us all off somewhere for the day, just as if we were still at Cortina."

Yes, of course he would, Boyne said; on Scopy's book he would. She lit up at that, asking where they'd better go, and finally settling that, if the rain ever held up, a day at Versailles would be jollier than anything. . . But it must be soon, she reminded him; because in a few days Mrs. Wheater was going to carry them all off to Dinard.

Yes, she pursued, she really did feel that Mr. Dobree, just in a few weeks, had gained more influence over her mother than any one else ever had. Judith had had a long talk with him that morning, and he had told her frankly that he was doing it all out of interest in the children, and because he wanted to help her—wasn't that dear of him? Anyhow, they were all going to stand together, grown ups and children, and put up a last big fight. ("On Scopy's book," Boyne interpolated with a strained smile.) And they were to have a big house in the country, with lots of dogs and horses, she continued. And the children were never to go to hotels any more. And Terry was to have a really first-rate tutor, and be sent to school in Switzerland as soon as he was strong enough; in another year, perhaps.

Boyne sat watching her with insatiable eyes. She looked so efficient, so experienced—yet what could be surer proof of her childishness than this suddenly revived faith in the future? He saw that whoever would promise to keep the children together would gain a momentary hold over her—as he once had, alas! And he saw also that the mere change of scene, the excitement of the flight from Cortina, the encouragement which her mother's new attitude gave her, were so many balloons lifting her up into the blue. . . "It will be Versailles, don't you think so?" she began again. "Or, if it rains deluges, what about the circus, and a big tea afterward, somewhere where Chip and Nanny could come too?" She looked at him with her hesitating smile. "I thought, perhaps, if you didn't mind—but, no, darling," she broke off decisively, "we won't ask Mr. Dobree!"

"Lord—I should hope not; not if I'm giving the party." He found the voice and laugh she expected, gave her back her banter, discussed and fixed with her the day and hour of the party. And all the while there echoed in his ears, more insistently than anything she was saying, a line or two from the chorus of Lemures, in "Faust," which Rose had read aloud one evening at Cortina.

Who made the room so mean and bare—
Where are the chairs, the tables where?
It was lent for a moment only—

A moment only: not a bad title for the history of his last few months! A moment only; and he had always known it. "An episode," he thought, "it's been only an episode. One of those things that come up out of the sea, on a full-moon night, playing the harp. . . Yes; but sometimes the episodes last, and the things one thought eternal wither like grass—and only the gods know which it will be . . . if *they* do. . .

"L'addition, mademoiselle? Good Lord, child; four *éclairs?* And a Dobree dinner in the offing! Ah, thrice-happy infancy, as the poet said. . . Yes, here's your umbrella. Take my arm, and we'll nip round on foot to the back door of the *Luxe.* You've eaten so much that I haven't got enough left to pay for a taxi. . ."

From the threshold of the hotel she called to him, rosy under her shining umbrella: "Thursday morning, then, you'll fetch us all at ten?" And he called back: "On Scopy's book, I will!" as the rain engulfed him.

On the day fixed for the children's picnic Boyne lay half asleep on the deck of a South American liner. It was better so—a lot better. The morning after he had parted from Judith at the door of the *Nouveau Luxe* the summons had come: "Job yours please sail immediately for Rio particulars on arrival"; and he had just had time to pitch his things into his portmanteaux, catch the first train for London, and scramble on board his boat at Liverpool.

A lot better so. . . The busy man's way of liquidating hopeless situations. It reminded him of the old times when, at the receipt of such a summons, cares and complications fell from him like dust from a shaken garment. It would not be so now; his elasticity was gone. Yet already, after four days at sea, he was beginning to feel a vague solace in the empty present, and in the future packed with duties. No hesitating, speculating, wavering to and fro—he was to be caught as soon as he landed, and thrust into the stiff harness of his work. And meanwhile, more and more miles of sea were slipping in between him and the last months, making them already seem remote and vapoury compared with the firm outline of the future.

The day was mild, with a last touch of summer on the lazy waves over which they were gliding. . . He closed his eyes and slept. . .

At Versailles too it was mild; there were yellow leaves still on the beeches of the long walks; they formed golden tunnels, with hazy blueish vistas where the park melted into the blur of the forest. But the gardens were almost deserted; it was too late in the season for the children chasing their hoops and balls down the alleys, the groups of nurses knitting and gossiping on wooden chairs under the great stone Dianas and Apollos.

Funny—he and the little Wheaters seemed to have the lordly pleasure-grounds to themselves. The clipped walls of beech and hornbean echoed with their shouts and laughter. What a handful the little Wheaters were getting to be! Terry, now, could run and jump with the rest; and as for Chip, rounder than ever in a white fur coat and tasselled cap, his waddle was turning into a scamper. . .

In the sun, under a high protecting hedge, Miss Scope and Nanny sat and beamed upon their children; and Susan flew down the vistas after Chip. . .

Boyne and Judith were alone. They had wandered away into one of the *bosquets:* solitary even in summer, with vacant-faced divinities niched in green, broken arcades, toy temples deserted of their gods. On this November day, when mist was everywhere, mist trailing through the half-bare trees, lying in a faint bloom on the lichened statues, oozing up from the layers of leaves underfoot, the place seemed the ghostly setting of dead days. Boyne looked down at Judith, and even her face was ghostly. . . "Come," he said with a shiver, "let's get back into the sun—." Outside of the *bosquet,* down the alley, the children came storming toward them, shouting, laughing and wrangling. Boyne, laughing too, caught up the furry Chip, and swung him high in air. Bun, to attract his attention, turned a new somersault at his feet, and Zinnie and Beechy squealed: "Martin, now's the time for presents!" For, since the Princess Buondelmonte had been so shocked by their cupidity, it had become a joke with the children to be always petitioning for presents.

"Little devils—as if I could ever leave them!" Boyne thought.

"Tea, sir?" said the steward. "Ham sandwiches?"

XXXII

BOYNE was coming back from Brazil. His steamer was approaching Bordeaux, moving up the estuary of the Gironde under a September sky as mild as the one which had roofed his sleep when, nearly three years earlier, he had dreamt he was at Versailles with the little Wheaters.

Three years of work and accomplishment lay behind him. And the job was not over; that was the best of it. A touch of fever had disabled him, and he was to take a few weeks' holiday in Europe, and then return to his task. His first idea had been to put in this interval of convalescence in America; to take the opportunity to look up his people, and see a few old friends in New York. But he was sure to find Rose Sellars in New York, or near it; he could hardly go there without being obliged to see her. And the time for that had not yet come—if it ever would. He looked at his grizzled head, his sallow features with brown fever-blotches under the skin, and put away the idea with a grimace. The tropics seemed fairly to have burnt him out. . .

Rose Sellars had been kind; she had been perfect, as he had foreseen she would be. He knew that, after a winter on the Nile with Aunt Julia, she had returned to her own house in New York; for, once re-established there, she had begun to write to him again. From her letters—which were free from all recriminations, all returning to the past—he learned that she had taken up her old life again: the reading, the social round, the small preoccupations. But he saw her going through the old routine with transparent hands and empty eyes, as he could picture the ghosts of good women doing in the world of shadows.

His own case was more fortunate. His eyes were full of visions of work to be, his hands of the strength of work done. Yet at times he too felt tenuous and disembodied. Since the fever, particularly—it was always disastrous to him to have to interrupt his work. And this flat soft shore that gave him welcome—so safe, so familiar—how it frightened him! He didn't want to come in contact with life again, and life always wooed him when he was not at work.

It was odd, how little, of late, he had thought of the Wheaters. At first the memory of them had been a torture, an obsession. But luckily he had not given his address to Judith, and so she had not been able to write; and Mrs. Sellars had never once alluded to the children. His work in Brazil lay up country, far from towns and post-offices; but bundles of American newspapers straggled in at uncertain intervals, and from one he had learned that the Wheater divorce had been pronounced in Mrs. Wheater's favour, from another, about a year later, that Cliffe had married Mrs. Lullmer. There had been an end of the story . . . and Boyne had lived long enough to know that abrupt endings were best.

As his steamer pushed her way up the estuary he was still asking himself how he should employ his holiday. All his thoughts were with his interrupted work, with the man who had temporarily replaced him, and of whose judgment and temper he was not quite sure. He could not as yet bring himself to consider his own plans for the coming weeks, because, till he could get back to Brazil, everything that might happen to him seemed equally uninteresting and negligible.

At dinner that evening, at the famous *Chapeau Rouge* of Bordeaux, the fresh truffles cooked in white wine, and washed down with a bottle of Château Margaux, insensibly altered his mood. He had forgotten what good food could be like. His view of life was softened, and even the faces of the people at the other tables, commonplace as they were, gradually began to interest him. At the steamer landing the walls were plastered over with flamboyant advertisements of the watering-places of the Basque coast: Cibour, Hendaye, St. Jean de Luz, Biarritz. A band of gay bathers on a white beach, under striped umbrellas, was labelled Hendaye; another, of slim ladies silhouetted on a terrace against a cobalt sea, while their partners absorbed cocktails at little tables, stood for Biarritz. The scene recalled to Boyne similar spectacles all the world over: casinos, dancing, gambling, the monotonous rattle and glare of cosmopolitan pleasure. And suddenly he felt that to be in such a crowd was what he wanted—a crowd of idle insignificant people, not one of whom he would ever care to see again. He fancied the idea of bands playing, dancers undulating over polished floors, expensive food served on flowery terraces, high play in crowded over-heated gaming-rooms. It was the lonely man's flight from himself, the common impulse of hard workers on first coming out of the wilderness. He took the train for Biarritz. . .

The place was in full season; but he found a room in a cheap hotel far from the sea, and forthwith began to mix with the crowd. At first his deep inner loneliness cut him off from them; that people should be leading such lives seemed too absurd and inconsequent. But gradually the glitter took him, as it often had before after a long bout of hard work and isolation; he enjoyed the feeling of being lost in the throng, alone and unnoticed, with no likelihood of being singled out, like Uncle Edward, for some agreeable adventure.

Adventure! He had come to hate the very word. His one taste of the thing had been too bitter. All he wanted now was to be amused; and he hugged his anonymity. For three days he wandered about, in cafés, on terraces above the sea, and in the gaming-rooms. He even made an excursion across the Spanish border; but he came back from it tired and dispirited. Solitude and scenery were not what he wanted; he plunged into the Medley again.

On the fourth day he saw the announcement: "Gala Dinner and Dance tonight at the *Mirasol*." The *Mirasol* was the newest and most fashionable hotel in Biarritz—the "Palace" of the moment. The idea of assisting at the gala dinner took Boyne's fancy, and in the afternoon he strolled up to the hotel to engage a table. But they were all bespoken, and he sat down in the hall to glance over some illustrated papers. The place, at that hour, was nearly empty; but presently he heard a pipe of childish laughter coming from the corner where the lift was caged. Several liveried lift-boys were hanging about in idleness, and among them was a little girl with long legs, incredibly short skirts and a fiery bush of hair. Boyne laid down his paper and looked at her; but her back was turned to him. She was wrestling with the smallest of the lift-boys, while the others looked on and grinned. Presently a stout lady descended from a magnificent motor, entered the hotel and walked across the hall to the lift. Instantly the boys stood to attention, and the red-haired child, quiet as a mouse, slipped into the lift after the stout lady, and shot up out of sight. When the lift came down again, she sprang out, and instantly resumed her romp with the boys. This time her face was turned toward Boyne, and he saw that she was Zinnie Wheater. He got up from his chair to go toward her, but another passenger was getting into the lift, and Zinnie followed, and disappeared again. The next time it came down, two or three people were waiting for it; Zinnie slipped in among them, flattening herself into a corner. Boyne sat and watched her appearing and disappearing in this way for nearly an hour—it was evidently her way of spending the afternoon. And not for the first time, presumably; for several of the passengers recognised her, and greeted her with a nod or a joke. One fat old gentleman in spats produced a bag of sweets, and pinched her bare arm as he gave it to her; and a lady in black with a little girl drew the latter close to her, and looked past Zinnie as if she had not been there. . .

At last there came a lull in the traffic, the attendants relapsed into lassitude, and Zinnie, after circling aimlessly about the hall, slipped behind the porter's desk, inspected the letters in the mahogany pigeon-holes against the wall, and began to turn over the papers on the desk. Then she caught sight of the porter approaching from a distance, slid out from behind the desk, waltzed down the length of the hall and back, and stopped with a yawn just in front of Boyne. For a moment she did not seem to notice him; but presently she sidled up, leaned over his shoulder, and said persuasively: "May I look at the pictures with you?"

He laid the paper aside and glanced up at her. She stared a moment or two, perplexedly, and then flushed to the roots of her hair. "Martin—why, I believe it's old Martin!"

"Yes, it's old Martin—but you're a new Zinnie, aren't you?" he rejoined.

Her eyes were riveted on him; he saw that she was half shy, half eager to talk. She perched on the arm of his chair and took his neck in her embrace, as Judith used to.

"Well, it's a long time since I saw you. I'm lots older—and you are too," she added reflectively. "I don't believe you'd have known me if I hadn't spoken to you, would you?"

"Not if you hadn't had that burning bush," he said, touching her hair. His voice was trembling; he could hardly see her for the blur in his eyes. If he closed his lids he might almost imagine that the thin arm about his neck was Judith's. . .

"Well, how's everybody?" he asked, a little hoarsely.

"Oh, awfully well," said Zinnie. "But you don't look very well yourself," she added, turning a sidelong glance on him.

"Never mind about me. Are you here together, all of you—or have the others stayed at Dinard?"

"Dinard?" She seemed to be puzzled by the question.

"Wasn't your mother going to buy a house in the country near Dinard?"

"Was she? I dunno. We've never had a house of our own," said Zinnie.

"Never anywhere?"

"No. I guess it would only bother mother to have a house. She likes hotels better. She's married again, you know; and she's getting fat."

"Married?"

"Didn't you know about that either? How funny!

She's married to Mr. Dobree," said Zinnie, swinging her legs against Boyne's chair.

Boyne sat silent, and she continued, her eyes wandering over him critically: "I guess you've had a fever, haven't you—or else something bad with your liver?"

"Nothing of the sort. I was never better. But you're all here, then, I suppose?" His heart stood still as he made a dash at the question.

"Yes; we're all here," said Zinnie indifferently. "At least Terry's at school in Switzerland, you see; and Blanca's at a convent in Paris, 'cos she got engaged again to a lift-boy who was a worse rotter than the first; and Bun and Beechy are in Rome, in their father's palace. They hate writing, so we don't actually know how they are."

"Ah—" Boyne commented. He looked away from her, staring across the deserted hall. "But Chip's here?" he asked.

Zinnie shook her red curls gravely. "No, he isn't here either." She hesitated a moment, swinging her legs. "He's buried," she said.

"Buried—?"

"Didn't you know that either? You've been ever so far away, I suppose. Chip got menin—meningitis, isn't it? We were at Chamonix, for Terry. The doctors couldn't do anything. It was last winter—no, the winter before. We all cried awfully; we wore black for three months. And so after that mother decided she'd better marry Mr. Dobree; because she was too lonely, she said."

"Ah, lonely—"

"Yes; and so after a while we came to Paris and she was married. It must have been two years ago, because the steps were with us still; and Beechy and I wore little pink dresses at the wedding, and Bun was page. I wonder you didn't see our photographs in the 'Herald.' Don't you ever read the 'Herald'?"

"Not often," Boyne had to admit.

Zinnie continued to swing her legs against the side of his chair. "And it's then we found out what Mr. Dobree's Christian name is," she rambled on. "We had work doing it; but Terry managed to see the papers he had to sign the day of the wedding, and so we found out. His name's Azariah. We never thought of that, did we? It's the name of a man who made millions in mines; so I s'pose when he died he left all his money to Mr. Dobree."

"Made millions in mines?"

"Well, that's what Scopy said. She said: 'Not know that? You little heathens! Why, of course, Azariah was a minor prophet.' "

"Oh, of course; naturally," Boyne murmured, swept magically back to the world of joyous incongruities in which he had lived enchanted with the little Wheaters.

"So we think that's why he's so rich, and why mother married him," Zinnie concluded, with a final kick on the side of the chair; then she slid down, put her hands on her hips, pirouetted in front of Boyne, and held out the bag of pink glazed paper which the old gentleman who wore spats had given her. "Have a chocolate? The ones in gold paper have got liqueur in 'em," she said. Boyne shook his head, and she continued to look at him attentively. At last: "Martin, darling, aren't those *Abdullahs* you're smoking? Will you let me have one?" she said in a coaxing voice.

"Let you have one? You don't mean to say you smoke?"

"No; but I have a friend who does." Boyne held out his cigarette-case with a shrug, and she drew out a small handful, and flitted away to the lift. When she came back her face was radiant. "It's awfully sweet of you," she said. "You always were an old darling. Don't you want to come upstairs and see mother? She was a little tired after lunch, so I don't believe she's gone out yet."

Boyne got to his feet with a gesture of negation. "Sorry, my dear; but I'm afraid I can't. I—fact is, I'm just here for a few hours . . . taking the train back to Bordeaux presently," he stammered.

"Oh, are you? That's too bad. Mother will be awfully sorry—and so will Judy."

Boyne cleared his throat, and brought out abruptly: "Ah, she's here too—Judy?"

Zinnie stared at the question. "Course she is. Only just today she's off on an excursion with some P'ruvians. They've got an awfully long name—I can't remember it. They have two Rolls-Royces. She won't be back not till just before dinner. She'll have to be back then, because she's got a new dress for the dance tonight. It's a pity you can't come back and see her in it."

"Yes—it's a pity. But I can't." He held out his hand, and she put her little bony claw into it. "Goodbye, child," he said; then, abruptly, he bent down to her. "Kiss me, Zinnie." She held up her merry face, and he laid his lips on her cheek. "Goodbye," he repeated.

He had really meant, while he talked with her, to go back to his hotel and pack up, and catch the next train for anywhere. The place was like a tomb to him now; under all the noise and glitter his past was buried. He walked away with hurried strides from the *Mirasol;* but when he got back to his own hotel he sat down in his room and stared about him without making any effort to pack. He sat there for a long time—for all the rest of the afternoon—without moving. Once he caught himself saying aloud: "She's got a new dress for the dance." He laughed a little at the thought, and became immersed in his memories. . .

Boyne dined at a restaurant—he didn't remember where—turned in at a cinema for an hour, and then got into his evening clothes, and walked up through the warm dark night to the *Mirasol*. The great building, shining with lights, loomed above a tranquil sea; music drifted out from it, and on the side toward the sea its wide terrace was thronged with ladies in bright dresses, and their partners. Boyne walked up among them; but as he reached the terrace a drizzling rain began to fall, and laughing and crying out the dancers all hurried back into the hotel. He stood alone on the damp flagging, and paced up and down slowly before the uncurtained windows. The dinner was over—the restaurant was empty, and through the windows he saw the waiters preparing the tables again for supper. Farther on, he passed other tall windows, giving on a richly upholstered drawing-room where groups of elderly people, at tables with shaded lamps, were playing bridge and poker. Among them he noticed a stout lady in a low-necked black dress. Her much-exposed back was turned to him, and he recognised the shape of her head, the thatch of rippled hair, silver-white now (she had kept her resolve of not dyeing it), and the turn of her white arms as she handled her cards. Opposite her sat her partner, also white-headed, in a perfectly cut dinner-jacket; the lamplight seemed to linger appreciatively on his lustrous pearl studs and sleeve-links. It was Mr. Dobree, grown stouter too, with a reddish fold of flesh above his immaculate collar. The couple looked placid, well fed, and perfectly satisfied with life and with each other.

Boyne continued his walk, and turning an angle of the building, found himself facing the windows of the ballroom. The terrace on that side, being away from the sea, was but faintly lit, and the spectacle within seemed therefore more brilliantly illuminated.

At first he saw only a blur of light and colour; couples revolving slowly under the spreading chandeliers, others streaming in and out of the doorways, or grouped about the floor in splashes of brightness. The music rose and fell in palpitating rhythms, paused awhile, and began again in obedience to a rattle of hand-clapping. The floor was already crowded, but Boyne's eyes roved in vain from one slender bare-armed shape to another; then he said to himself: "But it's nearly three years since I saw her. She's grown up now—perhaps I'm looking at her without knowing her. . ."

The thought that one of those swaying figures might be Judith's, that at that very instant she might be gazing out at him with unknown eyes, sent such a pang through him that he moved away again into the darkness. The rain had almost ceased, but a faint wind from the sea drove the wet air against his face; he might almost have fancied he was crying. The pain of not seeing her was unendurable. It seemed to empty his world. . .

He heard voices and steps approaching behind him on the terrace, and to avoid being scrutinised he mechanically turned back to the window. And there she was, close to him on the other side of the pane, moving across the long reflections of the floor. And he had imagined that he might not know her!

She had just stopped dancing; the arm of a very tall young man with a head as glossy as his shirt-front detached itself from her waist. She was facing Boyne now —she was joining a group near his window. Two or three young girls greeted her gaily as she passed them. The centre of the room was being cleared for a pair of professional dancers, and Judith, waving away a gilt ballroom chair which somebody proffered, remained standing, clustered about by other slender and glossy young men. Boyne, from without, continued to gaze at her.

He had not even asked himself if she had changed—if she had grown up. He had totally forgotten his fear that he might not recognise her. He knew now that if she had appeared to him as a bent old woman he would have known her. . . He watched her with a passionate attentiveness. Her silk dress was of that peculiar carnation-pink which takes a silver glaze like the bloom on a nectarine. The rich stuff stood out from her in a double tier of flounces, on which, as she stood motionless, her hands seemed to float like birds on little sunlit waves. Her hair was moulded to her head in close curves like the ripples of a brown stream. Instead of being cut short in the nape it had been allowed to grow, and was twisted into a figure eight, through which was thrust an old-fashioned diamond arrow. Her throat and neck were bare, and so were her thin arms; but a band of black velvet encircled one of her wrists, relieving the tender rose-and-amber of her dress and complexion. Her eyes seemed to Boyne to have grown larger and more remote, but her mouth was round and red, as it always was when she was amused or happy. While he watched her one of the young men behind her bent over to say something. As she listened she lifted a big black fan to her lips, and her lids closed for a second, as they did when she wanted to hold something sweet between them. But when she furled the fan her expression changed, and her face suddenly became as sad as an autumn twilight.

"Judith!" Boyne thought; as if her being Judith, her being herself, were impossible to believe, yet too sweet for anything else in the world to be true. . . It was one of her moments of beauty—that fitful beauty which is so much more enchanting and perilous than the kind that gets up and lies down every day with its wearer. This might be—Boyne said to himself—literally the only day, the only hour, in which the queer quarrelling elements that composed her would ever join hands in a celestial harmony. It did not matter what had brought the miracle about. Perhaps she was in love with the young man who had bent over her, and was going to marry him. Or perhaps she was still a child, pleased at her new dress, and half proud, half frightened in the waking consciousness of her beauty, and the power it exercised. . . Whichever it was, Boyne knew he would never know. He drew back into an unlit corner of the terrace, and sat there a long time in the dark, his head thrown back and his hands locked behind it. Then he got up and walked away into the night.

Two days afterward, the ship which had brought him to Europe started on her voyage back to Brazil. On her deck stood Boyne, a lonely man.

(2)

THE END

VIRAGO MODERN CLASSICS
&
CLASSIC NON-FICTION

The first Virago Modern Classic, *Frost in May* by Antonia White, was published in 1978. It launched a list dedicated to the celebration of women writers and to the rediscovery and reprinting of their works. Its aim was, and is, to demonstrate the existence of a female tradition in fiction, and to broaden the sometimes narrow definition of a 'classic' which has often led to the neglect of interesting novels and short stories. Published with new introductions by some of today's best writers, the books are chosen for many reasons: they may be great works of fiction; they may be wonderful period pieces; they may reveal particular aspects of women's lives; they may be classics of comedy or storytelling.

The companion series, Virago Classic Non-Fiction, includes diaries, letters, literary criticism, and biographies – often by and about authors published in the Virago Modern Classics.

'Good news for everyone writing and reading today' – *Hilary Mantel*

'A continuingly magnificent imprint' – *Joanna Trollope*

'The Virago Modern Classics have reshaped literary history and enriched the reading of us all. No library is complete without them' – *Margaret Drabble*

VIRAGO MODERN CLASSICS
&
CLASSIC NON-FICTION

Some of the authors included in these two series –

Elizabeth von Arnim, Dorothy Baker, Pat Barker, Nina Bawden, Nicola Beauman, Sybille Bedford, Jane Bowles, Kay Boyle, Vera Brittain, Leonora Carrington, Angela Carter, Willa Cather, Colette, Ivy Compton-Burnett, E.M. Delafield, Maureen Duffy, Elaine Dundy, Nell Dunn, Emily Eden, George Egerton, George Eliot, Miles Franklin, Mrs Gaskell, Charlotte Perkins Gilman, George Gissing, Victoria Glendinning, Radclyffe Hall, Shirley Hazzard, Dorothy Hewett, Mary Hocking, Alice Hoffman, Winifred Holtby, Janette Turner Hospital, Zora Neale Hurston, Elizabeth Jenkins, F. Tennyson Jesse, Molly Keane, Margaret Laurence, Maura Laverty, Rosamond Lehmann, Rose Macaulay, Shena Mackay, Olivia Manning, Paule Marshall, F.M. Mayor, Anaïs Nin, Kate O'Brien, Olivia, Grace Paley, Mollie Panter-Downes, Dawn Powell, Dorothy Richardson, E. Arnot Robertson, Jacqueline Rose, Vita Sackville-West, Elaine Showalter, May Sinclair, Agnes Smedley, Dodie Smith, Stevie Smith, Nancy Spain, Christina Stead, Carolyn Steedman, Gertrude Stein, Jan Struther, Han Suyin, Elizabeth Taylor, Sylvia Townsend Warner, Mary Webb, Eudora Welty, Mae West, Rebecca West, Edith Wharton, Antonia White, Christa Wolf, Virginia Woolf, E.H. Young